Other books by Stanley Ellin

NOVELS

Mirror, Mirror on the Wall
The Bind
The Valentine Estate
Stronghold
The Panama Portrait
The Winter After This Summer
The Eighth Circle
The Key to Nicholas Street
Dreadful Summit
The Luxembourg Run
Star Light, Star Bright
The Dark Fantastic
Very Old Money

SHORT STORY COLLECTIONS

Mystery Stories
The Blessington Method and Other Strange Tales
Kindly Dig Your Grave
The Specialty of the House and Other Stories (1948–1978)

House of Cards

House of Cards

Stanley Ellin

A Foul Play Press Book
W · W · Norton & Company
New York · London

For my daughter, Sue,
with love and admiration

Contents

—So, dear reader, of all methods of divining the Future, the Tarot cards are supreme. Furthermore, where the cards in the various suits in Tarot cast a light on hidden Destiny, those twenty-two cards which are The Master Trumps illuminate it, as it were, with a veritable flash of lightning.

These are The Master Trumps and their meanings.

The Fool is the card of *Flesh* and *Folly*
The Magus is the card of *Subtlety*
The Priestess is the card of *Mystery*
The Empress is the card of *Fruitfulness*
The Emperor is the card of *Virility*
The Pope is the card of *Salvation*
The Lovers is the card of *Profane Love*
The Chariot is the card of *Aggression*
Justice is the card of *Honor*
The Eremite is the card of *Loneliness*
The Wheel is the card of *Rewards*
Courage is the card of *Success in Action*
The Hanged Man is the card of *Duty*
Death is the card of the *End of Hope*
The Angel is the card of *Peace*
The Devil is the card of *Violence*
The Tower is the card of *Disaster*
The Star is the card of *Hope*
The Moon is the card of *Fear*
The Sun is the card of *Joy*
The Judgment Day is the card of *Trial*
The World is the card of *Journeying*

And all twenty-two made into a pack and placed face down are the *Universe*.

from *La Mystère du Tarot*
by Sophie de Laennac

PART ONE

The Fool

1

This *discothèque*, the Club Barouf, was different.

All the other *discothèques* I had ever been in were on the Left Bank and were small, candlelit holes. This one was on the Right Bank, on the Boulevard Montmartre, and it was a huge, garishly lit place, as big as a barn but furnished with only the bare essentials, a banquette along the walls, an assortment of cheap, unmatched café tables and chairs, and a dozen amplifiers mounted overhead around the room.

My friend Louis le Buc, who had sent me out into the rainy evening for an interview with the owner, had told me that the Club Barouf was a converted roller-skating rink. It looked like it.

The owner's name was Jacques Castabert. He was a sleek, sad-eyed little man who seemed to have the cares of the world piled on his narrow shoulders. His office was a cubicle with plywood walls in a corner of the dance hall, and there was just enough room in it for his desk and chair and a rickety bar stool.

"Monsieur Reno Davis?" he said to me as I stood in his doorway, dripping with the icy February rain; and when I nodded he waved me to a seat on the bar stool. "Coffee? A cigarette?"

"Thanks. I could use them."

We talked about the weather while I was having my coffee and cigarette, and I saw he was sizing me up narrowly.

"How long have you lived in Paris?" he suddenly said.

"Six years. Two years in Italy before that."

"Then that explains it. The six years, I mean. Your French is excellent. Maybe a little too common, a little too much Boulevard Magenta, but excellent. And you're a pugilist?"

"Was. I gave it up a couple of years ago."

"And since then?"

"I've been trying to become a writer."

"Ah, another of those." He made a face. "But obviously you haven't become one yet."

"Obviously."

"Then what have you been living on?"

"Odd jobs now and then. Tourist guide. Translator for a magazine publisher. I was bouncer at Le Hollywood Strip on the Boulevard de Clichy for a while. That's why Louis le Buc thinks you might be able to use me here."

Castabert sternly shook his head. "I don't need a bouncer. I need a diplomat. Are you a diplomat?"

"When I have to be."

"I hope so. Let me explain. The kids open the place here in the evening, and you won't have trouble with them. But later on, the snobs will show up, the chichi crowd from the Faubourg Saint-Honoré, and when they and the kids rub up against each other there can be complications. That's what you're to stop before it starts. But no rough stuff, you understand. No muscle. The Grands Boulevards haven't been fashionable since grandpa cut his milk teeth, so it's a miracle we're getting any upper-crust trade at all, and I don't want it scared away. Is that clear?"

"Yes. Then I've got the job?"

"If you want it for a hundred francs a week. The whole thing's an experiment anyhow. Maybe later on—"

"All right. But I'll need two weeks' pay in advance. My good suit is in the pawnshop and I'm a little behind in my room rent. Two hundred francs right now would square everything."

Castabert's eyes closed tight. He put a hand to his round little belly as if seized by a pain there.

"That's how it goes," he muttered. "I'm the money tree. Come and pluck me." His eyes opened. "You'll get your two weeks' pay in advance. I don't know why, but there's something about you that inspires confidence. I know I'm being weak-minded;

you'll wind up cutting my throat and robbing the till, but I'll take my chances on it."

"Thanks. When do I start?"

"Tonight. But one final word—"

"Yes?"

"Keep away from any of those teen-age chicks around here, because if you get one of them pregnant, I'm ruined. Just remember that no matter how skinny a kid looks, how stringy she is, she can be as fertile as a rabbit."

"I'll remember that," I said.

I learned that first night on the job what Castabert meant about complications. Until almost eleven the customers were mostly kids, and I had an easy enough time with them. But after eleven a new element entered the scene, a new odor pervaded the outside foyer of the club. Now, instead of smelling from youthful sweat and cheap pomade, it was filled with the scent of damp mink and sable and of very expensive perfume. The Faubourg Saint-Honoré customers had arrived, and I led party after party of them through a gauntlet of hostility to the choice banquettes. En route, the newcomers must have caught some of the remarks about them, but either blank-faced or openly amused, they appeared not to mind.

Only once was there a break in this pattern. When some pimpled and pomaded youth grandly announced, "Ah, the Jet Set. *Crapule* and company," a fat, putty-complexioned man in dinner jacket hesitated menacingly until the pert little blonde he was escorting jogged his elbow and shoved him on his way.

Watching this gathering of expensive people, it struck me that in them I had material for the sort of play Madame Olympe, my landlady and an avid reader of the scandal sheets, was always advising me to write, and that the Club Barouf might well supply me with grist for the creative mill just as all my previous employments had.

I even picked out the heroine of the play at a glance, a tall, slender, full-breasted girl with splendidly regal carriage who, in the middle of that mob, managed to seem isolated and apart from it. Dark-haired, with unbelievably large, sapphire-blue eyes and a warm, full-lipped mouth, she sat in brooding silence among her companions, neither speaking nor being spoken to. Later, when I glimpsed the wedding ring on her finger, I added a second character to my play, a husband who was an unappreciative clod.

As luck would have it, I met her before the night was over. There was a signal for help from a waiter near the door of the foyer, and when I went out there I found the girl, and the pert little blonde who had jogged the fat man on his way, and a crowd of youths, all in hot dispute over the use of the one telephone on the wall.

It was a dispute with elements of nastiness in it. The boy at the phone was a big, hard-looking case, a motorcycle crash helmet slung over his shoulder, who leaned against the wall, receiver to ear as if he were just settling down to a few hours' chat. His *copains,* with eyes narrowed and tight little smiles on their lips, were teasing their girl friends by loudly remarking on the attractions of the dark-haired beauty; and the girls, the most dangerous of all, I suspected, had been roused to venom by this and looked ready for some serious hair-pulling.

"Thank God," their intended victim said when I presented myself to her. She pointed a finger at the boy with the phone, who leered at her in response. "He's only pretending to make a call, do you understand? And I must use the phone immediately!"

"Oh, do try to restrain yourself, Anne," said the little blonde in an undertone. "It's not really that important. I assure you Paul is perfectly safe."

"Maybe it is that important," jeered a girl behind her who had caught this, a chunky Cleopatra. "Maybe she wants to make sure her fancy man is ready for her when she ducks away from her husband later on." And another girl remarked to me with curled lip, "She tried to pay André to give her the phone. She's the kind that thinks she can buy whatever she looks at."

Beauty seemed deaf to these provocations. "Isn't there anywhere else to call from in this wretched place?" she asked me tensely, and I realized from her accent that she wasn't French at all, but British or American. So the hostile crowd around her had a double score to settle.

"You can call from the owner's office," I said.

The cloakroom woman, placidly watching from her counter, shook her head. "Not a chance. Castabert went out for a bite to eat, and the office stays locked until he gets back."

"Then get this phone away from that overgrown bully," the girl commanded. "This is incredible. I tell you he's only pretending to use it!"

Her face was chalk-white now. She looked as if she might fly apart in another moment.

I turned to the boy holding the phone. "Let's have it, son."

"*Allez-vous coucher,*" he said coldly. "Beat it. I can't hear a thing with you and that dame yapping away. Why don't both of you get lost?"

Around me I heard a menacing grumble. I held out my hand to the boy, half expecting a blow in back of the head from one of his tight-lipped *copains*. "The phone," I said.

"All right, if you want it, come and get it."

He was a hefty specimen but he was only a kid, after all. When I meaningfully raised my fist he paled and swallowed hard.

"You want to get yourself killed, André?" someone finally said out of the hard-breathing silence around us. "He used to be a heavyweight fighter, that one. Go on, let him have the lousy phone."

"Go on, you might as well," said someone else, and André, making it plain he was surrendering only to humor them, contemptuously tossed me the phone.

I put it to my ear, heard the shrill yammer of a female voice at the other end, and to André's open-mouthed astonishment, tossed the phone back to him.

"I'm sorry," I told the dark-haired girl, "but it really is in use. So if you don't mind—"

"Oh, this is too much!" cried the little blonde, and there was

no question about her being a born and bred Parisienne. "We'll
go back to the table, Anne, and see if we can't get them to
leave." Then in excellent English she said scathingly, "You're
certainly not going to get any help from that big oaf, I can tell
you. He's no better than the rest of this scum."

I couldn't resist paying her back.

"If you'll let me finish what I was saying," I told her, also
in English, "there's a phone down the block at the tobacconist's.
I'll escort the lady there if she wishes."

The blonde looked momentarily startled, then angrier than
ever. "Ah, an American, is it? But if you think I'll withdraw my
comment because you understood it—"

"Dear God, never mind that," said the dark-haired girl. "Just
let me make my call."

I watched her from the tobacconist's counter while she was
in the phone booth, envying the man who owned her. Then the
shop door was suddenly flung open with a force that almost
shattered its glass; the fat, putty-complexioned man, his face
wrathful, stalked in and went directly to the phone booth. When
he rapped his knuckles on its glass, the girl turned to stare at
him with open hatred.

I left them there like that. It was my policy never to mix in
anyone's family affairs.

2

Before my first week at the Club Barouf was up, Castabert was pleased to take me aside and confide that he was much impressed by my capabilities on the job, and that if I continued to impress in this fashion, my future in his employ was bright indeed.

"You've got style enough to get along with the swanky crowd," he said, "but even more important, you understand, is that the kids seem to have made you some kind of hero and they're behaving themselves when the snobs are around. Of course, this can be dangerous, too. All you have to do is get careless with one of those imbecilic schoolgirls who stand around adoring you, and presto! we've got a fat lawsuit on our hands. You want to remember that."

I assured him I would.

"I hope so for my sake as much as yours," he said.

His admiration lasted exactly one day. The next evening when I came to work, the cloakroom attendant told me that the big cheese wanted to see me in his office as soon as I arrived, and, in saying this, she drew her forefinger slowly across her throat.

"What's wrong?" I asked.

She shrugged. "I don't know, but he's in a real sweat. I wouldn't keep him frying in the pan too long, if I were you."

Still, it was with a clear conscience that I went into the office. There I found Castabert seated behind his desk looking like a thundercloud.

"Well," he said without preliminary, "what kind of trouble are you in?"

"Trouble?"

"Yes, trouble! With the law? With a woman, maybe? Do you know what a scandal could do to me? Don't I have the right to be told what disaster is coming to strike me down before it arrives?"

"Sure, but what's that got to do with me? I'm not in trouble with anyone."

"Aha!" Castabert said triumphantly. "Then will you kindly tell me why you are under investigation?"

"Under investigation?"

"And will you stop repeating my words like a parrot? Yes, under investigation. This afternoon, someone was in my apartment —right there in my apartment, you understand—questioning me about you."

"Who was he?"

Castabert flung up his arms in a tragic appeal to heaven. "Who was he, this creature asks, when that is exactly what I'm asking him!"

"And I have no idea. Did you get his name?"

"Yes, Marchat. Max Marchat. It's right here on his card."

I read the card and shook my head.

"A lawyer," said Castabert, eying me narrowly. "Distinguished, good-looking, obviously very wealthy. Excellent manners, but underneath them a very tough cookie."

I shook my head even more emphatically. "I don't know him," I said, "but I'd certainly like to. Mind if I use the phone?"

The phone number was on the card. I dialed it and was startled to hear a metallic voice respond: *This is a recording. The number you have called is not in service. This is a recording. The number—*"

"Well," said Castabert, "what is it?" and I handed him the phone so that he could hear this monotonous message. He listened, then gently put down the phone.

"Very curious," he said. "A joke? No, this type Marchat is not

a man for jokes. A tough cookie. A very tough cookie, believe
me."

I lay sleepless in bed a long time that night, pondering my
history, wondering what there was about it that would lead any
lawyer to purposefully investigate it. At sixteen, I had fled from
home in Nevada, leaving my parents to their unending war
with each other, and had lied my way into the Marines just in
time to see service in the even noisier war then being waged
in Korea. But both my parents were now dead and my service
discharge was honorable, so that offered no clue to the mystery.
And although at the unripe age of twenty-one I had undergone
six dismal months of marriage in New York, my ex-wife, from
last report, was now on her fourth husband and had no claims
on me.

My passport? My identification papers? My work permit?
All in order as far as I knew, but was it possible that somewhere along the way I had taken oath to a false statement and
made myself liable to a jail sentence? That was a really idiotic
thought, I realized just before I finally fell asleep, but being under investigation seemed to raise such speculations naturally.

When I woke in the early afternoon and threw open my shutters on the bustling Faubourg Saint-Denis I found myself shaking my head at my nighttime idiocy. I was still anxious to meet
lawyer Marchat and find out what he was up to, but not so
desperately anxious now that I would skip breakfast and a cigarette at the Café au Coin down the block. Louis le Buc and
some other regulars would be there for an *apéritif* at this hour,
and I relished the thought of tossing my mystery to them as a
conversation piece before I went to Marchat's office and had it
explained to me. Café conversation about literature or politics
in places like the Dôme or Deux Magots was tame stuff compared to what it could be in the Café au Coin when there was
someone's personal affairs to thrash out.

The café had another asset besides its conversationalists. The
Faubourg Saint-Denis was lined with food stalls of every de-

scription offering high quality for low prices, and if, on your way down the block, you selected a couple of oranges and a sausage for breakfast *á l'américain*, Jeanloup, the boss of the café, would squeeze the oranges and grill the sausage for you free of charge, provided you ordered a bottle of wine with them.

So it was to the Café au Coin, oranges and sausage in hand, that I hied myself with my riddle of lawyer Marchat. There I found Louis at a table in a far corner looking pinch-faced and mournful. When I asked how he felt, he said gloomily, "Like something the cat dragged in. I gave up smoking again yesterday, and I'm having a terrible time of it."

I was about to light a cigarette for myself while waiting for Jeanloup to prepare my edibles, but at this I shook out the match.

"No, no," Louis protested. "Light it up, pal. Enjoy it. That's the real test for me—holding off while I watch someone else enjoy it."

So I lit my cigarette, and after watching me exhale the first lungful of smoke Louis helped himself to my pack and lit one for himself.

"Did you see Olympe on your way out?" he said. Madame Olympe was our landlady and concierge, a virago in the grand tradition.

"No."

"Well, she had a visitor inquiring about you last night."

"What visitor?" I asked, with the unpleasant feeling that I already knew the answer.

"A lawyer named Marchat. When I was going down for dinner I saw your door open, so I looked in and there he was, inspecting the room like a sergeant in the barracks and pumping Olympe about you."

"And you let him?"

"I more than let him. I got him around to pumping me, too, so I could give him an earful about your noble character. What's it all about, anyhow?"

"I wish I knew. Last night, Castabert told me this same man had been at his apartment asking questions about me."

"Could it have something to do with that collection of books you've piled up? Are you trying to sell them?"

"No, why?"

"Because of the way he was combing through them. Olympe thought you might be trying to sell them to him, and that he was making sure they weren't stolen goods."

"Well, she thought wrong. Did he say anything about the books?"

"Yes. He said, 'So it seems our heavyweight favors the classics, no less.' He sounded amused."

"Well, I'm not. What right did she have to let him into the room at all?"

Louis shrugged. "He told her to. Look, kid, you're not getting the picture. This Marchat could make even a waiter at the Lido hop to attention by wiggling a finger at him. Anyhow, there's no need to stew over it. He gave me his name and address when I asked for them. All you have to do is look him up in the book and call him."

"Except that I already did and his phone's disconnected. What I'm going to do is go over to his office right after breakfast and straighten things out in person."

"But not in this mood," warned Louis. "At least, don't get all heated up until you know the score. Tell you what. I'll go along just to make sure you don't."

The address on Marchat's card was that of an old building in the Place Vendôme near its rue de la Paix entrance. Max Marchat, *avocat*, according to the brass plaque in the doorway, could be found on the second floor, so up the steep, creaking stairway we went, disregarding the raised eyebrows of the porter who sat behind his desk in the ground-floor corridor. There were two doors on the second-floor landing, and I tried each in turn, first tapping politely, then knocking loudly and rattling the knobs, but the doors remained closed.

Then the porter, a stout, white-haired old man who looked as if he had been around as long as the building, slowly came huffing and puffing up the stairway and when he reached the top stood gasping for a few moments to catch his breath.

"What's all the racket about?" he finally managed to ask. "Who are you looking for? Marchat?"

"That's right," I said.

The porter shook his head pityingly.

"Well," he said, "if you boys had bothered to ask about it at the desk, we could have saved ourselves this miserable mountain climbing. And no use banging on the door like that, because no one's there to open it. The office is closed for good."

"Closed for good?" said Louis. "But where's Marchat?"

"That's what I'm trying to tell you, little man," said the porter. "Marchat's been dead for a month."

3

Rome had been my nesting ground when I first met Louis le Buc, but the meeting took place in the prize-fight arena at Milan. After a bout I had there, Louis had hunted me out in the dressing room to shake my hand and remark what a pleasure it was to meet a fighter who could obviously fell a horse with one blow.

"I didn't know they made heavyweights like you any more, big boy," he said. "Today, it's all dancing around and shadow-boxing. It's enough to make a man cry, watching those cream-puffs. Come on, let's have a drink, and I'll make you an offer you can't afford to turn down."

He was a bright-eyed, big-beaked little gamecock of a man in threadbare clothes and an oversized beret, a would-be cynic whose acid manner could not conceal an immense good nature.

The beret, I later discovered, was worn indoors as well as out for the same reason Caesar had always gone around wearing his laurels—to conceal a shining bald scalp.

His offer, it came out over a succession of drinks in a *caffè* in the Galeria, was to take him on as manager, return to Paris with him, and settle down there in a city where the wine was drinkable, the food edible, and the women, whether willing or unwilling, at least vivacious. So, since I had few ties to Italy and some of them already had marriage on the mind, and since my American manager was homesick for New York and willing to cut me loose for a small payment, I became the protégé of Louis le Buc. It never dawned on me when I signed with him to ask if he knew anything about managing a fighter or if he even knew anything about fighting, which, I soon learned, he did not. But even if he had confessed this to me then and there, I would have signed with him. The best friendships are the ones where you meet someone by chance and intuitively know on the spot that here is a true friend. That's how it was with Louis and me the instant we shook hands in the dressing room of the Milan arena.

For a while things went well in Paris, although Louis' innocence of our business proved a constant problem. I had a tremendous punch, it's true, but I was a shade too slow to be more than a fairly good club fighter at my best, and a smaller, faster man might occasionally jab me dizzy before I could catch up to him. And Louis, who knew as little about matchmaking as he did about a left hook, had a penchant for signing me up against small, fast men rather than dangerous-looking big sluggers. Then he would watch agonized from my corner, suffering every punch with me, and becoming a more sickly green each round.

"That's enough," he would say while the seconds were repairing the damages. "You'll be mincemeat before this is over. You'll be crippled for life. I'm throwing in the towel," and a couple of times did throw in the towel, thus turning a possible victory for me into total defeat.

But, all in all, we did pretty well for a while, making fair money, spending it only a little faster than we made it, sharing the amenities of Madame Olympe's *pension* where we were entirely at home among the café waiters, bookies, lottery ticket peddlers and bath-house attendants who occupied the place, until the day came when I started to lose fights more often than I won them. In the end, it was Louis who forced me to throw the towel in on my career.

"You've had it, kid," he said. "Maybe you can take more of this, but I can't. Now is the time to quit and start writing those books you always wanted to write, while you're still in one piece and I'm not a complete emotional wreck. And if you don't make a big success out of writing books, we'll still get along somehow."

We did, because Louis in a pinch always managed to come up with a way for one or the other of us to make a few francs. It was for good reason, he liked to point out, that his real name had long ago been forgotten by the Faubourg Saint-Denis and replaced by the title of *le Buc*. That had nothing to do with taking bets from local horse players, but came about when, as a bright young lad, he would stroll each morning of the tourist season to Brentano's bookshop on the Avenue de l'Opéra which stocks a handsome collection of English-language pornography, buy a choice volume for twelve or fifteen francs, then walk over to the nearby Café de la Paix and sell the book to some evil-minded and uninformed tourist for fifty francs.

"I might have cleaned up a fortune that way before the cops moved in and started grabbing all my profits," he said wistfully, "but it was always one book a day and no more. I have your weakness, kid. Once I've got enough in my pocket to take it easy in the cafés the rest of the day, I figure tomorrow will take care of itself. Cafés have been my ruination. Cafés and idle talk and beautiful, avaricious women. But that book-selling business was what I call a good deal. A big return on a small investment, and everything strictly legal. Damn those grafting cops anyhow."

Actually, as I came to see, none of Louis' women were much in the *femme-fatale* department, but were, one and all, hard-

working, high-spirited salesgirls or secretaries, usually twenty
years younger and a head taller than he, who would start off by
being fond of him and wind up adoring him.

"Because," as he once pointed out to me, "they know I'm all
ears when they talk to me, I'm interested in whatever they have
to say. And of all things any woman wants from her lover once
they're out of bed, that's what she wants most."

Which, of course, is very close to the truth.

When Louis' latest, a buxom redhead who worked as typist
in the Ministry of Commerce and who was an avid reader of
mysteries, heard about the Marchat affair, she told me eagerly
that it would be no trouble at all for her to get me a dossier on
the late Max Marchat. And since this meant I was doing something about the matter instead of angrily wondering about it, I
accepted Véronique's offer with thanks.

Louis had arranged a double date for my first night off from
work. That night, Véronique brought the dossier with her, and
while waiting for my date to join us in my room, she and Louis
and I went through it carefully, line by line. It offered not the
slightest clue as to why anyone would want to adopt Max Marchat's identity and undertake an investigation of me.

The record was straightforward and respectable. Marchat
had attended a good school, practiced law in Paris, headed an
investigating commission in Algeria during the troubles of 1960
for which service he had been decorated by the government,
and then had re-entered the practice of law in Paris, where he
had died at the age of sixty as the result of a fall down the stairway of his offices. His wife had died ten years previously. They
had had no children.

"What a record," said Louis. "Obviously, here is a man
now occupying the dullest corner of heaven."

"But this business of dying from a fall down a stairway,"
hopefully said Véronique, the mystery addict. "Couldn't that
mean something?"

"Did he fall or was he pushed?" Louis said. "No, my darling,
for someone to kill Marchat so he could then pretend to be Mar-

chat for the benefit of a man who never even knew Marchat—
that would be the absolute height of lunacy."

"Yes, it would," Véronique promptly agreed. "Maybe that's
the answer. Some crackpot wants to torment Reno."

"Except," I said, "that from his description he is anything but
a crackpot."

We were still on the subject when my girl, Eliane Tissou,
finally arrived, full of apologies for being late. She had had to
work overtime at her office again, but that was life in the Compagnie des Gants during the season, *n'est-ce pas?*

It wasn't hard for her to get our forgiveness, because, as even
Louis, who didn't like her very much, had to admit, she was the
prettiest little thing in the whole Tenth Arrondissement, and
with all the delicious volatility of a newly opened bottle of
champagne in the bargain. For the past two years we had been
sleeping together when in the mood, but marriage was a subject we both warily skirted. For myself, once bitten, twice
shy. For Eliane, bourgeoise to the backbone, marriage to a man
who refused to make something of himself was out of the
question.

So, by and large, we had a comfortable relationship, I remaining unreformed and unrepentant and Eliane keeping a
sharp lookout for some man who would make a good, sound
marital investment. The one frustrating aspect of the relationship for me was that she, the only one of the six pretty daughters
of the butcher Tissou on the corner to remain unmarried, still
dutifully lived at home with Papa and Mama. That meant
getting out of a warm bed before dawn now and again to take
Eliane home a roundabout way. In the hallway of the top floor
of the *pension* was a closet with a ladder in it leading to the
roof. Then across the rooftops and down a fire escape from
which Eliane could step right through the window of her room
in the apartment above the butcher shop. Roundabout but
necessary, considering the payoff if Papa Tissou ever found
out what his daughter was up to.

Now, having made her apologies and been forgiven, having
commented at length on Véronique's new dress and hairdo,

having explained at machine-gun rate what life at the Compagnie des Gants was like, Eliane, a true Parisienne, wanted to know what the plans for the evening were. Because if Reno thought he was going to waste a whole week's pay—

"Keep cool, baby," said Louis, "because this one is all on me. The whole works. First, a stop at the Café au Coin to mellow the disposition, then Cary Grant in his latest, then the de luxe treatment at the Bourneville. How does that sound?"

The Bourneville was a café on the boulevard which was to other cafés what the Club Barouf was to other *discothèques*. It was a gigantic place which offered entertainment and a de luxe section with heavily starched tablecloths and a *prix-fixe* dinner.

"It sounds great," said Eliane. "It's your turn anyhow, and I need something like that to cheer me up. This business of Reno and that dead lawyer has me all on edge. I'll keep waiting in the office for some strange man to walk in, tell me he's Max Marchat, and ask what I know about Reno. Every time someone knocks on the door I'll go right up in the air like a rocket. It's absolutely gruesome."

"It's no fun for Reno either," Louis said unkindly. "Now how about getting started before we're late for the movie?"

Getting started meant a wait while the girls huddled before my dresser mirror redoing flawless make-ups, and while they were at it, Madame's voice resounded from below. "The telephone, Monsieur Reno! Monsieur, the telephone, if you please!"

"Don't answer it," Louis advised. "I've got a feeling it's Castabert telling you there's trouble at the club and you are now about to lose your night off."

"I know," I said. "I've got the same feeling."

But since I urgently needed my job, such as it was, I resentfully trotted downstairs to the phone in the hallway of the ground floor. When I picked up the phone it was not Castabert's high-pitched whine that greeted me. It was the deep, well-modulated voice of a total stranger.

"Monsieur Davis," he said, "we've never met, but my name is

de Gonde—Claude de Gonde—and I'm calling about a matter of great importance to you. That is, if you regard the offer
of an excellent and well-paid position as important."

"One moment," I said sharply. "Are you by any chance familiar with the name Max Marchat?"

"Yes. I'll explain that when we meet."

"Why not explain right now?"

"Because I'm only an agent in this matter, a third party. I'd
prefer we all meet together before making any explanations.
But really, none of this is as baffling as you make it sound. It
concerns a job that will pay you a great deal more than the Club
Barouf for much pleasanter work. Honest work, too. I'm not
asking you to smuggle diamonds or any such nonsense."

"I'll take your word for it. What are you asking me to do?"

De Gonde hesitated. "Well, I didn't intend to go into details
just yet, but apparently I must. My client wants you to undertake the instruction of her child in some not-too-difficult school
subjects. He's a little boy of nine, and, I may say, a very nice
one. Does that allay your suspicions?"

It not only allayed my suspicions, it suggested that I was
the victim of a thundering case of mistaken identity.

When I told this to my caller he said, "Why should you think
that?" in a voice that suggested I had insulted him.

"Because, Monsieur de Gonde, tutoring isn't my line of work.
You must have some other Davis in mind. Probably someone
attached to the University."

"I have not. As for your qualifications, I've investigated them
thoroughly and find them satisfactory. The one remaining
question is when we can have our meeting."

"I'm afraid there's a question to settle before that," I said
warily. "Just how much does this job pay?"

The voice was now distinctly chilly. "Monsieur Davis, as an
American you may like to do business over the telephone. I
don't."

"That's too bad. But if the job doesn't pay enough—which I
suspect it doesn't—there's no sense holding meetings about it."

"I see," said de Gonde. "Well, in that case, you may be in-

terested to know that the payment offered is three thousand
francs a month." Then he asked with bright malice, "Do you
think that would be satisfactory?"

I stood there stupefied. Even in the States a man could get
along nicely on what amounted to six hundred dollars a month.
The way I lived in Paris, it meant I could bank most of that
salary every payday and within a year accumulate enough cap-
ital for a long, golden period of complete freedom. Then I came
down to earth. This was too good to be true. There must be a
catch to it somewhere.

"Three thousand a month?" I said, just to make sure.

"Yes."

"All right, I'll take it."

"I thought you would. But are you sure you don't want to
meet my client and her child before making your decision? As
I've said, the boy is really a charming little fellow, if a little
difficult at times. His mother can be very difficult."

"Aren't all mothers?"

"What? Oh, yes, but this one—well, it's not necessary to go
into that now. I'll just take for granted you'll be able to solve
any problems as they arise."

"Fair enough."

"Then all that remains is to settle your affairs with the Club
Barouf. Its proprietor has a wagging tongue, so, you see, I
know about your debt to him. Two hundred francs, is it not?
But you won't have to concern yourself about it. I'll attend to it
promptly. And tomorrow morning I'll send my car for you at
nine so that you can enter on your new duties at once. Is that
satisfactory?"

"Yes, but as to your paying off Castabert—"

"No, don't give it another thought. Tomorrow, then."

I hung up the phone in a daze, and only then was struck by
the alarming realization that my caller's name might not be de
Gonde any more than it had been Marchat, that he had left me
no address, that this whole thing might only be one more move
in some macabre game he was playing with me.

In the directory beneath the phone I found the name de
Gonde, but that might mean nothing. Claude de Gonde, rue de

Courcelles. When I dialed the number, I was braced to hear a metallic voice tell me that this was a recording and the number now out of service, but almost at once I heard de Gonde's voice at the other end of the wire.

"Monsieur Davis?" he said before I spoke a word.

"Yes," I said, taken aback.

"Good. I was waiting for you to return my call. And now that you're assured I really do exist, good night, monsieur. The car will be at your door at nine promptly."

Whatever else he might be, I thought when he abruptly hung up, he must be a superb chessplayer.

I went upstairs, two stairs at a time, and somewhat incoherently broke the great news to my friends. Only one of them failed to respond with enthusiasm. Louis shook his head glumly and said he didn't like the smell of the whole thing.

"Oh la la," Véronique said merrily. "You're just jealous."

"Jealous!" said Louis in an aggrieved voice. "If I had a jealous bone in my body, do you think I'd take you to see Cary Grant?"

"Joking aside," Eliane put in, "at least now we know who was pretending to be Max Marchat."

"And who is he?" Louis demanded. He glowered at me. "Admit it. It's just too much money for any such job. And look how the arrangements were made. Whoever heard of such intrigue when it comes to hiring a tutor for a kid?"

He was right, of course. But if looking at it the way he did was going to cost me three thousand francs a month, I preferred to keep my eyes tight shut.

4

The car that pulled up before the *pension* at exactly nine in the morning was a magnificent gray Mercedes limousine. Its chauffeur, a hard-faced, leathery man of about fifty, wore a gray livery.

"I'm Georges Devesoul," he said curtly when I gave him my name. He jerked a thumb toward the seat beside him. "Let's go. Company's waiting."

When he swung the car around the corner past the weather-beaten arch of the Porte Saint-Denis—the poor man's Arc de Triomphe, as Louis once described it—a thought struck me.

"You're Monsieur de Gonde's chauffeur, aren't you?" I said.

"Yes."

"Is it his son I'm supposed to be tutoring?"

"His nephew. Madame de Villemont's son. Didn't he tell you?"

"No."

"That's who it is. A real case, too. He'll wind up as crazy as his mama, if she has her way about it," he said bitterly.

"Monsieur de Gonde mentioned something about her being a problem."

Georges made a grimace. "Problem? That's a pretty fancy word for someone who's had to put in time *à Charenton!*"

That meant time in an insane asylum. Louis' words of caution now sounded loud in my ears. For the first time since de Gonde's phone call, I began to wonder if I shouldn't have looked before I leaped.

"That bad?" I said.

"That bad. She had too many troubles and just cracked up under them. She's soft. No backbone."

"What kind of troubles?"

"I suppose the worst kind for a woman. Her husband was an officer in Algeria, a fine man, one of the best, and I know, because I was his orderly there. She and he were wild about each other, they were like a pair of honeymooners. Then those stinking Algerian mobsters caught up to him. One morning Madame kisses him good-bye when he leaves the house. Two minutes later, he's spattered all over the street in front of her eyes by a bomb tossed into his car."

"My God!"

"Then when we moved to Paris," Georges said grimly, "she got into a mess with a young fellow who went for her big, a real wild-eyed type. When she put him in his place, he killed himself. Drowned himself in the Seine. That's how it goes with her. She's got fifty million francs in the bank, and all it seems to buy is bad luck. She knows it, too. That's why she cracked up. If it wasn't for the family, she'd probably have been put away for keeps by now."

What, I wondered, had made Claude de Gonde think I was qualified to deal with a psychotic?

"Does Monsieur Claude live near Madame de Villemont?" I asked hopefully.

"They all live together. The whole family. Except the grandma, that is. Madame Cesira. She says she can't stand the mausoleum we're stuck in, so she's got herself this apartment on Île Saint-Louis."

"Mausoleum?"

Georges grunted. "We pulled out of Algiers in a hurry when everything blew up there, and this was the only furnished place near the Parc Monceau big enough for our whole gang. Half the rich *colons* out of North Africa headed in the same direction, but we had to be the ones stuck with this miserable stone-pile."

Colons. The late Max Marchat had led an investigating commission in Algeria in 1960, so he must have known the leading

colons there, the long-time French settlers who virtually owned
the country. That would explain the connection between him
and de Gonde, although not why de Gonde had posed as
Marchat for my benefit.

It gave me something to think about as we drove along,
Georges now maintaining a tight-lipped silence as if sorry he
had spoken so freely.

For anyone who wants a quick trip up an ascending economic
scale, there is nothing like the ride westward along the Grands
Boulevards. The neighborhood around the Porte Saint-Martin
and the Porte Saint-Denis is shabby lower class; then for a
few blocks there is a jazzy, neon-lit stretch of movie theaters and
showy cafés like the Bourneville; then past the Opéra there is
the middle-class shopping district where the landmarks are those
Macy's and Gimbels of Paris, the Galeries Lafayette and Au
Printemps; finally, as a climax, one enters the luxuriously upper-
class world of the Plaine Monceau.

At the rue de Courcelles, Georges turned off the boulevard
and pulled the car to a halt before an enormous stone building
in the middle of the block. A high wall surrounded it, and the
huge arched doorway in the wall was barred by a wooden carriage gate solid enough to repel an invading army.

Georges got out of the car—a chunky, barrel-chested, bandy-
legged figure, he moved with the gracelessness of an ape—and
unlocked the door set within the gate, stepped through it, and
pulled open the gate from the inside. Then he re-entered the
car and steered it into a courtyard.

"Well," he said, and gave me a sly, sidelong look, "what do
you think of it?"

He knew what I thought of it without my telling him. The
building suggested a fortress hacked out of rock, it was that
ponderous and barren of decoration. It surrounded the cob-
blestoned courtyard on three sides, and its rows of windows
stared down at me like all-seeing, coldly hostile eyes. And the
size of it, the expanse of its brooding façade, was overwhelming.

"Why so big?" I asked. "How many are there in the family
anyhow?"

"Enough. Madame de Villemont and the kid have one apartment. Monsieur Claude and Madame Gabrielle—she's Madame Cesira's older daughter—have another. Monsieur Edmond and Madame Matilde—she's Madame Cesira's younger daughter —have still another. That's three apartments big enough for a regiment apiece just to keep them all out of each other's hair. Then there's this Bernard Bourdon, Monsieur Claude's private secretary and a real pain in the neck, who likes plenty of room for himself. And up there on the top floor under the eaves are the rooms for the permanent staff. Right now there are eight of us, so when you move in it'll make nine."

That jolted me. "Move in? Do you mean I'm supposed to live here?"

"Why the hell not? If you're to take over the kid—"

"As his tutor, not his nursemaid."

Georges spat hard on the ground. "Go on," he said coldly, "don't tell me you really figured to collect three thousand a month for sitting with the kid over his books a couple of hours a day. You couldn't work that kind of swindle on anybody, even in America."

I looked up at the stony, silent walls around me, and suddenly the raucous, bustling, heart-warming Faubourg Saint-Denis seemed light-years away, the smoky little Café au Coin more desirable than Maxim's, the shabby arch of the Porte Saint-Denis more beautiful than the Arc de Triomphe.

But three thousand a month!

When I entered the mansion I found myself in a vast rotunda, big enough for a circus, whose ceiling was the roof of the building itself, three stories above my head. On either side of me were open doors revealing a succession of spacious chambers, and before me was a broad marble staircase which ascended to the pillared entrance of the second-floor landing.

"In that wing," Georges said, pointing, "the Grand Salon, the ballroom, the conservatory. In the other wing, the dining room used for big shows, the Grand Gallery—pictures and stuff —then the library and card room. At the far end is the conference room used for business meetings. One thing to remember. Don't hang around the doors there when a board meeting is going on."

"No market tips," I said.

"No market tips. No snooping. Those corporation bigshots are dividing up the pie for themselves, not you and me. Now we go through this door behind the staircase and straight down the passageway to the kitchen."

The narrow, low-ceilinged passageway was marked at intervals by steel doors which looked as if they had been recently installed.

"Storage rooms," said Georges in answer to my query, "and this one is the gun room where all the hunting equipment is kept. It's a repair shop, too, so if you hear someone banging away like a blacksmith you'll know why. And right through there is the kitchen."

The kitchen looked capable of serving a battalion of gourmets at a sitting. Gathered there around a long table were some people leisurely comparing a collection of lottery tickets with the list of the week's winning numbers in the morning paper. One of the hopefuls, a flinty-eyed matron, proved to be not only the housekeeper in charge, but also Georges' wife, Madame Thérèse. After Georges introduced me to her, she, in turn, introduced me to the rest of the staff. One of them, a youthful domestic with a bouffant hairdo and ripe figure, ogled me with marked interest until Madame Thérèse rapped her knuckles on the girl's forehead and acidly remarked, "Obviously, our Jeanne-Marie has never yet seen a man in her whole life, poor, deprived thing."

Still, it was Jeanne-Marie who was delegated to lead me to Monsieur Claude's apartment where the family was waiting, and as I followed her through a door opposite the one by which I had entered the kitchen, I wondered how long it would take me just to learn my way around this labyrinth.

Our destination turned out to be a wrought-iron cage containing the traditional French elevator, a car barely large enough for two passengers.

"This way, handsome," said Jeanne-Marie, waving me into

it. She joined me, making no effort to keep any distance between us. "So you're coming to work in the mental ward," she gibed as the elevator started a groaning, chain-rattling ascent.

"Is it that bad?"

"You'll find out. When's your day off from the job?"

"They haven't told me yet. What's Madame de Villemont like, anyhow?"

Jeanne-Marie gently rubbed her hip against mine. "She's like somebody who gives ideas to men who ought to know better."

"What does that mean?"

"Nothing. Just don't you get any ideas about her like that last character they had taking care of the kid. Then you won't have to go drowning yourself in the dirty old river. That would be a terrible waste, big boy."

So it had been the child's last tutor who had killed himself over Madame de Villemont. Hard to believe that in this practical day and age men were still capable of such idiocies, but if ever a place seemed capable of inspiring them, it was this gloomy castle on the rue de Courcelles.

The elevator stopped, but Jeanne-Marie remained where she was, now leaning warmly against me, her face upturned expectantly. Instead of seizing the moment, I reached over her shoulder to push open the door. If I stayed on the job, there would be time later for such games.

Jeanne-Marie drew away sharply and gave me a withering look. "*Tiens,*" she said, waggling a hand in a wonderfully expressive gesture, "*un zozo des zozos!*" which, words and gesture combined, stated that I was a supreme innocent of innocents, and God pity the girl who wasted her good intentions on me.

The elevator opened on a corridor running the length of the building. It was impossible to tell what vista the windows ranging along one wall overlooked since they were completely shrouded by faded red velvet drapes. The walls, too, were covered with the same kind of material, the chairs and tabourets arrayed against them were dispiritingly ugly, and the lighting from tarnished gilt wall brackets was pallid and shadowy.

The whole effect, in fact, was that of a corridor in a bad dream, just the place for a neurotic, tragedy-ridden woman to walk while nursing her bitter memories. Then it struck me that I didn't really know whether Madame de Villemont walked this passageway or was a recluse in her apartment, or, for that matter, was altogether bedridden. I had to be prepared for anything when I met her.

So I braced myself against surprise when Jeanne-Marie knocked on a door and announced us and was told to enter, but not against the one surprise that awaited me.

There, of all the company gathered in the room, the first to catch my eye was the girl of the Club Barouf, the distracted American I had rescued from her tormentors the night I started work there, and in that instant of recognition I knew who Madame de Villemont was.

5

I knew she was Madame de Villemont because this made sense out of what had been happening to me since our first encounter. And because she sat rigidly upright in a straight-backed chair, distinctly apart from the others in the room, hands tightly clasped in her lap, face very pale, eyes shadowed with apprehension, the total effect somehow suggesting that she, the family problem, was on trial here.

I also recognized as her companions at the club that night the pert little blonde and the bloated, sour-visaged man seated at opposite ends of a couch. Nearby, a pleasant-looking, matronly woman in eyeglasses, embroidery work in her hands, was sunk into the depths of an overstuffed armchair, and on its arm was perched a young man with a soft, pretty, girlish face so supercilious in expression that he seemed to be smelling something bad.

If these seemed to be the jury at the trial, the man facing me from across the room, feet planted apart, arms folded on his chest, could be cast as the judge. As ascetically lean as the man on the couch was grossly fat, his thin, tightly compressed lips pale even against his sallow complexion, he had the strong features, the stubborn jaw and level eyes, the almost palpable air of authority of someone born to command. This, I was sure, had to be Claude de Gonde.

After Jeanne-Marie departed, he was the one who brusquely introduced me to the gathering, and I found my surmise was right. He was Claude de Gonde and the woman with the eyeglasses and embroidery was Madame Gabrielle de Gonde. The couple on the couch were Edmond Vosiers and Madame Matilde Vosiers. The two women, I already knew from what Georges, the chauffeur, had told me, were the daughters of the *doyenne* of the family, Madame Cesira, who appeared to be the only member of it absent from the proceedings. And, finally, the supercilious young man was Bernard Bourdon, private secretary to Monsieur de Gonde. When, in response to my nod of greeting, Bernard murmured, *"Enchanté,"* and slowly looked me up and down with the eye of a connoisseur, I understood why Georges had commented unpleasantly on him.

As for my new employer, Madame Anne de Villemont, she said nothing when I made an awkward little bow in her direction, but only gave me a regal lift of the chin like Nefertiti of Egypt acknowledging the obeisance of a peasant before the royal throne. It stung me, but, I warned myself, I was getting three thousand a month as balm for such stings. And there was something else that helped keep my temper down. The feeling that she was holding herself in tight restraint. That underneath her hauteur was an explosive tension barely under control. It made an electric aura around her as strong in its way as the sense of command emanating from de Gonde.

In fact, the whole room was charged with this tension. De Gonde's abrupt manner, the way Madame Gabrielle stared at me from her armchair, embroidery needle poised in the air, a

sudden loud clearing of the throat by Vosiers, the angry glance
his wife darted at him for it—they all seemed on edge.

De Gonde was not in a mood to waste words on me.
Madame de Villemont, he said, had been impressed by my
tact and resolution in handling an ugly scene at the Club
Barouf, had decided I might be the right person to take her
fatherless son in charge. As it happened, the child was un-
usually intelligent, extremely sensitive, but in a very bad way
emotionally. Charming, but unstable.

"Hysterical," snapped Vosiers. "Bound hand and foot to his
mother's apron strings. Can't be away from her without coming apart at the seams."

"He's only a child," Madame Matilde sharply reminded him.
"And he's been through a great deal."

De Gonde cut all this short with a peremptory gesture.

"The cure is our concern now, not the cause." He addressed
himself to me again. "And the cure may lie in his being super-
vised by a capable, athletic sort of a man with a reasonable amount of patience and understanding. Also, Madame de
Villemont is an American like yourself. She feels that perhaps
American methods—"

"I don't know anything about any methods," I said bluntly.
He struck me as someone you could be blunt with, and his response told me I had gauged him correctly.

"Then you'll have to improvise and use common sense," he
said. "Under any conditions, you'll get a fair trial. Now, if you
have any questions—"

"I have. Why did you pose as Max Marchat when you were
looking me up?"

"Because," de Gonde said calmly, "I didn't want you on my
neck if nothing came of this business. I presented myself to
your Monsieur Castabert as Marchat to conceal my identity and
avoid that."

"This Castabert," the pert Madame Matilde remarked to me,
wrinkling her nose in disgust. "Such an obscene little creature.
How could you stand him?"

"It was my job to, madame," I said.

What I didn't say was that in applying for that job, I had

been politely invited by Castabert to sit down, have a cup of coffee, light a cigarette. Not, as in the present case, kept standing before company, hat in hand. For the first time in my life I could really appreciate the feelings of the servant in the old-fashioned household where he was not supposed to have any feelings. Living here was going to be an enlightening experience.

"One other question," I said to de Gonde. "I've been told I'm supposed to live here in this house while I'm in charge of the child. But is that necessary?"

At last Madame de Villemont herself had something to say.

"Yes," she stated flatly. "It is necessary."

I turned to her in appeal. "But I could arrange—"

"If Madame de Villemont is to be free to come and go," interposed the matronly Madame Gabrielle, "you should be with the child as much as possible. And you'll find any room you choose on the upper floor quite comfortable."

"No." Madame de Villemont rose and stood gripping the back of her chair with both hands. "He's to have the room next to Paul's in my apartment."

Every face turned incredulously toward her. It was the stout Edmond Vosiers who recovered first.

"Impossible!" he exploded. "Out of the question! I won't tolerate it."

"He must be near Paul," said Madame de Villemont. "You agreed to that. All of you."

"But not to having a man live right there in your apartment," said Madame Matilde. Her voice was solemnly reproving, but her eyes, I saw, had a wicked glint of mockery in them. "What a scandal it would make. We'd never be able to face any of our friends again."

"Only if you choose to make something dirty of it," said Madame de Villemont.

"Now that's uncalled for," de Gonde said sternly. "And I warn you, madame, not to work yourself into a state."

"I am not working myself into a state. I am doing what must be done for Paul's good."

"My dear, we know that," Madame Gabrielle said gently.

"But Matilde is right. The servants will gossip, and the gossip will soon reach our friends. If you intend to start living life among them again as you promised you would, you can't afford that."

"And if I can't," demanded Madame de Villemont, "what sort of friends are they?"

"The truest," snarled Vosiers. "The most loyal. Your husband knew how to choose his friends. For his sake, you will not disgrace yourself before them."

"Besides," Madame Matilde remarked with raised eyebrows, "wouldn't this particular bedroom be Henri's—if he were still with us? What do you think Dr. Morillon will make of your little arrangement? Since he's such an expert on psychology, shouldn't he be asked about it?"

"He doesn't have to be asked about it; he can be told about it," Madame de Villemont said defiantly, but the quivering of her lips, the way she gripped the back of her chair for support showed that the defiance was hollow. Plainly, she was terrified by what Madame Matilde had said.

As if by some secret signal, everyone in the room now looked at everyone else. It was a subtly inquiring look that went from eye to eye and was answered by a barely perceptible nod, an out-thrust lower lip, a shrug. A silent vote was being held, and charity prevailed. The mother has to be placated for the child's sake, they must have decided, so placate her they would.

It was de Gonde, of course, who announced the verdict to her.

"If you insist, madame," he said wearily, "have it your own way."

Now I understood the tensions in the room. That little scene alone left me feeling like an overwound watchspring.

And what, I wondered, had the scene been like when Madame de Villemont first announced to her husband's family that she had chosen as his son's caretaker the bouncer of the Club Barouf?

6

Paul de Villemont was a strikingly handsome little boy who seemed both younger and older than his nine years. Much too small and slight for his age, he had his mother's lustrous, darkly blue eyes and a shock of pitch-black hair spilling over his forehead, and these features were in startling contrast to the pallor of his face. A strangely disturbing face, too. For all its childishness, it was already stamped with an adult wariness.

Following Madame de Villemont the length of the corridor to her apartment in the opposite wing of the building, I had been apprehensive about my meeting with the boy, and my first sight of him, all wariness, had increased the apprehension. But when we soberly shook hands, man to man, and I felt his fingers in mine as fragile and fleshless as the claws of a sparrow, felt the shivering tension in them, apprehension turned to pity.

He looked up at me, measuring my dimensions with open-mouthed awe.

"Uncle Claude told me you were once a pugilist," he said eagerly. "A champion of boxing. Were you really?"

"In English, *chéri,*" his mother said. "Remember that when you're with Monsieur Reno you must speak only English."

Paul threw her an impatient look, then repeated his question to me in excellent, almost unaccented English.

"Not a champion," I said. "But I was a professional fighter."

He nodded, indicating this was quite acceptable to him. "And will you teach me how to be one?"

"If your mother doesn't object."

"Do you?" he asked her tensely, his heart in his voice.

She hesitated.

"Oh, please," he begged.

"Very well, I don't object," she decided. "Not if you take care."

"Of course," he assured her, and then he remarked to me with a shrug, "That's how women are, always telling people to take care."

He sat on the edge of his bed furiously gnawing his finger-nails and staring at me wide-eyed as his mother explained my duties. Fridays were my time off, and Sundays Paul was delivered to his grandmother on Île Saint-Louis and left in her charge part of the day, but every other morning of the week was to be devoted to instruction. On hand was a syllabus for each subject prepared by the headmaster of the Lycée Monceau. Special textbooks on American history and literature had been imported from the States, and if I needed others they would be ordered immediately.

"Those are the important subjects," said Madame de Villemont. "Paul is an American and some day will be attending an American school. He must be prepared for that."

Paul's face became darkly resentful.

"I am not an American," he protested. "Grandmother says I am not. She says some day I'll go to school at Saint-Cyr to learn to be a soldier like Papa and Grandpa."

I saw Madame de Villemont stiffen.

"Enough," she said.

"But it's true," Paul assured me. "That's what Grandmother says. My father was a colonel in the paratroops and my grandfather was General de Villemont, a very great general. And my father died in action. That is the right way for a soldier of France to die."

"*Assez! Ça suffit!*" Madame de Villemont said between her teeth, and her face had drained of all color. "You know I don't want you to talk about these things."

"Grandmother does," Paul said cunningly. "And you told me to listen and be polite when she does. You told me—"

"Now I'm telling you you're a child and don't understand these things." Madame de Villemont took hold of herself with an effort. She turned to me inquiringly. "Do you know how to play baseball?"

"Yes."

"Good. I had a ball and glove sent from New York, and I'd like Paul to learn how to use them. They must be somewhere around here."

She looked distractedly around the room, which was littered with toys and games and construction sets as well as stacks of books and magazines most in ragged and well-read condition. In case these failed to provide enough diversion, there was also a large television set, a radio, and an elaborate tape recorder on hand. Materially, at least, Paul lacked for nothing.

The ball and glove proved to be under a pile of toys in a large chest. Paul finally dug them out with the air of doing everyone a great favor.

"Very well," said Madame de Villemont. "Now on nice afternoons, you're to go with Monsieur Reno to the Parc Monceau and learn how to catch and throw. If you wish, you can take your football, too."

"Oh, Mama, the Parc Monceau is for babies."

"It happens to be a delightful place. And when you're there you will not sit on a bench and read. You will practice playing ball with Monsieur Reno and do exactly as he says so that you'll become as big and strong as he is."

"Yes, Mama," said Paul, and if I had been in his shoes I would probably have sounded just as wearily cynical.

"And," Madame de Villemont said to me, "when the weather doesn't permit being outdoors you'll take Paul to whatever museum or gallery you think worthwhile. Or, if anything decent is playing, to a movie in the neighborhood. Evenings when I'm at home you won't have to take charge of him. There's usually a card game going on in the kitchen after dinner, and I'm sure you'd be welcome there. If I'm not at home, you will remain in your room and look in on Paul regularly. Your room is right through here," she said, leading me into it.

From its size and furnishings, it was a master bedroom. A huge double bed, an armoire big enough to camp in, a dresser, and a Gargantuan chest of drawers still couldn't dwarf it. It also had its own dressing room and bathroom. Then I saw that I had been brought here, not merely to be shown my accommodations, but to be told something in confidence away from Paul.

Madame de Villemont closed the door between his room and mine, leaving him hard at work cramming toys back into their chest. Then she quietly turned the key in the door and wheeled to face me.

Before she could get a word out there was an explosive crash against the door, then another—the sound of a small body being hurled wildly against it.

"*Ouvrez la porte!*" Paul screamed. "*Ouvrez! Ouvrez!*"

Madame de Villemont's hand went to her forehead in a distrait gesture. "*Chéri,* listen to me—"

"*Ouvrez! Ouvrez!*"

The child's voice rose to a demented shrieking. The battering at the door continued. A foot drummed against it so that it looked as if the panel were going to be splintered. "*Ouvrez!*"

With fumbling hands, Madame de Villemont turned the key and threw open the door. Paul stood there panting, his eyes blazing, his teeth set. He looked like some small, disheveled animal gone rabid. Suddenly he leaped at me, swung his clenched fist hard against my leg, and before I could catch hold of him, darted back into his room. With a sweep of the arm he sent his radio crashing to the floor. The lamp on his bedside table went next. He looked around, then headed for the shelves of books against the wall.

"*Chéri,*" his mother said helplessly, "please, please, listen to me."

Books went flying as he clawed them off the shelves.

Madame de Villemont, her face agonized, stood rooted there. This, her manner seemed to say, was all one could do until these storms passed. I walked into the hail of flying books, clamped a hand on Paul's shoulder, and whirled him around to face me. I squatted so that we were on eye level.

"Didn't you hear your mother?" I asked. "Do you really enjoy making her unhappy?"

He struggled frenziedly in my grip, building his hysteria to a point where it seemed dangerously close to going out of control altogether, but still I refused to release that grip on him. Then slowly the struggling subsided. Paul stood spent and gasping.

"Now answer me," I said.

With cool deliberation, taking careful aim, he spat full into my face.

I stood up. He had no idea what was coming; evidently nothing like this had ever happened to him before, so he was still leering at me in triumph when I brought the flat of my hand hard against the seat of his pants. I have a heavy hand. The leer dissolved into a yelp of anguish, echoed by a gasp from his mother.

Hands pressed to his seat, he retreated from me, step by dazed step, until he was brought up short by the bookshelves. He stood there staring at me as if unable to believe what had happened. Then, as realization dawned, his face started to work. He had too much pride to give way to tears but it took an effort to fight them down. I heard his mother's quick steps approaching us, and with a gesture from behind my back I stopped her where she was.

Paul finally found his voice. "You hit me," he said accusingly.

"I spanked you."

"It's the same thing."

I shook my head solemnly. "No, one only hits a dangerous man. One spanks a troublesome puppy."

"I'm not a puppy!"

"If you behave like one, you are one. Like this." I let out a series of shrill yapping sounds and waved my hands aimlessly in the air. "That," I said with disdain, "is Paul de Villemont being a spoiled puppy."

It was a perilous moment. The darkly blue eyes narrowed with outrage at the same time those lips couldn't help curling into a smile at the spectacle I had made. It was touch and go, and next time the hysteria might go all the way.

The smile won.

"You're silly," Paul told me, then turned to his mother. "Of course I'm not really like that," he assured her. "Am I?" he asked uncertainly.

"Not really." Madame de Villemont shrugged apologetically. "But just now—"

He didn't like that. The storm clouds started to gather again.

"Because you locked the door," he charged. "You went with him and left me alone."

Before she could answer, I said, "There are times when people want to talk in private. You and I will have times like that. When we do, would you want someone banging away at the door?"

Paul grudgingly shook his head. "But what will you and I talk about in private?" he asked suspiciously. "Only lessons."

"No." I thought of his mother, his grandmother, his doting aunts, the houseful of maids—all the women surrounding him while the men in his life were either dead or attending to business. "We'll have a lot to talk about besides lessons. Men's affairs. Things that don't really concern women."

He considered this soberly. "Yes, of course. Men's affairs."

"Now your mother and I must talk in private. Meanwhile"— I looked around at the havoc in the room "—you might try to do something about this mess."

I would settle for this temporary victory. Quickly, before he could respond, I ushered the startled Madame de Villemont into my room, and not trying to muffle the sound at all, twisted the key in the lock.

I turned to see Madame apparently braced for a fresh assault on the door, her face taut, her clasped hands tight against her breast. As silence prevailed, her hands slowly unclasped, fell to her sides. Still the tautness remained in her face.

"He likes you," she said breathlessly in a low voice. "I'm sure he does. I'm sure he'll listen to you."

"I hope so, madame."

"No, I'm sure of it. And that's important, because you won't have trouble keeping him close when you're away from the

house. Do you understand? When you're away from the house
with him you must never leave him out of your sight."

"Of course, madame."

Her voice took on a sharper edge. She was becoming her old
regal self again.

"And you're never to allow him to have anything to do with
strangers. Certainly, you're never to put him in someone else's
charge while you're off having a quick one at some bistro."

Up to that moment, I had been nurturing a growing sympathy for her because of her tragic past, her inability to cope with
her son, her whole neurotic state. More than a sympathy, in
fact, because she was one of the most hotly glowing, most
sensually exciting women I had ever come across. Now the sympathy instantly turned to chill dislike.

"Yes, madame," I said. "I'll see to it that both Paul and I stay
out of the bistros."

"Don't try to make a joke of it," she flashed back. "Can't you
see I'm in deadly earnest? Paul may be in danger, and you—"

"Danger?" I said in bewilderment. "Danger from what?"

"From kidnapers!"

"What makes you think so?"

"That doesn't matter. All that matters is to see he's protected
from them."

My bewilderment mounted. Aside from the fact that kidnaping was one of the rarest of crimes in France—to any Frenchman it was strictly *le crime américain*—neither Georges nor de
Gonde had even mentioned to me any threat of it against Paul.
But why hadn't they? One good reason came to mind.

"Hasn't the family been told about this?" I asked Madame.
"And the police?"

"It's not their business. No one must be told about it. No
one at all!"

So that was it. I might be lured into playing a part in this
fantasy, but never the police or the family, those unkind real-
ists.

"All right," I said reassuringly, "you can count on me. I'll see
to it nothing happens to Paul."

"I am counting on it," said Madame. Then, to my mystification, she quickly crossed the room to the massive chest in its far corner and pulled out the bottom drawer. "Give me a hand with this," she ordered. "Get it out all the way and put it on the floor."

I did so, not without an effort since the drawer was almost the size of a steamer trunk and filled with red velvet draperies that reeked of camphor. Then she kneeled down and groped deep inside the empty space left in the chest, finally coming up with a small, cloth-wrapped bundle. She undid the wrapping feverishly, and there in her hand I saw a beautifully designed pistol, a Beretta, its muzzle aimed squarely at my chest.

"Here, take it," she commanded, and I promptly did so. I was relieved when I extracted the clip to see it empty, but even so, the cold weight of the gun in my hand made me wonder uneasily what was going on in this grim pile of stone on the outwardly serene rue de Courcelles. Under any conditions, I decided, object number one was to keep this gun out of Madame de Villemont's hands. And since I wanted no part of it either, the man to deliver it to was Claude de Gonde. As head of this household, he was as much in charge of Madame as I was of her son, and the deadly weapon she had stored away was his problem, not mine.

She watched me thrust the gun into my belt. "You'll have to get bullets for it. Do you know where to?"

"I think so."

"Good. Now put the drawer back. You can hide it behind that drawer when you're not carrying it." She watched me replace the drawer, and then said abruptly, "I want you to move in here as soon as possible. Today, if you can."

"There's no reason I can't. But I'll need some place for a load of books. Madame Vosiers mentioned the rooms on the upper floor. If I could use one of them as a study on my time off—"

"No, I want you here close to Paul. I'll have a bookcase put in here for you, and a desk, and proper lighting. But you're to stay away from the upper floor. You wouldn't have much privacy there anyhow, once the maids get a look at you."

"I'm sure Madame is wrong."

"Is she?" Madame de Villemont reached out and plucked something from my shoulder. When she held it out at arm's length I saw it was a long golden strand of hair which must have been glittering on my jacket since I had ridden the elevator upstairs. "It looks to me," she remarked, distastefully letting the strand fall from her fingers, "that Jeanne-Marie has her own ideas about that."

"I'm afraid I don't know what Madame means."

"Yes, you do. Madame means that her son is a highly observant little boy, and she doesn't want him living in an atmosphere of bedroom intrigue. So stay away from the girls here, especially Jeanne-Marie. Someone else in the house already has a claim on her anyhow, and there's nothing the silly little bitch would like better than to use you against him. Don't let that happen or you may find yourself in serious trouble. Is that clear?"

"Yes, madame." Serious trouble suggested that it was one of the upper echelon who had the claim on Jeanne-Marie. Since the compatibility between de Gonde and his wife seemed genuine, and since the supercilious Bernard Bourdon would certainly find a pretty boy much more enticing than a pretty girl, I had the feeling that Edmond Vosiers was the man.

Madame de Villemont did not choose to linger on the subject.

"Do you have a driver's license?" she asked.

"Yes, I have."

The last of my succession of sports cars had gone for eating money long ago, but, like any good American, I had kept my driver's license up to date.

"Then you can borrow one of the cars in the garage whenever you need it. The garage attendant keeps the keys to them. You'll need one now to move your things here. I'm counting on you to be back in time for dinner. I'll have a place set for you."

That seemed to be the end of the interview. Madame de Villemont led me to the door of my room, which opened directly on the second-floor corridor.

"If you want someone to show you the way to the garage—" she said.

I felt the Beretta weighing down my belt, a cold, heavy reminder of what had to be done as quickly as possible.

"No, madame," I said, "I'll find my own way."

As soon as she closed the door behind me, I headed directly for Claude de Gonde's apartment.

7

De Gonde and his wife were there alone. When I drew the gun from my belt and handed it to him he looked at it incredulously, and Madame Gabrielle clapped a hand to her mouth in horror.

"My God," de Gonde said to her, "I could swear it's Henri's! The one that disappeared after his death." He turned to me. "He was Colonel de Villemont, my wife's brother, Madame de Villemont's late husband. Where did you get this? How did you get it?"

He listened intently as I answered that, obviously much shaken by my story.

"Yes," he said when I had concluded, "you've behaved with good sense, letting me know about it at once."

He dropped into an armchair and sat there lost in thought. When he abstractedly put a cigarette between his lips and leaned forward toward me, it took me a few seconds to realize he was waiting for me to light it. I had almost forgotten I was a servant in this house. I lit the cigarette, and de Gonde inhaled deeply. "Now what?" he said grimly to his wife.

"I'm not sure," she said. "Perhaps the best thing is to tell all this to Dr. Morillon immediately."

They looked at each other steadily, and again, as during the family conference, I had the uneasy feeling that much more was being communicated by this meeting of eyes than I was supposed to understand. And up to now, little Paul de Villemont had lived most of his life in this shadowy world of meaningful glances, whispers behind doors, veiled secrets. If I could be put on edge by one day as an inhabitant here, it was shockingly clear what must be happening to him.

De Gonde held up the gun on the palm of his hand. "And in view of this," he said, "Dr. Morillon should also be told he's wrong about Madame taking a turn for the better. One doesn't need medical charts to recognize the symptoms of a growing paranoia. This weapon, the terror that the child might be kidnaped—"

"Isn't it possible," I said, "that she did receive such a threat?"

Madame Gabrielle shook her head. "There never was any threat, Monsieur Reno," she said gently. "You see, my brother —Madame's husband—was a leader of our country's forces in the struggle against the terrorists of the Algerian FLN and was marked for death by them. They finally did succeed in murdering him. After that, Madame was seized by the idea that Paul was intended to be one of their victims, too. It was an obsession with her. But we thought that with the ending of the war, with Algeria's getting her independence, she would forget this fear. It was so long ago, too. But now it seems we were wrong about it."

"At least we have one comfort," de Gonde said to me. "Since you've managed to win a degree of Madame's confidence, you can warn us if measures must be taken to protect her against herself. Or, for that matter, to protect the child from her."

"Ah, no!" said Madame Gabrielle. "She would never do anything to hurt Paul! How can you think she might?"

"Because I don't know what to think any more," de Gonde

said wearily. "Can someone irrational be judged by rational standards? She was difficult even when Henri first married her—"

"She was an adorable child," Madame Gabrielle remonstrated.

"But always difficult, always violently emotional. Now, in her present state, she's impossible to deal with." He shook his head hopelessly.

"I'll call Dr. Morillon at once," said Madame Gabrielle. "He can talk to her this afternoon."

"About this?" De Gonde hefted the gun. "No, that would destroy her confidence in Reno. Such confidence is too valuable to risk. For the first time since Henri's death we may have a way of penetrating that wall she's built around herself. The doctor should be told about the matter, but under no conditions should he approach her about it. I'm sure he'll agree with that policy."

"Perhaps," said Madame Gabrielle doubtfully.

"He will have to," de Gonde said. He handed me the gun. "As for this," he told me, "simply return it to its hiding place. If Madame questions you about it, tell her you're unable to obtain the ammunition it requires."

"Do I have to? I'd much rather tell her I just don't like to have anything to do with guns."

"But that won't serve the same purpose," Madame Gabrielle pointed out. "It might alienate her instead of winning her trust in you."

"Well—"

"Please. Not even Dr. Morillon has been able to overcome her secretiveness so far. You may be able to. For the child's sake alone will you help do that?"

"Yes, madame," I said, still not liking the smell of this whole arrangement.

That seemed to cover the subject for the time being. I was already at the door when de Gonde suddenly called me back. He sat contemplating me narrowly for a long time while I stood wondering what now.

"How serious are you about your writing?" he said abruptly, taking me by surprise.

"Very serious. I've gotten enough encouragement from some editors to believe I'll be published sooner or later."

"Do you know Charles Leschenhaut?"

"I know about him." Leschenhaut was the editor of *La Foudre*, one of the most recent literary magazines to appear in Paris, and already, within a couple of years, one of the most talked about.

"He's an old friend of mine," said de Gonde. "If you have no objections, I'll arrange for you to meet him and show him your work. His personal interest can mean everything to getting a career started."

Objections?

So, at least, I had that much to sustain me as I drove back to the Faubourg Saint-Denis. I needed something to sustain me because the thought of packing out of my room in Madame Olympe's *pension* after six contented years there was a depressing one. Madame Olympe may have been the classically bilious concierge, but the room itself, only one flight up and with a window overlooking the lively Faubourg Saint-Denis, was a jewel. Reasonably cheap, it was spacious, clean, free of all insect life, cool in the summer, warm in the winter, and, above all, was furnished with a bed big enough for me to stretch out in full-length. It was not a room to give up lightly.

Even worse was the thought of separation from Louis, my boon companion for almost every day of these six years. Something had to be done about that during the time I'd be quartered at the grim fortress on the rue de Courcelles.

Louis wasn't in his room when I arrived, so I left the car, a neat little red Renault, parked in front of the *pension*, and walked down the block to the Café au Coin where he was sure to be at this hour along with most of the shopkeepers of the Faubourg Saint-Denis on their late-morning break. I found him at a table next to the bar where the service was quickest, sharing a bottle of wine with Maguy, the grizzled old cop on the beat who had dropped in for a glass of something to fend off the February chill.

Louis took in my mood with a flick of the eye, and promptly

ordered a sandwich for me and another bottle of wine. In any crisis, he always said, food and drink were the vital restoratives. While Jeanloup, thus happily given an excuse to detach himself from the clutches of a well-dressed, sharp-looking, fast-talking salesman who had him pinned down at the bar, prepared the sandwich, I briefly described my new situation.

"What's wrong with that?" demanded Maguy, a moralist who strongly disapproved of my way of life. "It might teach you something, being with high-class people like that. It might make a respectable citizen out of you yet."

"Oh, stuff it," Louis said glumly. "That name de Villemont sounds familiar," he said to me. "Any relation to General Sebastien de Villemont?"

"The kid is his grandson."

"High class all right. And if they're *colons,* they're the most poisonous kind of high class. That's why you'd be crazy to give up your room here. They're not your kind of people. You'll never stick it out with them."

"If I could do it for a year it would give me a real bankroll to work on. And de Gonde said he'd give me a personal introduction to the editor of *La Foudre.* You know what that can mean."

"Even so, you have a temper of your own, and you're not used to being pushed around by people like that. You could have a showdown with them and be out of there next week for all you know."

"I still can't see paying Olympe for an empty room on the chance of it." I knew what was on his mind. "Look, this doesn't mean breaking up the old partnership. I have to be out with the kid afternoons. We can get together then any time we want."

"And play games with the kid?" Louis said, but I knew from his tone that the worst of his worries had been settled.

"Anyhow," Maguy said to me, stuffing his mouth with a piece of the sandwich Jeanloup placed on the table, "why don't you rent the room to somebody yourself? That way you could have it back any time you wanted it."

The salesman standing at the bar an arm's length away

turned around interestedly at this. "Somebody say something about a room to rent?"

I couldn't help staring at him. Although it was a miserable, wintry, slate-colored day, he was wearing oversized wraparound sunglasses, the kind the youthful patrons of the Club Barouf went in for. And one side of his face was deeply scarred from cheek to chin.

He saw me staring before I could look away, but he didn't seem perturbed by my bad manners.

"*Plastique*," he said dispassionately, patting the scarred cheek. *Plastiques* were the mean little bombs the anti-government *Organisation de l'Armée Secrete* terrorists had used indiscriminately around town during the height of the Algerian troubles a few years before. "I was in the wrong place at the wrong time when it went off. One of those couscous joints on the Faubourg Montmartre."

"Lousy OAS bastards," growled Maguy. "We had a sad case with a *plastique* right down the block here. You were there at the time, weren't you?" he said to me.

"Yes," I said shortly. He knew I didn't like to talk about it.

"Anyhow," Louis said to the salesman, "you were lucky to get off as well as you did."

"Was I?" The man lifted the sunglasses, and I saw that instead of an eye in the socket on the scarred side of his face was only a milky glistening whiteness. "That's why I wear these things. I tried a black patch, but the customers said I looked enough like a pirate as it was." He smilingly replaced the glasses. "Hope you don't mind the flapping ears, but are you guys serious about renting a decent room around here cheap? I need one, but everything I've seen so far is either a cockroach nest or sky high in price."

It reminded me of the mansion on the rue de Courcelles, the way Louis and I gave each other a questioning look and came to the same answer instantly, without a word being spoken.

Thus it was that I packed into the Renault only my clothing, typewriter, and a few of my books and manuscripts, and gladly saw Léon Becque, salesman extraordinary of carpeting, linoleum, and other floor coverings, in temporary possession of my room and whatever I had left in it. He immediately proved to be the ideal tenant. Once his bags and sample cases were stored away in the room, he insisted on paying me a week's rent in advance, which gave me more than enough to stand treat in the Café au Coin for the rest of the afternoon.

As the phrase goes, I was feeling no pain by the time I arrived back at the mansion on the rue de Courcelles shortly before the dinner hour, but the sight of those massive gates and gray, forbidding walls was as sobering as a cold bath. I parked the car in its proper place in the garage, and, with the help of a youthful garage attendant, bore my belongings to the kitchen. There, Jeanne-Marie, without invitation, hefted my typewriter and package of books and accompanied me to the elevator. This time there was no room at all for her after my luggage was stowed aboard, but still she managed to squeeze in beside me and share my ascent.

"Well, handsome," she said, "did you find out which is your day off?"

"Fridays," I said.

She made a face. "And I'm off Thursdays. That's all right. I can always find someone to switch around with."

"Fine," I said. "I'll see if my girl friend can't get Fridays off from her job too, and we'll make it a foursome."

Jeanne-Marie glowered at me. *"Ce matin un zozo, et maintenant vous faites le mariolle, hein?"* which was to say I had certainly undergone the transformation from bumpkin to wise guy in short order.

"Don't you believe I have a girl friend?" I asked amiably.

"Look, it's not any plain ordinary girl friend you've got on the brain right now."

"What does that mean?"

"You know what. It means you had a good look at Madame de Villemont so now there are some interesting ideas buzzing around in that thick skull. Well, you can forget them, because Madame already has all the men she needs to warm her bed."

Quick, unreasoning anger flared up in me, but I fought it down.

I patted Jeanne-Marie's cheek without affection.

"Such a pretty little girl," I said. "Such a dirty little mind."

She slapped my hand away.

"Don't you put on airs with me, teacher," she said coldly, "because you're the one who's got a lesson coming. And you're an American, too," she threw at me as a parting shot when I hauled my belongings out of the elevator. "You're the one who ought to know how American women are about anything that wears pants!"

I entered my room to find that Madame de Villemont had been as good as her word. There was now a bookcase and writing desk among its furnishings. Also, as lagniappe, there was Paul de Villemont curled up on my bed, his nose in a book. He scrambled excitedly to his feet when he saw me, his face lighting up.

"I was waiting for you," he said. "Look at me! Georges took me to the big store today for it. How does it look? Magnificent, no?"

Looking at him, I saw I wasn't the only one present carrying a pistol. He was dressed in full cowboy regalia of gaudy shirt, chaps, and tooled-leather, high-heeled boots, and around his skinny shanks was draped a cartridge belt with a toy six-shooter in it.

"Magnificent," I said. I had hoped to return his father's gun to its hiding place in the chest of drawers as soon as possible. Under the circumstances, all I could do was hastily thrust it under my mattress while Paul clumped around the room to show off his boots.

"The real thing," he assured me. "There's a lasso, too. You know. A rope for catching people."

"Sure enough," I told him admiringly. "You'll be ready to take on every rustler in Paris."

When I placed my typewriter on the desk, he immediately turned his attention to it.

"What's this for?"

"Writing stories."

"What kind of stories? What are they about? Can I read them?"

"Hey, what are you?" I said. "A question machine?"

He gave a nervous little cackle of laughter.

"You sound like Grandmother," he said. "She says I ask too many questions, too. Only she doesn't make it sound funny, the way you do. Did you meet her?"

"Not yet."

"You will. And you'll hate her."

"Perhaps not."

"Yes, you will!" Suddenly, from out of nowhere, the storm clouds were on us again, black and menacing. The child's teeth glinted behind lips curled back in a snarl, the eyes narrowed at me; the unhealthy color now mottling the pale face made it look bruised. "You will hate her! She says bad things about Mama!"

"Stop it, Paul!" Utterly confounded by this pitifully small, snarling image of hate, I found myself furiously shouting back at him. I took control of myself. "Enough of that," I said quietly. "Now come give me a hand unpacking these suitcases."

He remained at bay. "I'm not your servant!"

"I'm asking you to help me as a friend, not a servant."

"I'm not your friend! I don't want to be your friend! I don't need any friends!"

"Of course not." I saw the opening and quickly moved into it. "But what about me? I'm a stranger in the house. I don't know anyone here. It didn't bother me before because I thought I'd find at least one good friend to count on. Now that I know how you feel about it—" I let my head droop disconsolately.

I had gotten through to him. Slowly, the rigid little jaw unclenched, the bruised look faded, the fury in the eyes turned to frowning bewilderment. I sat down on the edge of the bed, my back to him, my head in my hands. I waited.

"Reno?"

"Yes."

"Don't be sad." He approached me as timidly as a puppy approaching some new and baffling object. "Please, don't be sad, Reno."

"I can't help it."

"Yes, you can." He tugged at my sleeve, and when I still refused to raise my head, he gave me a sharp, angry wallop on the shoulder with his fist. "Listen to me! I'll be your friend."

I raised my head. "Will you really?"

"Yes."

"I'm very grateful." I put an arm around him and took him on my knee. For a second he strained against the arm like a snared animal, but when I only tightened my hold he relaxed and leaned back against me. "After all," I said, "it's no fun being lonely."

"No." He looked up at me doubtfully. "But what do friends do?"

"Oh, everything. Help each other out, talk to each other, play games together—"

A voice from the doorway broke the spell. "Is something wrong?" It was Madame de Villemont, her hand to her breast, her expression fearful. "I heard your voices. From the way it sounded, I thought perhaps—"

"No, madame, there's nothing wrong." But there was something very wrong. As Paul slipped from my knee and turned to face his mother, my hand still resting on his shoulder, I felt the shivering tension that seized him, saw the way his face mirrored her anxiety. It gave me a sympathetic understanding of de Gonde's weariness with the situation. The child couldn't be separated from his mother, and she couldn't seem to mask her feelings from him, protect him from them. I felt pity for her, too, mixed with my anger at this unwanted intrusion. After all, as de Gonde himself had said, it's impossible to judge someone irrational by rational standards. "Paul and I were just having a little talk," I said.

Madame took herself in hand. "Well, you can continue it at dinner. It's almost time, Paul, so go wash up and wait at the

table for us. And please take off that gun. Cowboys don't wear
guns at the table."

Paul looked up at me. "Is that true?"

"I'm afraid it is, partner. They'd seem mighty unneighborly
otherwise."

"Is a partner the same as a friend?"

"In this case it is."

"Okay, partner. *Au'voir.*"

He clattered out of the room on an imaginary horse, and his
mother quickly closed the door behind him and placed her back
against it.

"You didn't tell him about the gun I gave you, did you?" she
said in a low voice.

"Of course not, madame."

"Good. Were you able to get the bullets for it?"

"No."

Something about the way I said it put her on guard.

"Did you try to get them?"

"Yes," I said uncomfortably.

Madame de Villemont stared at me. I stared back at her, trying to brazen it out.

"You're lying," she said at last.

That stung all the more because it was deserved. I thought of
the de Gondes pleading with me to make up a story about the
gun that would appease Madame, would win me her confidence for her own good, but I would have to let them down.
I wasn't built to play the game their way.

"You're right," I said. "The truth is I don't want any part of
a loaded gun. There's always a chance it'll go off when you
least expect it to."

Her breath quickened. She struggled for words.

"You fool!" she burst out. "Do you think I took you into this
house as some sort of joke?"

De Gonde was wrong, I thought with a sense of shock. The
whole family was wrong. Looking at this woman, I could swear
she was not imagining the dangers that so terrified her. She

knew something that her family and her psychiatrist didn't know. Something she didn't dare reveal to them. Something real.

"Madame," I said placatingly, "I came here as Paul's tutor, not as his armed guard. But if you'll tell me—"

"All I'll tell you is that you're being paid to follow my instructions without question!"

So, even sooner than Louis had prophesied it would, the showdown had come.

"Madame, there are some instructions no one in his right mind follows without question."

"That's too bad. Especially when the only other choice you have is to pack up and get out of here."

My valise and carry-all lay open on the bed. In silence, I closed the valise and locked it.

"Now what?" Madame demanded.

"That should be obvious. I'm packing up and getting out of here."

She watched unbelievingly as I drew the zipper around the carry-all and set it on the floor.

"You can't be serious," she said. "Simply because I want you to follow instructions—"

"Commands," I said. "Without question. But I've already served my time in the Marines."

"My God, you are thin-skinned, aren't you?"

"I'm glad you finally noticed it, madame. Better late than never, I always say."

With that as my farewell, I gathered the typewriter under one arm and the package of books under the other, took the valise and carry-all in hand and managed to get myself through the door while Madame de Villemont stood there watching me. Then I remembered the dismal object that had caused the whole crisis. I deposited my belongings on the hallway floor and wearily went back into the room to take the gun from beneath the mattress and return it to its original hiding place in the chest.

Through all this, Madame de Villemont remained immobile.

Then, when I straightened up and turned toward the hall door again, she came to sudden life. She crossed the room to me and caught hold of my arm. From the way she hastily withdrew her hand, I was sure she had gotten the same exciting shock from that contact that I had.

She was imperious Nefertiti descended from her throne, with eyes wide with panic.

"*Monsieur Reno*," she said, forcing herself to say it, "*je vous en prie—*"

"I beg you"—but spoken in French as if the English for it were unknown to her.

I had never expected she would condescend to say it. It was all she needed to say.

PART TWO

The Tower

1

Of course, the family had been right. The arrangement, as it had warned, was made to order for gossip. My door opened into Paul's room from one side, Anne de Villemont's door opened into it from the other; neither door was ever kept locked. Every evening, the three of us ate dinner together *en famille* in the dining room of the apartment. The constraint at the table was exactly the constraint one would find between a husband and wife not on very good terms with each other. I knew, because during my short-lived marriage to a woman whom Madame resembled in more ways than one —she was as rich, as strong-willed, and as sensually attractive —that was the way it had usually been at the table. To the furtive eyes and avid ears of the maids who waited on this table, it would also be the constraint of two people sharing a guilty secret.

Furtiveness was the hallmark of all the servants in the house. They made up a suspicious, tight-knit little confraternity devoted to the too silent step, to the covert, sidelong glance, to the whispered voice behind the half-closed door so that only the voice could be heard and never the words. Those occasional nights, when, on edge with boredom, I joined a party of them at a game of cards or dominoes in the kitchen, they gave me the feeling I had entered a meeting of conspirators who had no intention of allowing me into their inner councils. The rank miasma of this slyness and secretiveness permeated the whole house. It made the kind of poisonous atmosphere in which gossip had to flourish. Gossip about Madame de Villemont and her son's tutor especially, since Madame was in the family's bad graces anyhow, and the tutor, for all his polite ways, only an American roughneck hauled in from the gutters of the Tenth Arrondissement.

Regrettably, from my point of view, this gossip did not have the least foundation in fact. Regrettably, because no matter how much I detested her own secretiveness which easily matched that of the household help around her, no matter how I was angered at the way she selfishly made Paul a victim to her tensions, no matter how I resented her habit of addressing me with a "You will do such-and-such" which was her idea of giving instructions, I was, after all, a healthy male and Madame a highly desirable female. It would have taken very little encouragement from her to land us in bed together.

The encouragement was not forthcoming. However, what I did earn from her after a while was a wholehearted respect for my methods with Paul and an effort to co-operate with me in those methods.

This came about as the result of a crisis between Madame and me at the end of my second week in the house. With no training in how to serve as pedagogue and nurse to a morbidly fearful, violently emotional child who had been bound too long and too tightly to his mother's skirts, I devised a rough-and-ready program for him of no nonsense during lessons each morning and plenty of nonsense for the rest of the time we spent together.

At the end of the second week of this regimen I saw it wasn't working and I saw why. When Anne de Villemont asked me for a progress report, I came out with it.

"If you mean progress at his school work, he's doing fine. If you're talking about his physical condition and the state of his nerves, there is no progress. He won't eat enough; he doesn't sleep well; whenever you look at him he's biting his nails until they bleed; he has fits of shakes sometimes like somebody with the D.T.s. You know that as well as I do."

"Yes." Anne de Villemont looked up at me haggardly. "I've been wondering what you can do about it."

"Nothing," I said bluntly. "But I know what you can do about it."

"I?"

"Who else do you think is responsible for the state he's in? Don't you realize how you've infected him with your fears, your emotionalism? You're not blind. Watch him when you walk into the room. He might have been laughing at something one second before. Then he sees you and starts to go to pieces again. You're afraid of something—afraid for him, afraid for yourself —and he can smell the fear whenever he's near you. That's what's destroying him."

Anne de Villemont stiffened. She came to her feet with outrage. "Have you forgotten yourself completely? Do you know whom you're talking to? Is it your impression you were hired to worry about my well-being? You weren't. Paul is your only concern."

"I know it, madame. That's why I'm telling you the truth, much as you don't want to hear it. Paul is my concern. And if all I've been hired for is to be his attendant until he's taken off to an institution—"

It was calculated cruelty, and it worked. Eyes blazing, Anne de Villemont flung up a hand as if to aim a blow at me. The hand froze in midair, fell to her side. The woman seemed to disintegrate before my eyes.

"But what can I do?" she whispered. "What can I do?"

"Why are you so afraid something will happen to Paul?"

Her lips became a tight unyielding line. She shook her head.

It would be hopeless, I saw, trying to make headway against that granite resistance.

"All right," I said, "granting you are afraid something will happen to him, you can't let him know that. You'll have to hide your feelings, bury them deep. You'll have to keep tight control of yourself whenever you're near him. I don't think it'll be easy, but will you at least try to do it?"

She did. And because of the magic change that started to take place in Paul after that, she was encouraged to keep trying.

In a way, it made things harder for me. Away from Paul she would frequently slip back to the familiar, arrogant, overwrought Madame de Villemont I detested, but now there were times when I saw the woman who might have been, and so discovered that one might dislike a woman and still be jealous of her.

Times such as those evenings when she would come into Paul's room after dressing for an evening on the town, Djilana, the maid she had brought with her from Algeria, following at her heels, anxiously making a last little adjustment of a wisp of hair, of the drape of her gown, and Madame would, with an apparently light heart, pose and pirouette for her son in a wicked imitation of a high-fashion model on display.

"Well, what do you think?" she would ask him.

At nine, he was already Frenchman enough to take these things very seriously.

"But you're making fun, Mama. How can I tell unless you stand still and stop being funny?"

Then she would stand still, hands clasped, eyes demurely downcast, while he solemnly made a circuit around her.

"It's very beautiful, Mama. Don't you think so, Reno?"

And to this I would say "Very" in the most casual of tones, inwardly snarling at Madame's escort for the evening whoever he was.

Talk about Tantalus!

2

Raw weather made early spring a museum and movie season for Paul and me, but early in May we started to go afternoons to the Parc Monceau, which was easily the most staid and stuffy piece of greenery in Paris, a stronghold of prim nannies and nursemaids, of expensive children in elegant play clothes. It was hardly the place to play baseball or football, but play them we did every day before an audience of disapproving nannies and the policeman on the beat, who had to be regularly bribed not to interfere.

The one advantage of the place was that it lay within walking distance of the house. Transportation was our problem. Georges was usually too busy to drive us anywhere—he was chauffeur for the de Gondes and Madame Cesira on Île Saint-Louis as well as for Madame de Villemont—and I was strictly forbidden to take Paul out in a car myself, whether one from the garage or a taxi. Since travel by bus or Métro was flatly ruled out, it meant that most afternoons Paul and I had no way of getting very far from home. Thus, such wonderlands as the Musée Grévin whose mirrored chamber of illusions suddenly becomes a steaming Amazonian jungle, and the Conservatoire des Arts et Métiers with its model railroads and factories and mines were usually out of bounds. When it came to movies, the chic little theaters in our district did not show cowboys and Indians but only, as Paul acidly pointed out, a bunch of silly people kissing each other all the time.

I could understand his increasing boredom and frustration with life in the park—they made for some bad scenes now and then when he would slip back into one of his almost uncontrollable, shaking furies—but this was one subject on which Madame was obdurate. We were intended to be kept on short leash outside the fortress walls and that was all there was to it.

Then Louis, a born agitator, began to meet us in the park every few days and mischievously planted seeds of revolt against maternal restrictions at every opportunity. The first flowering of these seeds came as a startler to Madame de Villemont at the dinner table one evening.

Paul, who was allowed to nurse a thimbleful of wine through dinner, this time finished his quota at a gulp and asked Djilana for more. When Madame, who, I had observed, occasionally used a full bottle of wine as anaesthesia against her bad days, changed the order to a glass of milk, Paul heaved his shoulders in weary reproach.

"Wine is more important than milk," he pointed out to his mother. "Milk only makes bones. Wine makes blood."

Madame de Villemont blinked at this. "And where did you get that piece of information?"

"From Louis."

"Who is Louis?"

"He comes to the park. He's Reno's friend, and now he's my friend, too."

Madame stiffened in her chair, a sure sign of trouble.

"Someone who came up to you in the park?" she said to me in a tight voice.

"No, madame. He used to be my fight manager. I've known him a long time."

The fear emanating from her had enveloped Paul. "He's very nice, Mama." His voice rose shrilly. "Don't say we can't see him any more. He's really very nice."

Madame relaxed a little. She even attempted a smile.

"Still, being a prizefight manager doesn't make him an expert on health," she told Paul.

"But he wasn't only that, Mama. He was a cowboy in America, too, and killed a lot of Indians. And he used to fight sharks in the bottom of the ocean with only his knife. Even if he is little he's very brave."

"You see?" Madame said gravely. "If he had drunk his milk when he was a boy he would have been big and very brave."

After that, she could recognize the agitator's handiwork without trouble.

"Wetting the skin every day is dangerous," Paul announced one evening when faced with his pre-dinner bath. "It becomes like a sponge and the germs get in very easily."

"Louis?" said Madame.

"Yes, Mama. Also, he says—"

Madame de Villemont gave her son a *je m'en fiche de Louis* look.

"It seems to me," she said, "that our little Louis certainly makes himself felt around here. I really ought to meet him."

So I arranged for them to meet—Madame walking with Paul and me to the Parc Monceau for the first time—and it turned out that Louis was the one to release us from our short leash.

He kissed Madame's hand with the air of a courtier; he dusted the bench for her with his handkerchief; he lectured her on child raising.

"Naturally, you're worried about the kid, madame, but it's selfish to plant him in a hothouse like the Parc Monceau because of that. He's at the age now where everything outside these gates would be magic to him. A ride on the Métro, a walk through the Flea Market with a couple of francs in his fist, a game of Wild West in the Parc des Buttes-Chaumont across town with the kind of kids who don't have a bunch of nursemaids breathing down their necks all the time—that's what he needs for his own good."

"I'm afraid I must be the one to determine what he needs for his own good, Monsieur le Buc."

"True, madame. But only if you don't let concern about your own peace of mind spoil your judgment."

She didn't like this impertinence, I saw, but she took it well. When she rose to leave, Louis again kissed her hand and said cheerfully, "Madame, if I were only a few years younger and a few million francs richer—" and Madame de Villemont made a charming little curtsy of appreciation for that. It was all so pleasant and meaningless on the surface that I never dreamed anything would come of it, but the next day Paul and I were, in effect, given the keys to the city.

So he rode in the Métro at last, proudly buying the tickets for both of us, and squandered money on a collection of rusty treasures in the Flea Market, and played football *à la française* in the Parc des Buttes-Chaumont with a gang of small rough-necks from the Boulevard de Belleville, coming home with both shins covered by black and blue marks which he proudly displayed to his quivering mother like battle wounds.

Liberté. Egalité. Fraternité.

3

I had little to do with the other members of the family.

Since my room overlooked the courtyard, I sometimes saw de Gonde and Vosiers setting out on foot for their offices on rue de Boetie nearby and a few times observed one or another of their wives depart for shopping or a social engagement—the chic little Madame Matilde at the wheel of her white Ferrari, the matronly Madame Gabrielle in the Mercedes limousine chauffeured by Georges—but I seldom met any of them face to face. When I did, I learned that each had his own unvarying way of responding to my polite greeting—Madame Matilde with an equally polite *"Bonjour, Monsieur Reno,"* always delivered with mocking solemnity; Madame Gabrielle with a quick, abstracted smile; Edmond Vosiers with a look of open dislike; and Claude de Gonde with a chilly, *noblesse oblige* inclination of the head.

For the most part, I preferred it this way. Not being natural servant material I didn't enjoy tugging my forelock to any of them, so the more distance between us, the better. But since Paul dutifully paid his respects to his uncles and aunts at regular intervals, they must have seen the change taking place in him, and it rankled a little that none of them saw fit to pat me on the back for my achievement. Even more to the point was that meeting with Charles Leschenhaut, the editor of *La Foudre,* which de Gonde had promised to arrange for me. As time went on, as weeks became months, and there was no meeting or even a mention of one, I came to the depressing conclusion that he had forgotten about the whole thing.

It turned out that I had done him an injustice on both counts.

Late one afternoon, I was waiting for the elevator on the ground floor, and when it descended into view I saw de Gonde aboard, his thumb working back and forth over his lower lip, his thoughts evidently far away.

"Bonjour, Monsieur de Gonde," I said as I opened the door for him, and he gave me that frigid inclination of the head, still lost in his thoughts. Then, as I was about to take his place in the elevator, he said, "One moment."

"Yes, monsieur?"

"How is the writing going?"

I decided I had everything to gain and nothing to lose by reminding him of his promise. "I've been hoping to get Charles Leschenhaut's opinion on that, monsieur. If you remember—"

"I remember very well," de Gonde said stiffly. "I've spoken to him about you. He'll meet with you here as soon as his schedule permits, and that should be very soon. He trusts you'll have something to show him worth his time and trouble. Will you?"

"I think so."

"Good." De Gonde slowly sized me up and down, his face expressionless. Then he said abruptly, "He knows the situation here. He knows you're doing well with Paul. That's in your favor, too."

And with that, he turned on his heel and walked off.

I was still wondering about this curious passage when there was another and far more disturbing one, with Matilde Vosiers. Midway along the drafty, red-velveted length of the corridor outside my door was the landing of the marble stairway to the rotunda. Approaching the landing early one Friday morning, pleased with the prospect of the whole day free before me, I was suddenly brought to a halt by the sight of Madame Matilde in negligee, her hands gripping the balustrade, her eyes fastened on her husband as he walked heavily down the stairs and strode across the rotunda on his way out. It was easy to see he was in a savage temper. He wore riding clothes, and with every step he swung his crop as if he were slashing away at weeds with a sickle. The great door to the courtyard was too heavy to slam, but his gesture when he pulled it shut was that of slamming it.

As the door closed, Madame Matilde turned and caught sight of me. Her hand flew to her cheek, covering it, but not before I had seen that the cheek was red and swollen and bore a distinct slash mark across it, a long ugly welt.

"What are you staring at?" she said furiously. "Is that all you have to do with yourself, stand and stare at people?"

It would have been hard not to stare. The negligee did little to conceal Madame's plump breasts and rounded haunches, and they, along with her disheveled prettiness, were sights I was never immune to. With an effort, I managed to fix my eyes unblinkingly on hers and keep them there.

"I'm sorry, madame." Then, because I was sure that no matter how painful Vosiers' riding crop across the face had been, the blow to her pride was even more painful, I said, "I was only concerned because you seem to have suffered a bad fall. The worn spots in this carpeting can be dangerous."

"Can they?" The angry eyes narrowed inquiringly. "Is that the story you intend to tell about this in the kitchen? Or will it be something a little more entertaining?"

"I'm not in the habit of telling stories anywhere, madame. I attend strictly to my own affairs."

She was still breathing hard, but the anger was now oozing out of her, little by little.

"Indeed?" She paid me the compliment of removing the concealing hand from her face. "You know, Reno, you're not at all one of the typical, smirking fools one finds infesting the house, are you?"

"I try not to be, madame."

"No. In fact, you seem quite the chevalier. Very much the chevalier. Someone who might deserve a little good advice in return for his chivalry. Would you be interested in it?"

I nodded, wondering what she was getting at.

"Very well then." Madame Matilde glanced over her shoulder as if to assure herself that the funereal length of corridor behind her was deserted, then in a low voice said to me, "The advice is to clear out of here. You don't belong in this place. For your own good, get away from it as soon as you can."

I saw she meant it.

"But why—?"

"No questions. Ask no questions of anyone here. That sad little *pédé* who was once Paul's instructor wasted time doing that, and what did it get him? Just leave here and don't look back."

"Not without some reason," I protested.

"And what would be your reason for remaining here? The money? A man like you can do as well elsewhere if he wants to. The charms of Madame de Villemont? Believe me, if that's what you're mooning after, you're living in false hopes."

For all its wild inaccuracy, this stung me.

"The princess and the peasant, madame?" I said with open sarcasm.

"No, the princess and her doctor!" Madame Matilde retorted. "Since it's hardly a secret here that she and Dr. Morillon—"

The words died in her throat. She must have seen from my expression that this was one secret, among many, I hadn't been let in on. What she couldn't know was that, when I recovered from the impact of it, I was taking this secret with a large grain of salt. It was too much an echo of Jeanne-Marie's malicious imputation about Anne de Villemont. It was the kind of gossip that could very well have been born in the kitchen, not the bedroom. And above all, since Dr. Morillon was a practicing psychiatrist, a respected member of his profession, he wasn't likely to risk his standing in it by having a grossly unethical affair with a patient.

"Madame," I said, but Madame Matilde's eyes, which had momentarily widened with terror at her own slip, were now veiled to me.

"I've said enough," she told me dully. "Too much. You make it impossible to do you a favor."

I saw there was no use trailing after her down the corridor, trying to get more out of her. On the way to the Café au Coin, where I was to pick up Louis and my amiable tenant, Léon Becque, so we could travel together in my car to the track at Auteuil, I mulled over what I already had. A cryptic warning. Word that Anne de Villemont and her doctor were having an affair. But the warning was too cryptic and the affair too unlikely to add up to very much. There was something else she had said, however—one small word she had dropped—which began to loom larger and larger in my mind until it overshadowed everything else in it.

She had referred to Paul's previous tutor as a *pédé*, and, as I knew from Paul, there had only been one other tutor in his life besides me. And there was only one single, explicit interpretation of that slang word *pédé*. Pederast.

Yet the description of my predecessor given by Georges when he drove me to the mansion my first day on the job there had been that of a passionate young man who had suicided because of a hopeless love for Anne de Villemont. There was a glaring discrepancy between that image and the one presented by Madame Matilde in a single unthinking word.

Now I remember how Claude de Gonde had insisted Georges chauffeur me to the mansion that day. Was this so Georges could tell me things he had been carefully instructed to tell me? In effect, to blindfold me before I arrived at the rue de Courcelles? On the other hand, if Georges had been sticking to the truth, why had Matilde Vosiers now been so careless with it?

I made poor company for the rest of the day while my mind was endlessly churning over the same futile questions and conjectures. I could hardly wait until I arrived back at the rue de Courcelles early in the evening and turned the Renault over to Pascal, the scrawny young garage-hand. He had been a worshipful friend of mine ever since he realized he had once seen me in the ring at the Palais du Sport.

To him I put the question directly. What sort of man had Paul's other tutor been? *Un pédé, peut-être?*

"You mean Monsieur Sidney Scott?"

"Yes. What was he like?"

"Oh, him." Pascal smiled broadly. "He was one of those, all right."

"Then how did he ever get the job taking care of the kid? After all—"

"How do you think? Monsieur Bernard was his *mignon,* and Monsieur Bernard throws plenty of weight around here." The smile suddenly disappeared from Pascal's face. "Look, champ," he said anxiously, "it's not smart to yakkety-yak about these things. Otherwise, we can both end up in the river like Monsieur Sidney, and the Seine is still damn cold this time of the year."

"You make it sound as if he was pushed in, *copain.* I thought he jumped in."

"I never said that, so don't put words in my mouth. The police report says he jumped, and that's good enough for me."

"And what made the police so sure about it?"

"Hell," said Pascal, "why shouldn't they be? That's what Madame de Villemont told them, and she was right there when it happened, wasn't she?"

"Madame de Villemont and who else?"

"But nobody else, of course." Pascal dug a knowing elbow

72

into my ribs. "How many people will you ever find hanging around the Quai d'Anjou on a February midnight?"

4

I phoned Louis early the next morning and told him to meet me at the round pond in the Luxembourg Gardens in the afternoon. When he joined me on my bench there, Paul was hanging far over the edge of the pond flat on his belly, trying to get some wind into the sail of his toy boat with his lungs.

As soon as my pupil saw who my company was, he came running over to us, the boat clutched against his chest and dripping water down his shirt front. One reason he enjoyed having Louis around was that then the rule about speaking only English to me had to be suspended. Louis' command of English was serviceable, but rudimentary.

"*Comment ça va?*" Paul greeted this old friend, and held up a leg to show the latest collection of bruises. "We won the last game, and I almost kicked a goal."

"Good. And the fingernails?"

"This time I really did stop biting them."

"Very good. And the weight this morning?"

"Thirty-one kilos."

"Say, you'll be a real fatso before you know it. Now go take your boat and sail it some more while Reno and I talk business."

"What kind of business?"

"Private business. So keep sailing that boat until we're open to the public again."

He waited until Paul was back at the pond, then said to me, "Come on, let's hear about it. What had you so hot and bothered on the phone?"

After I answered that at length, Louis sat in frowning silence for a long while.

"Well," he said at last, "you seem to be in with an unlucky bunch, all right. People they know have a funny way of falling down stairs and jumping into rivers, don't they? And the idea of a fag like this Sidney Scott killing himself over a woman—" He slowly shook his head. "No, there's a lot more chance Mama found that this type was trying to corrupt the kid and pushed him into the river for it."

"The hell there is. You've met her, haven't you? Does she look like somebody who'd commit murder?"

"Listen, pal, I have the same weakness for tall, beautiful, sexy-looking women you have, but that doesn't mean I wear blinkers around them. Sure, I met her. And what I saw, aside from all the assets, was that she's like a violin string wound up so tight it's almost ready to snap. Give a type like that enough reason for it, and she'll kill somebody before she can stop herself."

"I'd have to see it to believe it. Anyhow, what I'm getting at is her reason for hiring me as Paul's bodyguard. Up to now I never really thought there was anything to guard him against. Now I think there might be. Isn't it possible someone close to Scott jumped to the same conclusion you did and threatened revenge against Madame because of it? The cruelest way to hit her would be through Paul."

"It's possible," Louis said. "Anyone special in mind?"

"Yes, this Bernard Bourdon, de Gonde's confidential secretary. If he was Scott's *mignon*—"

"You can't hang a man just for that. What's he like, this Bernard?"

"Very pretty outside but poisonous inside. Sweet as sugar when he talks to you, but the eyes are dead, if you know what I mean. They're like a snake's eyes. They look right at you, and you can't see anything behind them."

"Sounds delightful," Louis said drily.

"If you like snakes. That reminds me. Be careful when we're on the phone. I wouldn't put it past Bernard to be listening in."

"A fine type all around," said Louis. "But take it from me, pal, this is a type for blackmail, not revenge. I knew a couple of boys in that line of work, and when you described that sweet smile and those dead eyes you could have been describing them. Yes, there's a good chance Bernard knows more about Scott's death than he should, so now he's got Madame de Villemont paying through the nose. I've watched this kind of thing being done. It's no joke, believe me."

"I'm glad you feel that way about it," I said. "Now tell me how I can get hold of the police report on Scott's death."

"You can't."

"Why not?"

"Keep your voice down or the kid'll wonder what you're so steamed up about," Louis warned. "As for that report, it concerns the family of General de Villemont, pal, and General de Villemont is now a sainted hero of France. You think the police are going to let anybody walk in and set off a scandal about the de Villemont name with their help?"

"How about Véronique? She got me that dossier on Marchat, didn't she?"

"That had information anyone in the Ministry of Commerce is entitled to look at. This is a criminal report supposed to be locked up tight."

"Suppose she typed up a requisition for it and had her boss sign it? She said a couple of times that he never looks at what he signs."

"He might look at this. Then she'd be in a fine mess."

"Why not leave that up to her?" I persisted. "Just ask her if she can get me that record without sticking her neck out too far."

"Why not ask her yourself?" Louis said coldly. "Tomorrow's Sunday, so you've plenty of time to do it while the kid is with his grandma."

"Not tomorrow. Grandma sent word she'd like to meet me,

so I'll be going along to Île Saint-Louis with him. And this is something I'd like to clear up as soon as possible."

He was, of course, the kind of friend who would faithfully carry out a request, much as he might hate to. He also had a flair for conspiracy, as I learned when he called that night while I was playing dominoes in the kitchen with Georges and some of the other help. It was the morose Georges who took the call on the kitchen phone and who, after handing me the phone, remained right within earshot. But I had nothing to worry about.

"Monsieur Davis?" Louis said brightly. "Ah, monsieur, that filly you asked me to place your bet on will be running this week. I'll keep you informed."

If there was anything that could put the inquisitive minds in the kitchen at rest, that was it.

5

The Ile de la Cité lies like a ship in the middle of the Seine, its sharp prow pointing westward, and behind it, like a barge under tow, lies Île Saint-Louis. The distance between the two islands is only the length of the little footbridge which connects them—a few steps altogether—but crossing that bridge means moving from one world to another. The Île de la Cité is alive with activity around the Palais de Justice, the Hotel-Dieu, and Notre Dame. Île Saint-Louis, except for a stray party of tourists now and then, seems lost in a centuries-old slumber.

Late Sunday morning, Paul and I were driven there by Georges, Paul tense and unhappy as he was every Sunday when faced with the imminent prospect of meeting his grandmother. When the car pulled up to the door of Madame Cesira's home I saw we were on the Quai d'Anjou where Sidney Scott had come to his end, and looking around at the sedate graystone and brownstone buildings along one side of the street, the embankment wall along the other, the trees freshly green, their leaves shimmering in a warm breeze, the river flowing beneath the lovely arches of the Pont-Marie, I had the feeling that this simply wasn't the right setting for death by violence. But of course, Scott had died in February. It would have been different then, especially at the midnight hours. And again the thought rose in my mind as it had so many times during the past two days—what was Madame de Villemont doing with the man on the Quai d'Anjou at midnight?

I thrust the thought aside as a maid led us up a flight of stairs to Madame Cesira's living room, a room filled with an indescribable clutter of bric-a-brac which must have taken a lifetime to gather. Madame was waiting there for us, a tiny little, white-haired woman with fierce eyes and a face almost monkey-like in its ugliness.

"Well," she said tartly to Paul after he had given her a gingerly kiss on the cheek, "haven't you been taught how to make introductions, you ninny?"

"Yes, Grandmama. This is Monsieur Reno. And this," he said to me, sullenly rattling it off as if he had learned it by rote, "is my grandmother, Madame Cesira Maria Montecastellani de Villemont."

"And what about your grandfather?" demanded Madame, which gave me quite a start until I saw Paul point to a framed photograph on the mantelpiece of a handsome, gray-mustached man in ornate military uniform.

"Yes, and that was my grandfather, General Sebastien de Villemont," he said to me. "A great general of the Army of the Republic of France."

"A very great general," said Madame. Her French, I observed,

was flavored with a strong Italian accent. She gave Paul an un-
gentle nudge. "Now leave us. You'll find the albums on the little
table next to my bed. But if you're going to be all over the bed
with them, you'll have to take off your shoes. I'll send you off
without lunch if you dirty my clean coverlet again."

Paul, plainly relieved to be dismissed even this unkindly, was
already tugging at his shoelaces as he disappeared into the next
room. "Those albums," Madame Cesira said to me, "contain all
the photographs, the documents, the newspaper accounts of the
General's career. Not a bad form of entertainment for the child
if it teaches him pride in his grandfather."

"I understand his father was also a fine soldier, madame," I
said, looking around. In Anne de Villemont's apartment there
was no photograph of her dead husband, and I had been wondering what he looked like. It was frustrating to find there was
no picture of him in his mother's apartment either.

Madame Cesira caught my meaning at once. "No, I prefer
not to have reminders of my son about me. That wound is still
a little too fresh." She seated herself majestically on a small
gilt chair, and small as the chair was, her toes barely touched the
floor. "You may sit also, so that we can talk. But take one of
those chairs that won't come apart under you."

"Thank you, madame." By now, she had me as much on edge
as Paul. "May I smoke?"

"You may not! I don't permit smoking here. If anything happened to the General's collection, it would be disastrous. Use
your thumb if you must keep something in your mouth like an
infant."

"That won't be necessary, madame." I actually found myself
sitting at attention with shoulders squared as those fierce eyes
drilled into mine.

"Do you know why you're here, Reno?"

"No, madame."

"It's because I want you to explain a mystery to me. My
daughters and Monsieur de Gonde himself—ordinarily, a man
of sound judgment—all seem to agree that you're a veritable
paragon. Now tell me how such a paragon came to be a penni-

less gladiator inhabiting the Faubourg Saint-Denis instead of making something of himself in his homeland."

"Perhaps because I wasn't really ambitious to make something of myself the way you mean it, madame."

"Did you ever try to?"

"Yes, madame. For a little while during the time I was married."

"When was that?"

"About ten years ago. The marriage lasted only a few months."

"Of course," Madame Cesira said coldly. "You had an eye for women, and women, I am sure, had an eye for you."

"No, madame. My wife married me because, as she once informed me, she thought it would be amusing to have a prizefighter for a husband. When she learned otherwise, she insisted I go to work in one of her father's companies, and after a couple of months I was as disillusioned with her and business as she was about me and prizefighting. We were divorced by mutual consent."

Madame Cesira made a contemptuous gesture. "You American men don't know how to handle your women, that's what it comes to. But what happened then? You fled the scene?"

"You might call it that. I had an offer to fight in Italy and went there. Then I came to Paris six years ago, and somehow never got home again. As for living on the Faubourg Saint-Denis, madame, it wasn't a hardship. I got along very well there."

"To me it has the same stink as Trastevere in Rome," said Madame Cesira. "Sickening, how that stench of the *canaille* is spreading everywhere today. Even the ancestral home of the Montecastellanis on the Via della Pilotta in Rome is now surrounded by the reek. Still," she nodded thoughtfully, "it can be an asset, knowing how to tolerate it. And while you were in Italy did you learn the language?" she asked, slipping into Italian. "Can you speak it as fluently as you speak French?"

"Not quite, but well enough to get by," I answered, also in Italian.

Madame Cesira leaned forward. "And do you know the mean-

ing of loyalty and discretion?" she asked sternly. "Do you believe
in them? Be honest with me."

"I find them comfortable virtues, madame."

"All to the good. Well, I have decided to do you a favor,
young man. Monsieur de Gonde's commercial interests extend
from here to Italy and beyond. I am going to recommend you
to him for some worthwhile position in his employment."

"Thank you, madame, but I'd rather you didn't."

"Why not? Believe me, you'll do well for yourself in my son-
in-law's service."

"Not if I were tempted to sit at my desk writing stories instead
of attending to his business, madame."

"Ah, so that's it." Madame Cesira's lips puckered sourly. "Yes,
I've heard of your ambition to win a place in the Academy, but
I hardly thought you'd choose to sacrifice a profitable career to
such nonsense. Stories, is it? Stories about what?"

"People I've met. Prizefighters and their women, petty criminals, clerks, café habitués—"

"You approve of such people?" demanded Madame Cesira
coldly.

"I don't approve or disapprove, madame. I just write about
them."

"A waste of time."

"That I must leave to the judgment of an editor Monsieur de
Gonde has kindly arranged for me to meet."

"Charles Leschenhaut. I know about it. Well, young man, I
trust you're braced for the truth about your talents because
that's what you'll get from him. A brilliant man, passionately
truthful. God knows how many enemies he's made because of
that, but he has the courage to face them down. A great man.
France hasn't seen his like in a long time. Another Louis IX in
spirit."

I tactfully nodded acceptance of this, although it was not how
I would have described Leschenhaut. From what I knew about
him, he had been a priest, had entered the worker-priest movement to help battle Communism, had been converted to Communism and unfrocked for it, and had eventually departed
from the Communist Party in a storm of invective to found *La*

Foudre, a magazine which attacked the Church, Communism, and any other institution which had won his enmity. And of course, in so doing, he had made *La Foudre* a French institution itself.

But mere iconoclasm could never have made Leschenhaut the power he was. It was his invention of a formidable new social theory which did that, and it was his enemies who jeeringly named it *la méthode Leschenhaut,* a name he promptly seized on and raised as a banner which drew a host of followers. Charles Leschenhaut had changed sides too often to be another Saint Louis, but he undeniably had charisma.

Certainly, I now had occasion to learn, he had had a potent effect on Madame Cesira. Once on this subject she remained there, growing more and more vitriolic about my indifference to Leschenhaut's political philosophy, or, as I incautiously let slip, all political philosophies. How, she demanded, could one remain neutral in the battle of ideas? If I were typical of the American people, no wonder my wretched country was such a weak-kneed colossus, unable to move this way or that.

I had a bad time of it until lunch, when Paul joined us at the table. I was grateful he remained at the table after lunch instead of leaving me alone to his grandmother again.

"Will you tell Reno's fortune with the cards, Grandmama?" he asked hopefully.

"There are some people who don't believe in fortunes," Madame Cesira said with malice. "There are some people who don't believe in anything. What good is it to tell their fortunes?"

"But Reno would believe in it, Grandmama. He believes in magic."

"White magic," I said. "Sympathetic magic."

Madame Cesira's lip curled. "How fortunate my magic is only that kind."

"The cards never lie," Paul said with a shrug of resignation. "My card is the nine of cups, and it means I'm going to Saint-Cyr and learn to be a soldier no matter what Mama thinks."

I cocked an inquiring eye at Madame Cesira. "Persuasive magic, madame?"

"Don't be too clever, young man," she said coldly.

Still, she rose and went to her escritoire and from it drew a beautifully done marquetry box. When she removed the worn deck of cards from the box and spread them face up on the table I guessed what they were although I had never seen anything like them before.

"Tarot?" I asked.

"Yes. Are you familiar with them?"

"I've heard of them. Especially this one." I picked up a card which depicted a young man trussed upside down by one ankle to a gibbet. "The Hanged Man, isn't he?" When I turned the card upside down I saw that the expression on the young man's face was that of beatific acceptance of his uncomfortable lot. "Not that hanging seems to bother him very much, does it?"

"You see," Paul said excitedly to his grandmother, "he turned it around just the way I did! That's very good," he told me. "If you don't turn around The Hanged Man to see if it really hurts him, it means you have a donkey head."

"One also shows he has a donkey head by giving away such secrets," sniffed Madame Cesira. "In all his life, your grandfather never let his tongue wag carelessly."

She deftly shuffled the deck, had me cut it, then dealt out part of it before her, face up. The remainder of the deck was placed aside. Now Madame studied the cards spread out before her and removed one.

"This is The Magus and will tell us nothing. But the card that fills its place—"

Madame Cesira turned up the top card from the remainder of the deck and placed it in the space left vacant by The Magus. She stared at it.

"My God," she whispered. "The Tower."

If she was putting on an act, it was a good one. She seemed really shocked by the sight of that pasteboard with its vividly colored picture of a stone tower, tongues of flame belching from its windows, bodies hurtling from it.

Her tone and manner were infectious. Paul's face went white, his eyes became enormous.

"That's very bad, isn't it?" he said tensely, and I quickly said, "No, it isn't. This is only a game, Paul. It doesn't mean anything."

"It does! And what do the cards around The Tower say, Grandmama? Are they bad, too?"

Madame Cesira took irascible notice of her grandson's state.

"Stop behaving like that," she ordered in a hard voice. "What a weakling, to faint away at the sight of a card. A fine soldier you'll make."

Paul squared himself on his chair and took a deep breath. "I'm not fainting away, Grandmama. But The Tower is a bad card, isn't it?"

"Yes," said Madame Cesira, "it warns of disaster and ruin. But that's the advantage of the Tarot. It warns what may be coming so one can take measures in time. Now let's see what surrounds The Tower so that we know what measures must be taken. Above it is the two of pentacles." She raised her eyes to mine. "This tells us that matters which trouble the inquirer are only in his mind. They do not exist at all, but by letting himself think they do, he is being drawn into danger."

I was jolted by that myself. It sounded as if she knew I was at work digging up her family skeletons.

Madame Cesira pointed a wrinkled finger. "And here below The Tower," she said to me, "is the king of cups. There is a powerful man who may become either your good friend or your deadly enemy. This is now being weighed in the balance, so take care not to weight the balance against yourself."

And who, I wondered, was the king of cups? Bernard Bourdon? But what could this woman know about my suspicions of him? Had Pascal the garage-hand told anyone about the questions I had asked? Not likely, when he seemed so terrified of Bourdon himself.

Suddenly it struck me that I was playing right into Madame Cesira's hands by thinking these thoughts. Simply watching my expression as I reacted to her nonsense, she knew she was hitting some target. There was every chance that my indifference to *la méthode* when we discussed Charles Leschenhaut had determined her to win me over as his follower with the help of the Tarot. Leschenhaut, in fact, made a far more logical candidate for king of cups than Bourdon.

I smiled at Madame. "The cards don't give names, I suppose," I said lightly.

"No, young man. Nor addresses and telephone numbers."

She swept the cards together with an impatient gesture and replaced them in their box.

"But there was more to tell, wasn't there, Grandma?" Paul protested.

"No more," Madame Cesira said shortly. "Besides, the cards change each time they're dealt. The next time they're dealt for Reno, everything may be changed for the better."

I sincerely hoped so, no matter what she was trying to tell me with her mumbo-jumbo.

Or was I only imagining there was a message in it?

I might be.

She had seemed really stricken when she had turned over The Tower, that gaudy card promising disaster to come.

6

One strange aspect of Anne de Villemont's relationship with the family was that while she had little to do with any member of it in the house, she only left the house on her evenings out in the company of Edmond and Matilde Vosiers. No other escort ever showed himself on the premises.

I ascertained this by spying on her several times after she had left the apartment and was safely on the elevator. I would take my position at the balustrade overlooking the rotunda and watch as she came into sight below, arm in arm with Madame Matilde and with Vosiers glumly trailing behind. It was always the same, the three of them and no one else.

Then, just as I had once caught Madame Matilde watching her husband from this vantage point, I was fairly caught in my turn by Bernard Bourdon. I started when I realized he was standing beside me, and he said apologetically, "I'm sorry. I didn't mean to take you unawares."

Perhaps because I disliked and distrusted him, I read meanings into his voice and manner that weren't really there. But it seemed to me that the voice was too sweetly apologetic, the manner too ripely ingratiating. As I had told Louis, it was impossible to know what went on behind those pale eyes shadowed by their long, dark, girlish lashes. The only thing one could be sure of was that they were coldly observant eyes, strangely at variance with that soft-lipped, pretty face. When I looked into them now, it was like looking into opaque gray glass where the only thing to be seen was your own tiny double image.

"Were you looking for me?" I asked.

"Yes." He watched a maid pull open the door downstairs and the trio depart through it. "Monsieur Edmond is getting fat as a pig," he remarked. "Paris must agree with him. Back in North Africa he was bad enough, now he's getting to look like a Strasbourg goose, the lazy bastard. It takes a man like Monsieur Claude to know how to keep in shape. Or you, for that matter. You always look in the pink."

The way he smilingly surveyed me from head to foot made my flesh crawl.

"What's on your mind?" I said, anxious to get clear of him as quickly as possible.

"Two messages. First, someone called while you were out this afternoon and said the filly you bet on had won and you could collect your bet any time." Bernard nodded at the downstairs door through which Anne de Villemont and the Vosiers had just departed. "Too bad you couldn't be there to hand out some advice on how to win bets. Tonight would be the night for it."

"Why?"

"Because tonight's another night at Spinosi's," said Bernard as if this were self-explanatory. Then seeing from my puzzled expression that it wasn't, he said, "Madame de Villemont doesn't keep you in touch, does she? Spinosi's is that classy gambling joint out at Saint-Cloud. She drops a load of money there once or twice a month."

"How do you know it isn't the Vosiers who do the dropping? Maybe Madame de Villemont is just along for laughs."

"Well, if she is," said Bernard, "she certainly likes to pay plenty for them. After all, Reno, I'm the one who brings her the checks to sign. Do you know how much they add up to every month?"

"How much?"

"Oh, only about a hundred thousand francs or so, give or take a few thousand. Not bad, eh? And that's been going on a couple of years now. Georges says that when they come rolling up in the car Spinosi does everything but stand on his hands for Madame. Smart boy, that one. He can tell you how to handle the goose that lays the golden eggs."

From the house's point of view that wasn't a bad description of a customer who gambled away what amounted to twenty thousand dollars every month. My father had made his living running crap tables for the house. I had absorbed his cynical contempt for the compulsive high-stakes gambler very young.

"What's your other message?" I said to Bernard.

"An invitation from Monsieur Claude to be his guest at dinner next Friday. Charles Leschenhaut will be there and wants to meet you." Bernard winked at me. "Dinner, no less. You are coming up in the world, aren't you?"

"Maybe I am. Thank Monsieur Claude for me and tell him I'll be present."

"Of course," said Bernard. "And remember, my dear Reno, my own door is always open to you. Really, it's time we came to know each other a little better, isn't it? So if you find yourself fed up with dominoes in the kitchen sometimes, it's only a few steps down this hall, and there I am."

Afterward, when I should have been rejoicing at the news that at last I was going to meet Leschenhaut, I found myself brooding over the disclosure of Madame de Villemont's gambling fever. Fever? There was never an eager expectancy about her when she left the house with the Vosiers. Only a sort of unhappy resignation, as if she were prepared for an expected and necessary punishment at the hands of fortune.

But a punishment for what?

7

Before going upstairs to look over the police report on Sidney Scott's death in the privacy of Louis' room, I placed Paul in Madame Olympe's charge and left him being stuffed with *café crème* and pastries. Not only did Madame Olympe have a soft spot for cats and small children as long as they were well behaved, but here in the flesh was the scion of one of those rich and powerful families she was always reading about in Paris *Match* with such avid interest. When I introduced them to each other, she cooed over the scion like a pouter pigeon and bore him off to his refreshments with a tender respect no tenant had ever earned from her.

Upstairs, I found Léon Becque with Louis, arranging a double date for the evening. Becque seemed abashed to see me, and when he departed soon after I walked into the room, gave me an awkward good-bye.

"What have I done to him?" I asked Louis.

"It's what he's doing to you. You know who he's taking on that date tonight? Eliane Tissou. You know who he's been seeing almost every night? Eliane Tissou. But that's your fault, pal. The way you've been neglecting her lately, you can't blame her for making eyes at Becque. Or blame him for liking it."

"I don't blame them. Maybe he's the right man for her. She ought to know by now that I'm not."

"She does," said Louis.

The police report Véronique had obtained for me was in a folder sealed in a large envelope, and Louis had scrupulously left the seal unbroken. I tore the envelope open and invited Louis to sit down beside me on the bed so that we could read the contents together.

The cover of the folder was marked *Confidential* in bold red letters. Under this warning was a sticker addressed to Monsieur Adrian Driot-Steiner, Ministry of Commerce, and since Véronique had a few times described her boss as a mean-tempered, pompous little bureaucrat, I could only hope for her sake that word of this escapade never reached him.

I opened the report. The first page was a copy of the requisition for it which Driot-Steiner had unwittingly signed. Attached to this was a note on police stationery saying, "In answer to your request we enclose—" and concluding with flowery regards to Monsieur Driot-Steiner.

After that came a police surgeon's report dated February twelfth two years previously, describing in scientific lingo the cadaver of Sidney Scott. The gist of it was that the deceased had expired from an excess of water in the lungs, and that there were no marks of violence on the body or any of its organs.

Some photos of Scott shown gruesomely dead did not invite closer study. There was also a police form setting forth the information that Sidney Scott had been born in Upper Letcham, Kent, England, and had died at age twenty-five, a baccalaureate of Cambridge University, a poet by profession, and without any criminal record.

All this was only a preface to the interview of Madame de Villemont by Inspector of the Police Toucart. It surprised me to see that the interview was dated March fifteenth, more than a month after Scott's death, but this oddity was immediately cleared up by the interview itself.

Question (by Inspector Toucart): Madame, you do not mind having it entered in this record that for the past month you have been confined as a patient in the sanitarium of Dr. Felix Linder at Issy, a sanitarium for the treatment of emotional disorders?

("'Madame, you do not mind—'" Louis said admiringly. "Ah, but it's great to be rich and beautiful. You can almost hear those violins playing in the background.")

Answer (by Madame de Villemont): No, it's all right.

Q: And you are now sufficiently well to discuss the events of February twelfth?

A: Yes.

Q: Very well. Then please describe those events, starting with the telephone call you received at about eleven o'clock that night.

A: Yes. Madame de Gonde called from Île Saint-Louis to say that her mother—my mother-in-law—had suddenly suffered a heart attack. She asked would I please come to her bedside as quickly as possible and bring my son with me.

Q: Again for the record, madame: your mother-in-law is Madame Cesira de Villemont, widow of the general?

A: Yes.

Q: And at the news of this sudden illness, what did you do? Please be specific.

A: I was reading in bed. I got up and dressed. Then I woke my son and dressed him, too. Then I went upstairs to the servants' quarters. Monsieur Scott was asleep in his room there. I woke him and asked him to drive me to Île Saint-Louis.

Q: Why? Were you afraid to drive by yourself at that hour?

A: I don't drive. My husband was killed in a car, and I've had a deathly fear of driving since then.

Q: I see. And this Monsieur Scott was your son's tutor?

A: Yes.

Q: How long had he held the position?

A: I don't quite remember. Only a few weeks at most.

Q: So Monsieur Scott then drove you to Île Saint-Louis. I have been informed that others in your household had already been driven there by your regular chauffeur, Georges Devesoul.

A: Yes, they had.

Q: And when you arrived there where your limousine and chauffeur were at hand, did you tell Monsieur Scott he was now free to return to the rue de Courcelles?

A: No. I had my son with me. It was Monsieur Scott's duty to look after him.

Q: Was it? But, madame, soon after you entered the apartment of Madame Cesira, you put your son to sleep in her maid's room while the maid herself remained with him. So it would appear that Monsieur Scott had little to do with looking after the child that night. And still you did not tell him to leave?

A: I suppose I didn't think of it. There was so much excitement.

Q: I see. The crisis soon passed, did it not?

A: Yes. After Dr. Linder made his examination, he said that Madame Cesira had not suffered a heart attack but only a digestive trouble.

Q: The best of news. This is the same doctor who directs the sanitarium at which you were a patient?

A: It is.

Q: A psychiatrist called in to attend a heart case?

A: He's also a medical doctor. My mother-in-law has a great deal of faith in him.

Q: Apparently she has. Can you recall who else was present during the crisis?

A: Monsieur and Madame de Gonde, Monsieur and Madame Vosiers, and some others.

Q: Dr. Hubert Morillon?

A: Yes, he's an old friend of the family.

Q: And Monsieur Charles Leschenhaut?

A: If you know all this—

Q: I must verify certain statements made by others, madame. Please continue.

A: Well, Charles Leschenhaut was there because when my mother-in-law was told a priest should be called, she asked for him.

Q: Although she must have known he is not a priest? That he was unfrocked many years ago?

A: She would not be bothered by that, Inspector. She is intensely devoted to Charles Leschenhaut and his works.

Q: But still—well, never mind. Can you recall anyone else being present at the time?

A: No.

Q: The chauffeur, Georges Devesoul?

A: He was waiting in the limousine in front of the house. At least, that's where he was when Monsieur Scott and I left the apartment.

Q: You were the first to leave?

A: Yes.

Q: Leaving your son asleep in the maid's room?

A: Yes. The maid said she'd be up all night anyhow, attending to Madame Cesira, so it was no bother for her. Once that was settled, I asked Monsieur Scott to drive me home.

Q: And then?

A: Then we went downstairs to the car. But we didn't get into it. It was parked across the street—on the embankment side—and Monsieur Scott took my arm and led me away from it. He said he had something desperately important to discuss with me.

Q: What did he tell you?

A: That he was—that he had conceived a passion for me.

Q: You were surprised by this?

A: Very much so. Until then I had no idea he saw me as anything but his employer. Now he told me he had been struggling against his feelings for some time and couldn't keep them a secret from me any longer. While he was saying this, we reached the stairs that led down to the water's edge. He started down them. I asked where he was going, and he said I'd find out soon enough. I went after him and caught hold of his shoulder, but he pulled away.

Q: You suspected his intentions?

A: I don't know. I suppose I did, but at the same time I didn't really believe he'd throw himself in the river. It seemed just too ridiculous, the whole scene. At the foot of the steps I told him so. I said there was no reason we couldn't go home and discuss the matter sensibly. That wasn't what he wanted. He said I was to tell him straight out whether I thought he and I could make a life together. He said everything depended on my answer.

Q: And how did you answer?

A: I didn't. I wanted to lie to him about it, but I couldn't bring myself to do it. And I didn't dare tell him the truth. Suddenly he walked to the river. The next moment—

Q: You saw him leap in?

A: Yes. Then I screamed for help.

Q: Are you sure of that, madame? No one seems to have heard you, and this area is very quiet, especially at such an hour.

A: But I wasn't up on the embankment; I was below it. I assure you I did call for help.

Q: And when no one responded?

A: I ran up the stairs to the embankment and down the street to where Georges was waiting in the limousine. I told him what had happened, and he left me there and went down to the river to see what he could do. It was too late to do anything. He couldn't even see Monsieur Scott. He came back and helped me into the house, where someone called the police. That's all I remember clearly. When Dr. Linder saw the state I was in he gave me a sedative.

Q: That was his privilege. Well, you have been most co-operative, madame. I trust you will not object to signing a transcript of this interview?

A: No, but I've been advised by my lawyer to let him see the transcript before I sign it.

Q: And he is—?

A: Monsieur Max Marchat, Place Vendôme.

Q: I'll have a copy sent to him. Meanwhile, madame, you have my sympathy for the ordeal you have undergone. Thank you again for your co-operation.

"And thank *you*, dear Inspector Toucart, you poor fish," jeered Louis as I closed the report and thrust it back into its envelope. He cocked his head at me. "Did you notice what was missing from that song and dance?"

"The same thing you did. Madame Vosiers knew what Scott really was when it came to women, and the kid in the garage knew. That means everybody in the house knew, from top to bottom. And there's not a word about it here."

"Not a word," said Louis. "Not a whisper. Which proves I was right from the beginning. Madame de Villemont shoved this guy into the drink, and that whole bunch went to work covering up for her. And what a job they did! The sweetest part was getting this Dr. Linder to keep the police away from her until the alibi was all polished up."

"I'm not so sure about that part of it. She might have had a breakdown after what happened, no matter how it happened. But there are plenty of holes in her story without that. And there must have been plenty of holes in what everybody else had to say. I have a feeling Toucart suspected that, too."

"So do I, poor bastard," said Louis. "But what could he do when he's dealing with the uppercrust? Take them all into the back room and beat the truth out of them?"

"They're not all uppercrust," I said. "And there are other ways of getting the truth—"

With that in mind, when Paul and I got home I sent him off to make his way upstairs by himself, and then dallied in the garage for a few words with my admirer, Pascal.

All the cars were in place now, the big Mercedes, the white Ferrari which was Madame Matilde's pet, the red Renault which was mine, a couple of commonplace Fiats, and a battered Citroën which had been converted into a pick-up truck. Pascal wasn't in sight, but after a few minutes he appeared through a small door in the rear of the garage, a box of scrap metal in his arms. I helped him heave the box into the truck, and when he could draw breath he said, "There were a couple of guys working on the boiler, and that's the giblets." He mopped sweat off his face with the back of his hand. "What can I do for you, champ? You want to take the Renault out again? Need some fresh gas?"

"No, just taking a breather before I start chasing after the kid again." I looked down the line of cars and shook my head. "You've got a big job all right. It takes a good man to keep six wagons like this in top shape."

While Pascal didn't actually do it, he gave the impression of shyly scuffing his toe in the ground.

"Oh, I guess I can handle the job," he said. "I've been around it long enough."

"You mean, working for the family here?"

"And in North Africa. That's where I'm from. Couldn't you tell from the way I talked?"

I shook my head admiringly. "From the way you sound, you could have been born and raised in Paris."

"Not me," he said, much pleased. "I'm a *colon* same as everybody else around here. Jeanne-Marie and Monsieur Bernard and I were all together in the same orphanage in Oran when Monsieur Claude signed us on. We were all snotty-nosed kids then, but you learn your way around, working for a family like this."

"Good people to work for," I agreed. "I guess the only one you wouldn't know too well is Madame de Villemont. After all, if she never did any driving for herself, she wouldn't have been down here very often."

Pascal gaped at me. "Never did any driving? Now where would you get that idea? Until that night when she had the big trouble with Monsieur Sidney she did all her own driving!"

8

I had expected the dinner at which I was to meet Charles Leschenhaut to be an informal little affair probably held in the de Gonde apartment. As I visualized it, there would be an excellent meal, impeccably served, and there would be considerable talk, especially, if I gauged my man properly, from Leschenhaut himself.

I had primed myself for the occasion by reading all the recent issues of *La Foudre*. It wasn't easy to nail down an exact definition of the theory Leschenhaut promulgated in his magazine—*la méthode*—but what I could make of it suggested he was all for turning France into a gigantic beehive where everyone was a busy little bee toiling away at a task set him by a wise and truly patriotic leadership.

Here, said *La Foudre*, was the answer to our present crazy social structure, this anarchistic shambles where every man selfishly goes his own way, where the cultivated minority must bow before the ignorant majority, where the state itself is left defenseless against the barbarians outside its gates and the subverters inside. Change this, apply *la méthode Leschenhaut*, and all would be well.

However, what really concerned me were the stories Leschenhaut published, because here were the clues to his literary tastes. It was encouraging to see that he was not an editor who demanded that fiction be propaganda for his cause. Obviously, one did not have to preach *la méthode* in a story to win publication in the magazine. This was a great relief to me. I had half

a dozen manuscripts ready to offer Leschenhaut, but none of
them sang the delights of life in a glorified beehive.

So, primed as it were for an informal little dinner with the
maestro where Claude de Gonde and Madame Gabrielle would
be on hand to keep the conversational ball rolling, I was taken
aback when Paul remarked the day before the dinner, "Djilana
says you're going to Uncle Claude's grand party. How can I
watch with you, if you're going to be there?"

"What grand party?"

"The one tomorrow night for Monsieur Leschenhaut. Mama's
going to be there, too, and even Grandmother. Everybody will
be there."

Two or three times before, Paul's bedtime had been delayed
so that he and I could covertly watch from the balustrade of the
second-floor landing as the family entertained in style. Our view,
of course, was restricted to the rotunda where the guests entered and briefly circulated before making their way off to
the Grand Salon, but it still provided a good picture of un-
limited décolletage, bemedaled uniforms, and Legion of Honor
ribbons. Anne de Villemont, down below among the company,
knew we were there and had no objection to it. In fact, she would
now and then glance up at us as if to inquire how we were en-
joying the show; and once, in a rare, light-hearted mood, while
a stout little dignitary with a vast, snowy-white beard and totally bald head was in the very act of solemnly kissing her hand,
she tipped Paul a broad wink which sent him into a fit of giggles.

That was all very well, but it gave me a picture of meeting
Leschenhaut under impossible conditions. As soon as the lesson
period was over and Paul sent off to his lunch in the kitchen,
I sought out Madame.

I found her standing at the window of her living room, holding apart the heavy drapes and staring at the emptiness of the
courtyard.

"Madame?"

When she released the drapes and turned toward me the room
fell into semi-darkness, its only lighting from a table lamp. It
gave me the feeling I often had at night in my own room—of
eyes at keyholes, of ears at door panels, of a soft breathing over

my shoulder, of a sly watchfulness surrounding me. There was something about the monstrous size and massiveness of everything in the house that seemed to breed that feeling, and the manners of its servants intensified it. Now, with the thickening mystery of Anne de Villemont filling my mind, it was so acute that I was almost tempted to look over my shoulder to see if someone was in the shadows behind me, watching me.

"Yes, Reno?"

I explained my concern about the meeting with Leschenhaut, and Madame shrugged.

"You don't have to be concerned," she said. "No matter how Paul described it, it's only going to be an informal dinner. I'm sure Leschenhaut will give you his undivided attention at it."

"What makes you so sure, madame?"

"Woman's intuition, Reno. There are times when I can be fantastically intuitive."

She said it with such an excess of bitter self-mockery that I was thrown off my guard. I had been resolved not to ask her anything about the riddle of Sidney Scott, much as I itched to. It was too dangerous a subject altogether; raising it might well cost me my job and the three thousand a month that went along with it. Beyond that, while I might lust after Madame now and then, I didn't like her or trust her enough to want any more involvement in her curious affairs than I already had.

But now, as a piece of jigsaw puzzle suddenly fell into place, it was out before I could stop it.

"Leschenhaut was once invited here to meet Sidney Scott, wasn't he?" I said.

"How do you know that?" Madame de Villemont said sharply.

"Through backstairs gossip, madame," I lied. "Gossip is everyone's favorite sport around here."

"Yours, as well?"

"No, madame."

We stood facing each other in a long silence that was like a pressure in my ears.

"Go on," Madame de Villemont said abruptly. "What else were you told about Sidney Scott?"

I had gone this far; I might as well go further.

"That he committed suicide, madame, because a woman rejected him."

Madame's fine nostrils flared. "You don't have to play games with me. You know I was the woman."

"Yes, madame."

"Why that tone of voice? Am I to blame if Sidney Scott was a pitifully foolish and tragic young man?"

"I was also told," I said softly, "that he wasn't a young man to kill himself for a woman. Any woman."

I have seen men in combat who did not go down under the bullet that struck them, but who remained motionless on their feet in a state of unbelieving shock. Madame de Villemont was struck that way now, turned into a staring statue of horror. Then life returned to her. She swayed and caught hold of the drapes with one hand to steady herself. When I quickly moved toward her, she shook her head.

"A drink," she whispered.

A decanter and tray of glasses were on the sideboard. I poured her a stiff drink and watched her take it all down in one long gulp, reserving my pity for her until a final question had been answered, a question that had filled me with sick bewilderment every time it had risen to mind.

I waited until, with her eyes screwed shut and her teeth clenched, she had shudderingly gotten the impact of the drink.

"Sidney Scott was that kind of man," I said relentlessly. "How could you have ever let him take charge of Paul?"

"My God, do you think I knew what he was?" she said in anguish. "I didn't. I never knew until that night."

"The night he died? When you were with him on the Quai d'Anjou?"

"Yes. It was grotesque, incredible. He told me what he was, how wretched he was because of it. He told me I was the first woman he was ever attracted to, and that maybe I could save him. You see"— she gave a half-hysterical, sobbing laugh —"I was supposed to be therapy for him!"

It was an explanation that made sense.

"So that's why you hired me to watch over Paul," I said. "Because there's someone who doesn't believe Scott really killed himself, someone who's threatening or blackmailing you because of it."

She shook her head violently. "No! Your being here has nothing to do with Sidney!"

The explanation started to make much less sense.

"You mean," I persisted, "that the threat is from a different direction?"

"I can't talk about it. It's better for all of us if I don't."

This was too much like trying to catch hold of quicksilver. I wondered how a bluff would work.

"Madame," I said, "what if I told you that unless I know exactly what you've gotten me into here—and why—I'm leaving the house right now?"

"You can't!" She was completely her other self now, her imperiousness dissolved to quivering panic. She grasped my arm in supplication. "All you have to know is how much Paul needs you here," she said breathlessly. "And he's not the only one—"

She hesitated, searching my face for my reaction to this.

We were very close together. The eyes probing mine were so wide with panic that I had the sensation of swimming in sapphire-blue depths. The ripe lips were half-parted, the white, uneven edges of teeth glinting behind them. Then, to my astonishment, Madame de Villemont waited no longer. Her arms slid through mine, her hands clasping behind my back. Her head rested on my shoulder so that my nostrils were filled with the scent of her hair.

"This is what I mean," she said in a remote voice. "You're like a rock. You have all the strength I don't have."

My occasional dreams of finding myself in this position with her had been pleasant. The reality, I found, was even more so. But I trusted her as little as ever. I stood there, arms at my side, excited by the warm pressure of her body against mine, but refusing to fall victim to it.

"Madame—"

"*Ah, mais non.*" Her head turned on my shoulder so that her lips were almost touching mine. "*Je m'appelle Anne.*"

After all, one didn't have to trust a woman like this to take pleasure in her. I put my arms around her in a hard embrace and we kissed. Hotly. Lingeringly. But when my hands moved to explore that delectable body, the lady called quits. She yielded to the exploration for only a moment, then slowly drew away, breathing hard.

"No," she said. "Paul might walk in here any minute."

So he might. Or one of the servants for that matter. All of them in the house had the French habit of knocking once on the door and then walking in, whether invited to or not.

"All right," I said, "since you've produced such a convincing argument for my staying on here—"

"Dear God." She looked sick. Really sick. "Is that what you think it was?"

"I'm sorry," I said, and I meant it. She knew I did. The sickness faded from her face as I watched. But I didn't intend to let it go at that. Like an echo of Claude de Gonde, who was once driven to use the same words about Anne de Villemont, I said, "The truth is I don't know what to think any more. Can you blame me? All I know is that you're desperately afraid of something. Anne—"

"Anne?" Her lips curled in the palest shadow of a smile. "So you finally managed to say it."

"Because it's hard to when you're so damned evasive with me. Now let's have it. Did anyone ever really threaten to kidnap Paul?"

"No. But when you have money, isn't there always the danger—?"

"Not in France, so that's not the answer I'm waiting for. Let's try again. What is it that keeps you in such a state of nerves?"

"All right, I'll tell you." Her voice hardened. "It's this house. And now it's gotten to you the way it did to me. It doesn't matter what it's like outside; in here it's always Elsinore Castle at midnight with the ghost of Hamlet's father walking the parapet. Only here it's Sidney Scott's ghost that seems to do the walking."

"No," I said, "it isn't the house. You could always leave here."

"How? Do you have any idea what would happen if I tried to remove Paul from this museum?"

"But since he's your son—"

"He also happens to be the sole grandson of Madame Cesira Montecastellani de Villemont. And the sole nephew of her daughters. Try to remove him a healthy distance from them and see what happens."

"Have you tried?"

"Once. I made arrangements to travel to London with Paul, but it was no use. We got as far as Le Bourget, and there were Claude and Edmond waiting to bring us back." She shrugged helplessly. "Claude has the right to do that. I had a breakdown after Sidney's death and was tucked away in a sanitarium at Issy. The only way I could get out was to put myself in Claude's charge. Even then, I might still be there if Paul hadn't carried on so wildly when we were kept apart."

"So that's how it is."

"That's how it is." She sounded as if just talking about it had exhausted her. "I might as well be in prison as in this place, except that I have Paul with me here. But if I could only get away—"

"To where?"

"Back to the States. God, how I dream of it. I'd be outside French jurisdiction; I could get doctors and lawyers to clear up my psychiatric record. And what it would mean to Paul to be far away from here!"

She didn't have to draw me a picture. I vividly saw what it could mean to both of them. As it was now, every one of her bad spells undid part of my week's work with Paul, and every Sunday that he spent with the little martinet on Île Saint-Louis undid another part. But to be three thousand miles away from here—

"Why not?" I said.

Anne frowned at me. She pressed her hand to her forehead as if easing a sudden pressure there.

"You mean, you'd help us get out of the country?"

"I might."

"To New York? That's how I've been imagining it. No luggage, just take a plane to New York before anyone can find out about it, and rent a house there under a different name. New

York would be the best place, don't you think? It should be easy to lose yourself there."

"I said I might be able to arrange it. First, I want to lay the ghost of Sidney Scott to rest."

"Not now," Anne said pleadingly. "It's best for you not to know any more about it than you do right now. When we're in New York I'll tell you all the rest."

"We?" I said. "Then you want me to come along with you?"

There was more chance than ever now of Paul's suddenly walking into the room, but we were again very close together, her hands resting on my shoulders, mine on the lovely swell of her hips.

"*Mon cher,*" she said gravely, "I want very much for you to come along with us. Will you?"

"I will."

"And it should be soon. As soon as possible. Can you make the reservations for two weeks from today—an afternoon flight, first class—and use the name Dulac? Monsieur-'dame Dulac and son. That sounds anonymous enough, doesn't it?"

"At least as much as Smith. Any special reason for the Dulac?"

"No, it just sticks in my mind from a French lesson at school. *Monsieur et Madame Dulac et leur petit fils, Robert. 'Comment ça va, Robert?' dit Monsieur Dulac—*"

"I can guess the answer. '*Comme-ci, comme-ça, mon cher papa.*'"

Anne shook her head. "Things were never so-so for the Dulacs. They were always brimming over with optimism and energy. And you know—"

"Yes?"

"That can be a strange and wonderful feeling," she said.

9

Charles Leschenhaut lived up to all expectations.

His face had already been made familiar to me by photographs in the newspapers—it was the face of a lusty Friar Tuck without tonsure, a full-lipped, snub-nosed, sharp-eyed face under an unkempt tangle of dark hair—but no photograph had captured the dynamic force he was charged with, the electricity that emanated from him.

"Your protégé?" he said to Claude de Gonde as we shook hands. "But what a brute this one is, what a giant! And talented too, you believe? I wouldn't dare tell him otherwise. He might crack me apart like an eggshell if I did." Which was hardly accurate, considering that Leschenhaut, although a head shorter than I, had the physique of a bull and an iron handclasp.

"I once saw you fight in the Vel d'Hiv," he remarked to me. "About five years ago, I think, when you knocked out that big Senegalese."

"I was lucky that night."

"You were," said Leschenhaut wickedly. "If that black had sense enough to keep moving away from you the way he was doing, he could have chopped you apart piece by piece. And now you want to try your luck at writing. Your Hemingway was also a writer who was handy with his fists, wasn't he? An amateur boxer of sorts. Was he really good at it?"

"I've heard he was. But let's keep him out of it. I have some

stories to show you, and if you're expecting another Hemingway—"

"No, no, I'm not that much of a dreamer. All the same, I'm
prejudiced in your favor from the start. You look healthy to
me, and I've had a bellyful of decadent weaklings and whim-
perers. Would-be suicides without the guts to cut their own
throats, that's who manufactures our literature today. Now I
say to hell with the mourners for our sick society. Let's bury
them with that society and create a new world worth living in!"

It was refreshing to be caught up in this whirlwind, because
until Leschenhaut made his appearance the evening had gone
badly for me. When I had joined the company in the Grand
Salon I was depressed by the baroque magnificence of the
room and the tinkle of meaningless conversation in it. I was even
more depressed when Dr. Hubert Morillon walked in and
took immediate possession of Anne.

From what I had been told about Morillon I had somehow
come to visualize him as the caricature of the traditional psy-
chologist—bearded, bespectacled, pompous as a walrus—and
it was this which made it easy for me to reject Madame Matilde's
imputation that Anne was his mistress.

Then I met him, and was jolted to find myself face to face
with a tall, strikingly handsome man of about forty who looked,
not like my idea of a scientist, but like a ski instructor at some
place like Chamonix or Cortina. And this bronzed, blue-eyed,
rugged Viking type with hair so pale that it looks as if all color
had been bleached out of it has an uncanny appeal for women.
Morillon had a *diablerie* about him too, a dash and glitter which
I could only envy with all my heart. I might refuse to believe
Madame Matilde's gossip, but I couldn't deny that this doctor
looked like a fit man for Anne de Villemont; he was no one
to laugh off lightly. I had a strong sense of proprietorship over
Madame now, and the sight of her, head to head with Morillon
in a corner of the Grand Salon, bothered me. The way they
looked together gave a little too much credence to Madame
Matilde's words for my comfort.

However, when we were at dinner I felt better, watching

Anne's manner toward Morillon, who was her table partner. As dinner progressed, she seemed to grow more and more indifferent to him, discarding him altogether after a while in favor of the wine bottle. This, I knew from experience, was her refuge whenever she was having a bad time of it, so it seemed evident that the doctor was not making the impression on her he was hoping to make. It was a relief getting that settled in my mind. I could concentrate on Leschenhaut and the rest of the company then, instead of always having half an eye on Morillon, measuring him as a rival.

It was a curious gathering at that table. I knew the family, of course, including Madame Cesira, who was there in waspish good spirits, but the others were strangers to me, and a mixed lot they were. A foxy-looking little antique of a nobleman, le Comte de Laennac, and his apparently mummified wife; a hard-boiled retired colonel of the United States Army, Jesse Hardee, and his extremely youthful and pretty German bride Clara ("Colonel Bluebeard," I heard Madame Matilde whisper to Madame Gabrielle. "She's his fourth. When his wives reach their thirtieth birthday he trades them in for a new model."); and, of course, Leschenhaut himself.

I quickly learned that Anne had been right in her prediction that Leschenhaut would devote his attention to me at this gathering, an attention which largely consisted of barbed shafts aimed at the United States, the nation he held responsible for most of the troubles humanity found itself in today.

When I challenged this, he took me up with ferocious delight. America, he made plain, was a land of nincompoops, of libertarians, of fake idealists who encouraged the barbarians outside its gates and the subversives within.

Most painful, he declaimed, was that when on rare occasions, far too rare indeed, a nation like France awoke to the menace and tried to hurl it back, America served only to betray the effort. At Dienbienphu, in Algeria, in Egypt, America had betrayed the French to the enemy. In the Congo it had sold out all European civilization to the cannibals. What a bitter joke. Let the barbarians advance until their knives are at your throats, and then try to counter them by preaching peace and good will.

Or by such half-hearted military excursions as our pitiful effort in Southeast Asia.

"*C'est un cautere sur un jambe de bois*," he snorted at the conclusion of this indictment, meaning that my country was like a doctor who applied medicine to a wooden leg; and I observed with irritation that when Mrs. Hardee, the Teutonic child bride, had translated the gist of this in richly accented English to her husband, the colonel joined the rest of the company in applauding it. So with the colonel on Leschenhaut's team and with Anne now morosely devoting herself to the wine bottle, I found myself all alone in defending the American way, like a Yankee Horatius at the bridge.

The trouble was that Leschenhaut apparently knew much more about the American way than I did. To make it worse, while he was loudly demonstrating this, Madame Cesira turned the Comtesse de Laennac loose on me. Madame la Comtesse, it seemed, was a great authority on the Tarot cards and had written a splendid book about them. Up to here, Madame la Comtesse had been sunk in a deep reverie. Now she suddenly came to life, seized my wrist with an avid claw, and paying no heed to the booming Leschenhaut, addressed me at length on the mysteries of the Tarot.

Under fire from both sides, distracted by the way the colonel required his wife to serve as translator during the proceedings, I found it hard to understand what any of them were saying.

"And what is the first step to be taken by the state, monsieur?" This from Leschenhaut, aiming a stubby forefinger at me. "To instruct its people in the nature of the enemy. Yellow hordes, black hordes, mongrel hordes. And the second step—"

The colonel's sharp voice. "What's he saying, Clara? Damn it, don't sit there like a dummy."

"Somesink about hordes, *nicht wahr?* Suh yellows, suh blacks—"

"—so you see, monsieur," this from Madame la Comtesse, plucking at my sleeve, "—when you examine the card known as The Priestess you will observe she is holding the scroll of the Law. From this we know that the key lies in the Cabala. Therefore, we—"

"—and why this second step?" Leschenhaut, sweetly reasonable. "Because unless the state is splendidly monolithic—"

"—decided to call my little book *La Mystère du Tarot.*" Madame la Comtesse mercifully releasing me and turning to Madame Cesira. "Do you remember, Cesira, while you were reading the proofs you asked—"

Leschenhaut now triumphant. "—so even your own Thomas Jefferson believed in rule by an elite! And *la méthode—*"

"Damn it, Clara!" The colonel's voice briefly drowning out all others. "What's that he's saying about Thomas Jefferson?"

Afterward we all adjourned to the library, where card tables had been set up, but conversation still took precedence over cards. Here Colonel Hardee drew me aside and looked me over with concern on his craggy face.

"What do you think of him?" he asked, jerking a thumb in the direction of Leschenhaut.

"He's a clever man."

"He's a lot more than that, Davis. He's an inspired man. He sees the big picture like no one else around. He sees the termites gnawing away at the foundations of the house and he damn well intends to do something about it before the walls cave in." The colonel frowned. "You got every word he said, didn't you?"

"Yes."

"I wish to hell I did, but I'm tone deaf or something when it comes to foreign languages. Great thing, languages. A man can make himself useful anywhere if he's got an ear for them. You ever been in the army?"

"Marines."

"When was that?"

"Around the end of the Korean business. I was sixteen then, so I had to lie my way in, and when they got wise overseas they tossed me out."

"Honorable discharge?"

He was so much the commanding officer addressing the enlisted man, what with his sharp voice and closely cropped gray hair and military stiffness of spine, that I was hard put not to address him as "sir."

"Yes," I said, "it was an honorable discharge. I saw action a few times and was almost divisional middleweight champ and always kept my nose clean like a good boy."

The colonel nodded vigorously. "I thought so. I could tell right off you're my kind of man. Too bad you didn't think of making a career of the service once you came of age. Still, there's a lot of ways to fight the good fight even if you're not in uniform."

I never had a chance to ask him what good fight he was referring to. In the middle of the room a scene was building up between Anne and Dr. Morillon. Other voices fell as theirs rose. All faces turned toward them with surprise.

"I *will* leave," Anne said loudly. "I told you I want to see how Paul is."

Her arm was in Morillon's grasp. When she swung away from him, he didn't release the grasp but effortlessly drew her back to face him again.

"Djilana is watching Paul," he said angrily. "What could possibly happen to him?"

"Oh, all right! Will you believe I'm too exhausted to keep my eyes open any longer?"

"No, I will not," the doctor said scathingly. "You are not exhausted, madame, you're drunk. Very drunk. And you know how I warned you against that. You know how dangerous it can be."

"Hubert!" de Gonde said sharply. "What the devil kind of performance is this? What are my guests supposed to think of it?"

"Whatever they please," retorted the doctor. "As for what I think, it's that I'd better escort Madame to her room before she collapses on her face in front of your guests."

Suddenly the positions were reversed. Morillon started toward the door, but now Anne hung back. From the glassiness of her eyes, the slightly disheveled look of her, I saw she really was quite drunk.

It was Madame Cesira who stepped forward to break up this ugly tableau. She faced Anne wrathfully.

"Do you remember promising to do whatever the doctor advised?"

"I don't remember," Anne said thickly. "I don't want to remember. I'll do whatever I like."

"Even to having another breakdown?" demanded Madame Cesira in a voice that cracked like a whip.

That struck home.

Anne jerked free of the doctor's grasp. "All right, I'll go!" she said, but made no move to. Instead, she vaguely looked around the room until her eyes fell on me. She raised her arm and pointed at me. "I'll go," she said, "if you take me."

All at once, I was the focus of everyone's shocked attention. The only thing to do was try and brazen it out.

"I must go upstairs to get some manuscripts for Monsieur Leschenhaut anyhow," I said to the assemblage at large. "It won't be any trouble for me to escort Madame to her apartment."

Most of the faces around me registered pained resignation. Dr. Morillon's registered naked murder.

"You seem to forget your place," he said to me. "I've been told that you're paid to be Madame's servant, not her escort."

I may have flinched at that, but I took it in silence. At all costs, I warned myself, do not rock the boat.

My refusal to shove his words down his throat only added to Morillon's fury. A strange doctor, I thought. A man dedicated to the study of emotions who couldn't control his own.

"Are you deaf?" he demanded. "Must I repeat my words?"

Even Madame Cesira, his ally, recoiled at the violence boiling in him. "Enough, Hubert!"

He wheeled on her. "No, madame! If they leave this room together—"

We left together, Anne and I. But I had Morillon's expression vividly in my mind's eye as I took Anne up in the elevator, my arm around her waist, her body almost limp against me. There could be more trouble with the man about this, but my concern was leavened with a hot sense of triumph. There had been a showdown between this dashing doctor and me, and Anne had publicly rejected him in my favor. True, as a cynic like Louis might argue, she was too drunk at the moment to know what she was doing, but I was willing to believe *in vino veritas*. Anyhow, in a short time I would be escorting her and Paul out of the country, thus neatly settling any problem of a clash with Morillon.

As if reading my thoughts, Anne suddenly stirred and said in a blurred voice, "I've done something. What was it? Tell me what it was."

"Nothing at all."

"It was," she said fearfully. "I want to see Paul now. I must see him right now."

I comforted her as well as I could and delivered her to Djilana, who appeared to recognize the symptoms at a glance and who reacted to them with tight-lipped disapproval. I left the two of them standing together over the bedside of the sleeping Paul. There had been a time when Paul tossed restlessly all night, always on the edge of sleep but never quite entering it, when he would come violently awake two or three times a night with shouting nightmares; but all that seemed a thing of the past now, and he regularly slept as if he had flung himself into happy unconsciousness.

It didn't take me long to make sure the manuscripts I had ready for Leschenhaut were in order and to thrust them into my pocket and leave the apartment. The quicker the better, I knew. This was no time to linger and rouse obscene speculation in the company waiting below.

It was when I reached the landing overlooking the rotunda that I saw I had been too sanguine about the chances of avoiding a real clash with Morillon. It takes two to avoid a clash, and the doctor was standing at the foot of the marble staircase looking up at me with grim anticipation on his face. And, I saw with disbelief, he held in his hand a riding crop—undoubtedly supplied by the helpful Edmond Vosiers—which he slapped with a steady rhythm against the palm of his other hand.

It was an incredible scene, yet somehow in keeping with the baroque, tragic-opera setting provided for it here. It gave me the eerie feeling that Anne might be right after all, that maybe this monstrous house on the rue de Courcelles did have a baleful effect on everyone who entered it. It seemed to be like a looking-glass world where rationality and the ordinary emotions were discarded as soon as you stepped through the glass.

The doctor was not alone. With him were Claude de Gonde and Edmond Vosiers, de Gonde plainly angry about this turn events were taking and Vosiers just as plainly gloating over it. And leaning against the closed door to the dining room stood Charles Leschenhaut, hands in pockets. That meant a real complication if a brawl started. Leschenhaut knew I had been a professional fighter, had seen me in the ring. I could imagine his contempt if he saw me willing to practice my old trade against the doctor, big and fit as Morillon looked to be.

So, as I walked down the marble steps, I set my teeth against any possibility of a brawl. I would be the soul of forbearance. I would keep myself in control at all costs and hope that de Gonde could manage to exercise some restraint over Morillon. But when I reached the foot of the staircase where Morillon stood barring my way, the riding crop tap-tapping against his hand, I saw it would be hard for anyone to exercise restraint over him. He was the image of malevolence. He reminded me of an aroused cobra, cold-eyed and deadly, spreading its hood before striking.

"Ah, Monsieur *Larbin*," he said, laying heavy emphasis on this gutter word for a hired lickspittle, "have you finished attending to Madame for the present? Have you put her to bed and assured her you'll be back very soon to properly comfort her? How sad that you're now going to have to disappoint her."

"If you don't mind, Doctor," I said, "you're in my way. I'd like to speak to Monsieur Leschenhaut."

"You will not speak to Monsieur Leschenhaut. You will listen to me while I give you some vital instruction in psychopathology. In a nutshell, Monsieur Larbin, delusions can be dangerous. Especially delusions about your position in life. Wouldn't you agree that the time has now come for you to face reality?"

"I would, Doctor, because I find it highly unreal to get a lecture in psychology from someone holding a whip in his hand. I'd say you need some vital instruction in your own profession."

"For God's sake," said de Gonde, "that's enough of this."

"Not quite." The doctor shook his head. "Not until this scum has gone through that door back to the garbage heap he crawled from." He bared his teeth at me, and the riding crop slapped down hard in his hand. "That means now, do you understand?"

"I'm not sure I do, Doctor. If you're ordering this as Madame's medical advisor—"

"No, Monsieur Larbin, I am ordering it because Madame de Villemont will never again have a call for your services, gratifying as they may be to her."

"In that case, Doctor, when Madame de Villemont tells me to leave, I'll leave. Meanwhile—"

He struck then, quick as a cobra. Before I could get an arm up, the riding crop slashed across my face with a searing impact. And, half-stunned by that impact, blindly following instinct, all good resolutions washed out of my mind in that instant, I swung my fist square into Morillon's jaw, knowing as the blow landed that I had never hit anyone harder in my life.

He never knew what hit him. His head went sideways as if it were being wrenched from his shoulders, he sagged at the knees, and then went down flat on his face, arms outflung, one leg twitching a little.

Looking down at him, feeling the burning pain of the welt across my cheek, I suddenly saw the bloated corpse of Sidney Scott before me. Was it possible that Hubert Morillon, with his frantic jealousy, his seething temper, his willingness to use violence, was the one behind Scott's death? True, the police report had stated there were no marks of violence on the body, but wasn't there a chance that certain marks of violence wouldn't show on those blackened and swollen remains? That story of suicide in the report had sounded thin from the time I first read it, and Anne's confirmation of it almost as thin. But Morillon—?

Leschenhaut came walking up as de Gonde kneeled worriedly over my inert foe.

"He'll be all right," Leschenhaut said placidly, and I was glad to see him take it this way. "He's a tough one, our doctor friend. He'll live to make a few more mistakes like this before he's done for." He put a friendly hand on my shoulder. "Just like that careless black at the Vel d'Hiv, wasn't it?" he said. "One little mistake, and down he went. Now if you can only handle words as well as you handle your fists—"

But de Gonde, observing that Morillon was struggling back to consciousness, looked up at us and shook his head grimly.

"Do you really believe this has settled the matter?" he said, and I knew what he meant.

He was telling me that no one could deal with Dr. Hubert Morillon the way I had and expect to get away with it.

10

Next day, when I went down to the kitchen for the usual late-morning coffee break, I learned that I had desecrated an idol. I was sure when I walked into the kitchen that news of my fracas with Morillon had already circulated through the gathering there, and I expected the swollen, purpling welt on my cheek to draw sympathy. Instead, I found everyone there banded against me in cold hostility. It seemed that I had been given the unusual honor of dining with the family and had then proceeded to disgrace myself and the entire staff. I had gotten drunk. I had made eyes at Madame de Villemont. I had assaulted a guest who had resented this, and what a guest! What a man Dr. Morillon was. What a privilege to have him in the house. And what a horror to have him depart from it, bruised and battered by my drunken assault.

When I tried to defend myself, Jeanne-Marie promptly put me in my place.

"No, big boy, we're not buying that bill of goods," she sniffed. "Not with the kind of man Dr. Morillon is, and not when Monsieur Edmond said right out it was plain unprovoked assault. Take my word for it, if you weren't the only one around here who could manage the kid, you'd have been out on the street for good last night."

It left me wondering just how Dr. Hubert Morillon, who certainly wasn't part of their world, had come to earn such popularity with the help.

I was still wondering about it when I went upstairs. Each room of Anne's apartment—as with all the upstairs apartments—had a door opening on the gloomy, red-velveted main corridor, and as I walked down the corridor I saw Madame Matilde emerge from Anne's bedroom where, I was sure, she had been vividly describing the scene in the rotunda last night. Judging from what I had just encountered in the kitchen, the fact that Madame hadn't witnessed the scene would only add to the bias and color of the description, so when we met face to face I was braced for more hostility. But Madame only flicked her eyes over my damaged cheek with detached interest.

"A lovely day, isn't it, Reno?" she said.

"Yes, madame."

"You won't mind then, if I take your pupil for a little drive in the Bois? At least, I hope you won't mind. He's waiting in the car now, and I'd hate to disappoint him."

She was being too solemn about it.

"It's up to Madame de Villemont," I said warily. "If you have her permission—"

"Oh, I have," Madame Matilde said sweetly. "But we know whose decision really matters around here, don't we?"

With that, she went off down the corridor, leaving me feeling like a large, slow-witted mastiff that has just had a losing encounter with a nastily clever little poodle. Yet I found myself pitying her rather than disliking her. Marriage to a brutal, sour-tempered lump like Edmond Vosiers entitled her to all the pity she could get.

I knocked on Anne's door, and when she called for me to

come in I found her in bed looking wretchedly at the tray of food Djilana was offering her.

"I've come to report on Paul's progress, madame," I said, "but if you're not well—"

"No, I'm well enough for that." She waved Djilana out and waited until the door had closed behind her. Then she said bitterly, "Yes, I know. I made a fine mess of things last night, didn't I?"

"Forget last night. How do you feel now?"

"Ashamed of myself. Look at your face. That was my fault."

"Stop it. I'm here to give aid and comfort, but if you're going to carry on like this—"

"I won't." Anne shook her head weakly. "I promise I won't. Now lock the door, then sit here beside me and hold my hand. That might help."

I followed instructions willingly, and when I took her hand I found it cold and clammy.

"And all because of a few glasses of wine," I said.

"And a few glasses of cognac so I'd get up enough courage to join the festivities. Brandy courage. When that started to wear off I used the wine for a booster. Next thing, there I was on my high horse, galloping right off to disaster."

"I wouldn't worry about it," I said. "Your doctor wasn't quite the disaster he thought he'd be."

Anne squeezed my hand hard.

"That's where you're wrong. Hubert can be very dangerous. There are some people—friends of his who settled here from North Africa—who are fanatically devoted to him. They haven't changed in their ways since that whole sickening business in Algeria. You know what that means, don't you?"

"I'm not sure. Are you trying to tell me that a respectable citizen like Morillon, a professional man at that, has a gang of cutthroats at his beck and call?"

"*Mon ange*, I'm telling you to be careful of him. Of everyone else here, for that matter. When I made a fool of myself last night it put them all on guard against us. It'll be harder than ever now to make a move they don't know about."

"Then we'll rise to the challenge," I said, humoring her.

"I'll get the plane tickets through someone else so that I won't have to go near a ticket office. And my ex-fight manager lives in New York. I'll call him on an outside phone during the week and have him lease a house for us under the name of Dulac. Or an apartment if that's quicker. I can cable him whatever money he needs for it."

"Yes, the money." Anne had been listening to my plan of action as if it were a love lyric. Now she roused herself. "There's a traveling case in that chifforobe," she said, and fumbled through the purse on her bedside table until she found a small key which she handed to me. With it I opened the case and removed an envelope with a packet of banknotes in it. "It's ten thousand francs," Anne said. "Will that be enough?"

"A lot more than enough."

"Keep it all anyway. You never know what extras might have to be paid for."

It was pleasurable to stuff that bulky walletful into my pocket. It made the still unreal promise of the future very real now. But there remained some dark clouds overhead that troubled me.

"Anne," I said, "about Dr. Morillon—"

"Yes?"

"Tell me the truth. Did he have anything to do with Sidney Scott's death?"

"Darling, I've told you the truth about Sidney's death. Why can't you believe that? Why do you refuse to believe it?"

"Because from what I've put together about Scott and Morillon—"

"No, you have to stop thinking about Sidney! You're the one Hubert is jealous of; you're the one he hates, not poor dead Sidney!" Anne drew me down beside her on the bed again. "That's what frightens me. That something might happen to you because of me. I don't want anything to happen to you."

Her arms went around my neck; her weight bore me down until our mouths met in a kiss that went on and on until I found myself blissfully drowning in warm, perfumed flesh, gladly suffering the sharpness of those small teeth cutting into my lips. There was something wonderfully ingenuous about this woman's embrace. She was like a schoolgirl who, being kissed for the first time, joyously discovers how much she likes it and plunges with an awkward ferocity into the game.

When she released me, I said, "If that was an invitation—"

She smilingly shook her head.

"In that case," I said, "I'd better go while the going is good."

"I think you should. But whatever you do, *mon ange,* take care. I mean that with all my heart."

Back in my room I did some hard thinking about that warning. Added to de Gonde's grim concern about the consequences of my manhandling Hubert Morillon, it hit home. I had seen Morillon in action the night before. The thought of how he would act if he ever learned I was going to take Anne out of the country made the sense of menace in the air real and palpable. It was like a cold current sluggishly stirring through the room and nuzzling me between the shoulder blades.

It was hard to laugh off a premonition as strong as this. I went to the chest where I had stored Colonel Henri de Villemont's Beretta. It didn't matter that it was unloaded; in fact, I preferred it to be. I was sure that, aside from military action, I could never bring myself to aim a loaded gun at someone and actually pull the trigger. But letting it be known over the grapevine in the house that I was going around armed was a healthy ounce of prevention. Morillon's devoted friends, whoever they were, would think twice about jumping me in some dark alley on the doctor's behalf.

I pulled out the drawer of the chest, set it on the floor, and lay on my belly to thrust a hand deep into the recess where I had hidden the gun. I inched forward on my belly, reached the hand out until my fingertips met the wood in back of the chest. I swept the hand back and forth, my nails scraping the wood.

The gun was not there.

My first angry thought was that someone who knew about the gun—Anne, Claude de Gonde, Madame Gabrielle—had surreptitiously removed it, but as the anger cooled I realized none of them would have had any reason to conceal this fact from me.

What about Paul? He had been in the next room when I had hidden the gun away, he might have seen me do it, might have taken this shiny weapon as a delightful toy to play with in secret. The chest drawer was heavy, but if he had the patience to empty it he could have handled it easily enough.

The idea disturbed me. The gun itself didn't matter since it was unloaded, but until this moment I hadn't imagined there were any secrets left between Paul and me. We had grown so close together that he now confided to me every opinion, every problem, every little sin he committed during the day. Whatever he had on his mind would be talked over gravely, man to man, and I came to see that he was constantly searching for precise definitions of right and wrong this way. Even more important, I found that no matter how he raged against some of my strict rules now and then, these rules were what he wanted. Without realizing it, he was happy they were there, marking the boundaries of what was permissible and what wasn't.

So I felt acutely guilty, searching his room for the gun. The room was as orderly on the surface as Djilana could make it, but the drawers of its dressers and cabinets when I pulled them out were magpie's nests. I searched through every one, probed under the mattress of the bed, dug under the cushions of the chairs, emptied the huge toy chest and had to replace its contents like the pieces of a Chinese puzzle before I could fit them all back in. Nothing.

My last hope was the bookshelves, but the only thing I found hidden behind a row of books was a cardboard folder. In it was a photograph, a family portrait. A smiling Anne stood against a dazzling whiteness of Moorish architecture, a scarf tied around her blowing hair, her eyes squinting into the glare of sunlight, and standing before her was Paul as a very small toddler. But what drew my close attention was the man beside Anne, an arm about her shoulders. He looked like an attractive *boulevardier* who had gone into military life. Tall and darkly handsome, his lip decorated with the *boulevardier's* trim mustache, a paratrooper's beret cocked jauntily on his sleek black hair, he was the schoolgirl's dream, the hero of all the movies ever made about dashing Frenchmen in the Foreign Legion.

When I returned the picture to its folder I noticed an inscription on the back of it. "To my dear mama from her worthless son, Henri," it read in translation, which explained how Paul had come by it. I had surmised long before that Anne, like Madame Cesira, preferred not to have pictures of Henri de Villemont around to reopen fresh wounds, so Madame Cesira must have entrusted Paul with this photograph of his father to be kept in private. Thought of Madame Cesira also enlightened me as to why the man's face in the picture should look so hauntingly familiar. It was, allowing for the difference in age, very much like the face of General Sebastien de Villemont in the picture on the mantelpiece of the old lady's apartment overlooking the Quai d'Anjou.

Still, it was Henri's pistol, not his photograph, which was my real concern. An unpleasant possibility came to mind. When I had first brought the gun to the de Gondes they had said something about Dr. Morillon's being told of it. At any time between then and now he might have decided to do something about it on his own. Servants were always in and out of the apartment. It would be a simple matter to bribe one to remove the pistol when I was away from my room.

There was only one way to settle this. Claude de Gonde had insisted on returning the gun to me when I handed it to him. As far as I was concerned, that made him responsible for now finding out what had become of it.

11

It was Madame Gabrielle who opened the door of the de Gonde apartment to me. She was entertaining guests, the room was full of chic, middle-aged women chattering away at the tops of their voices, and whatever she read in my face led her to immediately step out into the hallway and close the door behind her.

She peered at me anxiously through her glasses. "What is it? Is something wrong?"

I saw no point in alarming her. "Nothing is wrong, madame. I only wished to speak to Monsieur de Gonde for a few minutes."

"Oh." She pressed a hand to her bosom and sighed with relief. "After that dreadful affair last night I didn't know what to expect."

"That affair was my fault, madame. I apologize for it."

"What nonsense. Is that what you want to talk to my husband about? Is it possible that because of last night you feel obliged to leave Madame de Villemont's service?"

"Do you think I should?"

"My God, no," Madame Gabrielle said. "I assure you that if you do leave, Paul would be the only one to really suffer. Before you came here he was such a sad little ghost of a child. Now—well, do I have to tell you how strong and alive he's become? There have been too many upheavals in his life already. Your departure could be the most shattering of all because he'd feel that his friend and hero had deliberately deserted him. Although"— Madame Gabrielle could not help smiling a little at this —"he has confided to me that his hero can be a very cruel taskmaster when it comes to schoolwork."

"Only when the student is lazy," I said. "But I have no intention of deserting Paul. What I wanted to talk about with Monsieur de Gonde concerns something else altogether. Do you know where I can find him?"

"At present, he's attending a business meeting in the conference room. But I suspect," Madame Gabrielle said wryly, "that it may take hours for the meeting to decide the fate of the world."

My feeling was that, business meeting or not, de Gonde would be glad to give me a few minutes on a matter which concerned him so vitally, but before I could make my departure, Madame Gabrielle insisted on leading me into her living room and introducing me to the guests there. At first, I imagined this to be merely a gracious gesture in my direction—after all, to these patrician ladies I was a servant in the house—but I quickly saw that the gesture had an ulterior motive. The pink-cheeked defiance with which Madame Gabrielle presented me to her friends, their startled expressions, raised eyebrows, and bright, false smiles, all made it plain that Anne de Villemont and I were objects of scandal to those present, and that Madame Gabrielle was publicly declaring her faith in us. If I had liked her before for her unfailing kindness, her obvious concern for Anne and affection for Paul, I had to wholeheartedly admire her now for her courage in facing down these glittering birds of ill-omen perched around the room.

I took my leave as soon as I could and went directly to the conference room downstairs. It was the last room of the house's west wing, the one immediately beyond the game room where the disastrous scene between Anne and Morillon had taken place the night before, and its massive doors were tightly closed. I heard the drone of a voice on the other side of the doors and hesitated there, straining my ears to make out what was being said. I didn't want to break in on the meeting during an important speech and decided that if this sounded important I could wait it out.

I wasn't given a chance to wait very long. The next instant, I felt a pressure between the shoulder blades and a soft voice said, "Please do not move. This is a gun, and if you make one little move it will certainly go off."

I froze in my awkward listening position.

"Very good, monsieur," said the voice. "Now clasp your hands on your head and turn around to face me."

I did so, and found myself looking at a boy—he couldn't have been more than twenty—who regarded me with an expression of sleepy indifference, although the gun he held aimed at my chest was certainly at the ready. It was a heavy, long-barreled revolver with a silencer attached to it.

I tried to put on the same front of indifference as the boy. "What's that all about?" I said, nodding at the gun.

"It's about my instructions, monsieur. There's always a chance that someone may bruise an ear pressing it against that door. I'm here to see this doesn't happen."

Too late I remembered Georges' warning my first day in the house that the conference room was guarded against eavesdroppers during business meetings. While the boy kept the gun against my breastbone and frisked me with his free hand in a thoroughly professional manner, I said, "Look, I'm the tutor of Monsieur de Gonde's nephew and only wished to speak to Monsieur for a minute. If you'd put that cannon away and call him out here—"

"But of course. You always prepare to speak to someone by listening at his keyhole. Only it's Monsieur de Gonde who does the calling here. Since he doesn't want to be bothered now, you might explain yourself to his secretary instead. Do you know Monsieur Bourdon?"

"Yes."

"We'll soon find out," said the boy.

A side door in the game room opened onto a narrow staircase. Hands still clasped on my head, I was prodded up a flight of steps and along the second-floor corridor to the door of Bernard Bourdon's apartment. When I was ushered through the door by a jab of the pistol, Bernard, seated at a desk, pen in hand, gaped at me, his mouth wide open with astonishment, and then burst into helpless laughter.

"What a scene!" he managed to say. "I knew that sooner or later something like this had to happen."

"But this type—" the boy started to say angrily, and Bernard cut him short with a wave of the hand.

"Yes, yes, idiot, this type is a dangerous spy sent by the oil companies of America to learn how many holes we intend to dig in the Sahara Desert next year. You've done a magnificent job in capturing him, and I'll see you get a medal for it. Now put that disgusting piece of machinery back in your pocket or wherever you keep it and go downstairs."

White with rage, the boy thrust the gun into his belt and drew his jacket over it. As he started to open the door, Bernard cheerfully remarked, "And next time, hero, try a little more brain power and a little less fire power. Otherwise, you'll be dragging Madame de Gonde herself up here one of these days, and how I'll explain that to Monsieur de Gonde I don't know."

When the boy was gone, savagely slamming the door after him, Bernard pityingly shook his head. "He takes his job seriously, that Albert."

"A funny sort of job," I said.

"Not at all. In case you don't know it, Reno, industrial espionage is all the rage today. It can be worth a fortune to overhear a few secrets, get a look at some contracts, learn a formula for a new product. It should be. If the wrong people got an earful of that meeting downstairs, the Bourse could go crazy when it opens Monday. Anyhow, I'm sorry you were bothered by that fool. What was it you were trying to do when he pulled his gun on you—see Monsieur Claude?"

"Yes."

"He'll be tied up in conference quite a while. Would you want me to deliver him a message?"

"No."

Bernard regarded me quizzically. "You don't like me very much, do you?"

"I haven't thought about it one way or the other."

"I suspect you have. The sad part, Reno, is that you and I

should be good friends, considering our position here. Maybe we're not members of the family, but we're a long way from being chefs or chauffeurs. It's possible that we even have an interest in the same literature, the same music, the same art. What could be a better foundation for friendship? It certainly offers more than a game of dominoes with those lumps in the kitchen."

What interested me in this appeal was not the meaning under it, the thinly veiled suggestion that I might fill Sidney Scott's place in his life if I chose to, but the fact that Bernard did not share the attitude of the lumps downstairs to my manhandling of Dr. Morillon. Instead of responding to first impulse and walking out of the room, I remarked this to him, and he shrugged.

"Monsieur Claude said you were forced to defend yourself and that's all there was to it. For myself, I can tell you that the scene wasn't unexpected. Anyone who becomes attached to your Madame de Villemont sooner or later finds himself involved in such ugly situations."

"Why?"

"Why? Because this is a woman, Reno, who seems to have taken the great Shakespeare literally. 'All the world's a stage,' he wrote, and so it is to Madame, who evidently regards herself as the heroine of a frantic melodrama playing off the people in her life against each other. Mad, quite mad, you see. The worst of it is that she happens to be extraordinarily attractive to men. At least enough to make even a man like Hubert Morillon behave like a fool."

"And me as well?"

"For the sake of her child, I hope not."

It intrigued me to hear such concern expressed for Paul for the second time within the hour. First by Madame Gabrielle and now by Bernard.

"What's Paul got to do with it?" I asked.

"Everything from the family's point of view. Consider, Reno, that of the de Villemonts, the de Gondes, the Vosiers, this is the one child, the sole heir, the family's most precious treasure. His upbringing means everything to these people. Left to his mother he was being turned into a neurotic, sickly little creature. In your hands he's being shaped into a boy his father might have been proud of. If anything happened to Madame de Ville-mont—"

"What, for example?"

"Do you really want to know," said Bernard, "or are you only looking for an excuse to hand me the same dose you handed Morillon?"

"I want to know," I said. To give Bernard his due, he seemed honestly concerned by these family problems.

"Then in the kindest terms," he said, "Madame de Villemont is not well. Her psychotic outburst last night—"

"She was drunk."

"That in itself is a bad sign to anyone who knows her. The point is, she's already spent time in a mental institution and may some day have to return there. In that case—"

"Who's the judge of her mental condition?" I cut in. "Dr. Morillon?"

"No, Dr. Felix Linder. He's recognized throughout the world as an authority in this field."

"But Morillon has a strong influence on him, doesn't he?"

Bernard looked annoyed.

"I'm sure they respect each other," he said, "but Morillon isn't in practice; he's simply an observer at the sanitarium. And what I'm getting at is that the last time Madame entered the sanitarium, it was almost disastrous for Paul. He had barely recovered from the loss of his father, and now he thought he had lost his mother as well. What everyone hopes is that if this emergency arises again, you'll be on hand to give the boy the sense of security he needs, the courage to get along without his mother, even the upbringing he ought to get. Does that make clear your importance to the family? Can you see why they all hope you manage to take a properly clinical attitude toward Madame?"

Somehow I managed to look squarely into those hooded eyes and nod polite understanding. The worst mistake, I knew, would be to get into any argument with Bernard where the secret of Anne's plans might slip out.

When I prepared to leave, Bernard said that if I were free for the afternoon—

I told him I wasn't and he took this graciously.

"But we must get together very soon," he said. "I'm especially anxious to hear about your meeting with Charles Leschenhaut. I'm a great admirer of his."

"And of the Comtesse de Laennac?" On his desk was a copy of her *La Mystère du Tarot*, its jacket garishly illustrated by a picture of The Hanged Man from the Tarot deck. It was hard to imagine the icily intellectual Bernard devoting himself to fortunetelling.

"Oh, that." He grinned mischievously. "The Tarot is Madame Cesira's obsession, dear lady that she is, and she's been on my neck for ages now, insisting I delve into its mysteries. All I can make of them so far is that old Sophie de Laennac is probably the worst writer who ever twisted the French language to her own idiotic purpose. If you'd like to borrow the book—"

I thanked him but declined the offer. I had already heard Madame la Comtesse deliver herself at length on the subject of the Tarot and wanted no more of that dubious pleasure.

When, in the privacy of his study later that afternoon, I told Claude de Gonde about the missing gun, he wearily said, "It must have been Madame de Villemont herself who took it. It couldn't have been anyone else."

"But she entrusted it to me, monsieur," I pointed out. "If she wanted it back, all she had to do was ask for it."

He pondered this, slowly rubbing a thumb up and down that hard jaw.

"Yes," he said unwillingly. "That's undeniable. But what other explanation could there possibly be?"

"Monsieur, I hope I'm not overstepping bounds, but if you told Dr. Morillon about the gun—"

He didn't like that.

"I did tell him about it, and you are overstepping bounds, young man. Don't judge Dr. Morillon by last night. If he behaved badly, it was because he was driven to it by Madame de

Villemont's obscene performance. His fault is temper, not lack
of honor. I assure you he had nothing to do with the gun's dis-
appearance."

I left it at that, wishing I could be as sure of it as he was.

12

Meanwhile, the whole week went by
without any word from Leschenhaut about the manuscripts I
had given him. Saturday, which marked the beginning of the
second week, I was in no state of mind for light conversation
when Paul and I went out after lunch, and I was grateful that
he was also in a silent mood, evidently brooding over some
deep problem of his own.

We did the historical bit that afternoon—a visit to Napo-
leon's tomb—and on the Esplanade des Invalides were caught
in a sudden downpour and forced to seek shelter in a *crêperie*
where Paul could stuff himself with leathery pancakes sweet-
ened with strawberry preserve and washed down by Breton
cider. He ate steadily but said nothing, highly unnatural for
him, and I was about to ask him what was on his mind when
he suddenly came out with it.

In the middle of his third *crêpe froment à la comfiture*, he
fixed his eyes on me and said in an accusing voice, "Do you
love Mama?"

I choked on my *apéritif*, then recovered myself.

"Of course," I said with a great show of indifference. "Don't
you?"

"I don't mean that way." He jabbed his fork into the limp pancake here and there as if stabbing it to death. "I mean, are you going to get married to Mama?"

I shrugged. "To tell the truth, I haven't been planning to marry anyone."

He brightened immediately. "Then the Tarot cards were right. Last time I went to Grandmother's I asked her to find out what the cards said about it, and they said Mama would never get married again."

And they would, I reflected, as long as Madame Cesira was dealing them out. If Anne remarried in the reasonably near future, it meant that her son, that heaven-sent heir to the de Villemont name, would be given a different name, a different identity, would be removed from the hands of the de Villemonts altogether, and I could see Madame Cesira's face harden at the thought. It might explain why there was never an escort calling for Anne on her evenings out. Orders could have emanated from Île Saint-Louis that suitable males were to be kept at a safe distance from this sultry, tempting young widow. And, since she was tightly ringed around by her husband's family, there wasn't much she could do about it.

That scene also gave me an insight into myself. Anne de Villemont was devious and secretive. Her moods, ranging from stony arrogance to panicky fearfulness, from the morbid withdrawal into herself to the hot yielding to me, were unpredictable. She was, after making her son neurotically dependent on her, incapable of managing him. She got drunk at the wrong time. She gambled recklessly and incompetently at the tables for stakes too high even for someone with her kind of money. I knew all this. And now that Paul had come out with the word, I also knew that, despite everything, I was in love with the woman. It had been ten long years since I broke up with my wife, and from that time to this I had been afraid to let myself go over the edge about any woman. Now I had the feeling I was making up for all those years in one jump. A wild, blindfolded jump, and a blissful one.

It was a relief to face that fact squarely. I raised my *apéritif* glass in a silent toast to it.

At about nine that evening when I was at my typewriter and when Paul had just settled down to the Alfred Hitchcock show on his television set—the dubbing of dialogue into French giving the American scene a decidedly Gallic flavor—I heard Anne addressing her son over the crackle of dramatic dialogue.

"I'm going now, *chéri*. And this must be the last program."

"Yes, Mama. You look very pretty."

"Thank you, sir."

"But the dress— It's very naked on top, isn't it?"

"Mais oui. C'est la mode."

That sounded interesting. I got up to investigate *la mode* for myself, but then heard Djilana's voice.

"The jewelry, madame. After all, one must make the proper impression at a grand place like Spinosi's. Yes, this one, I think. And this bracelet."

Spinosi's. So this was to be one of those profligate gambling nights, and the thought vaguely depressed me. Apparently fate had decided that the woman I was to love would be of the kind that my father, viewing them from behind his dice table, most loathed. But then my father had loathed everybody he ever had dealings with, not excluding his own wife and child.

"Good night, *chéri*," Anne said to Paul, "and behave yourself. I'll be leaving as soon as I give Monsieur Reno his instructions."

When she came into my room, discreetly leaving Paul's door wide open behind her, I forgave her all profligacy on the spot. She was distractingly lovely. The dress left little of those ripe breasts and long, shapely legs to the imagination; the jewelry was a diamond and sapphire necklace and bracelet, and the sapphires almost exactly matched the color of her eyes.

I started to tell her this, but she hastily pressed a finger to my lips. Djilana was still there in Paul's room, her ears certainly pricked for any word of ours she could catch.

"Make sure the child has his glass of milk before bedtime," Anne said loudly, then came into my arms for a quick, hard kiss. "I've left lipstick on you," she whispered warningly as she broke away, and raising her voice again, "Good night, Monsieur Reno," she said in the tones of a kindly chatelaine, and was gone.

But the scent of her perfume remained with me, making it impossible to concentrate on my work. I very soon gave it up to join Paul at the television set, and afterward saw to it that he had his glass of milk and was tucked into bed. I had just stretched out on my own bed, hands under my head, to contemplate the mixed blessings of my situation when I had to get up to answer the phone.

With shock I realized it was Charles Leschenhaut who was speaking to me. What he had to say sounded like music. He had read my six stories, he jovially informed me at the top of his voice, and while four of them were beneath contempt, a couple were highly promising.

"The one about the musician in the strip joint especially," he bellowed. "*Ça te la coupe!* Right on the jaw, that's how it hits one. Also the story about the young husband who discovers his wife has asked her rich and loving papa to buy her a mink coat because he can't afford to. That really cuts to the bone. Were you the young husband by any chance?"

"Yes."

"I thought so. Well, two out of six isn't bad for a start, but both these little beauties need a lot of work before I print them. Your literary French is sometimes atrocious beyond belief. Anyhow, I'm busy as the devil all week, but next weekend I can give you two full days of my time. Are you interested in putting in a couple of days of hard work with me at my apartment?"

I was so dazed by this incredible good news that I said, "Yes, of course," before it struck me that next weekend, by Anne's schedule, I was supposed to be far away from Paris. Now the departure would have to be postponed. It seemed only fair to get Anne's nod of approval on this before I accepted Leschenhaut's invitation.

"There's one small problem," I told him. "Nothing of any importance really. You see, Saturday and Sunday are work days for me. I'll have to get Madame de Villemont's permission to take them off." He was too close to the family, I was sure, to be trusted with the exact truth. "Would it be all right if I spoke to her about it and called you back?"

"If you wish," said Leschenhaut, and gave me his phone number. Then he remarked, "There's no reason why Madame would be inconsiderate, is there? I know she has her—ah—eccentricities, but I don't imagine suppressing literary talent is one of them."

"No, I'm sure it isn't, Monsieur Leschenhaut. I'll call you back tomorrow."

If I had been free to do it after that call, I would have gathered together Louis and a few other cronies and gone out on the biggest drunk of my life. But trapped as I was, all I could do was try to pass along the good news by phone.

Even in that I was frustrated. When I called Louis, Madame Olympe informed me that Monsieur Louis and Monsieur Becque had already gone out for the evening, God knows where. When I tried Véronique's number, although I was sure she must be with Louis, there was no answer. In the end I settled down to wait for Anne's return, whenever it would be. I was so keyed up that sleep seemed impossible anyhow, so I turned out the light, stretched out still fully clothed on the bed again, and lay there alert for any sound of homecoming.

Nothing induces sleep like the determination to stay awake. Eventually I dozed off. I was brought suddenly awake by the throbbing of a car motor in the courtyard below. Then the motor was cut off, and in the silence that followed I made out the sound of muted voices and the clicking of women's heels over cobblestones.

I got out of bed and opened the door to the corridor an inch or two, no more than was necessary to see Anne when she passed by on the way to her room. Waiting there in the darkness, I heard the whine of the elevator ascending and the small clash of its gate opening and closing. There was a muttered colloquy at the elevator—the Vosiers and Anne making their farewells to each other, I supposed—and then footsteps approached.

My hand was on the knob of the door when I saw the flicker of light from the jewelry Anne wore at her throat, but the hand froze on the knob, the door remained as it was. Anne was not alone. There was a man with her, handsome and blond as a Viking, swinging her evening bag from his forefinger in time with the tune he was silently whistling through pursed lips. Dr. Hubert Morillon.

They passed by; the door to Anne's bedroom opened and closed; Morillon did not reappear on his way back to the elevator. I counted seconds, counted minutes, then finally gave up counting.

At break of day, I watched Morillon depart, rumpled and sleepy-eyed, knotting his tie as he strolled along the corridor. Looking down from my window, I saw Georges leap from the driver's seat of the Mercedes and respectfully usher Casanova into the car. As it passed through the gate, Pascal the garage attendant was right behind it to close and lock the gate.

My valise and carry-all were stored in the otherwise empty armoire. I dragged them out, flung them on the bed, and opened them. First to pack, and then to write a parting note, a few choice words telling Anne de Villemont exactly what she was. Djilana could attend to Paul until his mother read them.

I had flung my luggage on the bed with such violence that the sound of it must have penetrated Paul's slumbers.

"Reno?" he called in a faraway voice. "Reno, *j'ai peur!*"

I went to him quickly. He was sitting up in bed looking around fearfully, and when I squatted down beside him he flung his arms around my neck and clung to me. I held him close and felt his bony little body relax.

"There's nothing to be afraid of," I said.

"I heard a noise."

"Yes, because I let something fall. I'm sorry."

"But in my dream it was a bad noise."

"All right, next time tell me when you're dreaming, and I'll make only good noises," I said, and he giggled.

"You know I can't tell you when I'm dreaming because I'm asleep then. Why are you dressed? Is it morning already?"

"No, it isn't." I detached his arms from around my neck and pushed him flat, roughing him up so that he squirmed and kicked joyously. "Now back to sleep," I commanded, "and no more dreams."

"Will you stay with me?"

"Naturally. But only if you close your eyes and make believe you're asleep."

He was asleep within two minutes, but I waited a while before returning to my room. Then, after long and painful consideration, I put the valise and carry-all back in the armoire. It was impossible to disappear from the child's life this way. Whatever I felt about his mother, the parting from him had to be made as painless as it could be made.

The best way to handle it was to go through with the bargain. Madame wanted herself and her son conveyed to New York? All right, they would be. I would attend to it, bid an affectionate farewell to Paul, and head directly back to Paris. And since there was no reason why Spinosi's gambling establishment should be the only one to profit from Madame's foibles, I was going to wind up with a pocketful of money for my trouble. Enough to buy me my complete independence for a long time to come.

Independence from anybody and everybody, male or female.

13

My only duties on Sunday mornings were to see that Paul was fed and clothed and to deliver him to Georges for the weekly hegira to Île Saint-Louis.

I managed this with my eyes bleary and my nerves ragged, and when Georges brought the limousine around to the door, I saw he wasn't in any better shape. That was no surprise, since he had also been waiting attendance on Hubert Morillon until dawn. But the realization that by now every servant in the house must know how Madame de Villemont had spent the small hours of the night added the final drop of acid to the sourness of my disillusionment.

What I most wanted was to walk right into her room and tell her off in plain language, but I knew I was still too dangerously angry for any such confrontation. Just the thought of seeing the imprint of Morillon's head on the pillow next to hers filled me with a murderous urge to slap her senseless. Better in that case to cool off a little before the big scene.

So I set off for the Champs Élysées as fast as I could walk, and wound up at a café on the corner of rue Washington where Paul and I were occasional customers. Taking a back table on the sidewalk, I was reminded that the tourist season had begun. There was a sizable gathering of well-heeled voyagers around me, cameras slung over chair backs, guidebooks at the ready.

The idea of eating anything still turned my stomach as it had when Jeanne-Marie had brought up breakfast for Paul and me. I settled for a *café au rhum*—black coffee liberally dosed with potent West Indian rum in the Faubourg Saint-Denis style —and after a second one I felt a little better. After the third, I felt that the worst was over. I could now contemplate the image of Anne de Villemont with cold venom instead of boiling rage, could almost take pleasure in considering various ways of revenging myself on her. Six ounces of rum on an empty stomach is strong medicine. My head hummed with it; I felt crafty as Machiavelli plotting the downfall of an enemy.

It was providence which sent the instrument of my vengeance strolling by the café just then. I saw the girl on the sidewalk at the same time my waiter did, recognized what she was as promptly as he. She was small and pretty, with a trim figure and excellent legs, and was dressed with a chic that suggested she was the pampered wife or mistress of some rich denizen of the Étoile district. But her walk gave her away. She moved too deliberately, her face expressionless, her eyes flicking over the tables, taking in every man who sat there unaccompanied, appraising the possibilities with the accuracy of a pretty little electronic computer. A *poule de luxe* out to explore the rich tourist market.

When she finally headed toward an empty table nearby, my waiter, a footsore old veteran, snapped his fingers to attract her attention and gave her a warning shake of the head. I knew what was on his mind. At this early hour, there were too many watchful, bad-tempered American and British wives here with their husbands. Let word get around the tourist bureaus that the place welcomed professional temptresses and the family trade might very soon fall off.

The girl seemed momentarily embarrassed by the warning, then shrugged and started to walk away. Suddenly, Machiavellian inspiration seized me. I stood up—discovering in the process that my knees had mysteriously turned to rubber—and waved a greeting to Mademoiselle.

"So there you are, *chérie*," I said. "Do you know you've kept me waiting for an hour?"

She looked at me with surprise, then promptly picked up her cue.

"Oh, I'm so sorry, baby." She flashed the waiter a look of triumph as she sat down beside me. "I had so many things to do before I could get away. You know how it is."

"Sure. Anyhow, I have a forgiving nature. What would you like to drink?"

"What are you having?" she asked, and when I told her she shuddered and said, "My God, what a stomach you must have. *Café crème* and a cigarette will do very well for me, thank you."

The waiter departed, growling under his breath, and as I lit the girl's cigarette I said to her *sotto voce*, "It's only fair to tell you I'm not in the market right now. But when that miserable type tried to run you off the premises—"

"You felt it would be amusing to stick a thumb in his eye," the girl said, "and now he probably thinks you're my mackerel. Well, if it doesn't matter to you, it doesn't matter to me. I can always use a cup of coffee anyhow."

"Good. My name's Reno, by the way. What's yours?"

"Ghislaine."

"It's a nice name."

"It's just a name," the girl said indifferently. "Don't strain yourself, baby. You don't have to make conversation if you don't want to."

"I want to. However, there's a phone call to make first. Will you wait here meanwhile?"

"Yes. But not very long unless I get paid for it."

I found the phone in the back of the café. When Anne heard my voice over it, her own immediately became guarded.

"Yes, Monsieur Reno?"

"Is someone there with you?"

"No, but someone may be listening in. I've always had trouble with this connection. What did you want to tell me?"

"It concerns the reading list I've drawn up for Paul, but I'd rather discuss it in person, madame. Could you meet me here at the Café Chaudron? It's too pleasant a day to remain indoors."

"Impossible, Monsieur Reno. I don't think Georges has returned with the car yet."

"It's only a short walk, madame."

It took her a long time to come to a decision, and then at last she said, "Very well, monsieur; I'll bring my copy of the reading list with me," and hung up.

I kept the receiver to my ear. Sure enough, after a few seconds the silence in my ear was broken by the sound of another phone being carefully replaced on its stand. So someone had been listening in. Bernard, most likely. But when I pictured him at his desk, eavesdropping with wet-lipped avidity, what came sharpest to mind was his copy of La Mystère du Tarot on the desk, its jacket decorated with the grotesque illustration of The Hanged Man. It neatly symbolized me in my present state, emotionally dangling upside down by one ankle, but with a beatific smile on my lips.

I somewhat unsteadily made my way back to the table outdoors, and Ghislaine said, "Well, you certainly look pleased with yourself. That call must have been a great success."

"It was. I arranged for a friend of mine to meet you here."

"A rich friend?"

"Unbelievably rich."

Ghislaine drew on her cigarette with great deliberation and exhaled a cloud of smoke into the golden, hazy air.

"*Vous êtes un drôle de mec, bébé,*" she declared, which could mean either that she found me a disturbingly weird character or a remarkably fascinating one. "What's your racket?"

"I'm a writer."

Ghislaine nodded wisely. "So that's it." She seemed relieved at this logical explanation of my eccentricities.

After that, she settled down in her chair and drowsily took the sun, her face turned up to it, while I sat on tenterhooks, keeping a close eye out for Anne's arrival. It didn't take long. Whatever she thought when she saw I wasn't alone didn't show on her face. She took the seat I offered her, smiled at the startled Ghislaine and looked at me inquiringly.

"This is Ghislaine," I told her. "And this," I said to Ghislaine, "is the friend I want you to meet."

Ghislaine threw me a sidelong glance of loathing, then turned apologetically to Anne.

"Madame, I don't know what sort of joke your husband is playing, but believe me, I have nothing to do with it. If you will excuse me—"

She started to rise, but I caught hold of her wrist and forced her back into her seat.

"You're mistaken," I said. "I am not Madame's husband."

"Will you please tell me what this is all about?" Anne looked from one to the other of us. "I really don't understand."

"Nor do I," said Ghislaine, and to me she said witheringly, "Everyone is watching this, monsieur. If you want them to witness a scene that will curl their hair—"

"There's no need for any scene," I said. "I wanted you to meet Madame for a good reason. I've already mentioned that she's very rich. Unbelievably rich. And you can see for yourself she's also extremely beautiful and elegant, isn't she?"

"So?" Ghislaine said warily.

"So not to be subtle about it, I want you to clear up a mystery. I want you, as a professional in this line of work, to explain to me why such a woman as Madame would choose to go to bed regularly with a man she thoroughly detests."

Anne gasped. Her eyes, wide with shock, stared into mine; her hand went to her cheek as if it had been slapped. Then she came to her feet and blindly fled into the dim, concealing recesses of the café.

Ghislaine looked after her open-mouthed, then turned to me wrathfully.

"Ah, you brute! You animal! Now see what you've done? She's going to be sick all over the place."

She rose and hurried after Anne, leaving me alone to savor my splendidly brutal triumph. Bernard Bourdon had been right when he warned that Madame de Villemont doted on playing off the people in her life against each other. And she had been so sure, so pathetically sure, she could play me off against Hubert Morillon without being caught at it—

Ghislaine finally returned to the table.

"She wants to see you," she told me coldly. "She's sitting there in the dark crying her heart out, the idiot."

"Is she? Well, don't let her fool you. She's a great performer, that one."

"She's an imbecile, that's what she is. Just another stupid female who lets a man wipe his feet all over her because she thinks she's in love with him. You men are all alike. The only real pleasure for you is abusing women, isn't it?"

I held out my hand so she could see the edge of the fifty-franc note I had palmed, and she dexterously took possession of the money.

"*Chérie*," I said, "you didn't get to the game early enough to know the score."

I strolled into the café. Anne was at a banquette in a far corner, her face a pale oval in the darkness, her hands clasped before her on the table. The only other people in the room were the bartender and a waiter in close conversation. I sat down, and when the waiter bustled over I ordered a double cognac. The waiter looked questioningly at Anne, and she nodded. "The same," she said lifelessly.

Sitting there nursing my drink, I became aware of the saccharine strains of a ballad being piped by Radio Luxembourg through the speaker behind the bar. The sound of the music, the sight of Madame's melting eyes glimmering with tears— everything seemed calculated to make this a scene from *Tristan und Isolde* performed by a third-rate company.

"Turn off that damn thing, will you?" I said to the bartender, and when he seemed deaf to this I repeated it, bringing my fist down hard on the table to emphasize it. This time he hastily switched off the sound.

Anne leaned forward. Her hand hovered hesitantly over mine, then came to rest on it.

"You're very drunk, aren't you?" she said.

"Very."

"Please listen. Whatever you think—"

"Sweetheart, after last night I don't have to think. I know."

She abruptly withdrew her hand.

"Who told you about it?" she asked dully. "Matilde?"

"No. Your bad luck that I was waiting up to tell you some good news, so I got the picture all by myself. As for the news, Leschenhaut called me to say he'll take a couple of my stories if I work them over with him next weekend. I'm afraid our little jaunt to New York will have to be postponed until that's cleared up."

"Postponed?" Anne said unbelievingly. "You mean, even after what's happened you'll still get Paul and me to New York?"

"Strictly as a business proposition, and my price is twenty thousand dollars cash before we leave. If you're wondering how come I picked that figure, it's because I heard that's how much you've been dropping at Spinosi's every time you're there for the fun and games. How'd you make out last night, by the way? Win for a change? Is that what you were celebrating with Morillon?"

"Oh, please. If you're trying to punish me by talking this way—"

"I'm only trying to let you know how we stand with each other."

Anne took rigid control of herself.

"All right, I'll pay your price. But under one condition. The trip can't be postponed. We must leave Friday."

"Why?"

"It doesn't matter why." Her voice hardened. "You'll do what you're paid to do without asking questions, or we forget the whole thing."

I had the feeling she wasn't pulling a bluff. In that case, Leschenhaut would just have to stand by until I had her and Paul safely convoyed across the Atlantic.

"All right," I said. "We'll leave this Friday."

"And no one is to know about it. Absolutely no one."

"Except for a couple of people who are supposed to help me with the arrangements," I pointed out.

"You don't have to tell them too much, either."

"Oh, come on," I said. "You're making this sound like Eliza getting ready to cross the ice. Maybe you don't know it, but Orly airport is only half an hour down the road, and I've never yet seen a bloodhound in Paris."

"Don't be funny about it! Just listen and try to understand what I want done. Or are you too drunk by now to understand anything?"

"If I am, maybe it's better that way. And what am I supposed to understand?"

"Exactly what must be done Friday. Paul already knows his part. I've taken him shopping in the Galeries Lafayette a few times to get him ready for it."

"At the Galeries Lafayette?" Maybe I was too drunk to understand her.

"Yes. Georges always parks at the rue Mogador entrance and goes in with us. This time Paul will slip away once we're inside and meet you at the rue de la Chaussée entrance where you'll be waiting. You'll have a car, a rented one, and you'll drive straight to Orly and board the plane with Paul. I'll join you as soon as I can get away from Georges. If I can't, don't worry about it. Somehow I'll get a letter to you in New York that'll explain everything."

It took me a few seconds to grasp the significance of this.

"Are you serious?" I demanded. "Do you really expect me to

smuggle Paul out of the country by myself and try to keep him hidden away from his own family?"

"Oh God, all I expect you to do is go ahead without me if anything goes wrong. Doesn't it mean anything that I trust you so completely? Doesn't it prove that no matter what you think of me—"

She was abandoning that pose of hardness now. Her voice became unsteady; she yearned toward me, her hand reaching again for mine as if by its own volition—anything, but anything, to sell the customer a doubtful bill of goods. And, possibly, a dangerous one.

I drew my hand out of range.

"The price is still twenty thousand dollars, cash in advance," I said. "But now it's a real bargain."

I called Leschenhaut from the café as soon as Anne left. When I told him I wouldn't be able to keep the appointment with him he seemed to think I was pulling his leg.

"Impossible!" he snorted. "Surely Madame couldn't be so unkind. What reason could she possibly offer for such willfulness?"

When, without divulging Madame's reason, I convinced him that I was serious, he expressed his opinion of rich, psychotic, female Philistines in brutally frank language.

"And to be the slave of such a type—" he concluded. "No, my friend, you need more spirit, more iron in the soul. If you want to be a creative force, you can't let any woman lead you around by the nose, no matter how well she pays for the privilege."

That was uncomfortably close to the mark.

"Monsieur Leschenhaut," I said, "in a few weeks—"

"No, no, young man. A few weeks, then a few more weeks, and meanwhile I'm supposed to sit like a fool waiting for you to favor me with your presence. I want none of that, thank you. I'll return your manuscripts tomorrow. And give my regards to Madame. She may have saved both of us a great deal of wasted time."

It gave me a perfect score for the weekend. I had misjudged him almost as badly as I had misjudged Anne de Villemont.

14

In payment for Véronique's services as my travel agent, when I climbed the four steep flights to her apartment on the rue de Babylonne the next evening it was with a box of wild strawberries in one hand, a package of her favorite Sainte-Odile cheese in the other and a bottle of wine in each of my jacket pockets. The door to the apartment was unlocked. I pushed it open with my foot and walked in to see Véronique and Louis keeping each other dismal company, Véronique with her eyes red and swollen and Louis looking bleak.

"What's wrong?" I asked, and Louis said to Véronique, "You'd better help him unload that stuff before we tell him. There might be something breakable in one of those bags."

Véronique obeyed, and while she was at it said to me tearfully, "It's Monsieur Driot-Steiner. My boss. He's dead."

"Oh," I said. "Well, I'm sorry to hear it."

"Sorry?" Louis slapped his hand against his forehead. "You should be terrified to hear it. For God's sake, wake up, pal. Driot-Steiner. Adrian Driot-Steiner. Doesn't that name mean anything to you?"

Suddenly it did. That was the name signed to the requisition for the police report on Sidney Scott's death.

Louis was watching my expression. "*Alors,*" he said, "*il pige vite, notre Reno, hein?* Give him the least little clue and he catches on like a real genius."

"How did it happen?" I asked. "When?"

"When he was leaving the Ministry after work this afternoon," Véronique said. "A car was waiting there. It was just parked by the corner waiting. When he started to cross the street—"

"What kind of car?"

"A big black one. That's all anyone could make of it before it got away."

"Poor devil," Louis said to me, "he left the office at the same time every day and always crossed the rue de Grenelle at the same place. Such regularity can be fatal, it seems. Especially to types who get too interested in what happened to your Sidney Scott. What do you want to bet that Max Marchat was another one of those types?"

I tried to put cause and effect together but couldn't make them fit.

"Look," I said. "The only ones who knew about Driot-Steiner's signing that requisition were the police. Are you telling me that the police had him killed?"

"Why not?" Louis demanded. "The police have their share of rotten apples. And if someone like your charming Madame de Villemont is in the market for apples—"

"You've met her," I said. "Do you think she's the kind to go around hiring assassins?"

"*Elle t'allume, bébé*," Louis said pityingly. "She gives you hot pants, that's what I think, and that means you're in no shape to judge her. But ask yourself just one little question. If she didn't shove Sidney Scott into the drink and arrange to have Marchat and Driot-Steiner bumped off, who did?"

"An old friend of hers," I said. "Her lover, in fact," and since I was here on confidential business anyhow, I explained in detail Dr. Hubert Morillon's role in Madame's life. I wound up with her plan to leave the country, and I could see that neither of my audience was happy about it.

"But that woman must know what this Morillon is up to," Véronique protested. "Why isn't she just as guilty as he is?"

"Ah, for that you'd have to see her," Louis said maliciously. "Next to her, even Eliane looks like nothing."

"Oh God!" gasped Véronique, startling us. "What with everything that happened, I forgot all about it. I had lunch with

Eliane and Léon and they said they'd drop in here after the movies tonight."

Louis glared at her. "Couldn't you drop a hint that Reno would be here?"

"I did. That's why I think Eliane was so anxious to visit. She and Léon were engaged yesterday. She's wearing his ring, and I guess she wants to show it off to Reno."

"Let her show it off," I said. "The real question is what to do about the mess I've gotten us all into."

"What can we do?" Louis demanded. "Go to the police and get hit by a car the next day? Let's face it. We know too much and don't dare open our mouths about it."

"Which puts us in the same boat as Anne de Villemont," I said. "The fact is that Morillon killed Sidney Scott and she knows it. She might have been right there when it happened."

"True." Louis fell into a black silence, nervously working his hand back and forth across his mouth. "Wait a second," he whispered. "Now it comes clear. Now I begin to see the whole thing. Madame knows a little more than we think. She knows about someone else's death too."

"Whose?" I said. "Everyone else is accounted for."

"Not everyone, pal. Not Colonel Henri de Villemont, who had a bomb tossed into his car during the Algerian trouble. Tell me something. Who do you think did that job on him?"

"Some bomb-happy Moslem. Don't forget there were a lot of bombs being tossed around Algeria those days."

"There were. The French OAS terrorists were throwing them at the *sidis,* and the *sidis* were throwing them back, and what with those tin-pot Napoleons in the Foreign Legion figuring how to take over all France, it was a wild time, wasn't it?"

"We all know it was."

"All right," said Louis. "And during such a wild time it's easy to throw a bomb for something besides patriotic reasons. Remember that once the OAS took over, there were no more rules to worry about. Everything went."

"What about it?" Véronique said in bewilderment. "I don't see what you're getting at."

"I am getting at a spicy little situation which involves an army officer, his beautiful American wife, and his best friend. The scene is North Africa, so naturally the wife is bored to death. To relieve the boredom she has an affair with the best friend, who, although a man of science, is also a handsome, virile animal. But the affair becomes serious. A few stolen moments of bliss are not enough. Finally, the wife presents her case to the husband, sheds tears, asks for a divorce." Louis cocked his head at me. "Does this scenario make sense so far?"

"What about Paul?" I said. "You know how she feels about him."

"I do. That's why I'm sure she not only asked for a divorce, but also asked to be given the child. And what do you think his papa had to say to that?"

"A loud no, right along with his whole family."

Louis nodded sagely. "A very loud no. So Madame is caught in a terrible dilemma. Her solution? Well, to put it kindly, a woman in love sometimes thinks merely being in love is excuse enough for any madness. Even to joining with her lover in killing the nuisance of a husband who stands in their way."

I said, "I can't believe she was ever Morillon's partner in any murder."

"Maybe not a willing partner. But suppose she let Morillon get the idea she wouldn't mind seeing her husband dead? What if he took that at face value? Like it or not, she would be his partner afterward, and he'd make sure she knew that."

It was like watching the final pieces of the jigsaw puzzle being put together and a picture of hell emerging.

"Not that Madame and her doctor would be so crude as to handle the business themselves," Louis said relentlessly. "But with her kind of bank account, what could be easier than hiring the right man for the job? Someone hand-picked. One of those OAS baby-butchers.

"But once the job is done, what happens? Madame goes out of her mind with guilt and fear; she now detests her dangerous lover. But there's no escape from him. She is handcuffed to him by their partnership in murder. And that murder breeds others. Madame gets herself drunk one night and lets Sidney Scott in on her secret, so he's the next victim. Max Marchat somehow learns the truth about Scott's death, so he has to be knocked off. Poor Driot-Steiner is suspected of sticking his nose into the affair, so his number is up.

"Do you see what all this means? It means that if this bloodthirsty doctor ever gets the idea Madame has confided her secret to you—well, in simple language, pal, you have to get out of that pile on the rue de Courcelles quick. Tonight, if you can."

He and Véronique waited for my decision. But was there any choice of decisions? I had just had answered for me every question I had ever asked myself about Anne de Villemont. Above all, the question of why she was playing her double game now —going to bed with Morillon to keep him off his guard, and at the same time, using me to help her flee from him. After all, my wallet was stuffed with the ten thousand francs she had given me to arrange the flight.

"I'll talk to her tonight," I said.

"What can she tell you but a pack of lies?" Louis retorted. "No, all you do is wave good-bye to her. You can bunk with me in my room until Léon and Eliane set up housekeeping and he clears out of your place. That won't take long, now that he's got the ring on her finger."

Véronique glanced at her watch. "They'll be here soon. It's a shame they have to walk in on something as awful as this, tonight of all nights."

"Well," said Louis, "we can just tell them that if we're not as merry as we might be, it's because Reno's job is taking him back to the States at the end of the week."

We left it at that, and when Becque and Eliane made their entrance—Becque awkward in my company at first, then finally grinning from ear to ear with embarrassed delight when Eliane made a great display of the neat little diamond ring on her finger—everyone did his best to simulate merriment. It must have had a hollow sound to the astute Becque, however. His smile faded, was replaced by a puzzled frown.

"*Ça ne tourne pas rond,*" he said at last. "There's something wrong around here, friends, and no use trying to cover up. What is it?"

He was genuinely impressed when I told him I would be accompanying my young pupil and his mother to America at the end of the week.

"*De luxe*, I suppose, and all expenses paid?"

"That's right."

He nudged me with his elbow. "What a spot to be in, eh?"

As some philosopher once remarked, the most devastating humor is always unconscious.

Louis had not underestimated the impact Anne de Villemont could have on a man. When she opened her bedroom door to me and stood there in negligee, wide-eyed, her dark, lustrous hair caught up in a ribbon and falling loosely to her shoulders, she was enough to make a heretic out of Saint Anthony.

She knew at once that something was wrong. She closed the door behind us and leaned back against it looking at me with a mixture of fear and defiance.

"What is it?" she said.

"It's about the agreement we made. Twenty thousand dollars isn't enough."

"If you want more—"

"Not money. Answers to some questions."

"Oh God, haven't I made it plain there are things I can't tell you until we're away from here."

"You did. But we're not even starting to leave here until you tell me everything. And I mean everything. Now let's have it. What did Hubert Morillon have to do with your husband's death in Algeria? He did have a hand in it, didn't he?"

Too late, Anne shook her head in wild denial.

"Please go away," she said in a choked voice. "If you won't help me, please go away and forget you were ever in this house; forget you ever knew me. I'm telling you that for your own sake."

"I see. And was it also for my sake that you let me get the idea you were madly in love with me? Anyhow, enough in love so that I could handle you a little, sample the merchandise, as it were?"

"You bastard!" Anne said between her teeth.

"Now we're beginning to understand each other. It's about time, too."

"You don't understand anything!"

"Henri de Villemont," I said. "Sidney Scott. Max Marchat." I refrained from mentioning Driot-Steiner since that might be highly dangerous to Véronique. "Three dead already, and who knows how many more to go. Who can tell when Dr. Morillon might decide that a sanitarium in Issy isn't the best way of keeping the star witness against him quiet when she threatens to get out of hand? How does it feel to be the *petite amie* of a man who'll cut your throat the minute he stops trusting you to keep his secret?"

"That's my affair!"

"You've made it my affair too, sweetheart. And do I have to tell you it's very much a police affair?"

"You're not to go to them!"

"Why? Because you'd be implicated or because Morillon has friends among the police who'd turn me in to him?"

"He has friends everywhere." Now there was the familiar quivering panic in her voice. "Listen to me. Believe me. Everything depends on Hubert's being left alone, on his being allowed to do whatever he wants to. I've already told you that if anything happens to him, there are people who'd stop at nothing to avenge themselves for it on Paul. On Paul, do you hear?"

"Is that the story Morillon's been scaring you with? Who are these people? Has he ever named them?"

She refused to answer, but compressed her lips and slowly shook her head.

"So that's as far as the story goes," I said coldly. "For the rest—"

"I can't tell you any more. You know too much already. For Paul's sake—"

"No," I said angrily, "don't get started on that. For Paul's sake there's one thing you should have done long ago. As soon as you found out what Morillon was really like, you should have gone to Claude de Gonde and told him about it. He's devoted to Paul, he's as tough as Morillon, I'm sure he's too much man of the world to faint at whatever dirt you might tell him. As it is, he and everyone else in this house believe you were insane enough to deliberately murder Scott. That should make them all relatively shockproof by now. And if it comes to a question of Paul's safety, they'd do anything to protect him. What can I do for him single-handed that they can't do a hundred times better?"

"You could get us away from here," Anne pleaded. "You said you would."

"Not under the conditions that prevail. Not when all I get from you are lies and evasions. What I will do is stand by until you tell Claude everything, and that has to be damned soon. Tomorrow, in fact. I promised Paul I'd take him to the fair at the Place de la Versailles tomorrow afternoon. While we're away you can get Claude in here, lock all the doors, and unburden yourself to him."

"I can't!"

"You'd better. And since I'll have a long talk with him after you've had your turn, there's no use trying to stall about it. A murderous specimen like Morillon can't be left to roam around loose, and you're going to see he isn't!"

I went to the door. Then I turned and saw that Anne was staring at me with the horror of one who sees the devil coming to claim her soul.

I said, "One final question. That gun you gave me has disappeared. Did you take it?"

"No," she whispered.

In the corner of her bedroom was a huge chest of drawers, a twin of the one in my room. The sight of it drew me like a magnet. I went to it, removed its bottom drawer, and thrust my arm into the empty space left there. My fingertips brushed something cold and metallic, and I hauled it out. It was the gun, and this time, I discovered, it was loaded.

I extracted the cartridges and displayed them to Anne in my palm. "Where did you get these?"

She remained silent.

"Either you tell me who gave you these things," I said, "or so help me God, I'll beat it out of you."

"Nobody gave them to me," Anne said dully. "They're from the gun room. I found out where the key was kept and took them."

I dropped the cartridges into my pocket and tossed the gun on the bed.

"When you see Claude, you can start by giving him that," I said. "It might convince him you're not quite as unbalanced as he thinks you are."

15

The Paris Fair—*la Foire de Paris*—is the exhibition put together now and then by French trades and industries, and if one is in a mood to be entertained by a display of electronic eggbeaters and jerry-built model homes, it can be entertaining. But I was in no such mood when I arrived at the Place de la Versailles with Paul, and Louis, who was waiting there for us, recognized this at a glance. So at his insistence as we walked along the avenue leading to the electric train display which was our reason for being there, we made several stops at wine booths where free samples were offered. Samples being forbidden to Paul, he worked off his energy by running up and down collecting the literature offered by each booth.

Meanwhile, Louis and I had a chance to talk over my tangled affairs.

"You look like hell," Louis said. "I suppose you had that little talk with Madame, and she handed you one right in the eye."

"Not exactly." I briefly described the scene between Anne and me the night before. "She's probably with de Gonde right now, getting it all off her chest," I concluded. "After that, it's his baby."

"His monster," Louis said. "What do you think he'll do about it?"

"I don't know. Probably turn Morillon over to the authorities and sign Anne back into that sanitarium at Issy. Even if she isn't directly implicated in any of the killings, she's put herself on the wrong side of the law by covering up for Morillon. What the hell, a nice mink-lined sanitarium is still a lot better than the guillotine or jail or whatever is waiting for Morillon."

"The way you say that," Louis observed pityingly, "you sound like somebody shoved into that torture box in the Musée Grevin, the one with the spikes. You've got to stop eating your heart out about that woman. I suppose you've got the kid on your mind too." He nodded in Paul's direction. "What happens to him?"

"If de Gonde wants me to stay on until he gets used to being without his mama, I'll do it."

"Well, it won't be in town here. It'll be the scandal of the century, this mess, and once the papers get to work on it they'll chase the family right out of town."

"That won't bother me as long as I can keep in touch with Leschenhaut. I must have been out of my mind when I turned down his offer. I'm calling him up this evening to let him know that."

Louis nodded his approval.

"That makes sense." Then he added in an undertone, "If you want to show even more sense, keep your hand on your wallet. There's a smooth type like a pickpocket over there has an eye on it. What's in it, anyhow, makes it look so fat in the belly?"

It was the ten thousand francs I had forgotten to return to Anne in the heat of my scene with her, and I transferred it to a hip pocket, keeping a hand over it. The feel of that money made me marvel now at how close I had come to going through with the harebrained scheme to flee Paris. If anything kept Anne from joining me, there I would be, boarding a plane for America without luggage but with a child in my possession whom I was undeniably smuggling away to a secret destination. Madame

Cesira Montecastellani de Villemont's grandson, no less. I could see myself in handcuffs, trying to convince the sardonic French police that I was not a kidnaper, and this in a country where kidnaping is known as *le crime américain*.

The model railroad, our destination, lived up to its advertisements. It was laid out on a Lilliputian countryside a hundred feet long where an intricate web of rails wove through hills and fields and small towns and where a dozen tiny trains raced busily along on a schedule which miraculously kept them from colliding at switchpoints. A metal railing kept the public at a safe distance from the display, and it was just the right height for Paul to drape himself over it and suspend himself there by the armpits. Time went on and still he hung there, eyes glazed with wonder.

After a while he stirred from his trance and looked up at me. "Reno, do you think Grandmother would mind very much if I didn't go to Saint-Cyr and become a soldier?"

"I have a feeling she would."

"But if I told her I want to be the engineer of a train like that?"

"It's a lot easier getting into Saint-Cyr than the railroad union," Louis remarked. He dug an elbow sharply into my ribs. "There's the pickpocket type again," he muttered. "Only he's no pickpocket, that one. He's watching you like a hawk, and no pro would give himself away so stupidly twice in a row. Turn around fast and you'll see what I mean."

I wheeled around and at the far end of the railing, near the exit of the pavilion, I saw a youthful face, eyes fixed avidly on me. The next instant it was gone, but not before I had recognized the features of the boy who had once escorted me at gunpoint from the conference room in the mansion to Bernard Bourdon's presence. Albert, Bourdon had called him, and I remembered with foreboding the pistol thrust into his belt.

"You and Paul wait here," I ordered Louis, and sprinted to the exit. The promenade outside was filling up with sightseers now, but was still not so crowded that it offered ready concealment to the fugitive. Yet Albert seemed to have disappeared off the face of the earth in those few seconds. The tide of sightseers was all coming from one direction, the entrance of the fair grounds, and I moved with it down the promenade, peering into the face of anyone who, from the rear, bore any resemblance to my man.

I gave up at last near the entrance to the Alimentation Building, which seemed to cover at least an acre of ground and where I knew there was no use continuing any pursuit. Then it struck me that I might have been lured into doing just what I had done, follow a false lead intended to separate me from Paul. Carnival sounds filled the air around me—the snapping of banners in the wind, the hard-boiled Belleville accents of a barker proclaiming that he had on hand the one indispensable kitchen utensil, accordion music somewhere in the distance, a shrill chorus from some small schoolgirls trailing after a stout little nun *à la queue leu leu,* in single file like ducklings—but insinuating through it all what I heard in my ears was a whisper of menace, a chuckling, demented note of triumphant evil, the dry rasping of the cobra's scales as it slowly uncoils to confront its prey.

That was enough to send me racing back full speed to the pavilion where I had left Paul and Louis. I twisted and dodged through the gathering crowd, recklessly jostling aside anyone who barred the way, learning at first hand how a sun-filled carnival atmosphere could make a nightmare taking place in it that much more nightmarish.

I could have hugged Louis when I saw him standing with an arm around Paul, both of them exactly where I had left them, both absorbed in the workings of a toy world whose inhabitants were only the size of matchsticks and never dangerous.

I waited until I got my breath back and then went up to them, drawing Louis aside out of Paul's earshot.

"No luck?" said Louis.

"No, but I know where to find him as soon as I get back to the house. He's a guard hired to keep people away from the meetings they have there. Bourdon seems to be his immediate boss, and he might be able to explain what this is all about. In any case he'll know where I can look up the bastard. His name's

Albert, by the way, and the last time I saw him he was packing a gun."

Louis frowned at me. "If this Bourdon is his boss, how do you know he wasn't the one who set him on your tail?"

"Because he has no reason to. Morillon's the one behind this."

"To what purpose? Morillon seems to be a type who plans accidents, not shootings. Or is it possible," Louis said grimly, "that your lady friend never went to de Gonde at all, but went straight to Morillon and told him about your intention to expose them? That wouldn't leave him much choice, would it? His one hope would be to get rid of you before you spill the beans. Next thing we know, there's this species of gunman—"

"Do you think she'd let anything like that happen while Paul was with me?" I demanded.

"She wouldn't even know what was happening, pal. She runs in a panic to Morillon, tells him the disaster they face; he tells her not to worry, that he'll make a deal with you, and as soon as she's gone he picks up the phone and arranges for a quick assassination no matter how it endangers the kid. What the hell do you think the kid's safety could possibly mean to him at a time like this? You've got some brain all right, giving a woman like that warning you were going to pull the house down over her head!"

"And you've got some imagination, working up a sweat because we happen to run into a little squirt I once saw carrying a gun. If it wasn't just coincidence—"

"One bump is coincidence," Louis said. "Two could mean business. Also, when I got my first look at this Albert over by the wine booths he was with another type I'd hate to meet up with in a dark alley. Even bigger than you, shoulders like a barn door, arms like meat hooks on him. One of those animals spends all his time lifting weights, I guarantee. And a pretty little head too small for the rest of him, with golden curls on it like one of those Greek statues in the Louvre. Did you see anyone like that standing around when you ran outside?"

"No."

"Anyone like that ever show himself around the rue de Courcelles?"

"Not that I know."

"Oh, you'd know it all right, if you once got a look at him. This is a type who liked to pull the wings off flies when he was a kid, and you can see it in his face right now. It also shapes up as a type who might get a lot of fun out of pushing people downstairs or driving cars over them, if you know what I mean."

"I know what you mean. What do you want me to do about it? Run to the police and tell them you got a look at someone and knew right off he killed Sidney Scott and Max Marchat?"

"No," said Louis, "what I want you to do is get home right now and ask your Monsieur de Gonde what the hell is going on. Ask him what he knows about this Albert and his buddy being on your tail, and if he can't answer that, let him find out about it from someone who can."

What he said made sense. I was in no position to remain on the scene and invite trouble with Albert and his muscular friend while I had Paul in charge. So I explained to Paul that the time had come for our departure, that we would return next day to see the rest of the fair, and steered him, obedient but plaintively arguing the point, out of the pavilion and along the promenade leading toward the Place de la Versailles gate, Louis trailing close behind as a sort of rear guard.

I saw the big man before Louis did, recognized him at once from his description. Immense arms and shoulders bulging under a too-tight jacket, a disproportionately small head, the flawless features of a vacuous Adonis, and a crown of beautifully tended gold ringlets that would make any woman enviously wonder who his hairdresser was. Hands in pockets, he was leaning against a pillar, sleepily scanning the passing crowd. Then he caught sight of me and came wide awake. He turned to signal someone further up the promenade and started breasting his way through the crowd in my direction. The man he had signaled, young, hard-faced, looking as if he would be more at home in a black leather jacket than in the neat business suit he was wearing, fell in step with the crowd and sauntered toward me. Then I thought to glance behind me and saw Albert moving in. Three of them, all intent on the business at hand.

"Trouble," I said to Louis, pulling up short.

"Yes, I see it coming. One of them bumps us, next thing there's a fight about it, maybe a knife shoved into you. And right in the middle of the fair, too. You'd think this was rue Lepic on a Saturday midnight, the way those bastards are handling it."

Paul looked up from one to the other of us. "What bastards?" he asked.

"Big ears," said Louis. "Never mind that. Just keep your eyes on the ground, and if you see a diamond Véronique dropped around here this morning she'll give you a reward for it. Just keep looking and don't say a word until you find it."

The unholy threesome closing in around us had stopped in their tracks when we did and remained poised at a distance, the passing throngs eddying around them. We were not far from the graveled walk leading to a row of model homes, and just inside the walk was a phone booth.

I said to Louis, "That phone is our best bet. I figure the trouble is supposed to start before we can make it to the gate, but if I call de Gonde and tell him what's going on, he can be down here in no time. After all, our friend Albert is supposed to be on his payroll."

"What if de Gonde isn't there to take the call?" said Louis.

"Then Bernard will be, or even Bosiers. The main thing is for one of them to get the kid out of here."

When we moved toward the phone booth, Albert and his henchmen moved, too, closing in a little more, but when I entered the booth they remained at ease where they were. The roadway fronting the model homes led away from the promenade, but I knew that didn't worry them any. At the far end of the roadway was a board fence ten feet high which made this a blind alley offering no way of escape. Sooner or later, the trio knew, we would have to return to the promenade, where in the thick of the crowd anything could be made to happen.

I kept the door of the phone booth open as I dialed de Gonde's number, and Paul tugged protestingly at my jacket.

"How can I find Véronique's diamond if you make me stay here?" he demanded.

"Because she might have dropped it right here when she made a phone call this morning."

"She's unbelievably careless," Louis remarked. "The ground must be littered with her diamonds. Just keep looking."

I was getting no sound of ringing or busy signal on the phone, nothing but dead silence. I tried Bernard's number to no better effect.

"What's the matter?" Louis said.

"Plenty. This thing must be out of order."

Louis swore under his breath. "Did you try the operator? Maybe you can get through to her."

I tried the operator, while from my vantage point I watched Albert and his henchmen watching me. Then the operator's voice sounded in my ear. I explained my inability to get the numbers I had been calling, she asked me to wait a minute while she investigated the matter, and in less than a minute was back on the line.

"The numbers you have been calling, monsieur, have been discontinued."

"But that's impossible!"

"There is no use shouting at me this way, monsieur. All telephone service to the address you are calling has been discontinued."

I had a feeling of total unreality. The sunshiny fairgrounds, the watchful trio deployed among the passers-by on the promenade, Paul scrabbling in the gravel underfoot while Louis kept a protective hand on the collar of his jacket, the echo of the operator's voice in my ear—everything suddenly seemed part of a sinister dream.

"Monsieur?" said the operator impatiently, and I started from the dream to find it wasn't a dream but a wholly sinister reality.

"One more favor, mademoiselle," I said, and gave her Madame Cesira's number. "Will you please put this call through for me?"

Now it seemed like an endless time before she reported back. "Service to that number also has been discontinued, monsieur."

"It can't be! Please make sure of that, mademoiselle. This is a very important call."

"Monsieur, it doesn't matter whether your call is intended to settle an international crisis or merely to learn the time of day; service to that number has been discontinued."

Parisian operators have short tempers. Before I could say another word the line went dead again, and I had to grope in my pocket for another coin.

"What is it?" Louis said. "No answer?"

"More than that. No phone service. I'm going to ring the police and have them send a man here to get us out of this. There won't be any trouble once these thugs see a uniform heading toward them."

"Too late," said Louis. "Look."

Albert must have signaled the weight-lifter that we had remained under siege long enough. The big man came sauntering toward the phone booth, the others following his lead. As if to prove that Louis knew his customers, there was a flicker of light along a blade that the hard-faced one slipped from his pocket.

"Don't ask any questions," I told Louis. "Just get the kid out of here as quick as you can while they're concentrating on me and head straight for your room."

"I'd rather stay here," said Louis. "I can still deal out a good kick in the shins when I have to."

"Do what I tell you." I yanked Paul up by an arm and thrust him at Louis. "Both of you start moving right now!"

But their way was suddenly barred by Albert and the hard-faced man with the knife, and my way out of the booth was barred by the weight-lifter. This maneuver had been executed with such casual efficiency that no one in the passing throng was even led to glance our way.

The weight-lifter looked me up and down contemptuously.

"You've got a nerve," he said in an incongruously high-pitched voice. "You see citizens waiting to make a call but you think it's funny to stand here keeping that lousy phone warm. You sure as hell are looking for trouble, aren't you?"

His face, thrust against mine, was smooth-skinned and pink-cheeked as a baby's, and from it rose an overpowering flowery reek of cheap cologne. His eyes were veiled; his lips curled in a pout; the whole look of him, as Louis had remarked, suggested a child who was preparing for a quietly happy session of pulling wings off flies. But there was nothing childlike about his strength. Trapped in the confines of the phone booth I tried to push past that mountain of muscle, and his shoulder wedged into my chest, pinning me even tighter.

Through the door of the booth I saw Louis and Paul sandwiched between Albert and his hard-faced aide, Louis with a look of alarm on his face, Paul gaping at me; and I said to the weight-lifter in an amiable voice, "Look, let the little man and the kid go, and we can settle this between ourselves. You and me alone, or any way you want it."

"That's a good idea, you and me alone. We wouldn't want to scare the kid with any rough stuff, would we? My friend there can take him for a walk meanwhile. You want to tell the kid it's all right with you?"

So it was Paul who was the intended victim, and once he was hustled away into the crowd it would be too late to do anything about it. "Steady, big stuff," the high-pitched voice whispered with relish. "Try anything, and the kid might get his throat slit."

My hands were at my sides, but I still had a grip on the phone. I jabbed it viciously into the belly of the weight-lifter, and, although it was like trying to dent a block of granite, it made him grunt and fall back a step.

Those few inches between us were all I needed. I lifted an uppercut to his jaw which sent him staggering back out of the doorway of the phone booth. Then I burst out of the booth myself, following up the first punch with a wild right flush into that surprised face. The classically chiseled nose smashed to a pulp, blood spurted from it, the weight-lifter howled with pain, and yet, as if he really were granite, he refused to go down. His arms went out and clutched me to him, his breath in my face was a bloody froth. Half conscious, he still had enough strength in him to make my ribs crack under the pressure he was exerting.

An excited crowd was gathering around us now, coming on the run from every direction. Over the weight-lifter's shoulder I saw Albert suddenly grab Paul by the arm and try to pull him into the crowd, saw Louis wheel and deliver a stiff-legged kick—a lovely display of *la savate*—which caught Albert in the small of the back and sent him sprawling. The next instant, Louis

and Paul had melted into the crowd and out of sight. When
Albert came to his feet and started after them, I knew that he
must have been the one personally assigned to seize Paul.

I tried to heave myself free of the weight-lifter's grip, failed,
kneed him savagely, and this time he went down writhing.
Then I was after Albert as he furiously tried to push his way
through the crowd in pursuit of his victim. I caught him with a
flying tackle that brought him down full-length, women screaming and men swearing as we landed among them. The knife-
wielder dived on top of me; we made a kicking, squirming pile as
I rolled away, trying to dodge the knife blow I anticipated, and
then, incredibly, I was lying there alone.

I lurched to my feet and looked around dazedly. The crowd
was solidly around me, loud with comment, ready to join in the
battle now that it was over. As for the gang, they were all gone
now, even the weight-lifter, who must have found it an agony
to move, much less move fast. The reason was plain enough.
Through the onlookers I could see the kepi of a policeman heading my way.

To remain on the scene meant a waste of precious time. I
would be pinned down by questions, and then, most likely,
would have to go along to headquarters to answer for disturbing the peace. And all I wanted to do was get to the Faubourg Saint-Denis to make sure Louis and Paul had arrived
safely at Madame Olympe's.

I headed into the crowd away from the approaching *flic*,
and it parted before me like the Red Sea parting for Moses.
Then I realized I was drawing looks of consternation from
every side, and, once clear of the crowd, I glanced into the mirror of a vending machine to see why.

One quick look told the story. I was not only dirty and disheveled, but my face, shirt, and jacket were so spattered with
the weight-lifter's blood that I looked as if I had barely escaped
with my life from a train wreck. I cleaned my face with my
handkerchief as well as I could while making my way to the
Place de la Versailles gate, but that didn't do much to change
the general effect.

The driver of the first car in the line of taxis outside the gate flung open his door to me and said sympathetically as I clambered in, "What a mess! But take it easy. There's a hospital only a few blocks away on rue Raymond. I'll get you to it in no time."

"Never mind that. Did you see a man and a kid running out of that gate a few minutes ago? A little man with a big nose and a beret, and a boy about nine years old?"

"I saw a lot of people coming out of that gate. Are you sure you don't want a doctor to look you over?"

"No. Just get me to the Faubourg Saint-Denis as quick as you can."

The car moved forward and then stopped short. I saw the driver watching worriedly as two *flics* trotted through the gate and hesitated there, eying the street up and down. The cabby was a jaunty young man with his cap cocked on the back of his head and a cigarette thrust behind his ear, but all the jauntiness oozed out of him as the *flics* started toward us.

He turned to face me. "Say, pal, you're not in trouble, are you? If you are—"

"Get going!" I ordered.

"Now look—" the driver said, and I gripped the nape of his neck and said in a deadly voice, "Either you get going or I wring your neck like a chicken's. Which is it?"

We lurched away from the curb and down rue Vaugirard leaving the *flics* standing there in the middle of the street, futilely waving us back.

"They've got my license number," the cabby said gloomily. "You know what can happen to me now?"

"I'll explain to them if anything happens to you."

"You'd better," the cabby said. "And I want to be there when you do."

When we pulled up before Madame Olympe's, I flung him double the fare to placate him and said, "That's just a down payment. I'll be back right away, so wait for me."

I laid out my strategy as I ran into the house and up the stairs. I would remain here with Paul while Louis would take the cab to the rue de Courcelles and explain matters to Claude de Gonde. To de Gonde or Madame Gabrielle and no one else.

Anne was Morillon's puppet, Edmond Vosiers was his admirer, and I didn't trust Madame Matilde or Bernard Bourdon on general principles. No, the de Gondes were the only ones capable of relieving me of my duties as Paul's protector.

My footsteps thundered through the house as I raced upstairs. As I reached the head of the stairway, Léon Becque opened the door of his room and peered inquiringly at me through his dark glasses.

"My God!" he said. "What's happened to you? Are you hurt?"

"No. Is Louis here? Did you see him come in with the kid?"

Becque shook his head. I was aware he had crossed the hall and was close behind me when I flung open Louis' door and saw Louis and Paul standing there side by side facing me.

Then Louis leaped toward me, arms outthrust, I heard the roar of an explosion in my ear, and that was all.

PART THREE

The World

1

I came to hazily.

I was lying on the floor, my nose buried in a rug which filled my nostrils with the smell of dust. Then I felt something warm and wet trickling down my face and knew from the pain in my skull that this must be blood. I was wrong. The wetness touched my lips, burned them like an astringent. Cognac.

I braced my hands against the floor to push myself to a sitting position, and one hand brushed against something cold and metallic. A neatly polished, solid-looking black shoe pushed whatever it was out of my reach, and a familiar voice said, "No more guns for you, chum. Try that again and I'll mash your fingers into mincemeat."

"At least he's not dead," said another familiar voice. "I thought I might have killed him."

"Saved him a lot of trouble if you did," said the first. "Anyhow, it takes more than a whack on the head with a bottle to kill a type like this. Look at him, the sleeping beauty. If you hadn't cooled him off, he'd be a mile away by now and with all the money, too."

There were other voices clamoring in the background.

"What a monster!"

"Who would have believed it!"

"Yes, but when it comes to money—"

The shoe nudged me sharply in the ribs.

"All right, champ, the fight's over, so let's not play dead any more. Up, assassin. It's time for a nice little ride in the wagon."

I managed to get to my feet and stand there swaying as if I

were on the deck of a small boat in a high sea. Then the deck steadied, my vision cleared, and I could try to make sense out of what was being said to me and why.

It was my old acquaintance, Maguy, the cop on the beat, who confronted me, his eyes cold, his jaw set; and it was Léon Becque beside him, his dark glasses concealing whatever emotion he might show through his one good eye. Behind them were the cabby I had told to wait downstairs, and Madame Olympe almost filling the doorway with her bulk and barring the way to some tenants of the house and vendors from the stalls downstairs who craned their heads to witness this scene.

But there was something missing from the scene.

"Where's Louis?" I said to Maguy. "Where's the kid?"

He was standing between me and the bed. He moved aside and jerked his thumb at the bed.

"You want to make sure you did the job right?" he said. "Take a look, butcher."

I looked, and sickness rose in me, sticking in my throat so that I wanted to vomit but couldn't. Louis lay sprawled on the bed, his head hanging over its side, his eyes blindly staring at me upside down. His beret had fallen off exposing the waxen forehead and gleaming skull, and centered in the forehead was a small, dark, round hole from which oozed threads of blood.

For the past six years he had been my friend and family, a sort of hard-boiled, worrisome, affectionate older brother who was always there to lend a helping hand or to share my good times or bad times, and when the realization penetrated that he was really dead I was stricken by a sense of utter loneliness, a feeling of standing alone in a desolate world where everyone, no matter how familiar, was a stranger.

"Do you have to let him lie there like that?" I managed to say. "Can't you at least cover him?" and Madame Olympe remarked acidly, "Ah, but what tender sentiments now that it's over and done with."

"A little late for tears," someone else agreed.

I looked at the hate-filled faces pronouncing these strange words, looked at the scene around me, and now desolation was replaced by a wild rage at what had been done to Louis, by

fear at what might have happened to Paul, by bewilderment at
the sight of the money scattered over the bed and on the floor
at its foot. Thousands and thousands in banknotes lay there as
if a tree bearing them had been roughly shaken over the bed.
On the floor were also the shattered remnants of a cognac bottle—the quart bottle of Courvoisier Louis always kept on his
dresser—its contents soaked up wetly by the carpet, and near
the stain lay a gun.

The sight of that gun transfixed me. It was a Beretta, beautifully and efficiently designed, and it was either the gun which
I had flung down on Anne's bed the night before, or its perfect
facsimile. I reached down toward it, and Maguy shoved me
back.

"Is that yours?" he demanded.

"I don't know. I was given one like it, but I never carried it
with me. Who did this, Maguy? Who killed him? And where's
the kid, for God's sake? What happened to him?"

"What kid?"

"The one I'm supposed to be taking care of, damn it! Madame
de Villemont's son. He was right here when I came into this
room! Where is he now?"

Maguy turned to Becque, who slowly shook his head.

"He was here!" I said. "He was standing next to Louis when
I opened the door."

"There was nobody here but Louis," Becque said to Maguy
as if the words were being wrung out of him. "I was right at the
door and saw everything. Reno came running up the stairs like
a madman with the gun in his hand. He threw open the door,
and there was Louis counting the money on the bed. 'You thief!'
he yelled at Louis. 'You swindler! So you'd rob me, would
you?' and before I could do anything he fired that bullet into
Louis' head. Then he started toward the bed—I suppose he was
going to gather up the money—and I seized the bottle and
hit him with it. I don't know where I got the strength. Both of
them were my friends, and to have this happen before my
eyes—!"

I looked at Léon Becque and knew that at last I was looking
into the face of the enemy. Whether he was head conspirator or

only an accomplice, here in the open was one of those fanatic friends of Hubert Morillon who evidently lived only to serve him.

And how beautifully I had been duped into renting him my room, telling him my secrets, handing over to him Eliane Tissou who could explain my character to him, and Louis who could keep him informed of my every move.

From the day Léon Becque had entered my life, wherever I was—on the rue de Courcelles or the Faubourg Saint-Denis or any place in between—I had been under surveillance.

I lunged for Becque, and Maguy was instantly between us, his hand on the butt of his holstered pistol.

"Make one more move like that," he warned me, "and I'll blow a hole in you just the way you did to that poor slob laying there."

"Listen to me, Maguy. You know me. You can't believe I killed Louis. I tell you Becque is the one who did it!"

"With your gun? The gun I had to pull out of your fist while you were stretched out here dead to the world?"

"That's his gun, all right," the cabby put in loudly. "That's the one he aimed at me when he jumped into my car."

I wheeled on him, and he shrank back, fearful but defiant.

"What the hell are you talking about?" I demanded. "You know I never aimed any gun at you!"

"No?" The cabby held his arms wide in a gesture of outraged virtue. "You think I would have driven off with you otherwise, once I saw the cops chasing after you? You think I'm a type to help criminals make a getaway?"

I could see myself standing before a judge and jury while he testified to that, while Maguy testified to the way he had found me gun in hand, while Léon Becque testified to the murder he had seen me commit before his eyes. One by one, witnesses would swear to my guilt until the prison doors were locked behind me for good.

In all the world there was only one witness to Louis' murder who would tell the truth about it.

"Maguy," I said, "when I opened that door the boy was standing here with Louis. I swear to you he was here, and he's been kidnaped and is in danger. You must get in touch with his family at once. You'll have to tell them—"

"There was no one here but Louis," Becque said patiently, as if he were humoring someone with a hallucination.

"I know the child," declared Madame Olympe. "I opened my door as soon as I heard the gun. I would have seen the boy taken from the house. I saw nothing."

"Then he's still here in the house," I told Maguy, who slowly shook his head at me. "The kidnaper might be holding him in Becque's room for all we know. Why don't you search and find out?"

"There's nobody in Becque's room," an onlooker said from the hallway. "The door is open. It's easy to see the room is empty."

"You hear that, assassin?" Maguy said to me. "Empty. And what kind of kidnapers are you concocting who would take a child and leave a fortune in money lying around like this?"

In the distance I heard the demented, warbling note of the siren on a police wagon. It was an alarm that set my mind to racing frantically. I would be hauled to Santé Prison, and no matter what I tried to do in my defense—expose Morillon, involve Anne and the family in a gigantic scandal—it wouldn't clear me of Louis' murder. Worse, if I were locked up I would be unable to find Paul, and for his sake and mine I had to be free to find him.

The window was open, its curtain fluttering in the breeze. It was a long drop to the ground, I knew, but beneath the window was a canvas canopy over the fruit stalls against the building, and I could only pray the canopy would save me from a broken leg.

"Maguy," I said, bracing myself, "that's the bastard you want!" and shoved him with all my strength into Léon Becque. I saw them both stagger and fall, almost bearing Madame Olympe and the cabby down with them, and the next instant I was through the window and clinging to the sill by my fingertips. I looked down, saw the striped canvas of the canopy below, saw the crowd gathered in the street before the house staring up at me. I hadn't allowed for this audience, but there was nothing to be done about it anyhow. I heard Maguy bellowing at me as he

charged toward the window, heard the crowd shouting, and released my grip.

The canopy collapsed when I landed on it, and canvas and
I came crashing down on a table piled high with oranges. I
tried to scramble to my feet, oranges rolling every which way
under me and spilling out into the gutter, and when I did get
to my feet a couple of daring spirits grabbed at me and I had to
throw a few punches to clear a way to the cab. If the ignition
key wasn't in place I intended to get out through the other door
and make a run for it, but the key was there, and the cab, a
shining new Citroën, roared into life immediately. The next
instant, with a dozen pursuers futilely trying to keep pace on
foot, I was down the block and away at full throttle. I reached
the corner just as the police van, its siren deafening, swung
into the Faubourg Saint-Denis, and we almost crashed head-on.
I swung the wheel hard, careened up across the sidewalk and
down into the boulevard, horns honking furiously and drivers
raging at me as I threaded my way through them, and then I
got control of my nerves and let the cab be engulfed by the
traffic moving west toward the rue de Courcelles.

2

My thoughts moved in two directions at
once.

The immediate problem of escape I dealt with mechanically.
The traffic on the boulevard made a good camouflage, but pursuit, I knew, would be coming this way so I swung the cab into

the Faubourg Montmartre, cruised along a few blocks, and then turned west again on rue Saint-Lazare.

Slouched low in the seat to conceal the bloodstained jacket, the typical Parisian cabby's expression of boredom on my face, I drove with just enough abandon to pass, I hoped, for the real thing. About the reek of cognac which had soaked my hair and jacket, there was nothing I could do. There had been a time when the sharp fragrance of good brandy was pleasant to my nostrils. Now that it brought me only the picture of Louis sprawled out in death, his eyes staring at me upside down with glassy accusation, the smell was sickening.

What had happened after I flung open the door to that room and seen Louis and Paul standing there? All I knew for a fact was that Léon Becque had been close behind me, and Louis had suddenly leaped toward me, hands outthrust, as if to shove me out of danger. Then there had been the explosion of a gunshot, a blow on the head, and oblivion. When I had come to, Louis was dead and Paul was gone.

But no matter how murderously efficient Becque was, he could not have manipulated all this by himself. There must have been an accomplice behind the door with his gun ready. That was what Louis had been trying to save me from by flinging himself at me. That was why, probably in panic, the gunman had shot him down. The next instant, Becque had snatched up the bottle of cognac and smashed it over my head, and no better sacrificial goat could have been stretched out on the floor for his purpose. The accomplice had stilled any outcry from Paul and carried him away to some hiding place in the house. Becque had planted the gun in my inert hand, thrown open the window and shouted for the police, and the trap was sprung.

But those banknotes scattered over the bed and floor?

I clapped a hand to my pocket and knew, with a sinking heart, where that money had come from. It was the ten thousand francs getaway money Anne had given me; my wallet itself, with all my papers in it, would certainly be found in Louis' pocket. It was all the evidence needed to substantiate Becque's story that Louis had robbed me and I had killed him for it. No question about the murder weapon remained in my mind now. It was the late Colonel Henri de Villemont's pistol, and it rounded out an airtight case against me.

At least it was airtight if Paul couldn't testify for me. It was useless to count on Anne as a witness, with her child in enemy hands.

So now at all costs I had to get to Claude de Gonde before the police did. I wasn't sure how much of my story he might believe—the dimensions of Hubert Morillon's conspiracy were so staggering that I found it hard to believe in it myself—but de Gonde would do anything for Paul's safety. With his help I might elude arrest until I cornered Morillon or Becque and got the truth about Paul's whereabouts. Ten minutes alone in a locked room with either of them was all I wanted.

Yet, if the police got to de Gonde before I did, I was now walking right into their hands.

Tormented by this thought, twitching with the desire to step on the gas and cut through the jam-up of trams and buses heading in and out of their terminus in front of the Gare Saint-Lazare, I didn't see the traffic cop at the crossing until I was almost on top of him, and then at the sound of his whistle and furious motion of his hand I pulled up so short that there was a clash of bumpers in the rear. I cowered still lower in the seat and sweated it out while the cop venomously started toward me. The next moment, to my relief and mystification, he changed his mind and, while still glaring at me, returned to his post. Then I realized why. The rear door of the cab swung open and a passenger pushed her way in, a young woman carrying a very small child in her arms. Close behind followed a little girl of about six or seven and a plump young man with crew-cut hair and a prissy mouth. He was burdened with a large canvas valise in one hand and a couple of airline carry-alls in the other and looked hot and irritable.

"*Ah, non, madame!*" I said in despair, putting an arm behind me to bar the woman from entering any further. "*Mais non! Le taxi est dérangé!*"

"Crap," said the young man in plain American. He shoved

his family into the cab and clambered in after them, slamming the door behind him. "*Comprenez* English, Jack?"

"*Un peu, monsieur.*"

"*Beaucoup* more than *un peu*, I'll bet. So get this straight, Jack. I know the law just as well as you, and that means you take us wherever we want to go or I get that gendarme to come over here and find out what the hell is going on. *Vous allez* where *je demand*, or else. *Comprenez?*"

"*Oui, monsieur.*"

"Good. Make it the Hotel Lutetia, Boulevard Raspail. And by the short way, too. *Le vite route.*"

The cop was now furiously gesturing at me to get moving, so I did. The rue de Courcelles was a ten-minute drive along the avenue, and my idea was to pull up to the curb a block or two from the house on some pretext and leave my passengers to work out their own destiny while I risked making my way to the house on foot. I could only hope, as we swung into the rue de Rocher, that the peevish customer with the crew cut didn't know we were heading in the opposite direction from the Left Bank and Boulevard Raspail. If he did, it meant nasty complications.

But it wasn't crew-cut who made the complications, it was his wife.

"Larry," she said, "please take Bubba."

Larry snorted. "How the hell can I take him when I'm loaded down with these bags as it is? Anyhow, he's sound asleep. He's not bothering you, is he?"

"Please, Larry. It's getting worse. I feel awful."

"What is it? That lousy appendix acting up again?"

"It must be," the woman said with a gasp. "Oh, Larry, it's awful. It's killing me."

"All right, give me Bubba." In the mirror I saw Larry impatiently thrust the carry-alls on the little girl's lap and take the baby from his wife. Relieved of the burden, the woman doubled over, her face twisted with agony, her teeth biting into her lower lip. "Jesus, what perfect timing," Larry said, thus expressing my own anguished thought. "What a great vacation this turned out to be. The kids in our hair all the time, and now this. I told you to have that operation a year ago, didn't I?"

"Yes, but it's killing me, Larry," the woman moaned. "Oh, God, it's killing me. Do something. Please do something."

"For Chrissake, Alice, all I can do is get you to the hotel. They'll have a doctor there, or they'll know where to get one. You can hold out that long, can't you?"

We were a block from the rue de Courcelles now, and my foot started to bear down on the brake. This was the time and place to ditch the cab and make a run for the house. But I couldn't pull my eyes away from that mirror. Beads of sweat the size of marbles showed on the woman's forehead; her face was ghastly pale. Whatever Larry's opinion, it looked to me as if the pain was really killing her.

I took a deep breath, removed my foot from the brake, and bore down on the gas. We threaded the Place de Malesherbes and headed down the Avenue de Villers toward Neuilly, hemmed in by a maddening jam of traffic.

Over my shoulder I said to the woman, "We can make it to the hospital pretty soon if you can stand some fast driving. Can you?"

"I don't know." She was weakly crying now and rocking back and forth, the little girl watching her with wide, frightened eyes. "Yes, yes, I can, if you'll only get me there right away."

"Hey, you do talk English," Larry said to me in a voice of outrage. "You sound like an American."

"I learned how at the movies," I said.

Turning into the Boulevard Victor Hugo, I saw the two motorcycle cops cruising along the outskirts of the traffic. The first temptation was to steer past them; then I saw that here was the best possible answer to the immediate problem delivered right in my hands. For my own sake as well as the woman's I had to make speed, and what cop would ever believe that an accused murderer would deliberately pick him up as an escort? I blasted away on the horn until I got the attention of the team, and the motorcycles wove through the traffic, closing in on me, one on each side of the cab, the drivers menacing figures in their crash helmets and goggles.

I didn't wait for the one on my side to say the first word. I jerked my thumb over my shoulder and said to him, "It's an emergency, pal! Take a look."

One look at my passenger in her agony told him I wasn't overstating the case. He gunned his motor, waved at me to follow, and so with both motorcycles clearing the way we raced through Neuilly at full blast. At the hospital entrance the cops slewed their cycles to a halt, and one ran inside to announce our arrival while the other flung open the cab door and carried the woman in his arms through the entrance.

All I wanted now was to get away before the police reappeared, but it took Larry an endless time to maneuver his daughter and luggage out of the cab and climb out himself, the baby still sound asleep in his arms. Raging against this delay, I still pitied him as he tried to reach for the money in his pocket without losing his grip on the baby. The sight of his wife being carried into the hospital seemed to have washed all the bravado out of him. His face was as pallid as the woman's now; his lips trembled as if he were ready to burst into tears.

"How much?" he said, holding some folded banknotes through the window, and when I said, "Nothing. I just hope your wife makes out all right," he stood there, gaping at me as if unable to comprehend this.

"Look, it's on the house; there's no charge," I said angrily, trying to push away his hand, but it was too late. The cops were with me again, and while one led Larry and his brood into the hospital, the other companionably leaned an elbow on the windowsill and thrust his head inside the car to give me the word.

"She's in bad shape," he informed me, "but they think she'll pull through."

"Fine," I said, and raced the motor as a hint that I had important business elsewhere.

The cop started to withdraw his head, then changed his mind. He sniffed the air with a frown.

"You been taking your lunch out of a bottle?" he asked.

"No."

"It sure smells like it."

"No, that's just from a glass of cognac that was spilled on me. One of the guys I was eating with is a real comedian."

The cop regarded me closely, suspicion showing in his eyes. "It looks like cognac wasn't the only thing spilled on you. Those are bloodstains, pal. Don't tell me they're not."

"Sure they are. When I helped the lady into the cab she was bleeding from the mouth like a stuck pig. What the hell do you think made me head for the hospital so fast?"

"Oh," the cop said, evidently satisfied, and then knit his brow in deep thought. "Funny, I don't remember seeing any blood on her."

"Very funny," I said. Next thing, he would be asking for my identification. "Now I'd better get home and change these clothes before I take the hack out again. Thanks for the escort. I hope the tourists appreciated it."

I raced the motor again, and this time the cop took the hint. He withdrew his head, and I already had the cab rolling down the driveway when he called, "When do tourists appreciate anything? And this time, watch those red lights!"

I took that advice to heart, drove back into the city as cautiously as if I were trying to win a safety award, and parked a block from the house at the tail end of the hack stand near the Russian Church. Jacket muffling me to the throat, hands in pockets, I strolled to the gate of the house and let myself into the courtyard.

Standing there, I had the feeling that something was subtly wrong. Then I saw what it was. During the afternoon, the garage doors were always kept open and Pascal was usually servicing one or another of the cars, but now those doors were tightly shut. A few of the shutters at the house windows were always open in daytime, too, and now every one was closed. It was as if the house had been hermetically sealed against the world, and suddenly I remembered with misgiving that its phone service had been abruptly discontinued.

I put my key into the lock of the big door, half expecting to find that the lock had been changed, but the door opened readily. I closed it behind me, crossed the rotunda, and made my way upstairs to Anne's apartment. The door to it was wide open; the rooms were empty. Most bewildering was the sight of her dresser and dressing table cleared of all the personal belongings that ordinarily covered them.

I went down the hushed corridor to the de Gonde apartment. There, too, the door was open, the rooms empty, the dressers and dressing table cleared of everything. I stood blinking at Madame Gabrielle's dressing table as if this was all somehow a trick of my vision, as if by straining my eyes everything would come back to normal.

It was the same in the Vosiers apartment and in the rooms occupied by Bernard—an open door, empty rooms. The electricity was on and that was something, but not very much.

There was one hope left, the kitchen below, the ugly, reassuring face of Georges or, for that matter, the face of any one of the help. I ran downstairs full tilt, raced through the dank, narrow passageway behind the stairway of the rotunda and was brought up short by the door to the kitchen which, for the first time in my remembrance, was locked. I rattled the knob, threw my weight against the door in a fury of wrathful frustration, but there was no budging it.

And then a voice behind me said cuttingly, "Enough of such exercise, you idiot. Even if you break down that door you'll find no one behind it."

3

It was Edmond Vosiers.

Fat and sleepy-eyed, he stood in the passageway outside the door of the gun room. When I walked toward him he looked me up and down with open distaste.

"What a spectacle," he said. "What the devil have you been doing to yourself?"

"Never mind that. Where is everyone?"

"En route to the Château Laennac for a few days' vacation. Madame de Villemont is with them, if that's what you're getting at."

"No," I said, "what I'm getting at is that she didn't go willingly."

Vosiers raised an eyebrow. "What are you suggesting? That the woman's being carried off by force? Has she addled your wits so completely that you believe such nonsense?"

"Monsieur, is it also nonsense that Paul himself was taken from me by force a little while ago?"

"Indeed?"

"Do you think I'm joking?" I said angrily. "I tell you the boy is gone!"

"Of course he is." Vosiers glanced at his wristwatch. "Not fifteen minutes ago I had a phone call from his grandmother, who was with him at Le Bourget airport. At this very moment both of them are boarding the plane that will have them in Venice in time for their dinner."

It was stupefying news, but the man's tone convinced me he

was telling the truth. In that case, how had Paul been removed from the *pension* unseen? Then I understood how. In the hall closet on the top floor was the ladder to the roof. One could travel over a few rooftops and come down by way of a fire escape into the foul-smelling alley alongside Papa Tissou's butcher shop. Eliane Tissou had made that trip with me several times after a night of love-making in my room. As Léon Becque's fiancée she would surely have revealed the secret route to him. And whoever had been hidden behind Louis' door and gunned him down must have used that way of carrying Paul off.

"Monsieur Vosiers," I said grimly, "I think the police are going to arrive here very soon. You and I have only a little time left in which to reach an understanding."

"I fail to comprehend."

"Then listen closely," I said, and in very few words gave him a summary of the day's bloody events.

At the end of the account he looked at me skeptically. "And you mean our little Paul is the only one who can confirm this extraordinary alibi?"

"There's also Madame Cesira. The murderer was the man who delivered Paul to her. She could certainly testify to that."

"Could she?" Vosiers shook his head slowly. "And what if I tell you that the child was driven up to her door all alone in a cab, and in a state of hysteria, too. Believe me, she'd gladly see you guillotined for that."

Again someone was playing the game a move ahead of me. And what move was left to me now? To confess guilt by fleeing for my life, if I could even get out of Paris with the police barring all exits? To risk Paul's life by going to the police with my story?

No matter how I looked at it, I had been driven into a corner where there was only one way out. One desperate move to make that would either win or lose everything for me.

"All right," I said to Vosiers, "we still have to reach our understanding. I suppose you came here from your office to close the house and then join the family at the Château Laennac?"

"Yes."

"I'm going with you."

Vosiers stared at me in disbelief. "And make the chateau your refuge? But tomorrow the papers will be full of you!"

"Let me worry about that. Where is the chateau?"

"Near Dijon."

"Then I'll be there in time to talk to Madame de Villemont tonight. I must see her. Once she gives instructions to have Paul brought back here to appear with me before the police—"

"You take too much for granted," Vosiers cut in nastily. "What if no one wants to become involved in your problems?"

"*Alors, monsieur,*" I said between my teeth, "*il y aura du sport,*" which was my crude way of letting him know I was ready to kick over everyone's applecart. "I'm not the only one the papers will be full of. Think how delighted they'll be to discover that the daughter-in-law of the sainted General Sebastien de Villemont, no less, is up to her lovely neck in murder. You're wrong about her, monsieur. She is Hubert Morillon's mistress, not mine, and when I tell the police how she and Morillon arranged the murder of her husband in Algeria—"

"You're mad!" gasped Vosiers.

"Then you'd be wise to humor me, monsieur."

"Look," said Vosiers, "I'll give you money and the run of the house. Then, when you think it's safe to slip away—"

"No, you'll drive me to the Château Laennac and make sure the police don't get their hands on me. If they do, I'll have Morillon's name and the name of everyone in the family in headlines the next day."

The way I said it must have convinced him that my patience was fast running out.

"I suppose the sooner we leave, the better," he said sourly.

"It is. But I can't travel looking like this. You can keep me company while I clean up."

I had been through Anne's rooms on my first trip upstairs but not in my quarters. Now when I followed Vosiers into my bedroom, making sure he was always within arm's reach, I couldn't at first believe what I saw. Everything I owned had vanished. Books, typewriter, clothing, folders of manuscripts— everything. I pulled out drawers, peered into bathroom cabinets. Nothing was where it had been only a few hours before.

"What the devil are you looking for?" demanded Vosiers.

"All my things. Where are they?"

He shrugged. "I have no idea. I thought you had them removed."

"I didn't. But whoever did left me without a clean shirt and jacket. I'm afraid you'll have to help out with your wardrobe."

Hand on his collar, I steered him to his apartment. There I stripped off my befouled clothing and scrubbed down in the bathroom. One of Vosiers' shirts fitted me well enough, but I couldn't get my shoulders into any of his jackets. I finally settled for a cashmere sweater which made me look, according to the pier glass, as if I were set for an afternoon of tennis.

We went down the stairway of the rotunda, Vosiers leading the way, so it was by sheer good luck that he was the one who opened the huge front door to the courtyard.

"The police!" he said with alarm, and the next instant I pulled the door wide open so that I was tightly sandwiched between it and the wall.

"Leave it open," I warned Vosiers. "They might have seen you. If you shut it now, they'll know something is wrong."

Through the crack between the door hinges I had a chilling view of the three men in the courtyard. None were in uniform, but the pair walking toward the house moved with trained wariness, pistols in hand, while the third, standing on the alert inside the gateway, cradled a tommygun in his arms. The two men came to a halt not six inches from my hiding place behind the door. One was a grizzled, elderly man; the other was much younger and with a sharp, clever face.

"Monsieur de Gonde?" said the younger man.

"No, I am Edmond Vosiers, his brother-in-law. And who are you? What are those weapons for?"

"We're from the police, monsieur. I am Inspector Lenel and this is Detective Santange. We're looking for a murderer we have reason to believe is in this vicinity. An American named Reno Davis. He's in your employ, isn't he?"

"He was in the employ of my sister-in-law, but he was discharged this morning. And a murderer, you say?"

"Yes?"

"But he was here only ten minutes ago!" said Vosiers, and no one in the Comédie Française could have given those words a more bravura reading.

"Only ten minutes ago?" said Inspector Lenel.

"Right where you're standing. I was bringing my luggage down to the car—I'm preparing to leave for a vacation in the south and everyone else has already gone—when there was this banging at the door and there he was. And what a sight, Inspector. Bloodstained, disheveled, drunk to the world. He wanted money, he said. He had been robbed of the money given him the day before in final payment for his services, and now he insisted I make up the loss."

"How much was it?" asked Inspector Lenel. "Do you know the exact amount?"

"No, but it must have been a great deal. My sister-in-law agreed to give him a few months' unearned pay just to get rid of him."

"Could it have been about ten thousand francs?" Lenel persisted, and when Vosiers answered, "Yes, I believe it could," the Inspector turned to his colleague and said in a tone of triumph, "Ah, you see how it fits?"

It did. It was only too easy to see the prosecutor in court holding up that sheaf of banknotes spattered with Louis' blood and pointing out to the jury that here was the motive for my crime.

"But did you give him the money he asked for?" Santange, the elderly detective, said to Vosiers.

"No, I gave him just a couple of francs and sent him off as I would any beggar. But if I had known he was a murderer—"

"Ah," said Santange, "then you might have tried some heroics, and that would have been a bad business. He's a dangerous type, this American. He started the day by getting into a brawl at the Parc des Expositions and finished it off in style by shooting a man to death. Incredible you should ever have given employment to such a species of criminal in the first place."

"I told you that it was my sister-in-law who employed him. Madame Anne de Villemont. I'm afraid she's not a very good judge of character."

"The widow of General de Villemont's son, isn't she?" asked Lenel in a tone of more than casual inquiry.

"Yes."

"General de Villemont," Santange remarked fondly. "The Old Man himself. I served under him in the Normandy landing."

"That's to your credit, monsieur," Vosiers said with ice in his voice, "but in this house we do not refer to the general in such familiar terms."

"Of course, of course," Santange said hastily. "A thousand pardons. I didn't realize—"

By virtue of that one sharp rejoinder Vosiers was now in charge of the situation.

"Gentlemen, I'm on my way to the country," he said impatiently. "If there's no further help I can give you—"

The Inspector cleared his throat in apology. "We had hoped to make a search of the house."

"A search would be pointless. I told you I saw the man run out that gateway and disappear."

"But he occupied a room here?"

"He did."

"Well, that much I'd like to look at."

Vosiers was shrewd enough not to make an issue of this. He led the Inspector away while the elderly Santange remained in the doorway casually surveying the premises. It seemed impossible that he couldn't hear the thudding of my heartbeat; we were that close to each other. The sweat poured from me. I began to ache with tension as the minutes of waiting ticked by.

What, I wondered, was Vosiers telling the Inspector now that they were out of earshot. My mind raced. I had warned the man that if there was a double-cross I'd blow the lid off the family's dirty affairs. But was that enough to seal his mouth now?

Then I heard returning footsteps, heard the voices of Vosiers and the Inspector.

"But you have no idea where he carted off his belongings?" the Inspector was saying, and when Vosiers answered, "None," I went limp with relief.

"Too bad," said the Inspector. "It would have given us a lead.

But never fear, we'll catch up to him very soon. Since we have his passport, he won't find it easy to get out of the country."

"I trust not," said Vosiers. "And I'm free to leave now?"

"You are. By the way, I'll keep a man on duty at that gate twenty-four hours a day in case the creature decides to return here."

"On duty at the gate? Ah, but, Inspector—"

"No, no, it's not a personal favor. Just sound procedure."

Vosiers watched the team make their way out of the courtyard, then swung the door shut.

"You heard him," he said to me flatly. "That brute with the machine gun is remaining right there at the gate. So now you have no choice. You'll have to remain here when I leave."

I said with slow, deadly emphasis, "I told you I was going to see Madame de Villemont and have Paul brought back here to Paris."

"And how do we get out of here with that man at the gate?"

"I once saw Pascal carting scrap metal from the boiler through that small door in back of the garage, so there must be a passage between the cellar and the garage. We go through it, I hide in the car, and that's all there is to it."

"I assure you there is no such passage!" Vosiers said vehemently. So vehemently I knew he was lying.

"Then you'd better start digging one, monsieur," I told him. "Otherwise, you and I are going to be stuck here for a long time. And I don't think you'll find it easy to sleep nights, tied down to your bed."

Vosiers' eyes became pinpricks of hatred. "You oaf," he said softly. "You buffoon."

"The passageway, monsieur."

He stood there in an agony of indecision, gnawing his lip. Plainly, the last thing in the world he wanted to do was lead me to that passageway, although it was impossible to see why. When I took a menacing step toward him, he looked around wildly as if trying to find some last-second means of escape from the inevitable.

"I'll give you the ten thousand francs," he said hoarsely. "Remain here, and I'll make it twenty thousand."

"The passageway. We don't have all day."

It was not to the cellar he led me, but to the gun room. I
had never been in it before. Now I saw that it was a small room
handsomely paneled in oak, with a variety of rifles and shotguns mounted on the walls and with a glass case in one corner
displaying a collection of antique pistols. In the middle of the
room was a large workbench with rows of shallow drawers in
it. It must have been in one of those drawers, I thought,
that Anne had found the cartridges for Colonel de Villemont's
Beretta.

But there was nothing out of the ordinary about the room,
nothing to give one pause. Then Vosiers slowly and unwillingly
rolled the glass case away from its corner, and I saw something
very much out of the ordinary. He leaned his weight against
the wall there, and a panel of it silently swung outward revealing pitch blackness beyond. I followed on his heels as he
squeezed through the opening, my hand on his shoulder to
guard against any tricks, and the panel closed behind me.

"What about a light?" I said, as we were engulfed in darkness.

"It's not necessary. I know the way."

He didn't know it as well as he thought. He took two steps
forward, his foot kicked against something metallic, and I had
to steady him by the shoulder to keep him from falling.

"Now we'll do it my way," I said, and I swept a hand up
and down the edge of the panel behind me until I found a light
switch there. I pressed it, and then in the glare of almost blind-
ing illumination I saw what Vosiers had been so desperately
anxious for me not to see. Saw my incredible innocence in turning for help to Claude de Gonde, of all people.

It was a low-ceilinged room but immense in size and as full
of working equipment as a flourishing machine shop. I recognized the machinery. I had spent too much time in armorers'
wagons on the battlefront in Korea not to. This was the appa-
ratus for the repair and maintenance of weapons, and while
the size and shape of the metal packing cases on the floor might
suggest they were meant to store gardening tools, I knew that
they contained something far more deadly than rakes and hoes.

I was indifferent to politics; my reading of the daily paper was perfunctory; I had always tried to steer clear of discussions about governments and the riots and rebellions endlessly stewing against them. But I had lived in Paris through the Algerian crisis, had seen with my own eyes the terroristic tactics of the outlawed OAS—*l'Organisation de l'Armée Secrète*—as it made its fanatic, bloody last-ditch stand against the official decision to give Algeria its independence. Now as I looked around this room which was so beautifully equipped to assemble *plastiques* and repair machine guns, I thought of the high-toned family of *colons* inhabiting the luxurious apartments above it and of their friend Morillon; and all the intrigue I had been blind to since the day I first came to the mansion was illuminated as brilliantly as this room itself.

"Monsieur," I said to Vosiers, "you were right. I have been a fool. But now that I'm so much wiser, what do you, as a member of the OAS, suggest we do about it?"

4

For a moment Vosiers looked tired and beaten, the stiffening gone from his spine. Then he recovered himself.

"The OAS is dead," he said in a flat voice. "It's only a memory."

"Is it? The Sûreté may disagree after it gets a look at this layout."

Vosiers shook his head slowly. "But the Sûreté is not going to get a look at it."

"Because that would put my own neck on the block?" I said caustically. "No, monsieur, it isn't really necessary for me to report in person that I have the goods on Hubert Morillon and his friends. An anonymous phone call will do quite as well."

"It will," said Vosiers, "if you intend to destroy Paul."

"So you were lying when you said he was with his grandmother!"

"He is with her, but that changes nothing! Not even Madame Cesira can save the boy if Hubert is betrayed to the police. You must understand that." Vosiers' voice broke. "If Hubert is betrayed, Paul pays the price for it."

"And the price?"

"Death," Vosiers whispered. "Certain death."

His hand suddenly went into his hip pocket, and I emerged from my stupor just in time to pinion it there, squeezing the wrist until he groaned softly. When I withdrew the unresisting hand it was clutching only a handkerchief.

I released the hand, but then took the precaution of searching him for weapons. Vosiers bore this ordeal in silence, and when it was over he mopped his gleaming face with his handkerchief.

"You're strong," he said. "Muscular as a bull. But trample carelessly in this china shop and you will certainly kill my nephew. Hubert Morillon's safety comes before everything else. Believe me, this is a fact of life you must learn to live with."

"Believe you? Am I supposed to believe that you and your whole family are so completely in Morillon's power—"

"You make it sound as if the man is the devil himself!" Vosiers burst out. "Do you think he wants to see harm come to the child? He's the last one for that. But he has no choice in the matter. This arrangement was devised by his superior for Hubert's own protection. Those closest to you are the ones most likely to betray you. This way, no one would want to risk the child's life by such a betrayal."

I believed him then. It was impossible not to in the face of his sweaty anguish.

I said, "And who is Morillon's superior in this outfit? Who's the one willing to murder a child? Is it a fake rug peddler named Léon Becque?"

Vosiers shook his head. "I don't know anyone by that name."

"A smooth customer with one eye missing and bad scars on his cheek."

"I don't know him; I never heard of him. And there's no use asking further questions about it. It's not my affair to know the answers. Since the cause is just, I serve willingly in the ranks."

"As what? Butcher's apprentice?"

Vosiers emitted a hissing breath; his eyes glittered with rage.

"What would you know about these matters?" he said. "What did you ever own in your life that couldn't be tossed on a dump heap without regret? But my vineyards in North Africa brought me in a million a year until those Moslem savages destroyed them. So for the sake of my rotting vineyards and my ruined home where filthy *sidis* now squat on the floors to drop their dung, I serve as I'm told to without complaint. If I must be a butcher's apprentice to make the world fit to live in again, then I will be. It's as simple as that."

As simple as that. I thought of Louis' sightless eyes staring at me, a bullet hole between them, but I took a tight grip on my temper. Vosiers had to get me away from this house and lead me to Anne de Villemont. He would be no use beaten to a pulp.

"Let's get going," I told him. "We can cry over your sad story on the way to Dijon."

A door in back of the workshop opened on to the pasageway leading to the garage. Only one car remained in the garage, the white Ferrari, Matilde Vosiers' favorite toy, and our footsteps echoed hollowly in the emptiness around us as we approached it.

I opened the car's trunk. In it were a couple of well-worn Vuitton suitcases and a spare tire, and when they were removed —the luggage placed inside the car, the tire laid on the floor of the garage—I saw that whoever had designed the Ferrari had certainly not allowed for the possibility of transporting a passenger in its trunk. It would have been a tight fit for a skinny, undersized specimen; for me it would be like doubling up inside half a coffin. But I was in no spot to be fussy about the accommodations. Not while that cop stood watchfully at the gate cradling the tommygun in his arms.

At the same time, there was Vosiers to consider. I was sure he wasn't the man to risk trying murder on his own account somewhere along the road—he was an underling in the organization and would want the go-ahead from his leaders before taking such drastic action—but still I couldn't see myself letting him lock me in that trunk like a fowl placed in an oven for basting. So I searched around until I came up with a hammer and chisel, and while Vosiers watched with the anguish of a man who is having a chisel driven into his own heart, I knocked the catch off the inside of the trunk to keep it from being locked at all.

"Was that necessary?" he asked.

"I hope not. Do you know the woods the other side of Villeneuve?"

"Yes."

"Good. There's a dirt road that crosses the highway about a kilometer past the town. Take that road and park in the woods. When the coast is clear, tap on the trunk so I'll know it's safe to come out. And no tricks."

"No tricks," said Vosiers. He gave me a curious sidelong look, his lips twisting into an unpleasant smile. "As a matter of fact, I suspect my associates may find you much more valuable alive than dead."

"Keep that in mind," I advised him, wondering what he meant.

He waited while I fitted myself into the trunk, then lowered the lid on me. I heard the garage doors open, felt the car rock under his weight as he got behind the wheel, and we were on our way. There was a momentary delay at the gate, an exchange of words with the man on guard there, a heave and bounce of springs as we turned into the street, and then steady, surging motion.

5

So for the time being there was nothing left to do but lie there stifling, my knees under my chin, my arms clasped around them, and examine my situation. As far as I could see, it was bad but not fatal. For one thing, my recklessly walking into the lion's den this way, the fact that I could argue I was Anne's dupe and not her accomplice, should carry weight in the organization's councils. And for Paul's sake alone, de Gonde should be willing to meet my terms. Certainly they were easy terms. Let Paul clear me of murder without a word of the family's secret affairs being mentioned, let me return to my job of substitute father to the child until he was able to stand on his own feet; that was all I wanted. If I got that much, I might some day be able to move against the organization itself.

What about the organization?

All the evidence so far suggested it was divided into cadres kept secret from each other. The members of the household on the rue de Courcelles must make up one such cadre, the toughs who had assaulted me in the Parc des Expositions another which might include Léon Becque. It was even possible that Charles Leschenhaut belonged to some cadre of intellectuals. When I thought of it now, I realized how much the viewpoint of his magazine, *La Foudre*, echoed the aims of the OAS. And there must be still others, ruthless and well disciplined to judge from the stock of arms behind that gun room in the mansion.

OAS or not, this was a terrorist underground of the deadliest sort. Perhaps from the mansion itself had come the machine guns used by the squad of men who had nearly succeeded in assassinating de Gaulle that sweltering, emotional summer of 1962. And this underground army had to be flawlessly organized to have survived the retribution aimed at it by the government. A few of those involved in the assassination attempt had been tried and convicted but had never talked. The ringleaders had been tried and convicted *in absentia,* a farce if ever there was one. They had mysteriously vanished from the face of the earth, and not a trace of them could be found. Could it be that in the persons of Morillon and Becque they had reappeared?

If that were the case, it was easy to see why extreme measures would be taken to protect Morillon, a man already condemned to execution. But why was little Paul de Villemont made the hostage for him? Exactly whom had Vosiers been referring to when he said that those nearest to you are the ones most likely to betray you? Surely not the prime conspirators, the family of *colons* on the rue de Courcelles, nor any of its servants, hand-picked, and, as I had cause to know, fiercely loyal to Morillon. What it came down to was that there was only one person in that household who was not trusted by it —Hubert Morillon's mistress, Anne de Villemont.

To give her all the best of it, it was possible that when they first became lovers she didn't know of his activities. But sooner or later she learned about them and was thus made part of the conspiracy herself. Then at the first sign that she wanted to break with it, her child was made hostage for her good behavior.

And this, to use Vosiers' words, was the china shop I had gone blundering through like an enraged bull.

No thanks to Anne that I was still alive to reflect on my stupidities. And, as Louis had pointed out, the greatest folly of all had been telling her of my suspicions, telling her I was going to let the cat out of the bag. She must have immediately fled in terror with this to de Gonde or Morillon—one would be as bad as the other as far as I was concerned—and after that it was only a miracle that saved my life twice in one day.

I was the intended victim both at the Parc des Expositions and in poor Louis' room. I was The Hanged Man who threatened to pull down that house of cards on the rue de Courcelles.

Then miracle had canceled out miracle. I had managed to survive, but so had the house of cards.

6

In the woods beyond Villeneuve I crawled out of the car trunk feeling as if I had just come off the rack. When I was settled in the seat beside Vosiers, he swung the car into the highway leading south to Dijon and drove at a steady, unobtrusive rate of speed, both of us maintaining a tight-lipped silence. Night fell as we approached Joigny; a track of moonlight across the Yonne River kept pace with us as we moved along. It was the last thing I remember seeing until I was started out of a deep sleep by a jab in the ribs.

"If you're going to sleep, at least do it on your own side of the car," Vosiers said.

I was stretched out, my head on his shoulder. I sat up and peered into the darkness. All I could make out was a line of trees along one side of the road, as evenly spaced as the pickets of a fence, and along the other side the glimmer of a narrow canal.

"Where are we?" I asked.

"Near Dijon, but we turn off here for the chateau. We'll be there in ten minutes."

"What time is it?"

"Nine o'clock. Just in time for dinner. If you have any appetite for dinner."

I realized that my previous aches and pains were gone, but had been replaced by a ravaging hunger. I remarked this to Vosiers, and he nodded admiringly.

"You've got good nerves all right," he said.

We made a sharp turn into a lane between twin avenues of cypresses, the tires spraying up gravel as we jounced along. On a rise ahead I saw the chateau, silvery in the moonlight, an ancient building with a machicolated roofline bracketed between a pair of towers.

"The vineyards are on the other side of the slope," said Vosiers, then acidly commented, "De Laennac is a real genius in his way. It takes a genius to own land like this in the Côte d'Or and not be able to produce a decent bottle of wine."

There were several cars parked along the driveway, among them the familiar Mercedes limousine. As Vosiers pulled up behind it and cut the ignition, a couple of men emerged from the shadows of the building and walked up to us. One of them was my old admirer, Pascal the garage-hand. The other was a youth of the same vicious-looking cut as Albert and the knife-wielder at the fair. Both were armed with shotguns and neither blinked an eye when Vosiers got out of the car and said, pointing at me, "That one is to remain where he is until he's called for, understand? If he makes a move, you're at liberty to blow his head off."

"Yes, Monsieur Vosiers," said Pascal cheerfully, and leveled the gun squarely at my head from six feet away.

Vosiers disappeared into the building. As soon as the door had closed behind him, Pascal said to me, "What's going on, champ?" and while there was friendly concern in his voice, the gun barrel did not waver from its mark. "Whose corns have you stepped on?"

"Shut up, imbecile," his companion said tiredly to him before I could answer.

Pascal took the hint and kept his mouth closed after that.

The other youth lit a cigarette, pasted it to his lower lip, and narrowly watched me through the rising thread of smoke. When the cigarette was reduced to a stub he spat it out and lit another.

Time passed. Night dampness clouded the windshield of the car, and little trickles of water worked their way down the glass. I became aware of country noises around me, a rustling of warm breeze through the cypresses, a fitful croaking of frogs from some swampy patch nearby, an insistent chirping of insects.

I could imagine what was going on in the chateau. Vosiers had presented my case, the jury was now considering its verdict. How much did it weigh in my favor that I was here voluntarily, that I was the dupe of Madame de Villemont and not her willing ally? And wouldn't it be better at this moment to be hiding out in some dark corner of Paris, rather than waiting helplessly like this to be the victim of a neatly designed accident? No, I decided, it wouldn't be. At least, not for anyone who thinks that a quick, clean execution is far preferable to being slowly and relentlessly hounded to death.

The door of the chateau opened, but it was not Vosiers coming to bring me the verdict. It was a servant in uniform, bearing a dinner tray. As impassively as if he were waiting on the table inside, he arranged it on the seat beside me, poured me a glass of wine from the bottle on the tray, and to complete the incongruity of the scene, stepped back and remained at attention while I dined, the frogs and insects providing chamber music for us.

The dinner consisted of *coq au vin,* a half loaf of bread, a cut of cheese, and the wine, and I finished it all off ravenously, wondering if this was the condemned man's last meal. Still, I felt considerably more spirited by the time the tray had been cleared and removed.

Then Claude de Gonde appeared in the doorway of the building and paused there to light a cigar. When it seemed to be drawing properly, he sauntered up to the car.

"Remain on guard over there," he told Pascal and his comrade, and they promptly retreated to a position just out of earshot.

De Gonde opened the car door and slid into the driver's

seat. It was impossible to guess from his imperturbable expression what the verdict was.

"Monsieur de Gonde—" I said impatiently, but before I got any further he held up a warning hand and said, "No, don't bother to explain your situation. Monsieur Vosiers has already done that at length."

"I'm sure he has, monsieur, but there are still a good many questions to ask."

"And no questions," de Gonde said with finality. "The one thing I am here to discuss is your disastrous involvement in my family's affairs."

"In that case," I said between my teeth, "please remember that you were the one who hired me to become involved in them."

"I hired you to attend to my nephew so that he could grow up a sturdy young man instead of a sickly neurotic. After that, it was Madame de Villemont's folly alone which led to this present crisis. And you can't deny that you were warned against her by everyone who knew her."

The righteousness of this staggered me. In all sincerity, this man, a leader of a terrorist gang, saw me as the conspirator and himself as my victim.

"Whether or not I should have taken those warnings," I said angrily, "doesn't change the fact that Paul still needs me as much as ever. And God knows I need him, if I'm to clear myself of a murder charge."

De Gonde slowly shook his head. "You will have nothing more to do with Paul ever again. Absolutely nothing."

My heart sank. "Monsieur, you must know I'm not guilty of any murder. In all fairness—"

"That's a foolish word to use in these circumstances," de Gonde said contemptuously. "No, you and Paul are done with each other. You'll have to settle for another means of saving your skin."

"Such as?"

"In a day or two, you'll be taken to Marseilles and given passage aboard a certain ship leaving for Argentina next week. In Buenos Aires you will be provided with a modest allowance.

I don't see how you can object to this. You are—and I use the word kindly—an idler. You ask little in life but the chance to write books. Now the chance is being given to you."

"And the chance to become a permanent fugitive from the police?"

"Your plight is not unique, my friend. There are dozens of others in South America sharing it. I'll make sure you're welcomed by them with open arms."

Open arms, I thought, and closed fists with knives in them.

"You're going to a lot of trouble for me," I said bluntly. "Why?"

He wasn't prepared for the question; it threw him off-stride. He darted a quick, hard look at me, the cigar poised in mid-air, then recovered himself.

"Because I owe you a great deal for the good you've done Paul," he said. "Now I'm repaying you for that. Be wise. Accept the payment and don't tempt fate."

"But how do you know that once I'm safely away from here—?"

"Ah, so that's it," said de Gonde. "But would you really dare reveal your identity to the world and be convicted of murder? Would you deliberately risk the child's life for any reason at all?"

"That child saw the murder committed, monsieur. He may be able to point out the real murderer. How do you propose to keep him silent about it the rest of his life?"

This hit the mark. De Gonde's hand, which had been resting on the steering wheel, suddenly clenched into a fist.

"A child regards a scene of violence as play-acting!" he said explosively. "In a little while he forgets it."

"Does the murderer know that? What if he begins to worry that Paul won't forget so easily?"

The fist came down hard on the steering wheel.

"Enough!" De Gonde drew a handkerchief from his breast pocket, pressed it to his lips, and replaced it in the pocket, allowing time for his temper to cool. "The fact is, my friend," he said evenly, "you don't hold a single winning trick in this game. Even the one little ace you did hold has been trumped. By tomorrow night the entire contents of that arsenal on the rue de Courcelles will be gone from the house, so if you thought you could use your information about it—"

"Monsieur," I said, "to get several truckloads of arms and machinery past that gate with a suspicious cop standing there—"

"His suspicions will be put to rest by a high police official. Believe me, our organization has powerful friends in that department as well as in every ministry office."

"Organization? Monsieur Vosiers insisted that the OAS was dead and gone."

"He put it badly. It is not dead, but has been transformed into something much greater in function and purpose. Our new *Organisation d'Élite Internationale* is truly international. Its cells may be invisible but they are active throughout the world. The elite of every nation is awakening to the need for a new order."

"And expect to get it by terrorism and murder?"

"*La politique n'a pas d'entrailles,*" quoted de Gonde. All signs of temper were gone now. He was his old self again, completely under control.

"No one expects tenderness in politics," I said. "I'm only saying that your tactics seem not only inhuman, but futile. If they didn't work in Algeria—"

"Algeria was merely the opening battle of a great war. The battle was lost; the war will be won. There was even a time when I thought you, too, might be enlisted in it, but that was a mistaken judgment. So now make up your mind. Will it be Buenos Aires or not? Yes or no."

At least, precious time was being offered me. A week of it before I might have to board that ship at Marseilles.

"Yes," I said.

"Good. Meanwhile, you'll be given a room in the chateau and made as comfortable as possible."

"Fair enough. By the way, did Monsieur Vosiers tell you that all my belongings have disappeared from my room back in Paris? Perhaps you know what became of them."

De Gonde frowned. "I had the impression you yourself ordered them removed. I was there when the truckman came to cart them away, and he said he was acting on your instructions."

"May I ask Madame de Villemont about it?"

"Why not? The only thing you may not do here, my friend, is try to depart. I won't mince words. This place is closely guarded, and you wouldn't get three steps away from it before being shot like a rabbit. Bear in mind that whoever pulls the trigger will do so without the least compunction because you are, in effect, a dangerous criminal fleeing the police. Do you understand?"

"Perfectly."

"I hope you do. For the rest, I'll see about getting you suitable clothing and the necessaries for your trip abroad." De Gonde clapped an encouraging hand on my knee. "You'll enjoy life in South America," he said. "Let's make sure nothing prevents you from reaching there safely."

7

At eight o'clock every morning in the mansion on the rue de Courcelles, there would be a sharp knock on my bedroom door, and whether I answered or not, a maid would then open the door and wheel in a serving cart on which were Paul's breakfast and my coffee and croissant. Now I was jarred out of a sweaty, terrifying sequence of dreams by that same knock on the door, and I opened my eyes to see Jeanne-Marie make an entrance behind a serving cart.

The sight of her under these conditions was so familiar that for a moment I didn't remember where I was. Then I became aware of the dusty canopy over the four-poster bed I occupied, the huge room with its peeling walls and sparse minimum of furniture, the dank, musty smell in my nostrils of a country house moldering too long without proper care; and unpleasant enlightenment set in.

Jeanne-Marie pushed open window shutters, flooding the room with sunlight. Then she went to the dresser and, with a worried expression, leaned forward to study her face in the mirror over it. In her chic uniform, a tiny white cap pinned high on her extravagant coiffure, she made a very pretty anachronism in this room which might have been the donjon keep of a medieval castle.

"What are you doing here?" I said.

She looked startled, then stuck out her tongue at my reflection in the mirror.

"Good morning, lover," she said, "and aren't you in a sweet mood. One day away from Madame and you're all on edge, I see."

She took her time at the mirror before bringing me the breakfast tray. On it, besides the usual coffee and croissant, was a razor and shaving soap, a toothbrush, and a pack of cigarettes.

"The bathroom is right next door," Jeanne-Marie said, "and since you're first up, you won't get caught in the traffic." She helped herself to a cigarette from the pack and lit it. "As for what I'm doing here, I'll have you know I made the trip by request. You may not believe it, big boy, but there are some men who don't think your boss is the only female in sight."

"Like Monsieur Edmond?"

Jeanne-Marie sat herself on the foot of the bed and blew a cloud of smoke in my direction. "Well, what's wrong with that? He's all there, I can tell you. A real man despite that fat belly. And last night—!" She rolled her eyes wickedly.

"No!" I said. "You don't mean right here under Madame Matilde's nose?"

I couldn't have cared less what went on between this wench and Vosiers, but it struck me that I had to play it cool, had to win whatever allies I could before time ran out on me.

Jeanne-Marie nodded solemnly, but was obviously bursting with some priceless secret.

"Right under her pointy little nose," she assured me.

"*Formidable!*" I said with admiration through a mouthful of croissant. "But take care, baby. If Madame ever catches you two at that game, she'll hand you your head on a platter."

Jeanne-Marie seemed to find this excruciatingly funny. She choked with laughter.

"But she did catch us at it last night!"

"I don't believe you."

"I swear she did. My fat little rooster forgot to lock the door behind him when he came to visit, and suddenly there was Madame standing right in my doorway taking in everything with her eyes popping out of her head. Oh, she was in a fine state, all right. And do you know what?"

"What?"

"Monsieur Edmond didn't even turn a hair. He just looked at her as cool as you please, and she ran off without saying a word."

"She'll have plenty of words for you when she gets you alone," I warned.

Jeanne-Marie dismissed this with a lofty wave of the hand. "Not after Monsieur Edmond settles with her today. Naturally, Madame Cesira would never let them get divorced, but he's done sharing the same bed with sweet Matilde. He's planning to tell her that this morning. Once he does, she'll know her place." Jeanne-Marie sniffed contemptuously. "Couldn't even have a child for him, a man who'd give his soul for a houseful of kids. That's how much use she is."

"Well," I said, "in that case, no one can blame you for trying to cheer him up a little."

Jeanne-Marie warmed to this sympathy. "Yes, I guess you know how it is, don't you? Have you had a chance to see your lady friend since you got here?"

"No, but sometimes today—"

"Tonight, you mean, what with that gang of lawyers she'll be attending to all day."

"That's right," I said, as if this weren't news. "The lawyers come first. Meanwhile, would you do me one small favor?"

Jeanne-Marie lazily got to her feet. She swept the toiletries on my tray to the bed and picked up the tray. "I might."

"Well, there's a certain little Véronique back in Paris—she lives on the rue de Babylonne—and I'd like to get her out of my hair. Next time you go into Dijon, if you wrote her a picture postcard saying her friend Reno is having a fine time on vacation, and you signed it with Madame de Villemont's name—"

From the way Jeanne-Marie looked at me I knew I had been heading down a blind alley.

"Only a postcard?" she asked sweetly. "But why not a whole letter telling her why you're here and what she ought to do about it?"

"Do you know why I'm here?"

"Yes, my little lamb," said Jeanne-Marie. She motioned with her thumb at the door. "And so does that type in the hall outside and all his ugly friends around here with their hands on their guns. If you're smart, you won't ask them for such favors either, or you might become a very dead lamb."

After she was gone, giving me a broad wink as she closed the door to show me she bore me no hard feelings despite my *gaffe*, I tried to think what other possible allies I might find in this place. I could think of none. When de Gonde had ushered me into the chateau the night before, it was like being conducted into limbo. The foxy little Comte de Laennac and his mummified, fortunetelling wife were playing bridge with the Vosiers', and not one of them answered my greeting or even looked up at me. It was the same with Madame Gabrielle, who sat in an armchair busy with her embroidery. It was a servant who, after a consenting nod from de Gonde, answered my query about Madame de Villemont. She had been indisposed after dinner and gone directly to bed, he informed me, so that was that. To the rest of the company I was evidently a disembodied spirit, mute and invisible.

Nor did Jeanne-Marie have to describe the guard outside my bedroom or his friends. I had been guided upstairs to my room by a burly character who, although in mufti, wore a paratrooper's beret and jump boots. A half dozen others like him had been holding a low-voiced discussion at the foot of the staircase. Another pair lounged against the wall of the second-floor hallway, and one of them, thumbs in belt and jacket thrown open, displayed a shoulder holster with a gun butt protruding from it. No question about it. If the mansion on the rue de Courcelles was an armory for the *Organisation d'Élite Internationale,* the Château Laennac was one of its barracks.

8

Bathed, shaved, and dressed, I was ready to reconnoiter the enemy camp.

The objectives were clear-cut. Vosiers had let slip that Paul and his grandmother would be in Venice. Now all I had to do was learn exactly where in Venice they would be, get away from the chateau alive, cross the Italian frontier, find the child, take possession of him, and place both of us under the protection of the nearest American consulate. All this, of course, without money or passport, and with the police of every country this side of the Iron Curtain on the lookout for me.

I forced myself to examine my situation calmly, to move with slow deliberation, to push up the sleeves of Edmond Vosiers' now dirty and wrinkled cashmere sweater as if I were really preparing for a morning of tennis, but what I felt was a frenzy of helplessness. I felt as if I were bound hand and foot, writhing futilely under thoughts that were being driven into me like needles.

The thought of Louis dead and his killer roaming free was the most painful; and almost as tormenting was the thought of Léon Becque consoling Véronique for the tragedy and for my supposed part in it. I was sure he would remain close to her until I was safely in exile. After that, it would be good-bye to her and to poor Eliane who imagined herself engaged to this dashing salesman. Becque had more important missions in life than marriage.

Come to think of it, it was lucky Jeanne-Marie had refused to forward my message to Véronique. As long as Becque hovered close to her and Eliane, their best protection from him would be their innocent faith in him. Better to have them believe whatever he told them than to have him suspect they knew too much.

And finally there was the terrifying thought of the shadow over Paul. No matter how de Gonde tried to close his mind to the inevitable, if Louis' killer were someone Paul could identify, sooner or later that killer would try to get rid of this witness against him, child or not.

But it was no use standing helplessly while events were directed to their climax by the enemy. I knew my objectives. I had to start moving toward them before it was too late to make any move at all.

From the window, I had a depressing view of one of the obstacles confronting me.

The window overlooked a terrace at the rear of the building. A formal garden had been laid out on the terrace, but it was arid and untended, its hedges ragged and only a few clumps of flowers showing their withered heads. There was no water spraying from the fountain in the center of the garden, the basin of the fountain was empty, and on its rim sat a couple of the Foreign Legion paratroop types I had encountered the night before, each with a rifle propped between his knees. In contrast to this warlike display, the rolling terrain beyond the garden was green with vineyards which filled the warm, sunshiny air with a fragrance of ripening grapes. Only a few straw-hatted workers could be seen among the vineyards, and these, I was sure, must be loyal members of the Comte de Laennac's cadre of the OEI. It would be dangerous to employ others this close to headquarters.

I went out into the hall and made a tour of the second-floor corridors, under surveillance. A guard was loitering outside my door and stayed close behind me as I went along the corridor so that it was impossible to take even one step unobserved.

From the Gothic look of it, I surmised that the Château Laennac had been built in the Middle Ages, although it must have been restored a few times since then. The varying height and width of different passageways were clues to that, as well as the way I suddenly found myself going up or down a couple of steps to a different level on the same floor. And it had been a long time since the last cleaning up and repair of the place. The walls were all whitewashed plaster and all uniformly grimy with neglect; the wooden flooring was scuffed and dirty.

This was in keeping with the impression I had gotten of the downstairs rooms the night before. Everything decaying with time; furniture finished with brocades and *petit point* so worn that their original patterns had faded beyond recognition; and cavernous fireplaces with pitifully small fires in them that couldn't possibly take the chill out of the air. Outdoors the Côte d'Or was in the grip of early summer heat. Inside the chateau one got the feeling that no heat had penetrated these walls for centuries. Monsieur le Comte and his wife seemed used to this. The family, wrapped in sweaters and shawls, shuddered at it, and I shuddered with them.

The final turn of the second-floor corridor I was following led to an embrasure overlooking the driveway in front of the building. From this vantage point I could see Georges, in hip boots and with garden hose in hand, washing down the Mercedes. And where the driveway entered the aisle of cypresses leading to the highway beyond was another familiar figure briskly walking along. Bernard Bourdon.

Since these two were the only people in sight, I wondered if the driveway itself wouldn't be the easiest route for anyone trying to make a getaway from the house. Then I saw how wrong I was about that. From behind the cypresses a dog sud-

denly lunged at Bernard, a snarling fury held on leash by a
man who was almost dragged off his feet by the dog's efforts
to get at its intended victim. Bernard laughingly dodged away
from it, and when the man shouted a command the dog immediately went down low on its belly, pulling steadily against the
choking constraint of the leash, barking thunderously, but no
longer trying to leap to the attack.

The barking was answered from several directions. I saw
another dog at the far end of the driveway, this one without
a handler, detected at least three more slinking through the
greenery on either side of the cypress avenue. A few seconds
later, after Bernard had disappeared among the trees, there
was nothing at all to be seen or heard along the borders of the
estate; it was hard to believe there might be anything more
than a few harmless rabbits in that greenery. But I knew better
now. The boundaries of the estate were hermetically sealed.
Even if I managed to get out of the house, there was no way
of getting any distance from it on foot in one unbloodied piece.

Could I get through that front door at all? I went downstairs
and saw that the door was open, no doubt to invite some
warmth into this bleak interior. A couple of men lounged in
the doorway. They watched me incuriously as I came up,
but when I indicated I wanted to pass by, one braced his leg
across the doorway and the other patted the pistol butt in his
shoulder holster in warning.

In my mood of bottled-up violence, this temptation was too
much to resist. I swept a hand under the ankle of that leg
across the doorway, lifting it high so that its owner had to balance on one foot, teetering wildly and clutching at the door
to keep from falling. At the same instant, I caught hold of the
other man's wrist with my free hand, jamming it against his
chest so that he couldn't draw his gun.

It was a foolhardy thing to do—it was like grabbing a pair
of ravening tigers by the tail—and almost immediately I released both men and stepped back to show that it was all in
the spirit of good clean fun, no harm intended. I smiled, and
after a taut moment the pair smiled back at me, the one with
the gun motioning with it at the door as if to say that since I

was so determined to take a look at the world from the outside, it was all right with him.

I did step outside, so I learned my lesson the hard way. A third man was concealed on the other side of the doorway; he neatly tripped me as I went through the door, I pitched forward on the driveway, landing on my hands and knees, and, before I could get to my feet, was viciously kicked in the ribs. The impact of that heavy boot drove the air out of my lungs. I remained on hands and knees, gasping for breath, waiting for the next kick to shatter my ribs.

All this while, not a word had been spoken. We might have been acting out a pantomime for the benefit of Georges, a one-man audience, who leaned against the Mercedes nearby, following the action without interest. The three guards and myself were performers on this quiet, sunlit stage, and Georges was plainly bored with the performance. He made a gesture, and still badly winded I was hauled upright and steered back into the building by a gun digging into my spine. The show was over. If I hadn't grasped the point of it, Georges was telling me in effect, that would be my bad luck later on.

While I was regaining my breath in the entrance hall, cursing myself for not resisting temptation, a small car skittered to a halt in front of the building. From it emerged a tall, lean man, gray-haired, leathery, bristling with energy, and a handsome blonde girl, hollow-eyed and exhausted. At second glance I recognized them as a couple I had met at the dinner party de Gonde had given for Charles Leschenhaut—Colonel Jesse Hardee, late of the United States Army, and his German wife—and their presence here in this OEI nest now made plain what their relationship to de Gonde was.

The colonel marched through the door, his wife trailing behind, and one of the guards brought up the rear, their luggage under his arms. When the colonel saw me, he strode over to shake hands heartily.

"So you've joined the team," he said.

That meant he had the impression I was an active member of the OEI cabal. I didn't intend to waste the opportunity this offered.

"I guess I did," I told him.

"Fine, fine. Claude told me you were hanging fire, but I knew you'd sign on sooner or later. What the hell's your name again?"

"Davis. Reno Davis."

"I'll remember it after this. Look, son, you know the language, so do me a favor and tell that man to get Mrs. Hardee and those bags up to our room on the double. And tell him to have somebody from the kitchen bring her a pot of black coffee and some toast to settle her stomach. Tell him real toast, too; not a hunk of bread shoved into the fireplace on a fork."

After I had followed instructions, and Mrs. Hardee had been led upstairs, the colonel shook his head commiseratingly.

"Poor Clara won't get that channel crossing out of her system for the rest of the day No plane departures from London yesterday, so we had to settle for the boat. What's this hurry call about anyhow? And why here instead of Paris?"

"De Gonde is the one to tell you about it," I answered. "Meanwhile, how about some breakfast yourself?"

"I could stand some. Do you think you could tell them how to make ham and eggs American style? Clara never could because she doesn't know a damn thing about American cooking herself. You know, I'm really glad we got together this way, Davis. I've thought of you a few times since that party for Leschenhaut. I might have a red-hot proposition for you."

There was a long refectory table in the dining room with a few places set at it. I gave the colonel's order to the servant in charge, along with the recipe for ham and eggs *américain*. Since I was an old hand at this—I had learned from Jeanloup at the Café au Coin what French peculiarities must be overcome in order to make a breakfast taste American—the dish presented to the colonel was an unqualified success. At least it was to judge by the way it loosened his tongue.

He talked steadily and passionately through mouthfuls of food, and I hoped no one else would enter the dining room while he was at it. By contributing an occasional nod to this monologue, I learned that he was a leader of North American

Action—the division of the *Organisation d'Élite Interna-*
tionale which was working to bring the light to the United
States—and that my proper place was as part of this division,
preferably right at the colonel's side.

"Well, what do you think?" he said after he had spoken his
piece, and I shook my head regretfully, sure this would draw
him out still further.

"How long is it since you've been in the States?" he demanded.

"About eight years."

"Then you're out of touch, man. Damn it, everybody's waking
up to the fact that the ballot box is no answer for us. They're
all learning you can't get a hog to vote himself out of a full
trough. It's coming down to firepower now, sooner than anyone
dreamed it would. An armed underground that can pinpoint
the enemy and get rid of him the one convincing way, with a
bullet through his head. The trouble right now is that we've got
fifty different patriotic outfits in the country that know this, but
there's no co-ordination among them. Once they see that unity
within North American Action means an unbeatable force—"

"How do you expect to make them see it?"

"By delivering the goods. That means money, propaganda,
and weapons. The weapons are the real thing, too, nine-milli-
meter machine guns, lightweight for easy handling, and dead
accurate. We've got half a dozen caches of them from New York
to California already, and we'll have a dozen set up inside of a
year. Show an honest-to-god, red, white, and blue patriot this
kind of tool and you show him you mean business. But that's
my end of it. Your end would be the propaganda department, the written stuff. Clara's just no good at translating some
of those terrific things Leschenhaut turns out because her English is lousy, but you'd be a natural at it. You might even want
to try your own hand at that kind of writing."

"I've never done any of it before."

"Well, you could learn from Leschenhaut. Even when his
stuff is turned into Clara's kind of English, it can make your
hair stand up. And there's something else, Davis. There's the
business of talking man to man with all those patriots back

home who distrust the idea of OEI because it smells foreign to them. Let's face it, there are a lot of backwoods yahoos among them who need a lot of convincing if we're to organize on an international basis. You're a hundred-percent American; you're an ex-fighter, an ex-Marine; you're just the kind of guy who can do a great selling job on them."

"Maybe, but a few machine guns don't really add up to a movement. Now over here—"

"Yes, I know," the colonel cut in. "Over here is the lady friend, and don't tell me different. Remember I was there the night you and Morillon had that fracas over her. But man to man, Davis, what does hopping in bed with any woman mean compared to your patriotic duty? And your real duty is back home."

"I was going to say that here is where the action is, Colonel. Back home is where only talking goes on."

"The hell you say!" The colonel reached into his breast pocket and drew out a sheaf of papers, tissue thin. He slapped them flat on the table, and I got a tantalizing glimpse of what seemed to be rows of numbers. "You're thinking of eight years back, son, but here's the OEI table of command today, and these last three pages alone list fifty unit commanders on the North American Action payroll and dedicated to its program. Fifty of them, and that doesn't even include contacts who run outfits like rifle clubs and can be counted on when the time comes."

I didn't want to appear too anxious to see those pages. I took my time reaching for them, and then a shadow fell over them, a hand covered them. Claude de Gonde was standing behind me, his lips set in a deathlike smile, his eyes cold with anger.

"If you persist in meddling with affairs that don't concern you," he said to me in French, "you will have to be locked in your room," and then shifting to heavily accented English he said brightly to the colonel, "No, no, my friend, I am afraid none of this can be of interest to the young man." He carefully folded up the papers and handed them to the colonel, who tucked them back into his pocket, looking somewhat puzzled.

"I thought—" the colonel said.

"Of course, but Monsieur Davis was involved in a killing yesterday in Paris and is now on his way to South America only a few steps ahead of the police. At present, he must be considered *hors de combat.*"

"A killing in the line of duty?" the colonel asked calmly.

"Yes, but what difference does it make?" de Gonde answered. "For his sake as well as ours—"

"I need him in the States," said the colonel. "Have the same face job done on him that was done on Morillon—contact lenses, a few touches here and there—and I'll get him into the country by way of Mexico with no one the wiser. Why put a man like this in cold storage, Claude?"

"Because it must be done," de Gonde said shortly. "He is a very careless fellow, this one, colonel. I assure you he is not the man you take him for," and what intrigued me was the evasiveness of this, the refusal to come out with the truth about me. But I could see the reason for it. De Gonde had made a dangerous mistake taking me into his home; he had jeopardized the organization for his nephew's sake, and he had no intention of broadcasting that. Plainly anxious to change the subject, he now said to me, "Madame Vosiers is going shopping in Dijon later today and has kindly offered to replenish your wardrobe if you tell her what you need. She's in the sitting room waiting to make out the list."

"I appreciate that, but shouldn't I speak to Madame de Villemont first? She may know what's been done with the clothing I had in my room."

"I've already asked her about it," said de Gonde. "She has no idea what happened to your belongings."

"May I speak to her anyhow? It's not only the clothing; there are also my manuscripts. A great deal of work has gone into them."

"I'm sure of that, but you may not speak to her until later. She'll be occupied for a while with business affairs. She cannot be disturbed until they are settled. Meanwhile," de Gonde said pointedly, "Madame Vosiers is waiting. The sitting room is through that door."

"Too bad we couldn't work something out, Davis," the colonel said regretfully as I rose to leave, and thinking of that sheaf of papers in his pocket—a trump card in this deadly game if ever there was one—I couldn't have agreed more. To get my hands on them—

Matilde Vosiers was not alone in the sitting room. On a window seat were the little Comte de Laennac and the bulky Edmond Vosiers in low-voiced conversation. At the opposite end of the room a smoky fire had been kindled in the fireplace, and Madame Matilde, looking thoroughly miserable, sat on a couch beside the fireplace with a deal table drawn up before her.

She motioned me to join her on the couch, and when I did I saw close up how shockingly haggard she was under an excess of make-up. It was as if the years had caught up with her overnight, revealing the hitherto concealed lines of her face with cruel clarity, loosening the flesh of the face itself and making it look soft and jowly.

She took a notebook from the table and handed it to me.

"Please look at this," she said crisply. "I've already written down the essentials you'll need." Then her head moved closer to mine, her voice fell to an undertone. "For God's sake, keep looking at it. Pretend you're reading it carefully. Whatever you do, don't look surprised at what I say, don't turn around, don't blink an eye." Her voice rose. "I've marked the size of the pajamas as *grand patron*. Is that correct?"

"Yes, madame," I said, my eyes glued to the notebook.

"As for these other garments," said Madame Matilde, and again her voice became an undertone. "Now listen! It's been planned that you and Anne will be taken south by car tomorrow night. There's to be an accident on the road near Valence, so that the two of you will be found dead in the car at the foot of the mountain there. No, keep your eyes fixed on this book. Say something about the clothing you need. Say it loudly."

So that was why I had been allowed to remain alive this long!

"Madame," I said, and I had to clear my throat to get the words out, "I'll need one other pair of shoes at least, and they should be properly fitted. If I could go to town with you—"

"Impossible," Madame Matilde said sharply. "Monsieur Vosiers will accompany me to Dijon and do the best he can from this list. He's mad," she whispered. "Completely mad. They all are. The one protector Anne had was Hubert, and now he's turned against her, too, because of your affair with her. You must get away from here. Then it can't be made to look as if you and Anne were running off together. It also means she herself is safe for the time being."

"What are the papers she's attending to today?" I muttered, raptly addressing myself to the notebook, and in my mind was the French axiom which has it that he who signs his will may be signing his death warrant. "Is it her will?"

"No, that was made out when we first came to Paris from Africa. These are the papers making my sister and brother-in-law Paul's guardians, and with all rights to handle his inheritance as they see fit. Now listen. I can help you get away from here, but we must make a bargain."

"What kind of bargain?"

"This. I'll arrange to get back from Dijon at nine, and you must be waiting in the hallway by the door. When Edmond and I step out of the car I'll leave the motor running so you can get away in it before anyone can stop you. There will be a valise in the car with clothing in it and a train ticket to Paris. The Paris express stops here at nine-thirty. The train is best because they'll be watching for the car on every road."

"All right," I whispered, "the train it is. But you'll have to make it a ticket to Milan."

"You have no passport."

"Let me worry about that. Just book me for a compartment on a train to Milan."

"That train is half an hour earlier."

"Then get back here at eight-thirty. And I'll need money."

"I'll leave some in the valise."

"And one more thing. Where is Madame Cesira keeping Paul in Venice? What's the address?"

"Never mind that, you fool. Keep away from Paul and just consider your own neck." Suddenly, Madame Matilde's voice rose. "You must have a jacket, of course. I'll make a note of that."

She plucked the notebook from my hand as the form of

Edmond Vosiers loomed over us. He stood there, hands in pockets, looking down at us with suspicion.

"You're taking long enough at this," he said to his wife at last.

"Am I?" said Madame Matilde frigidly. "But if you're bored by watching this activity, monsieur, you can surely find better entertainment elsewhere."

Vosiers teetered back and forth on his toes, studying his wife's pale and angry face with satisfaction.

"Yes," he said, "I think I can. Much better entertainment," and then swaggered off to rejoin de Laennac on the window-seat.

Madame Matilde sat staring after him. The pencil she was holding snapped with a sudden sharp report and she flung it into the fireplace.

"Ah, the dog," she whispered. "He's laughing at me. Do you see how he's laughing at me?"

"Never mind him," I said. "What about the bargain? What's my end of it?"

"To kill him," Madame Matilde said. "No, don't look like that or he'll know something is wrong. That's better. Here, let me see inside your shirt collar for the size."

Her fingers inside the collar were icy cold and trembling uncontrollably. Her mouth was close to my ear.

"There's a gun under the seat of this couch. Get hold of it during the day. When you go to the car you must use it on him. Swear you will."

"Madame—"

Her fingernails dug into my arm. "You'll be close to him for one moment. It's all the time you'll need. It'll be like killing a mad dog. If you don't swear you will, there is no bargain. You'll be dead yourself and Anne along with you. Swear it on your soul."

"All right, I swear it." For the chance I was being given I would have falsely sworn to anything.

"How do I know I can trust you?" Madame Matilde asked.

"You don't. You'll have to find out when the time comes."

"But remember you swore it on your soul!" Madame Matilde

clapped the notebook shut. "That's quite enough," she said loudly. "After all, these things cost money. We don't intend to buy out the stores for you."

When I rose from the couch I saw from Edmond Vosiers' broad smile that this was the kind of talk he approved of.

9

I didn't delude myself about the bargain. My well-being was the least of Matilde Vosiers' concerns; what mattered to her was settling accounts with her husband. So I felt sure she had hidden a gun in the couch and that she would get the car back to the chateau at eight-thirty, since these items were essential to my part of the bargain. But there was a fair chance the car's motor would not be left running for a quick getaway, that there would be no train ticket or money left for me, and that whether or not I disposed of Matilde's erring husband for her, I would be disposed of myself as soon as I set foot outside the building.

Bad enough trying to plan my moves with this in mind. What made it worse was that Anne was going to be my partner in the enterprise without even knowing it. There was no way around that. She was marked for death as soon as she awarded legal guardianship of Paul to the de Gondes, those gracious representatives of the OEI; and the OEI was highly adaptable. If it couldn't arrange for Anne to share a fatal accident with me, it would very soon arrange for her to have an accident of her own.

And from my own coldly realistic point of view, Anne had a

passport which might help me get across the Italian frontier in her company. And she would know where to find Paul and could lead me to him.

We desperately needed each other now, that was what it came down to. Whatever I felt about her when I thought of how Louis had paid for her double-dealing and how I was expected to pay for it—this had to be put aside for the time being like a vial of acid locked away in a dark closet.

But I was wiser than I had been. Wise enough now, at least, not to trust Anne de Villemont. Faced with a crisis only two short days ago, she had promptly betrayed me to the enemy, and I didn't intend to have her do it again. So she was going with me when I broke out of this jail, but was not going to know that until the last possible moment.

Un vrai tour de passe-passe. A neat trick to get away with if I could. If I couldn't, it was likely to be the last one I would ever have a chance to try.

10

As the day wore on, I came to see the terms of my imprisonment. I was being allowed the freedom of the house, but unless I shut myself up in my own room, I was allowed no privacy. I prowled from room to room downstairs, always with a hard bitten OEI man keeping an eye on me. Where members of the household were present my guard kept himself discreetly out of sight. Where no one else was present he leaned against a doorpost in full view of me, yawning with boredom, but quick to move when I did.

This made it a touchy business getting hold of the concealed gun, a handy little automatic, fully loaded. I finally managed to do it by settling myself on the couch with an old copy of *Le Figaro* to mask my activity, and then by working the automatic up between the cushions, inch by inch, until I could bear it away in the folded newspaper. I stored it under the mattress of my bed and left the paper with it. *Le Figaro* was going to be even more useful than the gun when the time came.

Meanwhile, I wondered about the location of Anne's room, a vital piece of information I had no way of obtaining without arousing suspicion. The lawyers to draw up the documents concerning Paul's guardianship arrived before noon—four of them, as cold-eyed and efficient-looking as a school of sharks—and from the way they were received by Bernard Bourdon and Claude de Gonde, I gathered they were very much part of the OEI themselves. They finally left in the late afternoon. When de Gonde re-entered the chateau after seeing them off at the door, I fervently put to him my hopes of paying a little visit to Madame de Villemont. If I could be conducted to her room—

De Gonde was in high good humor now.

"Well," he said affably, "I suppose farewells are in order, aren't they? But there's no need to rush them. A long and tedious farewell is worse than none at all. And you'll have plenty of time to say good-bye to Madame tomorrow evening."

"Tomorrow evening?" I echoed, trying not to overdo the note of innocence.

"That's right. You see, my friend, I'm not as heartless as you may think. In a couple of days, an agent will pick you up at Valence to deliver you to your ship. Since Georges is driving Madame de Villemont and young Bernard down to Saint-Trop' tomorrow evening, I've arranged for you to travel with them as far as Valence."

To the place of execution, I thought, but all I said was, "That's kind of you, monsieur." Then I couldn't resist adding, "I suppose Georges and Bernard have instructions to make sure I don't get sidetracked along the way."

"They have. But for your own good, really. You're an atrocious bungler, you know. I shudder to think what might be-

come of you if you go wandering around on your own. The
way to avoid trouble on your journey south is to follow orders
closely and not test Georges' and Bernard's ability to enforce
them. Believe me, they're a dangerous pair to cross."

"I believe you, monsieur."

"And one other thing." De Gonde's voice hardened. "No more
baiting of Colonel Hardee. I prefer he doesn't know why you're
really here, but don't take advantage of that."

"I understand, monsieur."

My weary resignation to my fate seemed to impress him.

"I know all this is difficult for you," he commiserated, "but
then it's difficult for the lot of us. My God, when I think of
Madame de Villemont's stupidity, her heedlessness—"

"Her madness?"

He deigned to smile at this thrust.

"Frankly, it would have been better for you to believe she
really was mad. It would have kept you from involvement in
her wild schemes. But that's all water under the bridge now.
The damage has been done; we must simply make the best of
it. By the way, dinner is at nine. Would it help dispel your dark
mood if you joined us at the table?"

"I'm afraid I can't dress suitably, monsieur."

De Gonde waved that aside.

"Oh, life is informal here. Our host and hostess detest the
country; they regard it as a sort of jungle, and they're not Brit-
ons, you know, to dress for dinner in the jungle. Madame
Vosiers will be back in time to supply you with whatever you
need to wear."

"Then I'll be glad to join you at dinner."

When we parted I hadn't gotten the information I wanted
about Anne's room, but that warning against taking advantage
of Colonel Hardee reminded me of the OEI membership list
in his pocket. The organization was like a virulently poisonous
snake. Chop off a piece of its tail, and you're dead before you
can get in a second blow of the axe. But that membership list
might be the way to destroy the whole snake on the first try,
if—and there was the catch—if I had Paul safely in charge when
the try was made.

I found the colonel in a billiard room practicing shots on a table so thick with dust that the balls left tracks on it as they rolled. He was in shirtsleeves, and his jacket was neatly draped over a chair near the door I entered. I stationed myself beside the chair, wondering if the list were still in the jacket pocket, and when I cautiously reached a hand behind me I felt with jubilance the stiffness of folded papers. Then the colonel turned and saw me, and I had to quickly withdraw the hand.

"So there you are," he said. "Still going around like a tiger in a cage?"

"Well, it does get a little dull here after a while, sir."

"It does, but you'll have to get used to the quiet life. Yes, Claude told me all about how you knocked off that meddlesome bastard back in Paris. Too bad it had to happen with the cops practically looking over your shoulder, but that's the way it goes, son. Anyhow, you'll find there are worse places to be holed up in than Buenos Aires." He motioned at the table. "Care to have a game?"

"I'm not too good at it."

"It wouldn't matter if you were. The table's dead and the cues are crooked, but as they say back home, mister, it's the only game in town."

That was at five o'clock, and during the next two hours I was never allowed enough time unobserved to spirit those papers out of the jacket. The colonel played in military style, quickstepping to a position behind the cue ball, lining up his shot at a glance, and promptly firing away. It should have been a pleasure meeting an opponent who kept the game moving at top speed. Under these circumstances, it was anything but that.

I finally solved the problem by deliberately making a shot which lifted the ball right off the table and sent it bouncing into a far corner of the room. The colonel looked at me with surprise, then went to retrieve it. By the time he returned, his papers were safely tucked away beneath my shirt.

"Nerves," he remarked, as he tossed the ball back on the table. "You've got a sweet case of them, son." He took his jacket from the chair and put it on while I stood rigid, waiting for him to discover his loss. "And don't tell me it isn't the heebie-jeebies. You've been looking at your watch every two minutes since you walked in here, and that's a sure sign. What the hell, let's get up to my room and crack a bottle I stashed away there. That'll make you forget the time."

I followed him obediently, still braced for the fatal moment when he would clap an inquiring hand to his breast pocket, but we made it to his bedroom without incident, my guard trailing us at a distance.

In the bedroom, the colonel took a bottle of bourbon from a valise, found a glass for me, then disappeared into the next room to look for another for himself. When he returned with it, he said, "Clara's still sleeping off that channel crossing, poor kid. What the hell, she'll be as good as new tomorrow, but let's keep the party quiet anyhow."

I stood poised for trouble as he removed his jacket and carefully hung it away in an armoire. When he closed the door of the armoire and stretched out on the bed, glass in hand, I drew a deep breath of relief and downed my drink at a gulp.

"To the Day," said the colonel, following suit.

Since he had put me on guard about looking regularly at my watch, I now sneaked a surreptitious look at it. It said twenty after seven. That meant exactly one hour to go before I moved into action, and at any time during it the colonel might remember his list. Like it or not, I had to spend that final hour in his company.

It turned out to be a highly instructive hour. The colonel had evidently taken to heart the fact that I'd been away from our homeland for eight years; he now made it his business to bring me up to date about it. As he talked, refreshing himself from the bottle at regular intervals, he forgot about keeping the party quiet. His voice rose with passion. He got off the bed and stalked the room, now and then jabbing a lean forefinger at me like a prophet pronouncing doom, the sweat of emotion trickling down his face.

I listened with fascination to the bill of particulars. The seizure of high office, even the presidency itself, by subversives. The mongrelization of the race. The atheism fostered by traitorous churchmen. The filthy literature deliberately used by the forces of evil to corrupt the young and destroy the American spirit. The colonel's voice thickened; blotches of sweat showed through his shirt as he turned to the question of how he and his North American Action proposed to remedy these ills.

That was the terrifying part of it, his lip-licking anticipation of the day when the remedy would be applied. Those caches of weapons he had described at the breakfast table were not going to rust away uselessly. Where persuasion failed, a well-aimed bullet would succeed. And afterward there was the whip and club to insure order. It cast a new light on someone like Edmond Vosiers, who wanted to torture and murder for the sake of his lost vineyards, because that at least had a brutal logic to it. But the colonel's belief in his hallucinations, his eagerness to torture and murder for the sake of those hallucinations, was the madness of a paranoid maniac seeing devils menacing him from every corner.

Then it was eight-twenty.

"Colonel, if we're going to get ready for dinner—"

"What? Hell, plenty of time for that. And I'm five drinks up on you." He looked dazedly around until he located the almost empty bottle on his bedside table. He lurched toward me with it. "Here, you kill it."

The residue of the bottle half filled my glass. "Time to go when the booze is gone," the colonel said thickly. Then the bottle fell from his limp hand, he sat down abruptly on the bed and slowly went over sideways until he lay there, face buried in the pillow.

The guard patrolling the hall grinned when I left the room and lurched toward him in an imitation of the colonel's drunken gait. I raised the glass in a toast. "*A votre santé, copain.*"

"*Merci, monsieur. Vous avez sa pointe, hein?*" he jeered, a tribute to my acting since I was as sober as he was.

My room was nearby. I turned to the job at hand quickly and methodically.

I went to the window. The last rays of setting sun were fiery on the horizon. A different team of riflemen were seated on the rim of the fountain now; they looked up incuriously as I pulled the shutters together. Through the vents of the shutters I could feel a stirring of evening breeze, and that was all to the good.

From beneath the mattress of the four-poster I extracted the gun and the copy of *Le Figaro*. The gun I stowed in my hip pocket. *Le Figaro* I loosely crumpled into two wads of kindling. One I placed on the floor at the edge of the bed where the bedspread hung down over it; the other I piled on the bed itself. When I stood on the bed and dragged down an end of the canopy over it, a cloud of dust descended on me.

I stepped down from the bed, put a match to the crumpled newspaper on it and to the pile on the floor. The paper smoldered and burst into flame. The next instant, as if the canopy had been soaked in gasoline, a tongue of flame raced along it to the top of the four-poster. The bedspread took a few seconds longer to catch fire, then started blazing away merrily.

I went to the door as smoke thickened around me. I picked up the glass of bourbon I had left on the dresser, threw open the door, and staggered backward into the hallway. The open door provided a draft like a chimney. There was a roar of flame, smoke billowed out into the hall, and the guard raced up and looked at the holocaust with a stunned expression.

He took a step toward the door, then retreated from it. "Fire!" he bellowed at the staircase, and I heard the cry repeated in the distance, heard a woman screaming, and the sound of feet thundering up the staircase.

"We've got to get everyone out of here!" I shouted, and the guard wheeled on me, his face twisted with rage.

"You drunken fool!" he snarled and sent the glass flying from my hand.

"Look, we don't have time for that!" There was no need for me to play drunk any longer; I could be expected to sober up in the face of this disaster. "Where's Madame de Villemont's room?"

"At the other end of the hall. It's in no danger."

I was headed in that direction before he finished saying it, and I heard him pounding after me. "Wait! Hold it, or I'll put a bullet into you!"

I was sure he wouldn't, and I was right. I found the room at once because its door was already open a few inches and a frightened Djilana was peering out of it.

"Is Madame inside?" I demanded.

"Yes, what is it?" Djilana said fearfully. "Is there danger?"

"Great danger. A fire. You and Madame must go downstairs at once."

Then the guard was there, menacing me with a drawn gun. "Get away, damn it! You're not supposed to be here."

Djilana wailed like a lost soul. "He said there was a fire."

"It's nothing. It won't hurt you if you stay where you are," the guard assured her, but when her voice rose even louder in hysterical appeal to Allah, he said resignedly, "All right, all right, stop your howling and get downstairs with Madame."

"And tell her to bring her passport," I called over his shoulder. "Monsieur de Gonde wouldn't want it left lying around."

"Yes, yes, the passport too," Djilana said as she popped out of sight behind the door.

"All right," the guard told me, "now move."

He shoved the gun into its holster and followed close on my heels as I went back along the hallway. I had to get rid of him within the next minute or two, but this wasn't the time or place. A crowd of OEI men were now gathered around the door to my room furiously wielding extinguishers under the direction of Georges and Claude de Gonde.

It was a bad moment going past them but no one took notice of me as I slipped by and knocked at the colonel's door. Then I pushed open the door and strode into the room to see the colonel snoring away where I had left him.

"Give me a hand," I said to the guard who was watching from the doorway. "This smoke will choke him to death if we leave him here," and when the guard leaned over the other side of the bed he made the target I wanted. I hit him flush on the jaw, hit him another crusher for insurance as he sagged forward, his eyes blindly turning up in his head, and he went face down on the bed. In my fighting days Louis had sometimes mourned my lack of killer instinct. He would have had no complaint this time.

When I left the room I saw Anne and Djilana just starting down the staircase, pressing close to its banister to stay clear of the men dragging the garden hose up the steps. It wouldn't be long before the fire was under control and de Gonde could take notice of what else was going on around him. Following Anne down the staircase at a distance, all I could do was pray that Matilde would have the car outside on schedule.

The staircase led down to the entrance hall, the door to the outside world beyond was wide open, and the men supposed to serve as watchdogs there were busily uncoiling the hose snaking past them. With Anne standing hesitant near the door, it was the perfect time to make a break for it. But there was no car to be seen.

My watch said it was past eight-thirty. I stopped short midway on the stairs, wild with rage at Matilde. I couldn't stand frozen into inactivity like this, but in which direction should I move? The guard in the colonel's room would be stirring out of his coma at any minute, ready to sound the alarm against me. Could I risk losing sight of Anne and that open door to go back to the room and see to it that the man was gagged and bound?

Caught up by this question, I saw the headlights sweeping around the driveway without at first realizing what they meant. Then, as the gleaming whiteness of the Ferrari pulled up before the door with a screech of brakes, I was jolted into action.

What followed had a weird quality. I knew I was moving as fast as I could, but I felt as if everything was taking place at the maddening tempo of a slow-motion film. And I was not only performing in the film but was helplessly watching it unreel. At the same time that one Reno Davis was approaching Anne and putting an arm around her waist so that she gasped and tried to pull away before she saw who it was, the other Reno Davis stood apart, cursing the tedious amount of time every action took.

Then Anne saw who it was, and her body relaxed, yielding to me with relief. But only for an instant. She suddenly stiffened in resistance. "No," she said breathlessly. "I gave Claude my word we'd never see each other again."

"That's too bad." I was half carrying her toward the door.

"Walk, damn it," I said harshly for the benefit of the men at the door who were now watching us narrowly. "Don't you have sense enough to get out of a building when it's on fire?"

It worked. We walked past the guards, Djilana trailing behind us, and now we were outside the building and the car was only a few steps away. But Edmond Vosiers barred the way to it, his face almost comical with bewilderment. I saw Matilde, too, her face a mask showing nothing, and beyond her, Gabrielle de Gonde and the Comtesse de Laennac and a huddle of domestics, all turning to watch as I steered Anne toward the car, Vosiers making way for us as if he were moving in a dream himself.

As voices faded into silence, I became aware of the throbbing of the car's motor, the sweetest music I could have heard then.

Assurance, Louis used to say. *You can get away with anything as long as you behave with assurance.*

With assurance, I opened the car door and pushed Anne into the seat. She looked up at me with the same expression of bewilderment as Vosiers, but before she could speak I said, "It's all right. You'll feel better out here in the air."

Vosiers suddenly woke from his dream.

"What is this?" he demanded savagely. "What the devil is going on here?"

"This." I drew the gun from my pocket and leveled it at him. He stared at it incredulously, and in back of him the guards made a tableau of impotent fury as I slid behind the wheel of the car, the gun fixed on its blubbery target.

Only Matilde Vosiers dared break the spell.

"Shoot him!" she cried frantically to the guards. "He's trying to get away! You have your orders! Shoot him!"

It was her last hope, and she knew it. So far I had failed to live up to my part of our bargain, but if those men reached for their guns I might yet have to. It was such a little thing to ask. One bullet, and her husband would be paid for all his sins against her.

"For God's sake, no!" Vosiers shouted to his men in a high-pitched, quavering voice, and then I had the car rolling along the driveway, picking up speed as it entered the avenue of cypresses. A man with a leashed dog stood at the edge of the road, and as I passed he made a futile gesture at me and the dog lunged snarling at the car. There was no other sign of life along the way, no obstacle showing ahead.

"Listen to me," Anne said. "It's too late for this!"

I disregarded her, keeping my eyes on the rear-view mirror, waiting to see a glare of headlights move up behind us. Then I saw it and slowed down a little to make sure my route could be followed. As the car slowed, Anne suddenly threw open the door ready to jump. I flung her back into her seat and pulled the door shut, but immediately she started to open it again. Coolly and deliberately I slammed the back of my hand against her cheek. She made a choked sound of pain, then set her teeth against any further outcry and sat looking with blind defiance ahead of her.

"Let's get one thing straight," I said. "The police want me on a murder charge that I can't beat without Paul as my witness. And nobody in your gang intends to go along with that because they know it means the end for them. So now you and I are going to Venice to get Paul. It's as simple as that. But if you try any more tricks along the way, I'll take my chances on going straight to the police, no matter what it costs me or Paul. Unless you're with me in this all the way, there's nothing else I can do."

"You can do what Claude wants you to," Anne said. "Go to South America—"

"Sure, by way of Valence, which is where you and I are supposed to be found dead in an accident tomorrow. Neat, isn't it? A murderer gets his weak-minded lady friend to help him escape the law, and they pile up their car in the attempt. Too bad for her, say the police, but it sure as hell serves him right."

"Ah, no," Anne whispered, "dear God, no." But the look in her eyes as they stared wide-open at the brutal truth made it plain that she believed me.

"Dear God, yes," I said remorselessly. "And that means no more nonsense about turning back. Is that understood?"

"Yes."

"All right. Do you have your passport with you?"

She pressed a hand against the pocket of her cardigan. "Yes."

"Remind me to thank Djilana for that. Do you know where Paul is?"

"No. But Claude said he was with his grandmother and that they'd meet me in Saint-Tropez at the end of the week."

"Just in time for the funeral. Look, Vosiers happened to mention they were in Venice. Does that sound plausible?"

"Yes, the Montecastellanis have a summer place there on Torcello." Anne's voice broke. "But they'll take him somewhere else if they know we're trying to get to him, won't they?"

"If," I said.

To the north lay Paris; to the south Dijon—Milan—Venice. I swung the Ferrari north to Paris and bore down hard on the gas.

PART FOUR

The
Hanged Man

1

It was Georges who had once enviously remarked to me that Madame Vosiers' Ferrari was easily the fastest car in the family's garage, and now I was staking everything on that. I drove with a heavy foot on the accelerator, my hand on the horn to warn aside the scattered traffic along the way, but the traffic kept me from going all out, and the big Mercedes limousine trailing us clung to us like grim death.

Then at last I was on a deserted stretch of highway where the Ferrari could give me everything it had. Here the road was full of unexpected twists and turns, the glimmering canal on one side and an endless line of trees on the other seemed to cut right across my way again and again, and I had to fight the wheel to keep the car under control at this speed, the tires screaming as we wildly slewed back and forth. It was like racing along a course on which barriers were set at random angles so that you never knew when you would crash into one. The speedometer rose to the two-hundred-kilometer mark, passed it and kept rising. Then the headlights of the Mercedes began to dwindle smaller and smaller until they were dots of light that finally disappeared completely.

This was what I had been waiting for.

"Brace yourself!" I shouted, and as Anne thrust her hands against the dashboard I ruthlessly jammed on the brake, the car skidding lengthwise across the road, the smell of burning rubber pungent in the air. I didn't have time to study the terrain. I simply picked an opening between two trees and headed for it. The car rocked, bounced, and nosed downhill, coming to rest with the front wheels in a drainage ditch that ran along the foot of the low embankment on which the trees had been planted.

I switched off the lights and scrambled up to the head of the embankment, where I threw myself flat to watch the road. The Mercedes had not been as far behind me as I had thought; it roared past almost at once.

I slid down the embankment to the Ferrari and jockeyed it uphill in reverse.

"Now what?" Anne said as we turned south toward Dijon. "Italy?"

"Yes."

"We'll never make it. They'll be watching for us along every road across the border. You don't know them the way I do."

"That's a safe bet." I reached a hand behind me and felt the outlines of a valise propped against the seat. A cheap valise. It seemed to be made of cardboard. I lifted it and placed it on Anne's lap. "Open that and see what's in it."

She bent over the valise exploring it. "A jacket and trousers, a few pairs of socks in a paper bag, toilet things, some other clothing. What am I supposed to find in it?"

"Money and a railroad ticket to Milan. Look again, damn it."

She did. "Wait, there's something besides socks in this bag. Money and a railroad ticket. But what good is just one ticket?"

"What good would the other be without a passport to go along with it? How much money is there?"

Anne switched on the dashboard light and riffled through the banknotes. "A hundred francs."

So Matilde had kept her part of the bargain after all. Some day, if my luck held out, I might still pay her back by sending her husband to jail or the guillotine.

I said to Anne, "Do you have any money with you?"

"No."

"Any jewelry, anything negotiable?"

"Only my wedding ring." She started to strip the narrow gold band from her finger, and I said, "No, hold on to it. We'll cash it in if we have to, but even with what we can get for it we'll be on short rations."

"How short? Remember I don't have anything with me at all. I can't travel very far like this. I'll need some clothing and a few other things. A hundred francs is worse than useless if you're serious about getting to Venice."

She wasn't complaining, I realized, but only stating the case as she saw it. It struck me then that nothing in her way of life had equipped her to understand the value of money in small denominations. The casual shoes she was wearing cost more than a hundred francs, the evening gowns that filled her closet cost a few thousand each, the car we were in cost seventy or eighty thousand. To her, a hundred francs—twenty life-giving dollars—was what one stuffed into her purse for lunch money and a pack of cigarettes.

I said, "Let me put it like this. If you don't mind sitting with the peasants, train fare in sunny Italy comes to about five francs an hour. Since it's four hours from Milan to Venice, we allow forty francs for travel and ten more for getting around Venice. The food bill won't break us either. We can get a couple of days' worth of bread, cheese, and wine for twenty francs. That means we're left with thirty francs to luxuriate on. You can have half of it for your shopping."

"You're joking."

"The hell I am. Now put that money and ticket into your pocket and keep a hand on them. Do you speak any Italian?"

"Very little."

"Just as well. It means less chance of your giving the game away."

We reached the Dijon station ten minutes before train time, and I parked in a side street a block away from it.

"Listen carefully," I said, "because this is what you're to do step by step. You buy whatever Paris papers they have on the stand, then wait in the ladies' room until the train pulls in. Have you eaten dinner?"

"No."

"Then get a few chocolate bars, too. When the train comes in go straight to the compartment and make sure the window-shade is closed. The berth will probably be made up, but if not, tell the attendant you don't feel well and want it made up right away. And see if you can't take care of the customs declaration first thing. Got that?"

"Yes, but where will you be?"

"Hiding this car. It's too conspicuous to be left out in the open. Someone might recognize it."

"But if I'm left all alone and anything goes wrong—"

"Nothing can go wrong," I said, wishing I could believe it. "Now give me the compartment number."

Anne held the ticket under the dashboard light. "Compartment 2, Car 8."

"I'll meet you there. Get going. We don't have much time left."

She got out of the car, lugging the valise after her, and as she closed the door she said, "Please watch out for yourself."

"It's a little late for that, isn't it?" I said, and she looked as if she had been slapped across the face again. Then she turned sharply away and started down the street.

I found a garage on the next block, the man in charge getting ready to pull down its sliding door and call it a day. "Closed! Closed!" he cried, waving me back, and had to jump aside as I shot the car up across the sidewalk and into a filthy, oil-reeking interior.

He ran around to confront me as I emerged from behind the wheel. "*Peut-être vous avez le coco fêlé?* Stones in the head maybe? Didn't you hear me say I was closed? Isn't twelve hours a day enough time to give the lousy customers?"

"Cool off," I said. "I'm in no hurry. You can do the job tomorrow."

"What job?"

"Check the points, that's all. I'll be around in the afternoon to pick her up."

He was taking in the lines of the Ferrari now like a man studying Brigitte in a towel. "Well—" he said.

The train was pulling in when I got to the station on a dead run. I saw Anne climb aboard, but I laid back out of sight until the engine piped its departure warning before I sprinted for a car down the line. When I stepped into its vestibule, the train was already sliding out of the station. It gained speed, rattled over switchpoints, and was on its way southward through the darkness.

There were three cigarettes in the pack Jeanne-Marie had brought me at breakfast time, and even though it would be a long night ahead, I lit one now. I was on edge to take cover, but I had to make sure the train attendant was out of Anne's compartment before I got there. The cigarette might make me look a little more at ease while I lounged in the vestibule.

It might have made me look a little too much at ease. A party of sprightly, middle-aged women, American tourists led by a fussy little courier, crowded past me on the way to their berths, and one of them, a prairie version of Matilde Vosiers, regarded me with bright-eyed interest.

"God, these Frenchmen," she loudly whispered in pure mid-western American. "Look at that gorgeous thing, Adele," whereupon they all turned to examine me as they filed by, so that I felt like something behind bars in a zoo.

By the time I finished my cigarette, the corridors ahead were empty. I reached Compartment 2, Car 8, without running into any inquisitive officials along the way, found the door unlocked, and stepped inside, locking it behind me.

Anne was standing there in the narrow aisle between the made-up lower berth and the commode cabinet, which was about all the standing space the compartment offered. She looked completely unstrung.

"I'm glad you showed up," she said with a weak attempt at the light touch. "I was just getting ready to panic."

"Nothing to panic about. Did you get a customs declaration from the trainman?"

"Yes, I already signed it and gave it to him along with my passport. He has the money, too. I told him to change it to lire. And I asked about connections to Venice. He said we'd get into Milan at three in the morning, and a train to Venice comes through there about four. Otherwise, we could stay on board here in the Milan station until seven."

"Why would we want to do that?"

"It wasn't my idea. He seemed to think the early train to Venice wasn't my style. It's all third class."

"But the price is right and we'll be in Venice while your friends are still hunting around Paris for us."

Anne's nostrils flared. "Do you have to call them that?" she demanded.

"All right, just keep your voice down. You can be heard right through these walls. You're supposed to be traveling solo in here."

"Then what happens when the conductor comes back with the passport and money? Where will you be? There's no place in here to hide."

"You don't have much confidence in this deal, do you?"

"No. I want to have, but I don't."

"Then just do what I tell you to do. I trust you're wearing something under that dress?"

"The minimum."

"That's enough. Now get out of your things and hang them on those hooks so they're in plain sight. The shoes and stockings you can put on the commode."

She hesitated momentarily, but then obediently undressed while I stowed the gun under the pillow and stretched out on the bed. An extra blanket had been tightly rolled into a protective cushion between berth and wall, and I unrolled it and threw it over me. After Anne slipped under the covers I switched off the ceiling light so that the compartment was lit only by the pallid glow of the reading lamp at the head of the bed.

Anne was, in fact, wearing the stark minimum of underwear, and her body, where my hand met it, was cold gooseflesh. But she didn't flinch at my touch or try to withdraw from it.

"Can you reach the lock on the door from here?" I asked.

She stretched out an arm to test this. "Yes."

"Then when the trainman comes back, open it like that and take the passport and money without letting him in."

"What if he wants to inspect the valise?"

"He won't. Now let's see that newspaper. Which one is it?"

"*France-Soir.* It was the only one they had from Paris."

My spirits rose as I scanned the first few pages. There was no mention of Louis' murder in them, and that could mean it

hadn't stirred up enough interest to warrant a general alarm.
Then on page four I was handed the bad news. My picture was
there—an old one lifted from the sports files—and below it was
a detailed account of the killing. I read it, and it was like reading the prosecution's case against me as prepared by Léon
Becque, an airtight, unbeatable case.

I showed the news story to Anne and she nodded. "I read
it while I was waiting for the train."

"Is it the same story Claude told you about me?"

"Yes."

"Did you believe him?"

"He didn't pretend to believe it himself." She closed her
eyes and lay there quiescent. Then she said in a remote voice,
"When he told me it was your best friend I knew it was Louis.
It was horrible."

"Was it?" I said viciously. "I didn't know Louis meant that
much to you."

"I knew what he meant to you."

"Very touching."

"Oh, God," Anne said, "if you can't understand how I—"

"Never mind that. The man who killed Louis was the same
one who delivered Paul to his grandmother afterward. Who
is he?"

"I don't know. Probably someone sent by Charles Leschenhaut."

"Leschenhaut?"

"He's the head of the whole organization," Anne said wearily.
"He does the planning. He gives the orders."

So that was it. When I had stupidly let Leschenhaut know
I couldn't work with him on my stories the coming weekend
because Anne had other plans for me, he already suspected
what those plans were. And when his spy, Léon Becque,
brought Eliane to Véronique's apartment the next evening to
celebrate their engagement, he had learned enough to confirm
the suspicions.

I told Anne this. "It was my fault for being so damned gul-
lible," I said bitterly.

Her eyes opened wide, fixed on the curve of the ceiling over us.

"When it comes to adding up faults," she whispered. "When I think what I've done to you—"

I didn't argue that. It was only the truth.

"And Sidney Scott?" I said.

"Yes."

"What really happened to him?"

"They killed him."

"Who did?"

"All of them. They called me up that night to say Madame Cesira was dying and that I was to have Sidney drive Paul and me to Île Saint-Louis right away. They killed Sidney there. They drowned him in the bathtub the way you'd drown a helpless animal. I didn't see it because when I came in they gave me a drink with something in it that knocked me out completely. But Gabrielle de Gonde told me about it afterward. She enjoyed telling it to me, the sweet-faced, hypocritical bitch. How easy it was when you just lifted someone's ankles out of the water—"

"Why did they kill him?"

"Because I told him everything so he'd help Paul and me get out of the country. And that same evening he went to Bernard about it. I didn't know he trusted Bernard completely, didn't know they were lovers, until it was all over."

"So the whole story you handed the police—?"

"It was Leschenhaut and that doctor who runs the sanitarium—Dr. Linder—who made up the story."

"And," I said, "when Max Marchat, your nice respectable lawyer, read the transcript of the police interview he suspected you were lying. After a while he made the mistake of asking people embarrassing questions, and that was the end for him."

"How do you know about it?"

"Because once you know the OEI it's easy to work out the answers. Do you want to know another answer I just worked out? It's pretty risky handing over a quarter of a million dollars a year to an outfit like the OEI, what with all the snooping bank officials and tax collectors who might get curious about it. But you can hand it over by losing it in installments to someone named Spinosi who runs a gambling joint in Saint-Cloud. He doesn't keep the money for himself. He's an OEI agent and passes it on to them, doesn't he?"

"Yes."

"So with Leschenhaut the president of the club and Spinosi the treasurer, what does that make Morillon? Sergeant-at-arms? Chief executioner?"

I felt Anne stiffen at this, but she said nothing.

"Well?" I said angrily.

Still Anne remained silent. The infatuation for Morillon might have withered, but a loyalty remained, a feeling compounded of experiences shared, of torrid sessions in bed—

"Could I have a cigarette, please?" Anne said in a strained voice.

I had the pack halfway out of my pocket, then shoved it back. "I only have a couple left. If you don't have your own, you'll have to do without."

"Then I'll have to do without."

After that, she lay, hands clasped on breast, like the effigy of a crusader's wife on a sarcophagus lid. It was a knocking at the compartment door which started her out of that position.

"Madame, I have your passport and money."

I swiftly doused the reading light, drew the blanket over my head, and got a grip on the gun under the pillow.

"All right," I whispered, "you know what to do."

I felt Anne shift her position, heard the snick of the door bolt.

"The passport, madame. And this packet contains the twelve thousand lire."

"Thank you very much."

"But, madame, one must sign a receipt for the money."

I held my breath as Anne slipped out of the berth.

"The signature goes right here, madame. Ah, there we are. Good night. Sleep well."

The door closed; the bolt snapped back into place. Half-smothered, I threw aside the blanket and turned on the light.

My hot elation wasn't cooled any by the sight of Anne as she stood there, a few scanty inches of silk and lace this side of naked.

I had to force myself not to stare.

"We got away with it after all," I said.

"I think we did."

Anne put the passport into the pocket of the sweater on its hanger, handed me the money, and, without self-consciousness, slipped back into the berth. I reached for the light switch, pleasurably aware of the pressure of that bare shoulder and smoothly rounded hip against me as I moved, and Anne said, "No, leave the light on."

"Why? Afraid of the dark?"

"Yes."

I saw she meant it. I pulled out my crumpled pack of cigarettes and offered her one. "Maybe this'll help."

"How kind of you," Anne said coolly as she took a cigarette. Then holding it up in clear view, she slowly and deliberately shredded it to bits between her fingers and let the fragments sift to the floor.

The train roared through the farmlands of the Jura toward Switzerland, the compartment ceaselessly rocking and swaying, its walls creaking in a hundred different keys. And Anne and I lay wedged against each other in the narrow confines of that berth like a pair of prisoners chained together body to body, hating it, but at the same time—and I was sure this was as true of her as it was of me—feeling an uneasy excitement in the contact.

2

It looked strangely like a canal, but I knew it must be the Truckee River because of the Nevada state markers stuck into the ground along its banks. I was running away from home again, only this time, instead of taking the highway out of town, I was going to keep under cover of the thickets beside the river until I reached the California line. But the thickets held me fast, and whatever monstrous thing was following me was closing in now. Fire was the answer. Pine cones hung like belts of grenades from the scrubby trees around me, and all I had to do was hurl one at the pursuing Thing to send it up in a burst of flame. I reached for a pine cone. It was made of crumpled newspaper which turned to ashes when I touched it and floated like snowflakes to the ground. And the Thing thudded toward me with leaden steps—

I opened my eyes, quaking with terror. Around me was a reflection of dim light on metal, a luggage rack, a dark rectangle of window shade. Compartment 2, Car 8, of the Paris-Milan night express.

Anne lay against me deep in sleep, her cheek against mine, her arm across my chest. The sound of her regular breathing was the only thing to be heard in the eerie silence around us. Silence? That meant the train was standing still.

The silence was suddenly broken. A thump of footsteps in the corridor. Heavy, authoritative footsteps. And an authoritative voice.

"*Alors, chaque compartiment, vous comprenez.*"
French, but with a strong Teutonic flavor.
"*Oui, Monsieur l'Inspecteur.*"
I gently placed my hand over Anne's mouth. Her eyes opened, wide and staring.
"It's the police," I whispered. "Don't make a sound."
She nodded, and I withdrew my hand from her mouth. As noiselessly as I could, I climbed over her to the floor, switched off the bed lamp, and pulled up the window shade. The window was opaque with mist. When I cleared a patch of it with my fingertip I saw no human figures in the bluish, glass-distorted light outside, so I took the chance of raising the window and leaning out to look around.
An icy cold instantly enveloped me. The ground was covered with a crust of snow that glittered under powerful fluorescent lights; the only thing moving against the whiteness was a feather of steam from beneath the car ahead. I leaned out still further. Up the line loomed the black maw of a tunnel entrance.
I drew back into the compartment as a couple of uniformed men descended from the next car and walked briskly past me under the window, their shoes crunching in the snow.
"Where are we?" Anne whispered. "It's freezing."
"Simplon, I think. We're right near the tunnel. The Swiss police must be checking every train from Paris. Look, there's only one way out of this. We got away with it before; we'll have to try it again."
"But it's the police! If they walk in here and turn the light on—"
"That's what I want them to do. And what I want you to do right now is wait until I give you the signal, then scream your head off."
I cautiously pulled the compartment door open and took my place in the berth.
"But, Reno—"
"Shut up and listen. When they come in, tell them you screamed because a man ran in here and went out through that window. That's all there is to it. Now get that blanket over me

and crowd against me as close as you can. And don't do anything until I tell you to."

We waited. Those heavy footsteps moved down the corridor like approaching doom. There was a peremptory rapping
at the door of the next compartment. Then that guttural
French.

"Open up, please. Official business.."

I pressed my ear against the wall. A grumble of voices, the
official one rising in irritation.

"Regrettable, yes, but it can't be helped, monsieur. The man
is dangerous. And we know he's somewhere on the train. An
entire company of ladies identified him from this photograph."

So the bright-eyed prairie type and her companions had
taken too-good notice of me in the vestibule.

"Now!" I said to Anne.

She started to shiver uncontrollably, her teeth chattering in
her head. "I can't!" It was hard for her to even mouth the words.
"I want to, but I can't!"

"You can, God damn it! Think of Paul. Do you know how
easy it is to drown a helpless little kid? Do you know how he'll
look when they drag him out of the water?"

She screamed then, as if releasing everything pent up in her.
The footsteps next door thundered out into the corridor. The
compartment door banged wide open.

"Madame, what is it? What's happened?"

"A man!" Anne's body strained back against me. "He went
through that window!"

"Through the window? Son of a bitch, he's the one all
right!"

A deeper voice. The Inspector's.

"Naturally! So don't stand there looking out at the scenery,
lump. Follow him! Get after him!"

"He's already out of sight, Inspector. There's no one outside
here."

"Then he crawled under the car to the other side. He'll try
to make for the woods. Madame, forgive me, I know the state
you're in, but did you get a good look at him? Was he the one
in this photograph?"

"I don't know. It happened so suddenly. He just burst in here—"

"Yes, yes, of course. A terrible experience. But he won't be back, I assure you. I'll attend to him myself. A regrettable affair. Regrettable—"

The two official voices rapidly faded out of hearing, but another took their place.

"Madame—" This was the trainman oozing concern. "If there is anything I can do—"

"You can pull down that window, please. And the shade."

"Certainly. Ah, that's better, isn't it? But the train must start to move before the room will warm up properly and God knows how long we'll be stuck here. It's been half an hour already. I'm afraid you have very little chance of making a connection with the four o'clock train to Venice now, so if you wish to sleep late—"

"Wake me when we get to Milan anyhow."

"If you wish. And this time be sure the door is locked after I leave. After all, an attractive woman traveling alone—"

"It's all right. I'll take care of the door. Good night."

"And, madame, on behalf of the entire syndicate of French railways—"

"They're no sorrier about this than I am. Good night. I'm very tired."

"Good night, madame. Sleep well."

I heard him outside in the corridor answering the questions of some excited passengers. The pressure of Anne's body against me eased as she snapped the door lock. When I emerged from concealment she turned toward me, and I put a finger to my lips. Slowly the gabble of voices died away, and dead silence descended on us again. As time went on, I got the feeling that there was no silence in the world more complete and pitiless than that of a train standing motionless in an Alpine pass at midnight. My skin crawled with the tension mounting in me, but I had to stay where I was. The police, failing to pick up my trail outside, would probably return here on the sly to make another search for me. They knew I was aboard the train. They would never let me get away like this.

Anne's eyes were fixed on the ceiling, her lips drawn back, her teeth set. She looked like someone on the rack while its ropes were being tightened.

click—

The sound was almost inaudible. I wasn't even sure that I heard it at first.

—*click, click-click, click-click*—

"We're moving," Anne whispered unbelievingly.

We were. The walls of the compartment groaned. The tempo of the wheels increased. Suddenly a hollow din washed over us. We had entered the tunnel.

I put my lips close to Anne's ear. "We're still not out of this. That was my picture they showed you, wasn't it?"

"Yes. It was the same one they had in the *France-Soir.*"

"Then if the police are on the lookout when we hit Milan, they'll be able to identify me. The best thing is for me to get away when we slow down going through the yards and meet you in Venice."

"No," Anne said.

"I'll be there sometime during the day. All you have to do is wait in the station for me."

"No."

Her tone allowed for no argument about it.

"Fine," I said. "Then what happens when we reach Milan?"

"You'll think of something. You always do."

"Not always, lady. Only when I know what I'm up against." My sense of outrage boiled over. "Jesus, if you'd only told me everything from the start. You trusted me enough to bring me into the house, but from then on—"

"I told Sidney everything. You know what happened to him. I didn't want the same thing to happen to you."

"That was a mistake."

"Caring what happened to you?"

"Oh, why don't you try being honest for a change! What you cared about was having me get you and Paul to the States. All right, that makes sense. But the romance you cooked up between us, that touching love story you were acting out for my benefit—that wasn't the way to do it. There never really was a love story at all, was there?"

Anne took a long time to answer.

"No," she said at last. "There couldn't be."

I had finally forced the truth out of her. From the way it made me feel, it would have been better if I hadn't.

"It's Morillon, isn't it?" I said with cold contempt. "You know what he is, you hate him for it, but you can't get him out of your system, can you?"

"Must we talk about it?"

"Yes. I've always wondered how a woman could let a liar, a murderer—"

"You know he's become that only because he believed in what his organization is doing. He's sacrificed everything for it."

"Why? To make the world what Hitler and Stalin tried to make it? Only this time it would be Charles Leschenhaut who cracks the whip. Remember him? He's the man who made your own son a hostage. He's the man Morillon lies and murders for. But you're willing to forgive Morillon despite that."

"There's no use talking about it! All I want is to get Paul out of danger. I don't care what happens after that!"

"Then you'd better start caring. Do you think you'll be safe anywhere with what you know about the organization? Do you know the first assignment Leschenhaut would give that bastard Colonel Hardee and his Yankee storm troopers if you ever got to the States?"

"I'll find some place—"

"Not until the whole lot of them are finished off for good, and that includes Hubert Morillon. Now answer one question. If the time comes that you can get up in court and testify against him, would you do it?"

She didn't speak, but when she abruptly turned her head away from me I knew the answer. I took hold of her chin and forced her to look at me. Her eyes were glistening with tears.

"You damn fool," I said, almost pitying her, "do you really believe you can keep running the rest of your life? Just because you once thought you were in love with him—"

"More than that."

"More than that?"

"I married him," Anne said. "He's Henri de Villemont, my husband."

3

From the beginning he had been wily as the serpent which, dust-colored, lies in the dust and is not seen. More than anyone else, he was responsible for the creation of the OAS—*l'Organisation de l'Armée Secrète* in North Africa— but he was pleased to have others take the credit. When the *colons* turned against the government in 1960 it was Colonel Henri de Villemont who had directed their forces, although he chose to do it as an anonymity acting through his brothers-in-law. When the generals led the great revolt of 1961 it was this colonel who led the generals, fostered their Napoleonic dreams, soothed their distrust of each other, saw to it that they didn't drag their feet in moments of crisis, but always as a man behind the scene, a power behind the throne.

He was a fanatic but never a fool. He knew there might be setbacks along the way and wanted to be in a position to rally his forces again after them. A man couldn't do this if he were seized as a traitor by the government and left to rot in jail.

Of course, he had the means to function effectively while remaining anonymous. His brothers-in-law, Claude de Gonde and Edmond Vosiers, were leaders among the civilian *colons*. His wife was a childlike American heiress, as ignorant of politics as a kitten, and willing to provide him with whatever funds were asked for. His mother, his most rabid convert, had a ranking place in the influential social circles of the Continent. Above all, his father had been General Sebastien de Villemont, that great warrior, hero of the Republic, friend of de Gaulle and Leclerc, and one of the very first to openly attack Pétain for his betrayal of France to Hitler. The more the known leadership of the OAS came to revere the name of Pétain, the more Colonel Henri de Villemont publicly harked back to his father's condemnation of the old Marshal. Who then could suspect that this young officer had ties to the OAS, or, even more incredible, that he was one of its leaders?

Ironically, it was adoration for the father which had led the son along his treasonous course. There were a good many in the barracks of North Africa who wept openly that black day in 1954 when the shattering news of the defeat at Dienbienphu was announced, but Colonel Henri de Villemont did not weep. He sat alone in his quarters, sick with horror of an image he couldn't rid himself of—the French colors dragged in the dust by a gang of half-naked, dirty little Orientals—and thought of how his father had spent his life fighting for the glory of France and what had now happened to that glory. Dienbienphu was more than a defeat for France, it was a desecration of General de Villemont's memory. And the men really responsible for it—not the soldiers who had led the defeated army, but the politicians in Paris who had betrayed it—might as well have opened the general's tomb and spat on his moldering remains.

So where others wept and got drunk that day, Colonel Henri de Villemont sat dry-eyed and sober, examining the future. It would be the same in North Africa as in Indo-China, he saw. A war of the natives against the masters who had brought them civilization, an endless, dragging war which would finally break the nerve of the politicians and chop another member off the already mangled body of the Empire. There was only one way to avert this disaster. The army itself, the backbone of France, must be ready for the moment when the politicians would cry quits and must then settle with them once and for all.

But even the wiliest serpent may sometimes be detected as it slides through the dust. In 1960 a commission led by that ultra-respectable lawyer, Max Marchat, was sent from Paris to investigate army operations in Algeria and especially the curious activities of the officers there. Marchat himself had quickly been charmed to blindness by the engaging Colonel de Villemont. The colonel's wife possessed a vast fortune. Would Monsieur Marchat consent to act as Madame's legal representative in Paris and keep an eye on her interests for a substantial retainer? Monsieur Marchat, one eye on the lovely Madame de Villemont and the other on the retainer, would. So in his report to Paris there was never a word about certain rumors concerning Colonel de Villemont. After all, would anyone really guilty of treason hire the head of an investigating commission as his lawyer?

But one member of the commission, a trouble-making journalist, was not so easily persuaded. He saw the serpent, he went to work trying to pin its head to the ground, and when he had proven really dangerous he was disposed of in the American style. A car slowly cruised by him as he sat in front of a café in Bougie, a tommygun opened fire, and the journalist, as well as the waiter serving him, was riddled with bullets before the eyes of a dozen witnesses who, under police questioning, turned out not to have seen anything at all.

That was Colonel de Villemont's mistake. The journalist was gone but his notes remained, and when they fell into the wrong hands the colonel was now officially suspect. In the army revolt of 1961 he was marked as one of the OAS leaders; with the defeat of the revolt he knew he was marked for a firing squad.

What now? Suicide? Flight? Surrender?

It was Charles Leschenhaut, ex-priest, ex-Communist, editor of *La Foudre*, inventor of *la méthode*, the beehive society of the future, who provided a happier solution than any of these. The colonel and Leschenhaut had come to know each other well over the past few years; they admired and trusted each other. It was Leschenhaut who had once pointed out that when the OAS had seized power in France it must be transformed into an *Organisation d'Élite Internationale,* make contact with sympathetic organizations in every country, establish *la méthode* as the social system throughout the world.

Did the defeat of the OAS change the big picture, he now demanded of the colonel. Not at all. First, the hard-core leadership of the OAS must take measures to survive the blow. Then they must unit in the OEI and continue their work underground. Above all, this new organization must expand across borders, join with cells of disgruntled Stalinists the other side of the Iron Curtain and parties of gallant and stubborn neo-Nazis and neo-Fascists this side of it, to create an authority bigger than any one state. With Leschenhaut as chief executive of the organization and Henri de Villemont as chief administrator—!

Of all this, of her husband's role in the OAS, of his secret activities, Anne Devereux de Villemont knew nothing, and there was no one in the tight little circle of *colons* around her to enlighten her. No one back in the States to communicate with either. It may have been one reason why Colonel Henri de Villemont was so content with his marriage to this extraordinarily beautiful, but just as extraordinarily naïve and uninformed bride.

When she was five her parents, proper Bostonians, had died in an air crash and she had been taken in charge by an aunt and uncle who had room to spare in their Louisburg Square mansion. By the time she was twelve, the uncle, otherwise a chilly and taciturn man, was taking much more than a kindly interest in her, and so her outraged aunt had shipped her off to Mother of Mercy Academy in the suburbs where she spent the next six years safely out of her uncle's reach. The academy was more cloister than school; life there was narrow and lonely; and young Anne Devereux, shy and withdrawn, answered the loneliness by religious devotion and romantic dreams. The dreams became a reality sooner than she expected. After graduation, she was invited by the parents of a friend to join them and their daughter on a cruise of the Mediterranean, she was introduced to the dashing Colonel de Villemont by an official of the

American consulate in Algiers, and one month later was married
to the colonel.

The first year of marriage was strange and difficult for her.
As a husband Henri was courteous and dutiful, but not much
more. And the ingrown social life of the rich *colons,* the same
people saying the same things over the same iced drinks day
after sweltering day, bored her to distraction, sharpened her
temper and her tongue, sent her into pitched battle against the
members of her husband's family who made it their business
to supervise her every move.

Then, with the birth of her son, life became golden. It didn't
matter any longer that Henri neglected her for his other activities; she had Paul to fill her days. And as it turned out, Henri
was everything as a father that he had not been as a husband.
He adored his son, devoted whatever little time he could spare
from his duties to him, and talked about him to Anne with a
joyous affection he had never revealed for anyone before.

What he did not talk of, what Anne remained ignorant of
until the last possible moment, was his secret life as conspirator.
So when the moment came, she had to be told everything at
once. This behind locked doors with Madame Cesira and Charles
Leschenhaut in attendance as if to make sure the revelation was
properly witnessed.

The cool, dispassionate account of what her husband had
been up to during the past five years was enough to leave her in
a state of shock; what followed was still worse. Tomorrow
morning, the dark-haired, dark-eyed, trimly mustached Colonel
Henri de Villemont would be killed in the line of duty. Tomorrow afternoon, the blond, blue-eyed, clean-shaven, highly Nor-
dic Dr. Hubert Morillon would arrive at Madrid airport for a
conference with the eminent Dr. Felix Linder, who was in
need of a personal assistant in his sanitarium at Issy. Leschenhaut already had the passport ready, right down to its retouched
picture of the colonel. The hair dyes, contact lenses, and scholarly-looking spectacles which would complete the transformation of colonel to doctor were on hand. Most important, a cadaver resembling the colonel had already been obtained from the

morgue and was only waiting to be put to use. Too bad that the dazed, horror-stricken Madame Anne de Villemont had to be given all these details, but her husband had no intention of renouncing wife and child forever, of seeing the wife innocently move toward a bigamous relationship perhaps, and so there was no way of keeping the secret from her. The colonel might be officially dead, but the doctor was certainly going to be part of her life once she and the family were installed in Paris.

Did Madame understand all this? Did she understand that the one secret she must never breathe to another soul on earth was that her husband was still alive and very much kicking? That was Leschenhaut cruelly hammering at her. That was Leschenhaut cruelly saying, "And remember this. If Henri is betrayed through your carelessness or stupidity, it will be your son who answers for it. Wait!" he commanded, as even the imperturbable Madame Cesira started up at this. "Think it over, my friends. See if this doesn't assure that there won't be any betrayal of either Henri or our organization. I know what the child means to all of you. If I didn't, I'd be making a meaningless noise with this warning. But the warning is sincere. If you don't see it my way, just say so now and we'll part company. You'll have to go your own way then. My way lies with the organization."

He had left the room so that they could discuss it among themselves. De Villemont had paced the floor, gnawing his lip, his face drawn. Madame Cesira had sat like a statue of implacable justice.

"This is no joke," de Villemont had said at last. "Charles is a man of his word."

"Would you want him as your partner otherwise?" Madame Cesira had asked.

"True, but—"

"There was many a Roman's son who served as hostage for him," said Madame Cesira. "The child of the great King Francis took his father's place in a Spanish prison. Do you think I love Paul any less than you do? But, as your father always said, duty comes before love, honor before sentiment. This is so more than ever now, with a world at stake and with you the leader of the movement for its salvation. Besides, if your wife behaves herself properly"—Madame Cesira never referred to Anne by name but always as "your wife" or "my son's wife"—"no harm can come to Paul. It's up to her not to become the murderer of her husband and son."

And de Villemont had thought this over and finally nodded agreement. "Yes. It's up to her."

Anne was still in a state of shock when, early the next morning, the corpse resembling her husband was carefully dressed in his uniform, carried to the garage behind the house, propped in the rear seat of the staff car parked there, and driven by Georges to the street before the house where the body, slumped in a dozing position, could be remarked by any bypassers. Behind the curtains of an upstairs window, the family gathered to watch, Anne among them like the spectator at some macabre ritual, dreading to see the spectacle, but unable to take her eyes from it.

Georges left the car standing there and hastened up the steps of the house. The colonel, so the story would go, had forgotten his pistol on his dresser, had ordered Georges to bring it to him. Then down the street appeared a shabby little Citroën which drew up beside the staff car. A man leaped from it and in one quick motion flung a grenade through the rear window of the staff car. The planning had been perfect. It was not a fragmentation grenade that was used but a phosphorous grenade which exploded in a burst of white heat fierce enough to melt steel into boiling liquid. Then there had been a bad moment. A spatter of these boiling droplets struck the bomb-thrower in the face. He cried out and staggered back under the pain, but, half-blinded, managed to get behind the wheel of his own car and make good his escape. Meanwhile, the staff car went up in flames, the body in it incinerated to a charred lump of flesh and tattered uniform. The only clue to the man who had thrown the bomb was a handful of FLN leaflets he had tossed in the air as he sped away—the usual leaflets put out by the Algerian freedom movement demanding an end to French oppression.

Perfect planning. So perfect that the first witness to arrive on the scene was the agent who had been staked out in the house opposite to keep an eye on Colonel de Villemont and make sure he didn't slip the government net closing around him. He was to be arrested that day. The agent could hardly conceal his disappointment that some vengeful Moslem had taken matters into his own hands before the arrest could be made.

So Colonel Henri de Villemont had officially died, and Dr. Hubert Morillon was born. Dressed unobtrusively in mufti, carrying an attaché case filled with medical papers and a correspondence with Dr. Felix Linder, he had briefly joined the mob gathering around the blazing staff car, made a sage remark about the horrors of war, and taken a cab to the airport. It was the last Anne had seen of him until the family was transported to Paris and settled in the house on the rue de Courcelles. By then, plastic surgery, which shortened the nose a trifle and tightened the skin at the corners of the eyes, had transformed him so completely and subtly that she didn't even recognize this blond, blue-eyed stranger when he made his first appearance before her.

With the dossier on Colonel de Villemont marked "case closed, subject deceased," Dr. Hubert Morillon could freely move back and forth across frontiers knitting together the structure of the OEI and carrying out its assassinations (the attempt on de Gaulle in the summer of 1962 had been one of his few failures), but the price paid for this freedom was heavy. Aside from his political activities, the thing dearest to the man's heart was his son, but as Leschenhaut pointed out, it was best not to have any contact with the child until he was grown old enough to share the father's secret. A child's eye might penetrate the disguise, a child's tongue might wag carelessly—it was safer to stay at a distance than risk this. Safer, in fact, to stay away from the house on the rue de Courcelles altogether, because, while the servants knew the secret and could be trusted with it, there were old acquaintances one might run into who could not be trusted the same way. De Villemont's attendance at the dinner party given for Leschenhaut had been in flagrant disregard of this injunction, but he could no longer contain his tormenting desire to meet his son's tutor face to face. He had been hearing things about the young American who occupied his wife's apartment, he would find some way at the meeting of detecting whether or not he was being cuckolded, and according to the evidence presented at that disastrous party, he was sure he was.

Now, although the evidence had been misleading, here I was, lying in bed beside his wife while she told me all this, and doing what I could to remove his son from him. We had little to thank each other for, Colonel Henri de Villemont and I.

"The man who threw the bomb into the staff car," I said to Anne. "Was his name Léon Becque?"

"Not Becque. Léon Schaefer. He was an Intelligence officer in the Legion in charge of interrogating prisoners. He had a horrible reputation for cruelty. Why? Do you know him?"

"Under the name of Becque. He's the witness you just read about in the news story of Louis' murder. But if he got up to testify against me in court, and I could prove he was Schaefer—"

"It's no secret," Anne said. "He was in prison already as an OAS leader. He was released under the general amnesty," and the ray of hope I had seen before me went glimmering out. Algeria was ancient history, Léon Schaefer only a misguided revolutionary who had reformed and settled down to a peaceful civilian life as a rug salesman, and his story in court would remain as potent as ever. In the end, it came down to what I had known all along. The organization had to be completely destroyed at one blow.

I had the power to do that.

While Anne lay in silent reflection, I surreptitiously drew Colonel Hardee's membership list from beneath my belt and looked through it. My heart sank. All I saw were numbers. Page after page of them.

I slipped the papers back under my belt. No question about it, the list was in code. By the time it could be decoded, it would be too late to use it effectively against the OEI. I had plenty of time, however, to lie there and consider how I had risked my chance of escape from the Château Laennac for a handful of waste paper.

The train slowed and stopped briefly at Domodossola and

then sped southward again into a furious rainstorm which sent water sluicing against the window with an impact that sounded as if it were going to shatter the glass. But at least we were in Italy, and I celebrated this by inviting Anne to a breakfast of chocolate bars and then sharing my last cigarette with her.

This time she didn't waste a crumb of it.

4

We made the final leg of the run to Milan at breakneck speed through that steady downpour, and when the attendant tapped on the compartment door and announced we would be at Milan station in five minutes we had gained back enough of the time lost at the tunnel entrance to meet the four o'clock train to Venice. I desperately wanted to be on the train. Otherwise, the head start we had on our pursuers, the element of surprise I was counting on to snatch Paul away from under their noses, might all be dissipated.

The last five minutes seemed interminable as we slowed to a crawl approaching the station, winding this way and that through a maze of rails like a bewildered caterpillar hunting a resting place. Then we glided alongside the platform and came to a halt with a jarring of couplers.

The colonel's lady, whose bed I had been sinlessly sharing, was already up and dressed. She stood before the mirror on the door trying to do something about her tousled hair, her thoughts evidently far away and depressing.

"Never mind making yourself beautiful," I said harshly, and saw this had the hoped-for effect of stiffening her spine. "Just

switch off that light and take a look out of the window. See if
there are any police down at the exit gate."

She did and drew back from the window to report to me.

"It's not easy to tell from here, but I think there are."

"In uniform?"

"No, two men in raincoats, but they're looking at everyone
going through the gate. One of them keeps checking with a
sheet of paper he's holding. It could be that picture of you."

Could be? I knew damn well it was.

I stood there groping for a solution to this problem while
Anne obediently waited for instructions. I found myself enraged with her then for her faith in me, her unspoken confidence that I would now manage to pull a rabbit out of the hat
on demand. After all, she wasn't my woman, and whichever
way it turned out—whether Henri de Villemont destroyed me
or I destroyed him—she never would be. In one case I would
be dead anyhow. In the other case I would have brought about
her husband's death, and no matter how she felt about him now,
that would always lie like a shadow between us. Her upbringing
had been too rigid and narrow to allow logic to prevail. To her
the marital vows were not the amusing ritual they had been to
my ex-wife, but something profound and meaningful. For that
matter, I wasn't sure she still didn't find a powerful attrac-
tion in de Villemont's fanatic courage and virility and mag-
netism—

It was better not to dwell on it. The business at hand was to
get us out of the trap we were in.

Through the window I saw a couple of passengers walk by,
followed by a porter carrying their bags, and then the dimly
lit platform was empty. A baggage car, its doors gaping open,
stood on the track the other side of the platform, and beside it
were parked some handcarts of packages and crates waiting for
the morning shift to come on duty.

I took off my sweater and shirt and stuffed them into the
valise along with the gun and Colonel Hardee's papers, then
knotted my handkerchief around my throat. Too bad I didn't
have Henri de Villemont's resources for disguising myself, but
under the right conditions a grimy undershirt and neckerchief

and an unshaven jaw might serve as well as plastic ~urgery and contact lenses and hair dye.

I said to Anne, "I can't take a chance walking past the conductor. Is there anyone outside who might see me going through the window?"

"Just those men at the gate. But there are some people coming toward them. They probably won't be looking this way while they're checking them out."

"Tell me when they do, and I'll try to make it to that handcart across the way. When I start it moving, grab the valise and get out of here yourself. Use the door at the back end of the car. Then walk fast so that you can get ahead of me on the platform, but not too far ahead. At the gate ask those men a question—ask them where you get the train to Venice—anything, as long as you keep them busy until I get by. Can you do that?"

"I hope so."

"Well, you've got what to do it with." I reached out and pulled open the top two buttons of her blouse. "That's the kind of distraction a pair of cops ought to go for. And get that scared look off your face. Be bright and smiling when you talk to them. Are those people at the gate yet?"

"Yes. No one's looking this way now."

I let myself out of the window, dropped to the platform, and crossed it at a casual pace so as not to draw eyes in my direction. The handcart I had picked for my purpose was piled high with crates; it was the only one in sight that offered me full concealment from anyone I was steering toward. The crates must have contained machine parts, judging from the weight of the load. It took a gigantic effort just to get the cart moving, but once on its way it was not too hard to keep rolling. I had made fair progress when Anne passed me by without a glance, walking briskly, the valise swinging from her hand.

She reached the exit gate a car length ahead of me. Peering around my load of crates, I saw the two men in belted trenchcoats eying her as she approached them at a deliberately provocative, hip-swinging gait. That, added to the tousled hair and the blouse open almost down to the brassiere, seemed to put them into a blissful trance. The only trouble was that they were having the trance squarely in my path, and there was no way around them through the gate.

Both men came to quivering attention as Anne stopped before them.

"*Per favore, signores,*" she said as carefully as if she were reading it by phonetics from a textbook, "*dove il treno a Venezia?*" and the two men glanced at each other with knowing smiles. This knockout came from France, and these French girls—

I could see disaster ahead. They were totally oblivious of the cart which was almost on top of them now, and all I needed was an accident to have them give me their full attention.

There was only one thing to do about it.

"*Ehi!*" I shouted as I braced my heels, trying to drag the cart to a halt. "*Attenti, attenti, idioti!* You want to lose a leg under these wheels? Make up to the girls some place else!"

The men dodged aside just in time as the cart came to a standstill between them, and one of them, the one holding what I saw was indisputably my picture, snarled, "Watch out yourself, stupid. You know who you're talking to?"

"Never mind that," the other told him sharply, and walked around to lend me a hand as I strained to get the cart back into motion. I kept my head averted from him as we heaved together, shoulder to shoulder, heaved again, and then I was through the gate and away, my whole body clammy with tension.

I pushed along steadily, not daring to look around in case the police at the gate still had an eye on me. Ahead were only two trains showing signs of life. One was a sleek streamliner being loaded with ice and provisions, but that, I knew, must be a *rapido* being made ready for the morning run to Rome. The other, further down the shed, was undoubtedly the local to Venice, a couple of shabby, antiquated carriages hitched to a string of dilapidated freight cars. I steered the handcart toward it, and when I felt I was out of eyeshot of the plainclothesmen at the gate, I looked around expecting to see Anne not far behind me.

She was nowhere in sight.

I abandoned the cart where it was and moved to a position from where I could make out the figures of the two men at the gate. I could picture what had happened. Having cornered this luscious French doll with the big blue eyes, they weren't going to let her get away that quickly. Not, at least, until Anne had showed them her wedding ring and a flash of temper. The one holding my picture would be especially hard to discourage. With his wolfish face and trim mustache he looked like a type who fancied himself a real Lothario.

But, incredibly, only the two men were at the gate. No Anne.

And wherever she was, there was the money for the fare to Venice and the clothes that would allow me to travel inconspicuously.

In the few minutes since I had last seen her, I told myself, it was impossible she could have walked into the hands of the OEI. After all, I was its chief target, I was the one marked for its attentions. Yet, if this wasn't an OEI job—

Under any conditions, I couldn't remain where I was, wondering with a sick apprehension what had gone wrong. There weren't more than a dozen people to be seen in the whole vast cavern of the station, and in that emptiness I had the feeling of spotlights trained on me. I walked to the platform where the Venice train was standing and strolled past its two dismal-looking carriages, hoping against hope to see Anne in one of the compartments, trying to convince myself that she might have slipped by me while I was on my way here. Few of the compartments were occupied, none of them by Anne. They were the old-fashioned compartments, each with its own door and with wooden benches facing each other across a narrow aisle, anyone in them as visible as in a telephone booth, so there was no chance of missing her.

Then, as I began to retrace my steps, I saw her coming toward me, running as well as she could with the valise burdening her, and the apprehension in me turned into savage temper at having been given such a scare. When she breathlessly started to say something I cut her short by snatching the valise from her hand and shoving her bodily into an empty compartment, slamming the door behind us for privacy. I opened the valise on a bench and rummaged through it until I came up with a fresh shirt and a sports jacket. Fully clothed once more, I tucked Colonel Hardee's papers into my new jacket and thrust the gun into my hip pocket.

I turned to Anne, who was sitting there watching me with an expression of mounting bewilderment. "The money," I said. I didn't intend to again find myself in the spot I had just been in.

She wordlessly handed me the roll of banknotes, which seemed considerably depleted, and with it a pair of railroad tickets.

"What's this?" I said.

"The tickets to Venice. They cost five thousand lire so we should have seven thousand left. I didn't count it, but if you—"

"Is that where you were? You didn't have to buy these at the ticket window. We could have gotten them from the conductor. Of all the damn fool tricks—"

"Now listen," Anne cut in angrily. "When I asked that detective or whatever he is where I could get the train to Venice, he pointed to the ticket windows and said that was the place to ask. I couldn't just walk after you then, could I, the way he was watching me? I had to go to the windows. And while I was there it seemed logical to buy the tickets. What did you think had happened to me?"

"Plenty. And you can button up your dress now. The detective or whatever he is isn't looking any more."

"That's unfair!" She was so furious that she almost tore the buttons off, fumbling them into place. "I grant you've got reason to hate me, but not for this. Not for trying to help when I can."

"That's because I don't have your husband's charming disposition. You know, it would be interesting to see which of us he'd kill first if he walked in here right now and—"

As if timed with my words, the outside door to the compartment suddenly swung open. Anne gasped and cowered away as I whirled to confront the man looming in the doorway, my hand reaching for the gun in my pocket.

Then I saw I didn't need the gun. It was not Henri de Villemont who stood there, but a monk swathed in a robe which was the color and texture of an old khaki blanket and was belted with a piece of rope. He was carrying a worn carpetbag that looked a relic of a century ago. When he sat down and threw back his cowl, he revealed a freshly shaved tonsure and a bland, moonlike face with eyes that seemed distorted to twice normal size behind the powerful glasses he wore.

A man may be willing to fight lions barehanded, but not have the nerve to remove himself from someone's company, however unwanted it is. So I sat beside Anne while our traveling companion huddled in his seat facing us, hands clasped in his lap, distorted eyes fixed on us. It was hard to tell whether he saw me at all, or whether he was imprinting the image of my face, feature by feature, in his mind.

Then we were on our slow, racketing way through the city and into open country, sealed in that stifling atmosphere by tightly closed windows. It was no use trying to leave them open. When I did, a spray of rain spattered across all of us. The conductor who entered the compartment to collect our tickets, a fierce-looking little old man with a magnificent white mustache, shrugged at the sight of the wet floor.

"Let it rain in. Let it rain in," he advised. "Drowning is better than frying to death any time."

The monk stirred from his reverie.

"A fine choice," he grumbled. "But tell me, *signor il capitreno,* how long do we fry? When do we arrive at Venice?"

"Who knows? We have to deliver a can of sardines to every lousy stop between Ventimiglio and Venice. It can take forever. Don't worry about it. You'll have time enough to say all your prayers twice over before you arrive."

"And what about starving to death?" I said. "Is there a stop along the way where we can get something to eat?"

"At this time of morning?" The old man snorted. "Not a chance."

"A cigarette?" I hopefully produced the roll of money. "If you have some to spare—?"

"I smoke a pipe. Cigarettes are an extravagance."

He went his way, leaving me to digest this information under the gaze of those distorted eyes across the aisle.

Then Anne said abruptly, "Let's go out in the corridor."

"What for? It won't make the time pass any faster. You'd do better to try and get some sleep."

"Please."

There was a sharp urgency in her voice. Without further protest I followed her out to the corridor and to the end of the car. She turned to face me there.

"That man isn't a monk," she said.

"What makes you think so?"

"Didn't you see his hands? No monk would have his fingernails done like that. A manicure, nail polish—"

"I'm not an expert on these things."

"You don't have to be! Just use your common sense. It won't be the first time one of Leschenhaut's men has gone around like that and with false papers. And why do you think he got into our compartment when there are so many empties on the train? The best thing we can do is get off as soon as possible and not let him know we're gone. We can leave the valise. That should do it."

"Not if he's really OEI. It wouldn't fool him for a second. Any time the train stops and we're not in the compartment, he'll be watching for us right outside on the platform."

"Then what can we do?"

"I don't know. Anyhow, I'd rather take a chance you're wrong than get sidetracked at some godforsaken village this far from Venice."

That may not have satisfied her, but it silenced her. We returned to the compartment, and now I looked hard at the man's hands which were knotted in his lap. When he moved them to expose the nails I saw what Anne meant. The hands were leathery, blunt-fingered laborer's hands—the nails were conspicuously manicured and gleaming with polish.

The monk took notice of my interest. He looked down at the incongruously pearly nails and then at me.

"They interest you?" he said.

"Yes," I said flatly.

"Ah."

The carpetbag lay on the floor at his feet. He reached down toward it, but I was faster than he was. My hand was on it first, and as he drew back to avoid a collision of heads, I wrenched the bag open and groped inside it for the gun I knew must be there.

But there was no gun, only a greasy package that wafted a garlic aroma to my nostrils, a wine bottle, a cloth sack of what felt like onions, and some oddments of clothing. Too late it struck me that if the man had been carrying a gun, it would certainly be tucked beneath that robe in easy reach. A professional killer on the job would want his weapon where he could get at it instantly.

Feeling like a complete fool, I lifted the carpetbag to the bench beside its owner as if this had been my real purpose, but he easily saw through me.

"What did you expect to find?" he asked without rancor.

"Nothing. It doesn't matter."

He accepted this graciously. "Of course, Signore—?"

"Dulac. Jean Dulac. And this is my wife."

"Ah, yes, French. And not on tour either. Not at this hour and in such wretched accommodations. Perhaps you have some employment in Venice?"

I tried to think what employment I might have in Venice, traveling like this and looking the way I did.

"Yes," I said. "I'm a seaman on a ship docked there now. My wife is a stewardess on it."

"What a happy arrangement. And I, *signore,* am Fra Pietro of the Minorites of San Anselmo. What I had wanted to show you was the reason for my fingers being in this interesting condition." He lifted the bulging cloth sack from the carpetbag and hefted it before me. "Here it is."

"Onions?"

"Tulip bulbs. *Tulipa gesneriana.* For purity of form and splendor of color, the tulip is surely among the most magnificent of God's creations. I am gardener of our monastery in Chioggia and something of an expert on this subject, you see. In fact, a small text I prepared on it was recently published, and I was given the honor of presenting a copy to His Holiness in person. Do you know the *albergo diurno* beneath the railroad station in Rome where one may, for a few lire, relieve himself and wash his hands and face? Or even write a letter or have his clothing mended?"

"Yes."

"Ah. Well, when I arrived in Rome yesterday I stopped there before meeting His Holiness, and I noticed that my nails were a disgusting sight. A proper gardener does not work in gloves, and there are chemicals to handle and other things. A fine business, I thought. His Holiness will take one look at these paws and wonder what kind of pigsty we're living in there at Chioggia. Then I saw this woman dressed like a nurse in the *albergo diurno*—a horrible old crow or I would never have let the idea even enter my head—and she was very skillfully cleaning the nails of a respectable-looking gentleman. Well, I thought, desperate situations require desperate measures; she's the one to solve my problem. But to wind up looking like this! It's not only that His Holiness was obviously taken aback by the spectacle, there are some brothers in the monastery who fancy themselves humorists. I'm going to have a hard time with them, I fear."

I tried to keep my face straight but couldn't, and Fra Pietro wagged a finger at me. "Ah, you see? You yourself find it comical."

Anne had been following this with blank incomprehension. "What's he saying?" she whispered to me. "What's so funny, for God's sake?"

The mention of the name Dulac must have been the cue for her to speak in French, and I gave her credit for quick thinking. But she didn't intend to give me the same credit. When I translated the story of the manicure for her, she said, "And you believe him?"

"He's the real McCoy, *chérie*. Not everyone you meet is like your husband and his gang."

"Damn it, do you have to punctuate everything you say with that kind of remark?"

"We're in the presence of the clergy, *chérie*, so watch your language. And we're supposed to be married. Let's not make it one of those marriages people deplore."

"Of course, darling." Anne gave me a sweet, utterly false smile. "Then do tell the clergy about nail-polish remover. He can get a bottle somewhere around the station and settle his problem before he gets back to Chioggia."

When I passed this on to Fra Pietro, he was cheered considerably.

"I should have realized there would be such a thing. The world always offers us a chance to pay twice over, doesn't it? Once for the folly and once again for its cure. How can I thank you? Perhaps if there is some way I can help you in your trouble—"

I didn't like the sound of that. It suggested he knew more about us than he should.

"What makes you think we're in trouble?" I said.

"Your actions when I entered the compartment and when I wanted to open this bag. Also, these fingernails are more funny than frightening yet your wife seemed terrified by the sight of them. When she took you outside to describe them, you yourself returned in a state of alarm. Both of you behaved as if I were someone who threatened your safety."

"You'd make a good detective."

"Being unworldly does not necessarily mean being unobservant. You are in trouble then?"

"Let's say that I am. Would you be willing to help me without knowing what the trouble is?"

"Under such conditions," Fra Pietro said gently, "I can offer you and your wife consolation and a share of my breakfast. Beyond that—"

"Beyond that, would you offer the *signora* and a child refuge at your monastery if they showed up there during the day? All I can tell you is that they are in danger and should be kept out of sight for a little while."

"Would this be in violation of the law?"

"No."

"Then I will tell our abbot to expect their arrival, and he will see to it that they are taken to a convent nearby for shelter. Our monastery cannot offer hospitality to a woman, but the convent will do very well. The prioress is an obliging soul."

With this settled, Fra Pietro now opened his package of food and insisted we share it with him, so we breakfasted on tough, garlicky chicken, a chunk of hard bread, and some tepid water which, disappointingly, was what the wine bottle turned out to contain. The food raised my spirits a little, and when the rain stopped and the sunrise greeted us at Brescia, I felt fully alive again. Venice, then Torcello and Paul. Then the convent in Chioggia where Anne and the child would be safe while I attempted to knock down the house of cards built by Charles Leschenhaut and Henri de Villemont.

At nine o'clock—it had taken five hours to make the four-hour trip—we rumbled across the causeway over the Laguna Veneta and into the Venice station.

When we clambered out of the compartment Fra Pietro shook my hand.

"One last word," he said. "Change that story about being a common seaman. Your hand is strong, but it's a bit too soft for that line of work. At least promote yourself to ship's officer. It would be more convincing."

With that, he gave Anne a kindly nod, drew the cowl over his head, and trotted off toward the bus stand outside the station.

5

Anne was already heading toward the staircase leading down to the taxi stand on the Grand Canal when I caught up to her and brought her to a sharp standstill.

"Where do you think you're going?" I said.

"If you don't intend to waste time—"

"I don't intend to waste it; I intend to put it to good use. First of all, I'm going to the rest room and shave and clean up so everybody doesn't wonder what the hell I'm up to, looking like this. Especially the police. Meanwhile, you've got some shopping to do over at that stand. Get a couple of pairs of dark glasses— we'll go blind in this sunlight without them—and make sure to buy the cheapest they have. And something to put on your head, a babushka or whatever they call it. You can get us a pack of cigarettes, too, a local brand that doesn't cost much. Is there anything else you can think of that you really need?"

"I didn't come here to shop!" Anne said explosively. "How you can stand there talking like this—!"

Heads turned toward us as her voice rose.

"*Chérie*," I said pleasantly, "*mon ange*, the way I look right now, nobody would be the least bit surprised if I walloped you one for not showing me wifely respect. And that's what'll happen if you don't shut up and follow orders. We didn't get this far by being careless, so let's stick to that policy. Odds are that Claude is in touch with his friends on the police and doesn't know we're across the border yet. Another fifteen or twenty minutes won't change anything except that we'll be able to move around without looking like a pair of freaks just in from rue Pigalle. Is that clear?"

"Yes."

"Now, let's hear what you might need to make you neat but not gaudy."

"A comb. A lipstick. These stockings are torn—"

"The comb, all right. Lipstick and stockings aren't on the budget." I counted out two thousand lire into her hand, trusting that the remaining five thousand would carry us to Torcello and then Chioggia. "After you've done the shopping," I said, "you can freshen up in the rest room and get rid of those stockings. Do you see that table in the corner by the coffee bar?"

"Yes."

"Then meet me there when you're ready. If you're there first, keep a lookout for any of Henri's buddies. I suppose the OEI has a big contingent in Italy?"

"It has in Rome. I don't know about here."

"Well, don't trust any strangers, no matter how plausible they sound. And turn up the other chair at the table so nobody can move in on you."

When I emerged from the rest room, well-scrubbed, freshly shaven, odoriferous with the cheap, flowery toilet water Matilde Vosiers had included in my shaving kit, I found Anne waiting for me at the table. It took me a moment to recognize her. In dark glasses and with a cornflower-blue kerchief concealing her hair, she looked as anonymous as the other women around me who wore variations of sunglasses and kerchief.

She was having a *cappuccino*, and there was one cooling on the table in the place next to hers.

"Anyone bother you?" I said as I sat down to it.

"The usual. That's why I ordered the coffee for you. Having the chair turned up didn't seem to discourage them. That boy standing over there by the bar especially. He's been watching me in the mirror."

"Recognize him? Think he's OEI?"

"I don't recognize him. All I know is he certainly isn't a monk."

I looked into the mirror over the bar and found myself staring into the eyes of an Italian facsimile of Albert, the youthful gunman of the rue de Courcelles. This one, however, wore skin-tight jeans and a black sweater almost as tight, and there didn't seem to be room anywhere in them for a gun. There might be for a knife. The eyes in the mirror narrowed at me, the lips twisted in a little smirk. It was no use drinking *cappuccino* and wondering how safe it was to turn my back on this cool customer. I got up from the table and walked over to him, hand extended in friendly greeting.

"Well, think of running into you here," I said jovially, and when he dazedly offered me his hand in response to my greeting I pumped it with great good will, getting a tight grip on it so that he couldn't pull free. "How are you? And your mama and papa?"

"What are you talking about? I don't know you, do I?" He tried to pull free now, but I gripped harder and saw a look of anguish flash across his face. It was only raw pride which kept him from shouting with pain. "What do you want?" he gasped. "If your wife told you—"

"She told me you recognized her at once." The other patrons at the bar didn't even glance at us as I playfully patted the boy's pockets and arms. There was no weapon on him. "She wondered if you were too stuck up to have a drink with us. Like one of the elite, eh?"

His blank reaction to the meaningful word convinced me that the *Organisation d'Élite Internationale* meant nothing to him. All he wanted to do was get away from here as fast as he could. Who knew what a jealous husband might wind up doing? Especially a jealous husband capable of mashing one's hand to pulp with a little pressure of the fingers.

"I swear to you, *signore*—"

I released the hand. "Then you don't have time for a drink with us? You have to rush away?"

"Yes, yes. Immediately."

He warily backed away from me, then disappeared into the crowd eddying past. When I sat down beside Anne to finish my coffee, she said, "He was harmless, wasn't he? I'm sorry. It's getting so that I suspect anyone who even looks my way."

"That's being smart. Yes, he was harmless. Just one of those characters with an eye out for lonely tourist ladies who'd like a curly-headed guide to show them the town. Forget about him. How far away is Torcello? What's the layout there?"

"Have you been in Venice before?"

"A couple of times, but I never learned my way around." I refrained from explaining that this was not due to any lack of interest in sightseeing, but because in each case the company I brought from Rome—the first time a shapely blonde Briton, and the second time an even shapelier and blonder Swede—confined our activities to a tight little triangle whose points were the Piazza San Marco, the Casino, and the hotel bedroom we shared.

"Torcello's on the north side of the lagoon about five or six miles away," Anne said. "It's a strange place. Quiet and empty. So quiet you wouldn't believe it. I don't think there are more than a few dozen people living on the whole island."

"Where's Madame Cesira's house? Right on the lagoon?"

"No, there's a main canal that crosses the island and a few smaller ones that branch off from it. The house is on one of the smaller ones away from everything. I don't know the name of the canal it's on, but I'd know it if I saw it."

"If we get off at the landing, can we be seen from the house?"

"I think so."

"Suppose we landed further away from the house. Is there any cover along the banks there?"

"A lot of greenery."

"Trees?"

"I seem to remember some."

"Good. Did you get me sunglasses?"

She handed me the glasses along with a pack of cigarettes and a few coins. "That's all the change there was." Then she said, forcing herself to say it calmly, "There won't be any danger to Paul, will there?"

"Not as long as there's no danger to your husband; and he isn't involved in this operation. What kind of staff does the old lady keep at the place?"

"Just a permanent caretaker and his wife who attend to almost everything. And her personal maid."

"No guards?"

"Not ordinarily. But right now—"

"Right now no one's expecting company to drop in. The trick is to walk right in and walk out with Paul before the idea dawns on them that we're close by." I lit a cigarette for each of us, and Anne drew on hers with a long, shuddering inhalation that gave away the state of her nerves. "I wish to hell you didn't have to come along with me," I said. "If there was any way I could find the place without you—"

"You couldn't. Even if you could I want to be there with you. It would kill me, sitting here wondering what was happening. I swear I won't be any trouble."

"Then come on," I said. "It's time to get moving."

6

The taxi man was in shirtsleeves and wore a battered nautical cap on back of his head, but he had all the elegance of a young courtier painted by Bronzino. With kindly condescension he explained that the trip to Chioggia was out of the question. Torcello lay five miles to the north of us and Chioggia fifteen miles to the south. For the money I offered, the best he could do was take us to Torcello, wait while we picked up our son, and then return us to the Riva Degli Schiavoni in the city where there was a cheap public boat to Chioggia. I didn't like the deal but I accepted it. I couldn't offer him more than I had with me because I couldn't afford to risk a scene wherever we docked.

As we left our berth and made a sharp turn across the bow of a barge piled high with crates of Coca-Cola he said to me, "Where in Torcello? The Church of Santa Maria Assunta?"

"No, the Villa Montecastellani."

"I don't know where that is."

"The *signora* will show you where."

He grimaced as if doubtful a woman could find her way anywhere, but devoted himself to maneuvering us through the confusion of launches, gondolas, barges, and *vaporetti* clogging the Grand Canal. Then we steered into the narrow passage of the Riva di Noale where there was no traffic at all, the boat sending a heavy wash against the water doors of the stone buildings on each side. As we emerged into the open reaches of the lagoon and moved away from the city I had a close view of a side of it I had never seen before, a shabby, unglamorous waterfront of coalyards and barge piers and slums baking in the sunlight, a world apart from the Piazza San Marco. Even the water of the lagoon seemed to have nothing to do with the Adriatic whose tides filled it. It was slate-colored, streaked brown here and there by mudflats just below the surface.

Coming abreast of a line of gondolas following each other in precise order, our skipper slowed down so that our wash wouldn't disturb the gondolas. That, I knew, was an unusual courtesy.

"A regatta out here?" I said.

"A funeral, *signore*." He pointed to a small island ahead, a neat rectangle of greenery and marble monuments. "Somebody's getting a ride to the cemetery there. It might look crowded, but there's always room for one more."

We passed through the channel between the cemetery and the island of Murano and sped through silty water toward the string of islands low on the horizon.

"Burano," said the taxi man. "Then Torcello."

Burano was like a last outpost of civilization. Beyond it was a sea of marsh grass, the *barene*, and then a broad canal cutting through an island lush with vegetation. At intervals along the canal were signs of past habitation—a hut standing in a weedy clearing, a stucco mansion in the classical style with half the columns of its portico tumbled down, the roofless, windowless remnants of a stone structure that might have been a church decaying there since the Dark Ages. Somewhere on Torcello, I knew, life was going on, but along the canal we were traveling there was not a soul to be seen. It was as if the inhabitants had gotten warning of plague or invasion and abandoned it overnight.

Anne was staring ahead with the intensity of an explorer searching for the landmarks of a new world. Small canals traversed the main one, and as we approached a canal which looked like no more than a ditch running between stone embankments she suddenly said, "Here. *A sinistra. A sinistra.*"

The driver obediently turned left between the embankments, but shook his head. "The tide is out. There's hardly enough water in here to float a matchstick. And look at the way we have to cut corners."

He skillfully edged the boat around a turn that was almost a right angle, the embankment so close I could have reached out and touched it. "For a man who can handle a boat like you, this is nothing," I said, which was what he wanted to hear.

"Yes, I know my job." He looked more like a Bronzino courtier than ever as he casually spun the wheel with one finger. "But why anyone would want to live in this emptiness—"

That was understandable, coming from a city dweller. On one side of us was a wasteland of marshes. On the other side, the embankment was shaded by elms and weeping willows, and through the trees could be seen fields of wild flowers. The air was rich with the smell of brackish water overlaid by a lush scent of honeysuckle.

Outside of small pylons carrying telephone lines, it was beautiful, unspoiled, and menacing, the way a side stream of the Amazon might be where one saw only the natural splendors around him and not the savages lurking behind the trees with poisoned arrows fitted to their bows.

We inched our way around a bend and came in sight of a narrow footbridge spanning the canal in a steep arch.

"There," Anne whispered. "The boat landing is just past the bridge."

"Cut the motor," I told the driver, and he did. "Pull alongside the embankment here."

"Not here, *signore*. That stone would scrape the devil out of this woodwork. We can tie up to the tub there."

The tub was a small rowboat which was moored to the embankment thirty or forty yards below the bridge. We silently drifted toward it, and the boatman dexterously tied a line to its seat. He offered me a steadying hand as I stepped into the bobbing rowboat and up to the embankment, and then I saw that Anne was following.

"Wait here," I said.

"No. You might need me with you."

I might at that. And since she was already standing beside

me on the embankment with the boatman interestedly watching us from below, it was no time to make an issue of it.

"All right," I said, "but you're not to make a move unless I tell
you to."

"I won't."

There was another rowboat upside down on the ground beside the embankment, a splintery oar and some primitive fishing tackle resting against it. As I walked around it, Anne close
on my heels, the mossy loam underfoot yielded like a sponge.
It felt like the kind of ground where you could drop a seed and
have it take flower while you watched. There was a barely dis-
cernible path leading through a small grove of trees beyond,
and I followed it to what had once been a lawn but was now
a patch of untrimmed grass carpeted with marigolds. I pulled
up short before we reached this clearing and drew Anne behind a tree which kept us out of sight of anyone in the house
on the other side of the lawn.

It was not the home I had imagined Madame Cesira would
choose, not even as a temporary dwelling. It was the kind of
ugly, utilitarian box a prosperous Tuscan farmer might have
built for himself, and the only things to mask its ugliness were
the heavy growth of wisteria vine covering its walls as high as
the second-floor shutters and its two chimney pots, the classical Venetian chimney pots shaped like the funnels used as
smokestacks on old-fashioned steam locomotives.

Several pairs of shutters were swung open against the vine-
covered walls and a wisp of smoke trailed from one of the funnels, so there was a good chance someone was at work in the
kitchen.

"Where is the kitchen?" I said to Anne.

"Around the house, inside the back door."

"All right, that's where we're going." I drew Matilde Vosiers'
automatic from my pocket and checked it to make sure the
safety was on. "I don't expect to use this, so don't worry about
it."

"I'm not worried about it," Anne said between her teeth. "I'll
be glad to use it myself."

"Forget it. We're here to get Paul away, not start a war. The first job is for me to get up against the wall of the house. You follow when I give you the signal."

I scanned the windows where gauzy curtains hung limp in the lifeless, humid air. If anyone was on guard, gun in hand, behind those curtains, it would be all over for me before I got halfway across the lawn. I closed my mind to the thought, took a deep breath, and plunged across the lawn to the shelter of the house wall, rank grass and marigold stems whipping my legs as I ran. The ivy covering the wall was in flower and swarming with bees, but compared to bullets they were a positive pleasure.

I waited to see if any alarm had gone up in the house, then when silence still prevailed I signaled Anne to join me. Keeping against the wall we made our way cautiously to the back of the house.

What met the eye there was a scene of peaceful domesticity. A line of laundry hung drying in the sun, a few plump chickens *cut-cutted* back and forth beneath it, a pair of milch goats, their udders sagging, stood masticating some vine leaves. But what caught and held the eye was the girl lying spread-eagled on a blanket in the middle of the scene.

She lay on her back in deep slow-breathing slumber, arms and legs outflung as if inviting the sunlight to fill every pore, and her face and body gleamed with oil. A tall, slender girl, very young—she couldn't have been more than fifteen or sixteen— she wore the absolute minimum of bikini, the halter of which had been untied so that it was simply draped across the small, pert cones of her breasts.

I motioned Anne to remain where she was and stealthily crept up to the girl. Close up, I saw she was a Florentine type, blonde, fair-skinned, and with the sharply chiseled little nose one finds on Florentine portraits as far back as the de'Medicis. The closed eyes were probably gray. When I nudged the girl's shoulder with the gun the eyes opened, and they were gray. I aimed the gun between them and put a finger to my lips in warning.

A momentary fear showed in the eyes as they stared into mine, then it was replaced by a veiled interest. Either the girl found me more entertaining than menacing or she didn't appreciate the situation at all. Whichever it was, when I gestured her to stand up she did so with lithe ease, casually tying the bikini halter behind her as if to provide me with the best possible view of the breasts thrusting against it. Only when Anne appeared from around the house did the girl grasp that she wasn't the real object of my interest. She looked disappointed.

I turned her about-face and got my left arm tight around her naked, oily waist so there would be no chance of her breaking away and making a dash for it. That way I steered her toward the kitchen door, Anne following close behind.

"Who's inside the house?" I said into the girl's ear.

"My mother."

"Who else?"

"No one."

I didn't like the sound of that. I rapped on the door with the gun. The tall, handsome woman in housedress and apron who opened it and stood gaping at us bore a striking resemblance to the girl.

"Be quiet," I warned, "and nothing will happen to your daughter."

The woman glared at me. "Then take your dirty hands off her. Ah, *sciattone!*" she spat at the girl. "Pig! What did I tell you about going around naked?"

"Never mind that," I said. I shoved her back into the kitchen and we all followed, Anne closing the door behind us.

Recognition dawned in the woman's eyes as Anne moved toward her. "Signora de Villemont! So it's you, is it?"

"It is. Where is my son, Signora Braggi? Where is Paul?"

"Gone." The triumph in Signora Braggi's voice left no doubt that she was telling the truth. Anne swayed and braced a hand on the kitchen table to steady herself, and Signora Braggi openly gloated over this sign of weakness. In fluent French she said, "Gone an hour ago or more. Dr. Morillon himself came to take the child and Madame Cesira to the airport on the Lido. What more is there to say? Now tell this animal to take his hands off my daughter. For all her stupidity she's a decent girl. There's no need to punish her for your folly."

I maintained my tight grip around the girl's waist, and she stood at ease in this embrace, making no show of resistance.

"What plane are they taking?" I said to her mother. "Where are they going?"

"I don't know."

"How is Paul?" Anne pleaded. "Is he well?"

Signora Braggi stiffened into an image of outraged righteousness.

"After what you've put him through? After letting the poor little creature watch your lover here commit murder? And then abandoning the child so you could run off and have a time for yourself with this brute? Ah yes, you've been a splendid mother to the boy, *signora*."

"Enough!" I said. "Where have they gone?"

"I told you I don't know." But the way she said it did not carry conviction.

"Take that carving knife," I told Anne, "and cut down the clothesline in the yard."

It was Anne herself who tied Signora Braggi hand and foot to the kitchen chair with lengths of clothesline, tugging the knots fast with a savage strength that made the woman wince and cry out. Then, keeping a grip on the nape of the girl's neck, I turned her around so that her hands could be bound behind her. Her mother watched this with mounting horror.

"What are you going to do?" she asked hoarsely.

"Get the truth. Where have they taken the boy?"

"I don't know! Even if you torture me—!"

"I don't intend to torture anyone." I turned to the girl who stood there passively. "What's your name?"

"Daniela."

"You're a very pretty girl, Daniela." She eyed me warily at this but I could have sworn there was the shadow of a smile on her lips. "Now, so my visit here won't be wasted, you and I are going into the next room to have some fun."

"Murderer!" Signora Braggi struggled so hard against her

bonds that she almost overturned the chair she was tied to. "God himself will strike you down if you harm that girl! He'll fill your guts with a cancer so you'll rot away in agony! And your woman, too!"

"Maybe," I said, "but it'll be a little too late for Daniela by then, won't it? Now, where was Paul taken?"

The woman set her teeth stubbornly.

"You must be well paid by Signora Cesira to sacrifice your daughter like this," I said.

"Nobody buys my loyalty, murderer. Or my husband's. And he'll be back from the airport very soon. Any minute now. If you dare lay a finger on that girl, he'll cut you to little pieces."

"We'll see when the time comes, *signora*." I must have made a highly convincing picture of lust incarnate as I looked Daniela over from head to foot, then shoved her out of the kitchen into the room beyond. Even Anne started to put out a protesting hand but dropped it when I coldly said to her, "Stay out of this. Just keep an eye on the lady there so that she doesn't try any tricks. If she changes her mind about talking, I'll be waiting to hear about it."

I steered Daniela through a dining room and into a living room, leaving the doors open behind me. In Signora Braggi's mind, I was sure, was a clear image of the couch in the living room and our progress toward it. Still, even when we reached the couch there was no outcry from the kitchen.

"Your mother is a stubborn woman," I said to Daniela.

"Very." The girl regarded me slyly. "Who knows what might happen to me because of that."

"Aren't you afraid of what might happen to you?"

She pointed her chin over her shoulder to indicate her bound hands. "Not as long as I'm tied up like this. Otherwise, I might be expected to do something about it and that would be pretty frightening. This way I'm resigned to my fate. Go ahead and do your worst."

"Gladly." I undid her halter and pulled it off. Then I gently ran a hand over the unkempt blond hair which fell to her shoulders, gathering a few strands between my fingers. The girl swayed close to me, eyes half closed, lips parted with anticipation, and when I suddenly jerked the strands of hair loose from her scalp she screeched with honest pain.

"You bastard!" Her face was contorted, her eyes filled with tears. "That hurt!"

There was an echoing screech from the kitchen. "Let her alone!" Signora Braggi shouted. "I'll tell you what you want to know. Just stay away from her!"

I shoved the girl down on the couch. "Wait here and don't make a sound or I'll have you bald before I'm done with you."

I walked into the kitchen, and Anne looked a little sick when she saw the bikini halter dangling from my hand. Signora Braggi saw it, too. The sight seemed to choke the words in her throat.

"The child was taken to Rome," she whispered.

"Start at the beginning," I said harshly. "When was this decided on?"

"I don't know when. All I know is that Dr. Morillon suddenly arrived here early this morning and had me pack for Signora Cesira and Paul so he could take them to Rome. The child isn't well. Dr. Morillon said his friend, Dr. Linder, would come to Rome and attend him there."

So before I could call checkmate, the pieces had been moved again.

"Rome," Anne said dully, voicing my own despairing thought. "Oh, God."

With only five thousand lire left—not even ten dollars—most of which would have to go to our boatman, we couldn't take plane or train to Rome. That meant I would have to hitchhike it, risk being picked up by the police along the way. No matter how furiously I groped for an alternative, I couldn't come up with any. Meanwhile, Fra Pietro, our friend of the train, would have to see to it that Anne was safely deposited in the convent in Chioggia. I didn't need her as a guide in Rome, and I'd be better off without her on my hands.

When I drew her into the living room to tell her this she said, "Maybe there is another way. My mother-in-law keeps a car in the Autorimessa in Venice so that she can visit friends in Mestre and Padua. If it's there now—"

"Do you know anyone in charge of the Autorimessa?"

"No one in charge, but I know one of the attendants."

"Is there a phone in the house here?"

"Right behind you."

"All right, then call the Autorimessa and get hold of that attendant. Tell him you need the car right away and to see that it's ready with the tank full and an emergency can of gas in the trunk. And make sure he understands everything is to be charged to Signora Cesira. Is your Italian good enough to get that across?"

"No, but he speaks French."

She was trying hard to maintain her composure, but her voice was unsteady. "And what happens when we get to Rome and find they're gone again? They knew we were coming here, didn't they? Every move we make—"

"How could they know we were coming here when they couldn't possibly know we made it across the border?"

"But they did! Do you think it's just coincidence that they were one step ahead of us like this?"

"I think it's panic. Why should Dr. Linder come to attend Paul in Rome when the kid could be brought to him in Issy? It's because all the top echelon of the OEI will be moving out of France until we're taken care of. We're like a barrel of nitroglycerin to them right now, and if there's any chance of our going off with a bang, Rome or Madrid or Lisbon is where they want to be when it happens. Not that they won't know we're heading for Rome, unless we sink Signora Braggi and Daniela in that canal out there. That's all right with me. It means they'll figure on setting some kind of trap for us, but it also means they're not likely to try keeping a step ahead of us."

"What do we do? Walk into their trap?"

"Not if we can help it. Now make that phone call to the Autorimessa. I don't want our taxi man to get impatient and come wandering in here."

While she was at the phone I saw to it that the now sulky and resentful Daniela was more or less decently garbed in her bikini halter and then led into the kitchen to be tied to a chair in her mother's company. Signora Braggi took this opportunity to describe to me what my punishment in hell would be for abusing helpless women. Dante himself couldn't have described it more colorfully.

"Your daughter's still got her virtue," I said for Daniela's sake. "What more could you ask from a criminal type like me?"

"If anything delays my husband," Signora Braggi retorted, "the food on that stove will be ruined. It will be burned to a crisp."

To each his own sense of proportion. I turned off the flames under the pots on the stove as Anne came into the kitchen.

"Everything settled?" I asked her.

"Everything."

"Then let's get moving."

Outside the house, I saw that Signora Braggi would have still another reason for bloody vengeance against me. The remainder of the clothesline Anne had cut down lay on the ground, and goats and chickens alike were making dirty tracks across hitherto snowy laundry. I had a feeling that leaving the housekeeper with her food unburned and her daughter's virginity intact wasn't going to compensate for this outrage.

I retraced the way to the canal, Anne stumbling in her effort to keep pace with me. The heat of the sun was like a lead weight pressing down on the skull, and it was a relief to enter the path winding through the trees bordering the canal where the pale green of willow leaves offered some shade. Then we were in the glare of sunlight again, standing before the small boat which lay upside down on the ground at the side of the canal and staring unbelievingly at the water where our boatman should have been waiting.

There were no two ways about it. The man and his boat were gone, and with them my valise. As far as I could see up and down the canal, nothing floated on its glassy water but the rowboat we had been moored to.

In the marsh across the canal, reeds swayed in a tentative breeze. The reflection of willow leaves shimmering in the water disappeared and reappeared as the water rippled. A gull circled overhead, then lazily set off eastward toward the Adriatic in slow, voluptuous flight. The scene had an almost dreamily peaceful quality, but there was something very wrong about it.

It gave me a chilling sense of *déjà vu,* of having lived through it before in a sweaty terror. Then I realized where the feeling came from. It was from my recurring dream where I fled through thickets beside a stream of water while something evil pressed closer and closer to me in pursuit.

I had thrust the automatic into my hip pocket. I reached for it, and a familiar voice said, "No, that would be a mistake."

I turned to face the speaker, my hand conspicuously away from my pocket. The man I knew as Fra Pietro was not wearing his robe now but was dressed in a badly wrinkled silk suit. The patches of sweat showing through the jacket made plain the martyrdom he must have been suffering, wearing that suit beneath a heavy robe in the sweatbox of a compartment on the Milan-Venice train.

There were other striking differences in his appearance, too. The freshly shaved tonsure was hidden by a jaunty beret, the eyes distorted behind the strong glasses were cold with menace, and that beautifully manicured hand held not an olive branch, but a deadly-looking long-barreled pistol aimed square at my chest.

7

One thing I was sure of. If the man had intended to get rid of us as quickly as possible, he would have already done so. A couple of bullets in the head delivered from ambush, the bodies dragged over the footbridge that crossed the canal near the house and dumped into the swamp on the other side; it would have been over and done with in a few minutes. The fact it wasn't suggested this was not the fate planned for us.

That thought, along with the weight of the gun in my pocket, gave me the nerve to disregard his command to put my hands up. We stood facing each other about ten feet apart. Once that gap was closed, once I had been disarmed and marched with Anne back along the path to the house, the game was up for us. All I could do was try to forestall that moment.

So I remained with my hands at my sides, ready to make some move, although without any idea what move it might be.

"Hands up, please," repeated the make-believe Fra Pietro, and when I still disregarded the command he said patiently, "Don't be stubborn. Your boatman has been paid off and sent away; you're stuck here; accept the situation."

"Are you from the police?" I said.

"Hardly, *signore*. Also, I am Pietro Cimino, not any Fra Pietro. But I am devoted to the culture of tulips, and those were tulip bulbs in my bag, so I wasn't altogether deceiving you." He took a step toward me, peering at me near-sightedly, the gun steady in his hand. "Now, since we've settled the formalities, you will permit me to remove that weapon in your pocket. Then you will do exactly as I tell you and not attempt any heroics."

"Do what?" I said, and took a step backward. The rowboat lying overturned on the ground was right behind me. If I could get Anne down behind it out of range of any bullets, I would have more freedom of action myself.

"I am under instructions from my superior to detain you two until he arrives, and we will be much more comfortable waiting in the house. If you behave sensibly, you are in no danger. If not, I will be forced to kill you on the spot. Regrettable, of course, but I was warned you are highly dangerous and given discretion in this."

Out of the corner of my eye I could see Anne fixedly watching Cimino as if spellbound by his menace. That settled my hopes of signaling her to move as soon as I did.

"Who is your superior?" I said to Cimino, desperately stalling for time. "How do I know you're not a police agent?"

He cautiously moved one more step toward me.

"*Signore,* at whatever point you entered the country, there were others than the police waiting to oversee your activities. And my superior is a certain Dr. Morillon, whom I phoned at the airport immediately after leaving your company at the Venice station. You'll be able to ask him all your questions very soon. He should be returning here in a few minutes from the Lido airport. Then, *signore*—"

Anne had not really been spellbound by him. There was a blur of motion in the air, a howl from Cimino as he staggered back under the blow she delivered. Somehow, she had got a grip on the fishing pole which was resting against the rowboat and had brought it with a wild backhanded sweep across the man's chest. If I had had any warning of what was going to happen, I could have turnd the tables on him then. But I moved too late, and before I could get to him he had recovered his balance and was bringing his gun to bear on me. It would have been suicide to charge into it, so I did the only thing there was left to do. I twisted sideways and threw myself, shoulder first, at Anne, sending her head over heels over the rowboat, then followed after her with a diving leap that landed me almost on top of her on the other side of the boat, the canal side.

I heard the roar of Cimino's gun as I hit the ground, heard the bullet ricochet whining off the stone embankment of the canal, and rolled over to draw the automatic from my pocket. When I raised my eyes above the keel of the boat just for the length of time it would take me to squeeze off one shot in return, I saw Cimino, stooping low and with shoulders hunched, moving toward the boat. He saw me before I could get the automatic sighted, and as I promptly learned, near-sighted or not, he was a deadly marksman.

His bullet this time flicked across the edge of the keel inches from my forehead, whipping a spray of splinters into my face. Despite the protection of my sunglasses, I flinched involuntarily at that, and so missed by a wide margin when I returned the shot. The next instant, the man had scurried to safety behind a tree a few steps away from him. Unthinkingly, I fired again, saw bark leap from the tree, then hastily went down flat as he sent a bullet ripping into the rotting hull of the boat. Lying there, I had time to regret wasting that extra shot. When I had checked the automatic after it came into my possession it had been loaded with a full clip of seven bullets, and I had to get the maximum value out of every one of them to withstand any kind of siege.

And siege it was likely to be, judging from the spot Anne and I were in. From behind his tree, Cimino had us tightly pinned down. The one possible escape route was by way of the rowboat moored in the canal below us, but once in that clumsy-looking craft, moving along between the narrow banks of the canal, we'd be sitting ducks for Cimino. He had plenty of concealment along the banks from which he could dispose of us at his leisure. Still, for the time being he was pinned down, too. If I could only get Anne aboard the boat quickly enough and start it downstream—

Anne must have been half stunned by the brutal impact of the fall she had taken. Now she stirred against me and tried to sit up, but I pulled her down again.

"Stay close to the ground," I said. "We've got a real sharpshooter watching us."

"Cimino?"

"Yes."

"That's my fault. I wanted you to be able to get at him, and all I did was make it worse."

"The hell you did. We were done for that way. This way, at least, we have a chance."

"Not much of one." Anne nodded toward the bridge. "Look."

I turned my head, making sure to keep it below the level of the rowboat's keel, and saw a motorboat pull up at the landing beyond the bridge. Two men stepped from it, and while I couldn't make out the features of the taller at that distance, his pale, falsely blond hair and catlike ease of movement made him easily identifiable as Dr. Hubert Morillon. As Colonel Henri de Villemont, I hastily corrected myself.

At that instant there was the roar of a shot from Cimino's gun, the bullet passing close overhead with the whipcrack sound of fingers snapping in my ear. That, I knew, was a sig-

nal to the new arrivals, whom Cimino must have seen as soon
as they stepped up on the canal embankment. I saw them stop
and turn in our direction, and could tell from de Villemont's
pointed finger and his sharp address to his follower that he had
seen us and understood the situation. I prepared for attack from
that quarter, but none came. Instead, both men briskly moved
off toward the house and disappeared inside it.

Seconds ticked away and became minutes.

"What are they doing?" Anne whispered.

"I don't know. Phoning for reinforcements maybe. Or baiting us into making a try for that motorboat, getting us out into
the open that way."

"It might be worth trying for." Her voice was calm. "You
could get away alone, couldn't you? Somehow reach Paul—"

That and the sight of the waiting motorboat made a powerful
temptation, but I resisted it. Then it was too late to reconsider,
because the family Braggi—father, mother, and daughter, who
was now clad in a skimpy dress, all of them weighted down with
luggage—made their way aboard the launch. The canal was
too narrow here for the boat to make a full turn. It simply
moved off quickly and smoothly in reverse, and in a minute
the soft puttering of its motor had faded away in the distance,
and the silence of the *barene* settled over us again.

That departure settled the question of what the enemy intended for Anne and me. We were to be disposed of here, and
without Signora Braggi or Daniela inadvertently witnessing the
execution. They would be removed to a safe distance, and the
boat would then return to take away the executioners as well.
The house itself would undoubtedly remain locked and empty
for a long time to come. There was a good reason for that, a
reason de Villemont had to take into account when laying his
plans for us. The boatman who had brought us here might see
my picture in the papers; might, sooner or later, go to the police about me; and if the trail led them to this house, it would
be found deserted. That was how the OEI played the game,
always a few moves ahead of the opponent, always with alibis
prepared and escape hatches made ready.

Then a voice hailed me. Henri de Villemont's.

"Monsieur Davis."

From the direction of it, he had taken up a position not far from Cimino's, but I wasn't going to verify that by raising my head into the line of fire.

"Yes?"

"Don't you think the time has come for us to settle matters between us, Monsieur Davis?"

"On what terms, Colonel?"

"Excellent terms. More than you deserve." The voice hardened. "And I am a doctor, not a military officer. Please remember for your future well-being that it is Dr. Hubert Morillon you are dealing with."

That intrigued me. The man lied as easily as he breathed, but still this mention of my future well-being offered a glimmer of hope that I might have a future worth considering. Or was it that not even Cimino was supposed to know his superior's true identity?

"Well?" said de Villemont impatiently.

"I'm sorry, Doctor." I laid heavy stress on the "doctor." "It's hard for me to discuss anything with a gun at my head."

"That's easily solved. Take a look, monsieur, and you'll see I have much more faith in you than you have in me."

I did look then, warily raising my eyes just above the line of the keel, and what I saw filled me with a reluctant admiration for my adversary. He had moved away from any concealment and stood there in the middle of the clearing before me, the easiest target in the world, even for a small-caliber automatic like the one I had trained on him.

"You see?" De Villemont held his arms wide. "And as for my man—" He half turned and made a sharp gesture toward Cimino's place of concealment. However the gunman felt about it, one didn't lightly disobey that sort of command from Henri de Villemont. Slowly and reluctantly, Cimino appeared from behind his tree, and as de Villemont continued to stare hard at him, even more slowly and reluctantly thrust his gun away in a shoulder holster.

I got up and walked around the hull of the boat toward de

Villemont, keeping the automatic on him, and making sure he stood between Cimino and me.

"What gives you such faith in me, Doctor?"

"Your understanding of your position, Monsieur Davis. You already know Pietro is as efficient with his pistol as you are with your fists. Any attempt to kill me would, therefore, mean your own death, and, of course, Madame's. Beyond that, where will you go, what will you do, if by the wildest of miracles, you could dispose of both Pietro and me? Run in circles until the police catch up with you? Or even more likely, until my angry and vengeful friends do?"

"What do you offer instead?"

"Safe conduct out of the country. My boat returns here tonight, and under cover of darkness you can be started on your way to the Dalmatian coast. Later, your transportation to South America will be arranged."

"Penniless and without luggage?" I said, to sound him out. "My valise was in the boat Pietro sent away."

"Pietro is not that stupid. The valise is among those trees there. And money will be provided."

"And all my other belongings? My clothing and books and manuscripts that were taken from the house on the rue de Courcelles? What happened to them?"

"I will not dissemble," said de Villemont. "Charles Leschenhaut felt that instead of being an extraordinary fool, you might perhaps be an extraordinarily clever agent of the CIA or British Intelligence. Your belongings were therefore removed to his apartment, where he could investigate them at his leisure. He has now assured me that nothing indicates you are any sort of an agent."

"Just a fool."

"Very much so. But I must admit, one who has a way of getting what he wants." There was no humor in the cold smile he gave me. "In an amazingly short time, you have won the affections of my son, you have taken my wife as your mistress—"

"Doctor, if we were alone—"

De Villemont nodded contemptuously in Cimino's direction.

"That lout doesn't understand French. We're free to discuss your triumphs with all frankness."

"Will you listen to me?" I said angrily. "You're wrong about your wife and me."

"Am I? No, I'm afraid you've been found out, my friend. Still, I have no intentions of behaving about it like a cuckold in a bad joke. If you wish Madame as your escort when you leave tonight, I'd say I was well rid of her."

"And what then?" It was Anne, and she came to her feet before I could warn her not to. "What then, Henri?"

"Hubert," snapped de Villemont.

"Henri. Colonel Henri de Villemont." Anne almost spat out the words. "My husband, who would let his son be murdered to protect his own skin. What are the plans this time, husband? Last time, it was to be an accident in the mountains. What is it to be now? A drowning in the Adriatic?"

De Villemont was not disconcerted by this. He coolly looked his wife over from head to foot and seemed amused by the dirty, disheveled appearance she made.

"What a spectacle," he said. "Obviously, madame, you were never cut out for life as a vagabond."

"Don't try to put me off, Henri. For Paul's sake alone, let's be honest with each other. The organization wants my money, but it would be hard for them to get it until I'm proved dead. That's what you're arranging now, isn't it? Some convenient way of getting rid of me so that my body can be recovered to settle all legal questions of my will and Paul's guardianship at once!"

"My dear, if you persist in these delusions, you will most certainly wind up in the madhouse."

"I? Am I the one who butchers innocent people for the sake of an insane dream? Am I the one who made our son a hostage to a real madman like Charles Leschenhaut?"

"Yes!" de Villemont exploded. "If you had been understanding—if you had tried to make yourself my wife instead of my enemy, do you think I would have agreed to such a terrible arrangement? Do you think I love Paul less than you do? But look at where we are now, at the disaster you and your lover threaten. Isn't this proof that Charles was wise to demand such an arrangement? If it weren't for that, you would gladly have sent me, your husband, to the guillotine long ago, would have destroyed the one movement capable of making the world a fit place for my son to live in! You were the one, madame, who made the child a hostage!"

Disregarding my gun, he moved toward her as he spoke, but when I sharply said, "Hold it!" he stopped in his tracks and turned toward me, struggling for composure.

"Ah, yes, the valiant lover himself. Well, what is it to be? Since you both know the child is a hostage for my safety from the authorities, I don't see what you can do but accept the generous terms I offer. In exchange—"

"Yes?" I said.

"There is a certain membership list you stole from a drunken countryman of yours. It must be returned to me."

"Membership list?"

"Please, monsieur, let's not have these clumsy efforts at acting. Pietro has already established that the list is not in your valise; the inadvertent motion of your hand to your pocket when I mentioned it makes clear where it is. Hand it over, and our bargain is made."

"What if I'd rather entrust it to some friend, just to make sure the bargain is kept?"

It must have been his hand suddenly outstretched to me that was the signal to Cimino. But it wasn't that which triggered me into action, nor even the alarming realization that he had maneuvered us so he no longer stood as protective cover between his henchman and me. It was the unexpected dazzling glint of sunlight on Cimino's gun as he drew it, and at that flicker of light I moved quicker than I had ever moved in my life. I caught de Villemont's outstretched arm and almost yanked the man off his feet, getting him before me as a shield. In that instant, almost as if everything happened together, I heard the sound of Cimino's gun, felt the impact of the bullet going home in the man I was grasping, was aware of Anne's scream, and saw Cimino standing there, his face filled with horror, his gun still poised, but useless while de Villemont's body shielded mine.

Georges Devesoul had once mentioned to me the devotion Colonel Henri de Villemont inspired in his followers, and now I was given an awesome demonstration of it. Cimino stood there frozen for only a moment. Then, useless gun in hand, he charged at me, bellowing like a bull, blind to everything but the furious need to get at me. My first shot hardly staggered him. It took a second and a third to blast the life out of him and send him sprawling full length almost at my feet.

Through all this, de Villemont never released his grip on my jacket, but the strength was fast flowing out of him. It was only my supporting arm that kept him upright.

Anne ran to me. "Are you hurt?" she gasped. "Are you all right?"

"I'm all right. Give me a hand with him. I think he's had it."

She helped me lower de Villemont to the ground. The bullet hole in his side, on a level with his heart, was a testimonial to Cimino's marksmanship. If the sunlight hadn't flashed on his gun, that one bullet would have finished me off on the spot.

Anne kneeled beside her husband and drew out his handkerchief to futilely dab at the thread of blood oozing from the corner of his mouth. His eyes were closed. Then the eyelids fluttered open, the eyes fixed on her.

"Bitch," whispered de Villemont, and that was all. The eyes remained open and glassily staring; the face became gray as I watched; the sound of labored breathing was stilled.

Anne slowly stood up. She seemed helpless to remove her eyes from the sight on the ground.

"It's all right," I said. "Just don't look. Get to the house and wait for me there."

"What's going to happen to Paul now?"

"Nothing."

"But when Leschenhaut finds out—"

"All he'll find out is that your husband and one of his thugs settled with each other after getting rid of us. Anyhow, that's

what we're leaving him to find out. Now get up to the house
and don't be worried if you hear a gun going off by the bridge.
And whatever you do, don't answer the phone if it happens to
ring."

"I won't. But I'd rather stay here and help you."

"I don't need any help. Just that scarf."

After she had unknotted the gauzy piece of cloth from her
head and handed it to me I pushed her in the direction of the
path between the trees and she made her way toward it unsteadily. I waited until she was out of sight, then turned my
attention to the stage-setting I had to prepare.

The one thing I knew I had going for me was time. It was
now noon; Braggi, the caretaker, would not be returning with
the boat until after dark; there would be no excuse for my
overlooking any detail of this operation. As I stood there considering each detail, it struck me that I was finally giving up
the role of fool to which the OEI had long ago consigned me.
I was going to do some manipulating of my own instead of
always being manipulated.

First I recovered my valise from among the trees where
Cimino had stored it, and carried it to the footbridge that
crossed the canal near the house. Then I stripped off all my
clothing and, barefoot and naked, carted the two bodies to the
bridge. It was hard work with Cimino; it took all my strength
just to hoist that mass of blubber to my shoulder, and I had to
make an additional trip to get his gun, eyeglasses, and beret
and restore them to the body, which I laid out on the embankment across the bridge.

Looking down from the embankment at the marsh below, I
was sure that this was where I was to have been permanently
disposed of. Not Anne. She was right when she said she would
have to be identified as the victim of a fatal accident, if her
estate and her son were to be turned over to her husband's
family as quickly as possible. But anything as flagrantly crimi-
nous as a bullet through her head could tie up the estate in
court for years, and who knew that better than de Villemont?

So what if Pietro Cimino had been too zealous in his duties?
And what if the hot-tempered and murderous Henri de Ville-

mont had seen his gunman blow apart all beautifully laid plans by carelessly sending a bullet through Anne's head? And what if Cimino, instantly condemned to death for this costly mistake, paid his master back with a final, dying squeeze of the trigger finger?

That was the deduction my stage-setting had to provide. Braggi would be the first to come on the scene, but even if he failed to grasp its meaning some superior of his would very soon afterward take charge and draw the conclusions I was foisting on him.

So I arranged Cimino's body on the embankment facing de Villemont's on the bridge, placing the gunman's pistol in one of his hairy fists and Anne's kerchief in the other. When I turned my attention to de Villemont, I was gratified to find a small automatic strapped to his waist beneath his shirt. I fired three shots from it into the canal before laying it down close to his outstretched hand.

I touched nothing else belonging to either man. To the enemy I must appear dead, buried along with Anne in the muck beneath that marsh grass, and the dead can't pick pockets. There was hardly a chance in a million that someone knew the exact contents of de Villemont's wallet, much less Cimino's, but for all I desperately needed whatever money those wallets held, I refused to take even that chance. Never for me again the mistake of underestimating the enemy.

So, regretfully, I set the valise on the bridge and, even more regretfully, fired off the remaining rounds in my gun and thrust the gun into de Villemont's jacket pocket. There was no way around that. The whole Braggi family knew I had been armed and standing siege; the logical place for my empty weapon after I would have surrendered to de Villemont would be in his pocket.

Transporting those bodies on my shoulder had been bloody work. Even more bloody than I anticipated, I saw, looking down at my naked chest and belly. Sick to the stomach, I hastily lowered myself into the canal from the bridge, and, chest deep in brackish, sour-smelling water, scrubbed myself down as well as I could. I dried myself with my undershirt, dressed, wadded the undershirt into a tight ball and stuffed it into my pocket.

Only one thing remained to be done to complete the stage-setting. I quickly made my way to the house to attend to it.

8

Anne was waiting for me in the kitchen. From the way she was leaning back against the wall as if that were all that kept her from falling, and from her appearance—she still wore her sunglasses and her face was streaked with dirt and tears—I surmised she hadn't moved from the spot once she had closed the door behind her.

"What you need is a drink," I said. "Where do they keep the stuff?"

"In the pantry." She barely managed to get the words out.

There were provisions enough to feed a small army in the pantry—very possibly they were intended for just that purpose —and among the bottles there I found one of cognac from which I doled out a good-sized drink for each of us. Then like an automaton, Anne let me steer her to the kitchen sink where I removed her sunglasses, and supporting her around the waist with my arm, used a dish towel to give her a clumsy but thorough face wash. Finally, I swept aside the severed pieces of rope that had bound Signora Braggi to her chair and planted Anne firmly in the chair. Following my instructions at the Venice station, she had abandoned her ruined stockings in the *gabinetto* there. Now, when I removed her shoes and washed the dirt from her bare legs, I saw the ugly scrapes and scratches the dirt had hidden, and, for want of a better antiseptic, I simply doused them with cognac. Using iodine, I had attended to her son this way more than once, and it had been a point of honor with him never to flinch or gasp at the sting. Anne, however, both flinched and gasped. I was glad of that. It seemed to bring her out of the spell she was in.

"I'm sorry," she said weakly. "Paul would have been braver, wouldn't he?"

"That's why I'm not too much worried about him," I lied. "Feeling better?"

"Some. Anyhow, enough to get going." She shook her head despairingly. "But where? They know we'll be trying to get to Rome. All they'll do is take Paul some place else."

"Not this time. This time we've gotten a move ahead of them," I said, and when I explained how, Anne's breath quickened with excitement.

"If they think we're dead, we can get to Rome without any trouble," she said eagerly. "And when we're in Rome—"

"Yes, but it won't be as easy as it sounds. For one thing, the police are after me. For another thing, we've got almost no money left, and it may take time before any showdown. At least a few days. Maybe more. Not that it means any change in plans. I just want you to be braced for a hard time ahead."

"I'm braced. Can't we go now?"

"Not yet." I took out Colonel Hardee's membership list, the pages of maddeningly cryptic numerals, and showed it to her. "Did you ever see anything like this before?"

"What is it?"

"An OEI membership list in code. The one your husband was so anxious to get his hands on. Would you recognize the code? Would you know how to read it?"

Anne frowned. "No, but I did see something like it before. Paul once took a book from Bernard's desk when he was snooping around, and there was a page like this folded in it—all numbers—and he suddenly showed it to me and asked what it was while we were at the dinner table with the family. From the

295 HOUSE OF CARDS

arrangement of the lines, I think it was probably a letter to Bernard, or maybe one he was writing."

"What happened when the family saw you with it?"

"There was quite a scene. Claude, especially, was in a rage, and I remember Matilde Vosiers made it all the worse by saying I'd have to be a fortuneteller to understand it anyhow, and since I didn't believe in fortunetelling, what harm could I do? Claude was furious at her for making a joke of it."

"That's all? They didn't say anything about the code?"

"No. Even so—if they want this list so much—"

"I know what you're thinking, but you're wrong. Leschenhaut would never trade Paul for it, not when he finds out you and I are alive. He'd rather take his chances on the code's being undecipherable to anyone who tries to break it."

"I thought all codes could be broken."

"Maybe they can, sooner or later. But the kind of private code a brilliant man like Leschenhaut would cook up would take a long time to solve—weeks or months, for all we know—and we don't have that much time left to us. No, we must have Paul in our hands before anything is done about this list. Once he's safe with us and clears me with the police, they might be able to break the code fast enough to move in on the OEI and nail the whole leadership before it gets clear away to the Andes Mountains. If not, we're still in trouble."

"Then why can't we start moving now? Why stand here and talk about it?"

"Because we're leaving this list here."

"Leaving it?" Anne said in bewilderment.

"That's right. It's the finishing touch, the one thing that'll really convince the organization we were killed here and dumped into that marsh. But we're keeping a copy of the list. Now let's scout around and dig up some pencils and paper."

There turned out to be a supply of pencils in the house, but no writing paper. In the end, we settled for some immense sheets of white wrapping paper which the thrifty Signora Braggi had stored away in a kitchen cabinet, and by using both sides of each sheet we made do. Even going as fast as we could without pause, each of us alternating in calling out the numbers while the other jotted them down, it took almost three hours to transcribe the entire contents of the colonel's list. Each page was solid with digits, and there were anywhere from thirty to sixty digits a line, suggesting that each line probably contained a single name and address. I could only hope, as we wearily worked our way through page after page, that all this wasn't wasted effort.

When the job was finished I forced Anne against her will to join me in a lunch of bread, cheese, and wine, and then leaving her to clear up all traces of our presence in the kitchen, I went down to the bridge. I was sickened to find clouds of flies already swarming over the two bodies there, and I had all I could do to hold down my lunch when I brushed them away from de Villemont long enough to shove the original list into the breast pocket of his jacket. It took a final cognac back in the kitchen to wash the taste of that experience out of my mouth.

Outside the house, Anne started toward the canal, and I caught hold of her arm.

"We're not going that way," I said.

"But that's where the rowboat is."

"Use your head. If we took the boat, don't you think they'd know we got away?"

"But if we don't use the boat—"

"We'll walk it, that's all. We'll keep heading south until we hit the shoreline, then find somebody with a boat to give us a lift there. The ferry makes a stop at Burano, doesn't it?"

"The *vaporetto*? Yes."

"And Burano's near enough so that we ought to get a ride across to it from here pretty cheap. Then we take the *vaporetto* to the parking lot like nice tourists and pick up the car."

"But the *barene*. And all these canals."

"We'll find our way around them. Leave it to me. I'm a country boy, remember?"

As I soon learned, being a country boy from the banks of the Truckee River in Nevada didn't mean much when it came to finding a way through the maze of canals winding in every direction across Torcello where bridges were few and far between. It was easy going where we could walk an embankment, but when the canal we were following swung away from the south we had to leave it and strike out through almost tropical undergrowth, across fields where we sank ankle-deep in the loamy soil, through thickets which treacherously hid quagmires of silt. At the worst spots we pulled off our shoes, and Anne held them clutched to her while I, trousers rolled up to the knee, carried her in my arms until we reached easier going.

Throughout the journey I made sure to stay clear of any habitation that looked as if it might be occupied; and where we came on a vegetable patch or an orchard we took the long way around it. So it was almost dusk when we finally reached the shoreline and gratefully saw the water of the broad Laguna Veneta on fire with the setting sun, and the distant streetlights just going on across the chain of islands that led to the city itself.

Not far from where we emerged on the lagoon was a stucco box of a house in ruinous condition, but smoke curling from its chimney and a small felucca beached before it led us to it.

Its inhabitants turned out to be two Old Men of the Sea, incredibly wrinkled and ancient-looking, who were mending a net behind the house and who gaped at us in toothless, open-mouthed astonishment when we appeared before them. When I explained that the *signora* and I were tourists who had been separated from our party and would pay for a ride to the boat landing in Burano, I was prepared to meet exorbitant demands. Instead we were overwhelmed by hospitality. Yes, we would certainly be taken to Burano but first we must refresh ourselves with some food and wine. Indeed, if we wished to stay the night we could; the *signora* looked hardly able to stand on her feet.

In the end, after I managed to convey to them that time was of the essence, that our friends, our relatives, our little children would be worried about us, they finally transported us in the felucca to a jetty near the Burano *vaporetto* landing and would accept only the remainder of my pack of cigarettes as payment.

"No, no," said one of them in reply to my fervent thanks,

"we know how to treat visitors on Torcello. We're civilized people, not like that gang of lousy mercenaries around the Piazza San Marco. Tell them that for us, *signore*, when you get back there."

That, and the moonlight ride across the lagoon in the puffing little *vaporetto*, might have been idyllic under other conditions. As it was, I couldn't shake the feeling that eyes were following me, that among the passengers on the boat—most of whom seemed to be footsore, bad-tempered tourists, done in by a hard day's sightseeing—one, at least, was a hireling of the enemy, maneuvering to corner us as Pietro Cimino had so easily done.

It wasn't until the boat discharged us at the Autorimessa landing and I saw we were the only ones to step ashore there that I could shake the feeling. I waited behind the garage while Anne went to get the car. When she drove it around to pick me up, I was glad to see it was a neat black Fiat Millecento, the perfect car for inconspicuous travel.

Anne moved aside to allow me to get behind the wheel, and I said, "No, you do as much of the driving as you can. At least you've got a passport. I don't have any papers at all. That means that if the police stop us on the road for any reason, you might be able to talk your way out of it. If that happens, remember I'm just a hitchhiker you picked up. That's all you tell them."

"Is it only the police we have to worry about? What if the organization finds out the car is gone?"

"There's no reason they should. We're dead, aren't we? So they won't be worrying about the car while they're wondering how to dredge up your remains. You never signed over power of attorney to them, did you? I mean to Claude or any of the family?"

Anne shook her head. "They never asked me to."

"Because that would have made their plans a little too obvious. And you have been supporting the whole family, too, haven't you? I mean, besides the money you were turning over to the OEI through that gambling joint. Signing all the checks for them?"

"The first of every month."

"Well, the first isn't far off, so they'll be facing a financial crisis almost as soon as we will. They'll be ready to talk business."

"But if you're not going to use that membership list to bargain with, what can you possibly offer them?"

"What do you think?" I said, as we turned on to the causeway to the mainland. "Your remains."

PART FIVE

The Wheel

1

Money was the problem.

On our third day in Rome, at ten in the evening in a *rosticceria* in the Piazza Sonnino in Trastevere, we spent the last of it. The groceries I carried out to the car—cheese, cold macaroni, a couple of tissue-paper-thin slices of ham, a loaf of bread, and a jar of sulphurous Chianti drawn from the barrel of local vintage behind the counter—left me with two coins in my pocket, which together amounted to less than an American cent.

And prospects were dim. Anne's wedding ring was already in the pawnshop, replaced on her finger by an imitation-gold hunk of junk picked up in Standa, the Roman five-and-dime. Also in the pawnshop was my wristwatch and the set of tools I had found in the trunk of the car.

On the bright side, we had enough food on hand for a dinner and a breakfast, almost a full tank of gas, and no hotel bills to worry about. Whether we had the money for it or not, taking a room in even the most rundown *pensione* was too dangerous to risk, since it meant we would be asked for identification papers or passports.

So the car was our dining room and bedroom; and the *albergo diurno*—that complex of lavatories, baths, and beautification facilities in the bowels of the Termini, the main railroad station—provided the rest of our conveniences. As it was, the coins we had left couldn't even buy us admission to those conveniences any longer. And by noon the next day we would be out of food as well as money. The one cold fact that stared me in the face was that somehow or other we had to dig up a few hundred lire just to survive another day.

But dig it up how?

Anne de Villemont, whose fortune, by any estimate, amounted to about six billion lire, pulled our dinner out of the paper bags I handed her.

"Ham?" she said. "Isn't it expensive?"

"I thought you'd like to try some high living for a change. Don't let it bother you. We're all out of money anyhow."

"Completely out?"

"We couldn't even buy a newspaper with what we've got left. I've been wondering what to do about it, outside of slugging some prosperous-looking tourist and lifting his wallet. If that damn cook would only show up—"

Because that was what we were waiting for. Sooner or later, we hoped, the cook of the Montecastellani household, the household of Madame Cesira's devoted relatives, would show up and all unwittingly lead us to the family she served.

We had no choice in this; it was the only course we could take. From the time on Torcello when I had forced from Signora Braggi the admission that Paul and his grandmother were being removed to Rome, I was sure the Casa Montecastellani which Madame Cesira had once so vividly described to me would be their sanctuary in the city. Anne had agreed with me. According to her, the Montecastellani clan was divided against itself into neo-fascist and royalist factions, but all were united in fanatic support of the OEI, and their ancestral home on Via della Pilotta was a hotbed of its activities. And most important, Madame Cesira always stayed with her family when in Rome. On this basis I set my trap. All it needed, when we arrived on the outskirts of the city early in the morning, was a phone call to spring it.

That was when we hit bottom, when I called the Monte-castellani number, only to discover the line was dead. With all communications to the enemy cut off, we had come close to the end of our string. The end itself was the sight of the barred gate of the Montecastellani quarters on Via della Pilotta, as much a fortress as the mansion on the rue de Courcelles, the huge padlock on the gate and the sealed shutters at every window pro-claiming that the house was deserted.

But move we must, even if it was like moles blindly strug-gling through a labyrinth. So I left Anne in the parked car near the house and set out in desperation to explore the shops in the surrounding alleyways. Grocers, fruiterers, fishmongers —one and all shook their heads in response to my questions. Yes, they knew the family Montecastellani but only from a dis-tance. No, they wouldn't know where the family had gone. These bigshots, you understand, thought nothing of packing their whole ménage into a plane and flying halfway around the world at a moment's notice. I was already aware of that pos-sibility, and having it openly stated this way didn't make me feel any better.

It was in a butcher shop off the Via dei Lucchesi that I un-expectedly struck gold. I asked my question, braced for the usual depressing answer, but at the guarded look that came into the butcher's eyes when I mentioned the name Monte-castellani, I felt my heart leap. I repeated the question, trying to conceal my excitement.

The butcher, a grizzled, unshaven specimen, took his time answering. "Sure, I sell them their meat," he said at last. "They want the best, they know where to get it. But what's that got to do with you?"

I gave him a large mysterious wink and tapped the side of my nose with my forefinger to indicate that our discussion was confidential. When I motioned toward the back of the shop he led me there, not altogether willingly.

"Well?" he said.

"You don't have to sound like I'm the tax collector," I said. "I happen to be in the same general line as you. I sell to the Mon-tecastellanis too, but luxury stuff and fine wines. You know, the real imported goods."

"Imported from France," said the butcher with a great air of shrewdness. "You're French, aren't you?"

"That's right. How did you know?"

"The way you talk." He was full of self-satisfaction now, his guard coming down. "I know a Frenchie when I hear him."

"I can see that," I said admiringly. "Anyhow, this is one Frenchie in trouble. Who did the buying from you for the Monte-castellanis? The cook?"

"Naturally. I've been dealing with that bitch Rosanna for twenty years."

"And how much of a kickback does she ask for?"

"Five percent. I'd let her rot in hell before I paid her more than that."

"Well, she used to get five from me, but all of a sudden she said it had to be ten. You can't blame me for turning her down, can you?"

"Blame you? I wouldn't blame you for slitting her throat when it comes to that kind of thievery."

"Sure. The trouble is," I said woefully, "she took her trade to somebody else, and now my boss says get it back or get the hell out. So here I am, ready to talk business with her, and I don't know where she or the family went to."

"*Sfortunato.*" The butcher clicked his tongue sympathetically. "I don't know where myself. All I know is they pulled out a couple of weeks ago and took a villa somewhere around town."

"Has Rosanna been back here to do any shopping for the family since they moved?" I asked.

"Once, a few days ago."

"And she didn't leave any address?"

"No, all she said was it was a pain in the ass being sent all the way across the city for the kind of meat I sell. The miserable old hen. She knows she won't get a better cut of beef anywhere."

"So she'll be back, I suppose."

"Oh, she'll be back all right. Maybe tomorrow, maybe next week, but sooner or later she'll be back. For all her big mouth the trip doesn't really bother her, the way she comes rolling up in a limousine with a chauffeur to do her fetching and carrying."

"From Parioli, you think?"

"No, from the other direction, from the south side." He was growing impatient now; there were customers at the marble counter fronting the alley. "Look, friend, we're in the same way of business so I'd like to help you, but the truth is I don't know where you can find her. When she's in again I'll tell her you were around. You give me your card—"

"I'd rather you didn't tell her anything. If she knows I'm hunting for her she can afford to be stubborn as a mule. I'll get in touch with her some other way. Anyhow, thanks for your trouble."

I went back to the car, and Anne said fearfully, "Good or bad?"

"Both. They're still somewhere around Rome but I don't know where. Do they own a villa anywhere south of the city?"

"No."

"Then they rented or borrowed one. And the only lead we have to it is the family cook."

"Rosanna? You met her? How did you even know her?"

"I didn't meet her. But she buys from the butcher down that alley. What we'll do is lay low in the car on the Piazza della Pilotta there, and when she shows up we'll tail her back to the villa. Once we get the address we can get the phone number and then make our move."

"When is she supposed to show up?"

"The butcher says it might be tomorrow, or it might be next week. And I can tell you it might be never, if the villa is just that gang's first stop on their way out of the country."

"If they believe we're dead, they won't have any reason to leave the country."

"I know. That's what we're gambling on. Matter of fact, I have a hunch that now with the rue de Courcelles and the Château Laennac and even that sanitarium at Issy marked too hot for comfort, this villa here is intended to be the center of OEI activity for the time being. And with your funds cut off from it, the leadership from all around the Continent will be filtering down here to solve the problem. And there's the problem of Henri's death, too. As Leschenhaut's second-in-command, he'll be hard to replace."

What I didn't express aloud was my thought that if Louis' murderer was among the OEI leadership filtering down to the villa, Paul's life hung by a very thin thread.

After that, Anne and I kept butchers' hours in the Piazza della Pilotta, from seven in the morning until noon, and then from three in the afternoon until eight in the evening, the parked car heating up steadily during the daytime in the sweltering Roman summer until by late afternoon it was like an oven.

During the noontime break when the city settled down to its siesta, we drove to the *albergo diurno* in the Termini to refresh ourselves, and then to the slums of Trastevere across the river where we could buy food cheap and where there was small chance of anyone recognizing us. And after a bad experience our first night when a zealous policeman approached our parked car in the Piazza Mattrai in Trastevere to see if anything sinful was going on in it, we would drive out of town when darkness fell and find some isolated spot along a side road in which to get a few hours of broken sleep.

Meanwhile, although I doled out each coin like a miser, our money steadily drained away until, with the outlay for our meager dinner the third night, it was all gone. That night, to conserve precious gasoline, we stayed in the city, changing our parking spot now and then to keep policemen on the beat from taking an undue interest in us. We got no real rest this way, only fitful catnaps when it was impossible to keep the eyes open any longer.

What sustained me through this was Anne's nearness, her body against mine, her head trustingly on my shoulder as she dozed, the way she uncomplainingly bore the misery of the slowly passing hours. That was the way she had borne everything throughout our nerve-racking vigil of the past few days, faithfully following instructions to the letter, never asking the one question which must have tormented her as much as it did me—the question of what lay beyond for us if our vigil wasn't rewarded very soon.

At the same time, my admiration for her and the sensual pleasure of having her close couldn't rid me of the bitter realization of what she had done to my life. Worst of all was the nagging memory of the foolish little affair she had offered me as bait back in that house on the rue de Courcelles. A schoolboy's sickly romantic idea of an affair. At least, when I had finally asked her the question directly during the nightmarish train ride from Dijon to Milan, she had been honest about it. She had never intended me to be her lover. Cat's-paw, protector, agent of deliverance, yes, but not her lover. I was, after all, hired help, and that sort of thing was for Jeanne-Marie, not the convent-bred Madame Anne de Villemont of Louisburg Square and the Plaine Monceau.

Meanwhile, I was in possession of her, could take what satisfaction there was in drawing her close to me when she stirred uneasily in her sleep, loving and hating her as I did it. And despising myself for showing polite self-control under conditions where I had every right to be ruthlessly demanding.

This welter of emotions in me the night we ran out of money didn't make it any easier to concentrate on the real problem of the moment—how to lay hands on the few hundred lire needed for our survival—so it was almost dawn when the solution finally struck me. A little later and it would have been too late to put the solution to work that day. I promptly got the car moving, and as we turned into the Corso and headed northward Anne woke and looked around wonderingly.

I couldn't blame her. In the first gray light of morning, the Corso, usually jammed with traffic from curb to curb, was totally deserted. There wasn't a car on the avenue, not a single pedestrian in sight. We might have been the only people alive in the whole city.

"I've never seen it this way before," Anne said. "I didn't know it could be like this."

"It won't be for long. We'll have to work fast."

"Doing what?"

"Get those paper bags off the floor in back of the car and I'll show you. See if you can waterproof them with the waxed paper from around the meat and cheese."

"What are they supposed to hold?"

"Money."

We swung into the Via della Muratte and pulled up in the emptiness of the tiny piazza at the end of it, the incongruously cramped little square fronting the immensity of the Trevi fountain. There was no water jetting over the marble figures and carved rocks of the fountain now, overflowing its basins. The fountain was off, and the pool surrounding it was like a sheet of glass. Even in the dim light one could see the glimmer of the coins under the surface.

"That money?" said Anne. "But it's supposed to go to charity."

"The hell it is, not that I could think of a better charity than us right now. It goes to the guys who clean the fountain, and they're good for thirty, forty thousand lire every time they do it during the tourist season. I met one of them once when I had a bout here. He owns a couple of fighters, which he couldn't afford to do if these pickings went to charity. Now let's get our shoes off and start wading before the place comes alive."

She was knee-deep in the water before I was, gasping as the chill of it struck her, and then, stripping to the waist and rolling up my pants, I joined her. We were clumsy at our treasure hunting at the start, but grew steadily more adept at it. By the time the sun rose, brilliantly lighting the cornices of the buildings around the piazza, the bags we were filling were growing heavy with silver and copper coinage of every size.

I saw the man in uniform when it was already too late to escape his notice. He appeared from around the Trevi palace on foot, wheeling his bicycle beside him, and all I had time to do before his eyes swiveled in our direction was whisper to Anne, "Police! Keep that bag out of sight and play along with me," and with my own bag of coins clutched against my thigh in one hand, I threw an arm around her shoulders and fastened my lips to hers in a fervent kiss.

She was quick-witted enough not to put up any resistance. Then, as the man walked toward us, I realized she was more than yielding to the kiss, she was sharing it with a fierce, shuddering excitement, her lips hard against mine, her hand going around my back, the fingers digging into my naked flesh, her body locked so tight against me that we would have made a convincing tableau of unrepressed passion for the most cynical onlooker. It was as if the danger moving toward us, this threat to all our hopes, had set her on fire.

"*Ei, Marcello, Sophia,*" the man said with heavy irony, "*a che ora comincia l'intervallo?*"

"What?" I smiled broadly at him. "*Americano,*" I said, giving it the full midwestern twang. "*Non capisco.* No understand."

"*Naturalmente, un'americano. Uno pazzo.*" He jerked his thumb at our parked car. "*Andiamo, Signor Pazzo. Andiamo.*"

The trick was to get to the car without those bags of coin being detected, and Anne helped me in that by giving the man a fine display of leg and thigh as she stepped over the low retaining wall of the fountain. Still, he must have scented something suspicious about us as we awkwardly sidled past him to the car.

He eyed us up and down, then planted his bicycle on its stand and walked around to confront me. I passed Anne my bag of coin behind my back.

"*Uno momento,*" the policeman said coldly.

Now that I could, I held my empty hands wide in what I hoped he would interpret as helpless admiration at the scene around us.

"Beautiful! *Bella!*" I said, indicating the silent fountain. "It does something to you. *Amore.* You understand?" and it must have been my tone of inane rapture which convinced the man that I was, after all, only the harmless American lunatic I seemed to be.

"*Amore, merda,*" he snarled, and again gave me that gesture of dismissal with the thumb. I didn't make any long farewell of it. Barefoot and shirtless, I had the car away from there before he even got the bicycle off its stand.

There was plenty of time to return to the stakeout in the Piazza della Pilotta. What I wanted to do now was count our take and see how much of a haul we had made. I drove to the Borghese Gardens and parked in an untraveled lane, the rising sun filtering through the trees around us and flecking the ground with drops of gold. Still shaken by our close call, I took the jar of wine from in back of the car and helped myself to a long drink. When I offered the jar to Anne she shook her head.

"You deserve it," I said. "That was a great performance, Sophia."

"Was it?" She was looking at me steadily, those sapphire eyes unbelievably lustrous.

"Well, it was certainly convincing to the audience."

"And not you?"

"No."

"I love you," she said.

"God damn it—!"

"I love you."

"*Amore, merda.*"

"What does that mean?"

"You know what it means. It's the same as in French, sweetheart. *Merde.* Crap."

"Be as hard-boiled as you like. You know how I feel about you. You must know."

"Oh, I do. Especially after you told me in plain language there could never be anything between us. Any honest-to-God *amore.*"

"Can you blame me for that?" she asked. "What else could I tell you, when I had a husband and no way of changing that?"

"You could have told me everything long ago. You're supposed to trust the man you love."

"Don't be angry. Please, don't be angry." Her arms went around my neck, her breath was warm on my cheek. "I love you," she whispered. "It's as simple as that. Everything else is horribly complicated and terrifying, but not this."

"Anne, be reasonable. Right now we're like two people trying to walk a tightrope a hundred feet in the air and no net below. Even if we get across—"

"I know. Matilde told me what you once said about the princess and the peasant. I was already in love with you then, and that hurt so much—"

"Hurt or not, that's the way things are between us. I have my pride, lady. It's still got scars on it from the time I married money and was pointed out as a lousy fortune hunter."

"Pride, *merda!*"

"No, because you have your own kind of pride. That's why, as long as your husband was alive, you wouldn't go to bed with me. That's why, even at a time like this when we don't even know if we'll be alive tomorrow, you're just crazy enough to be thinking in terms of marriage. Of Darby and Joan walking hand in hand into the pretty sunset."

"It seems to me you're the one thinking in those terms," Anne said serenely.

"Not me. You're the one. Despite everything you've been through, the life you've led, you're still bourgeois to the backbone. You're as cockeyed conventional—"

"Crazy and conventional together?"

"Why not? It's a form of insanity to be conventional when the roof is coming down on your head."

"Yes, my darling." Those arms clung even tighter; those warm lips moving lightly across my cheek sent shivers through me. "But don't you see how simple it really is? You're stuck with me, and there's nothing you can do about it. I'm your woman. I need to be and I will be. It couldn't be simpler than that, could it?"

And as I crushingly bore her down, my hands grasping hungrily, our mouths glued together as if we were trying to devour each other, I knew that she was right. It was as simple as this.

The sun was already clearing the treetops when, satiated, disheveled, exhausted, we finally got around to the job of counting what we had gleaned from the kindly, superstitious tourists who had contributed their mite to the Trevi fountain. It looked like a lot and turned out to be very little. After discarding American pennies, British pence, French centimes, and the rest of the useless foreign currency scattered among our cash, the balance added up to only about a thousand lire, not quite two dollars.

But since the occasion certainly demanded it, I stopped on the way back to the Piazza della Pilotta and invested a hundred lire in a nosegay of violets for my woman.

2

The car was a black Cadillac limousine with the exaggerated tailfins of a few years ago. As it slid to a stop at the head of the alley leading to the butcher shop, Anne caught hold of my wrist.

"That's it!" she said.

"All right. Keep down in the seat so that they can't see you."

The woman who emerged from the Cadillac, however, in no way resembled my idea of the Montecastellanis' cook. From the butcher's scathing tone, I had somehow imagined her as a witchlike, malignant little crone. This woman, although white-haired and dressed in deep mourning, was tall, slender, and attractive. Her expression, when she slammed the car door behind her and leaned down to say something through the window to the chauffeur, was one of bright amusement.

"Are you sure that's Rosanna?" I said to Anne.

"Yes, of course. I'd know her anywhere."

Rosanna departed down the alleyway. It was almost half an hour later by the dashboard clock before she returned, the butcher following her, staggering under a loaded basket which he stowed away in the Cadillac's trunk under the chauffeur's supervision. When the limousine pulled out into the traffic I had my motor idling and ready.

The size of the Cadillac and the flamboyance of those tailfins made it easy to keep in sight as it crawled through the roaring, fender-to-fender jam of traffic in the center of the city and finally, with a triumphant burst of speed, entered the Via Ostiense, the broad highway running from the outskirts of town to Ostia. With the Château Laennac in mind, I had conjectured that the Villa Montecastellani would be one of those rundown, isolated properties on the way to Ostia, and now, as we raced southward past the sprawling wholesale-food market which was Rome's Les Halles, past the clay-colored Gothic bulk of Saint Paul's Basilica, it looked as if I had been right.

But not for long. As we approached the E.U.R., the Universal Exhibition grounds, the Cadillac, to my surprise, swung off the highway into an exit leading to the E.U.R. itself. I was in the wrong lane to follow this abrupt move, but I had no choice. Violating every law in the book, I cut right across the oncoming traffic and sent the Fiat slewing into the exit in hot pursuit. Luckily, there was no other car ahead of me to slow me down, and a minute later I sighted the limousine again as it entered the avenue crossing the grounds. I closed the gap between us, but not too much, and then realized that Anne had swiveled around in her seat and was peering with concern through the rear window.

"What's wrong?" I said.

"We're being followed. Take a look."

I looked into the rear-view mirror. The only car reflected in it was a dusty, weatherbeaten blue Citroën which was maintaining the same distance behind me as I was maintaining behind the Cadillac. I slowed down a little, and although the Citroën had plenty of room now in which to move up and pass, it slowed too, not closing the gap at all. That was an unpleasant sight to see.

"How long has he been with us?" I asked.

"I don't know. He stopped alongside at the red light on the Via Nazionale all the way back, and then when we pulled off at the exit here he was in the wrong lane, too, and almost had an accident when he followed us. Do you think it's the police?"

"Not in a French car."

"One of Leschenhaut's men?" Anne said calmly.

If I had ever loved her, I loved her now for the control she displayed.

316

"Maybe," I said. "The bad part is that if Leschenhaut knows you're alive it ruins my chance of making a deal with him."

"Then we'll try something else. If we can get hold of a gun—"

"It wouldn't help, and anyway we can't. All we can do is pray the guy tailing us is interested only in me and doesn't take you into account. Did you get a good look at him?"

"Yes. He's a sort of gray man."

"Gray man?"

"That's how it struck me when I saw him. He's wearing a gray straw hat and a gray jacket, and his face is completely colorless and unhealthy-looking."

"Sounds like a jailbird fresh out of clink. Did he see you?"

"I suppose so. He was right beside me at that traffic light."

"Hell. Up to now I thought we were holding the ace of trump or king of cups or whatever that de Laennac mummy calls it. Now—" Suddenly, unreasoningly, a light burst on me. I saw a book with a garish jacket, the gaudy picture of a man beatifically dangling from a gibbet by one ankle. "Anne, listen! What was it Matilde said about that letter in code? Wasn't it something about your not being able to read it because you weren't a fortuneteller?"

"Yes. But why—"

"And at that dinner party when I met Leschenhaut, Sophie de Laennac said it was Madame Cesira who had proofread her Tarot book. And that was the book on Bernard's desk, the code book!"

"Darling, I don't know what you're talking about."

"The book on Tarot! *La Mystère du Tarot.* Don't you see? That's what the code is based on. If we can only get hold of a copy—"

"No." Anne shook her head. "It still wouldn't be any use unless Paul is here with us."

That brought me back to earth with a thud. She was right. The decoded membership list could blow the OEI apart, but as long as Paul might be a victim of the explosion, it couldn't be triggered.

The limousine ahead made a right turn into Via Laurentina,

the perimeter of the E.U.R. and I followed, leaving the sports area behind. There was no sign of the dusty Citroën in the mirror, and I had a wild hope that its staying with us this far had only been a coincidence. Then it suddenly reappeared in the mirror, making the turn after us, weaving through a pack of youths on motor scooters to take up its position the same distance to the rear as before. That settled my plan to leave the Fiat when we reached the villa and explore the grounds on foot. As long as the Gray Man had us in his sights, the safest place to be was right inside the car, moving steadily along until we either shook him off or just ran out of gas.

To my right, the Exhibition Grounds now became a series of landscaped terraces at the crown of which stood the familiar glass mushroom of the Sports Palace. To my left, however, I saw that something new had been added to the local scene since my last visit here for a bout a few years before. A scattering of villas, modernistic in architecture, rose here and there from the slopes. And one of them, I knew, was the present stronghold of the Montecastellanis, the de Villemonts, the OEI leadership, including Leschenhaut himself. This was where he had to be right now to take charge of his forces, hold council, make decisions that needed to be made very quickly.

It was the last villa on the narrow, winding Via Altura which proved to be the Cadillac's destination. I was at the head of the street as the big car entered the driveway of the building. I made a quick note of the name of the building on its gatepost—it was, unimaginatively, the Villa Altura—and then shot past at high speed, turning at the end of the road back toward the E.U.R.

Anne was still keeping watch through the rear window.

"He's gone," she said suddenly as we re-entered the Via Laurentina, and the mirror told me she was right. There were a few cars behind us on the avenue, but none of them was the blue Citroën. And there was no sign of it anywhere on the terraced slope we had just descended.

It was hard to tell whether this was a good break for us or a bad one. On the one hand, it now left me free to make my phone call to the villa. On the other hand, it suggested that the Gray Man was an OEI scout and had pulled up at the villa to report on us. Yet why, I wondered, had he given up following us? Was he that sure he could pick up our trail any time he wanted to? If so, what made him so sure of it? More than ever, as I frantically searched for logical answers to these questions, I had the feeling of being surrounded by subtle, implacable enemies. Everyone seemed to be an enemy. Even the stout, *gemütlich*-looking couple overflowing the Volkswagen close behind me could be an OEI team assigned to keep us under surveillance.

I had to fight a temptation to bear down on the gas, to cut free of the traffic, turn the car southward again and race for some desolate hiding place in the hills of Puglia or Calabria where for a little while I could be rid of this sense of being a fly struggling in a spiderweb. Could, for a few days, a few weeks, eat, sleep, make love to my woman without starting at every sound and seeing murder in every pair of eyes that looked my way. For all I knew, once I made the phone call, flight might be the only way out. If Anne and I had already been found out by the organization, what else was left to us?

I made the call from a booth on the road opposite the Labor Building, that imposing series of arches rising six stories high in rows of nine, and had time to count all fifty-four arches facing me before the operator deigned to give me the number of the Villa Altura.

My fingers, when I dialed the number, were as clumsy to manipulate as sticks of wood.

"*Pronto.*" The man's eager voice suggested he was expecting an important message.

"I'd like to speak to Signora Cesira, please."

"Your name?"

"The name doesn't matter. Just tell her this call is urgent."

"Regrettable." The voice was now ice-cold and forbidding. "The *signora* is indisposed. She cannot take any calls. If you wish to give your message to Signor Montecastellani—"

"I don't. It concerns information I have about the *signora's* son."

"Ahh." The sound floated over the wire like a sigh and could have meant anything. "Very well. Wait, please."

I waited. From the booth I could see Anne behind the wheel of the Fiat watching me intently. We had arranged that if there were the least reason to suspect during the call that the OEI was on to us, we would make a getaway at once, heading south as far as our depleted supply of gas would take us. Even Anne had to admit that our first job was to shake off pursuit. Otherwise, we were really done for.

"*Pronto.*" Madame Cesira snapped out the word with venom. It must have been the cruelest possible blow when she was told of her only son's violent end on Torcello, but none of the fire had gone out of her. "Who are you, *signore?* What is this about my son. I have no son. He died in Africa long ago."

"Please, *signora,* no games. Your son was Colonel Henri de Villemont who died only a few days ago. I know, because I was there to witness his murder."

"You? Who are you?"

"Surely you recognize my voice."

"No, I do not. Wait!" Her voice became hoarse. "But it can't be! It's impossible!"

"Not at all. Like Lazarus himself, *signora,* I am Reno Davis risen from the dead."

Her shriek at that, as if she had actually seen a corpse sit up in its coffin, told me the best news I could have heard.

The Gray Man, whoever he was, had not reported on Anne and me to the OEI.

The enemy did not know Anne was alive.

3

"Signora?" It sounded as if she had let the phone fall. "Signora?"

There was a faraway confusion of voices at the other end of the wire. Then one drowned out all others in a rumbling basso of bad Italian. I knew whose it was even before it addressed me over the phone in excellent French.

"Monsieur Davis," said Charles Leschenhaut, "where are you?"

"Let's not waste time, Leschenhaut. The question is not where I am, but what I want."

"I see. You feel you're in a position to make demands on me."

"To make a deal with you. You get fifty million francs, and I get a half million of them and my passage out of the country. Does that sound reasonable?"

He understood at once what I was getting at.

"If you can produce the fifty million francs," he said.

"I can produce the remains of Madame de Villemont. That means I can point out exactly where you'll find them in the marshes on Torcello. You know she was killed there, don't you?"

"I was told she died there," Leschenhaut said smoothly. "But I was also told you shared her sad fate. If I was so grossly misinformed about you, how can I be sure that she—?"

"Oh, she's dead all right. You'll see for yourself soon enough."

"Will I? It's strange, Monsieur Davis. Everyone seemed to think you were passionately devoted to the lady. Yet you appear remarkably unmoved by her death."

"Why the hell not when she was only playing me for a fool all along? As far as I'm concerned, Leschenhaut, the one thing that'll make my troubles worthwhile is the cut I'll get of her money. And don't tell me half a million is too much for my end. Without my help it'll take ten years for de Gonde or you or anyone else to get that estate settled."

He digested that in silence for a few seconds, then said, "What you propose does seem reasonable. However, there must be a discussion of it with the principals here. If you give me your phone number and allow me a few hours—"

"*Chansons que tout ça, copain!* I'm wanted by the police, remember? And time is on their side. Whatever discussion is needed is taking place right now between the two of us. You know damn well nobody is going to veto any agreement you make with me."

"Agreement to what? I can hardly pull half a million francs out of my hat."

"I'll settle for fifty thousand down. In lire."

"By when?"

"Tonight after dark. I'll meet you, and we can drive to Venice together. And just to prove I'm not pulling any swindle, you can bring along anyone else you want. Is that agreed?"

"Agreed."

"I'll also expect transportation to South America, meaning tickets and passport. And," I added to make it sound all the more convincing, "I know forged passports come high. But whatever you have to pay for mine does not come out of my end."

"Agreed."

The phone booth was becoming stiflingly hot and airless, but with some sightseers close by I was afraid to open its door.

"Finally," I said, "I want evidence that the child is alive and unhurt."

"You have my word he is."

"That's not enough. Let's get it straight right now, Leschenhaut; if anything's happened to him the deal is off. I'll have to see him myself before we go ahead with it. Is he there with you?"

"No, he's living with Madame de Gonde not far from here.

But," said Leschenhaut, just as I hoped he would, "you will not pay him any visit."

"Why not?"

"Because he's been badly upset by the crisis you brought about. Dr. Linder, who is attending him, would never permit a meeting with you that could mean new emotional problems."

It was a neat way of telling me that he knew as well as I did that Paul was the major piece in the game, and he had no intention of allowing me the smallest chance of capturing that piece.

"Who said anything about meeting him?" I retorted. "All I want is one good look at him to make sure I'm not playing a sucker's game."

"I don't see how that can be arranged," Leschenhaut said flatly.

"There must be some way. Wait a minute—" I counted very slowly to ten. "Do you know the Metropolitana system?"

"No." His tone was wary. "I don't travel by subway here in Rome."

"I'm sure you can find someone to show you how."

"Perhaps. What then?"

"Just a short trip on the Metropolitana for you and the boy. You're near the E.U.R. station. Take the first train to the city after twelve noon and stay near the door of the last car so Paul is in plain sight from any station platform you pass. I'll be keeping under cover on one of those platforms, never mind which one. If I'm satisfied with what I see, I'll call you again at six and tell you where to pick me up for the trip to Venice."

"And if you're not satisfied?"

"I'll take my chances on getting away without your help. And I'll guarantee, Leschenhaut, you can dredge that *barene* around Torcello for the rest of your life without ever turning up what your friend Cimino left of Anne de Villemont."

"You have an ugly way of stating things, Monsieur Davis." He was stalling for time, studying the pieces on the board. "Do you know what your chances are for getting overseas without my help?"

"As good as your chances of producing evidence in court of Anne de Villemont's death without my help. And you're wasting time, Leschenhaut. Is it the Metropolitana at noon or not?"

Again that brooding silence. At last, Leschenhaut said with finality, "I'm sorry. The boy is being made ready now for a trip abroad to help him recuperate. The air flight is scheduled for this afternoon. I don't see how—"

"Too bad you don't. Good-bye, Leschenhaut."

"Wait!" I could hear him breathing hard. "All right, have it your way."

"Good. I'll call again at six."

I flung open the door of the booth to fill my lungs with fresh air, but the sense of suffocation choking me remained.

Anne yielded her place to me behind the wheel of the car.

"Did he agree?" she asked tautly. "Is Paul all right?"

"Yes."

She went limp with relief at that, but when I gave her the gist of the conversation with Leschenhaut she stiffened with fresh apprehension.

"Air flight this afternoon?" she said fearfully. "Do you see what that means? If anything goes wrong—the least little thing—Paul will be a thousand miles away by tonight and God knows where."

I couldn't dispute that. It was exactly what Leschenhaut had let me know in his devious way, and I believed him.

The Metropolitana is like a toy subway system, neat, clean, and orderly, with small trains and only ten stations altogether. It runs from the Termini south to Stazione Laurentina, just past the E.U.R. but only the first few stations after the Termini are underground. One of these is the Colosseum station, and that was the one I picked for the job at hand.

The dashboard clock marked noon when I parked the car at the corner of the Via dei Fori Imperialii just across the street from the Colosseum and within a few steps of the subway entrance. A short block away was the Via degli Annibaldi which led north to the center of the city.

I pointed it out to Anne.

"That's the shortest way to the Via Veneto," I said. "Do you know where the American embassy is?"

"Yes. But you'll be with me, won't you?"

"Once Paul is in the car you get to the embassy as fast as you can, whether I'm with you or not." The face she turned toward me was like death. "And don't work up any big scene about it," I said harshly. "Odds are I'll be with you. If I'm not, you'll have to handle everything by yourself."

"I love you. Don't you understand? You're as much a part of me now as Paul is. Do you think I could go off and leave you here, not even knowing what was happening to you?"

"You'll do what has to be done. For God's sake, Anne, you've been holding up fine so far. This is no time to come apart at the seams."

"I won't. I swear I won't. But I love you." Bypassers stared openly into the car as she fiercely clung to me. One gangling youth, his arm around a fat-rumped girl friend, whistled with admiration at the scene we made. "If anything happens to you—" Anne whispered.

A few minutes later, I walked to the subway entrance. Before descending the stairway I couldn't resist looking back to see her keeping tense watch on me. To the unknowing eye, the scene would be Rome at its loveliest. The timeworn stony ruins of the Colosseum outlined against the bluest of skies, the traffic almost playfully skittering by on the broad avenue, the beautiful girl in the front seat of a parked car rather fixedly smiling a farewell at her husband or lover who was preparing to enter the subway—then my view of her was obscured by a bulky tourist, flagrantly American in sunglasses and Hawaiian shirt, with cigar in mouth and camera slung around his neck, who took up a position between us to aim his camera at the Colosseum.

I closed my mind to what I was leaving and plunged down the stairway. At the stand I bought a copy of *Il Messaggiero* and a token for the subway stile. I pushed through the turnstile and walked toward the end of the platform where I judged the last car of the train would come to a stop.

Leaning against the wall, I studied the length of platform over the edge of my open newspaper. Of the few people in sight, none was conspicuously the OEI killer type. But I wasn't underestimating Leschenhaut. Between Stazione E.U.R. and the Termini were only seven platforms to cover so it would be easy for him to assign a man to each platform. Not for murder this time, but for my protection. In fact, if I ran into any trouble with the police while waiting here, it was likely some OEI agent would instantly move in to help me get away. It was a sweaty spot for Leschenhaut. I might be worth fifty million francs to him, and until he knew whether I was or wasn't, he had to make sure nothing drastic happened to me.

A train roared into the station and slid to a quick stop. No sign of Paul or anyone who might be accompanying him. The doors slammed shut; the train took off as if it were jet-propelled. Of the handful of people who had been waiting on the platform, only one had not boarded the train, a gray-haired, scholarly-looking man, soberly dressed, holding a book with his forefinger in it to mark his place. As the train disappeared into the tunnel, he glanced at his wristwatch, turned to peer hopefully at the empty staircase, then, with a headshake of irritation, went back to his book. An OEI man? It didn't seem possible. Yet it hadn't seemed possible for the gentle, moon-faced Fra Pietro to be one either.

Another train came through, again with no sign of Paul aboard. Still the scholarly-looking man remained close by, sunk in his book. But now I had other problems to consider besides him. What if Leschenhaut had decided at the last minute not to gamble for the fifty million? What if he really couldn't produce Paul? If Louis' killer had caught up to the child—

The station was full of noise as the third train raced into it, and as its doors jolted open all my terrors vanished on the spot. Facing me through the open door, just as he had faced me through the open door of Louis' room when I had last seen him, was Paul. Or at least, the pallid, huge-eyed, skinny little ghost of the Paul I had last seen. And as I flung the newspaper aside and moved toward him I saw, frozen into tableau, his primly bespectacled Aunt Gabrielle holding his hand, the ruddy, bull-necked Leschenhaut with an arm draped over those slight shoulders, saw the venomously pretty face of Bernard Bourdon and the thin-lipped, narrow-eyed face of Albert, the youthful gunman. And around them, other faces, tough OEI faces.

I heard Gabrielle de Gonde scream as I caught Paul up and burst out of the car holding him tight against me, heard Leschenhaut bellow. As I cleared the door, a pair of arms almost locking around my knees sent me staggering off balance onto the platform, and Paul's arms clasped my neck in panic as I made the effort not to go down full length. The scholarly-looking man was braced for me on the platform. Coolly, deliberately, he jammed the edge of his book into my belly with one hand, and with the other grasped Paul's jacket. Gasping for air, I wrenched Paul free and raced for the stairway.

"It's all right!" I assured him as he violently struggled against me now. "It's Reno! It's all right!" but halfway up the stairs, voices shouting and footsteps thundering right behind me, I knew it wasn't all right, knew I would never make it to the car this way without risking his life along with mine.

At the head of the stairway, avid hands grasping at me, I tore the child's grip loose from my neck and roughly shoved him onto the sidewalk in the direction of the parked car.

"Run!" I shouted. "Your mother's there! Run, damn it!" and at the same instant pivoted around, blindly swinging my fists to block off the pursuit of him. I hit someone, I don't know who, and then was hit myself across the side of the head with what felt like an iron bar. The impact was stunning. It sent me lurching weak-kneed across the sidewalk, and then I saw, leaping at me from out of the crowd of astounded spectators at the subway entrance, the wiry figure of Albert, the steel blade glinting in his hand.

I was too dazed to fend off the blow. I felt it on my shoulder almost like a friendly thumb jabbing me there, and then felt the searing pain of it flame through the shoulder. He would settle for that one thrust. Lips twisted in a leer of triumph he turned to run, but he was too late. A hefty arm caught him around the throat; a hand gripped his wrist and snapped it back and up. As the arm broke with the sound of a branch snapping, Albert screamed and went limp, sagging in the man's grasp. Blurrily, I realized with wonderment that the man was the same American tourist who had obscured my last view of Anne. There was no mistaking that Hawaiian shirt, that fat cigar still clenched in his teeth.

"Police!" he shouted furiously. *"Polizia!"*

Then the police were there, miraculously sprung from the ground, pistols in hand. A couple sprinted after a tall, lean figure, one of those I had seen near Paul in the train. Another collared Leschenhaut, who was clumsily running in the opposite direction. Others trotted down the subway steps, whistles shrilly blowing.

Through all this it was impossible to see if Paul had reached the car safely, if Anne had gotten away. The crowd was as thick around the scene now as it might have been in the Colosseum when gladiators met there. Suddenly, my arms were wrenched behind my back; I felt the cold steel grip of handcuffs, heard them click shut around my wrists. I was swung around and shoved toward a car, a familiar, dusty blue Citroën, pushed unceremoniously into it. Two men sat in the front seat. When the driver turned to look at me, I saw he not only wore a gray straw hat, but that his face had a gray, lackluster quality; his eyes were sleepy with apparent disinterest. Anne's gray man.

Leschenhaut, his hands also locked behind him in steel cuffs, was thrust into the car. The American tourist climbed in after him and dropped heavily into the seat between us, his stout thighs and fat buttocks crowding us.

"Ça gazouille," he said in good, hard-boiled, idiomatic French. "A neat job. Now let's move before we're all in the newsreels."

4

The car moved, the driver bearing down on the horn to clear a way through the mob surrounding us. I leaned forward, searching through the window for a glimpse of Anne or even the parked Fiat, and the big man in the Hawaiian shirt twisted his fingers in my hair and dragged my head upright.

"*Je ne suis pas à prendre avec des pincettes,*" he said jovially. "I've got a mean streak. Don't try anything that might stir it up, chum," and now I was sure he was no more American than Leschenhaut himself.

"Who the hell are you?" I demanded. "Where are we going?"

"You'll find out." He pulled a couple of pairs of motorcyclist's goggles out of his pocket. "Here, try this on for size."

"I've got a pair of my own in this jacket."

"These are more stylish."

He got a hard grip on the nape of my neck with those sausage-like fingers and snapped the goggles over my eyes. I discovered they were as completely opaque as if they were coated with black paint. It was impossible to see even a flicker of light through them.

"Now you," he said to Leschenhaut.

I took what joy I could from the fact that Leschenhaut was as much a captive as I was. The body of the snake still writhed dangerously, but, at least, the head was out of action for the time being.

The car stopped, started, turned a corner, then reversed itself. In a few minutes I didn't have any idea where we were or in what direction we were heading. All I could tell from our slow progress and the racket of traffic around us was that we were somewhere in the heart of the city.

The pain of the knife wound in my shoulder was getting steadily worse. It felt, after a while, as if someone were probing an inch deep into it with a dull scalpel. Then I became aware of a warm wetness trickling down my arm and into my palm.

"I think I'm bleeding," I said to Hawaiian Shirt. "I was stuck in the shoulder. You'd better take a look there."

He made a snorting sound through his nostrils, but peeled my jacket and shirt halfway down my back.

"You're leaking blood, all right," he said grudgingly. "Looks like an ice pick was used on you. In one side and out the other. But you'll live to have your head chopped off. Don't worry about that."

The car must have been equipped with a first-aid kit. I felt a cold spray of liquid numbing the wound and then a cloth being bound tightly and expertly around it. My shirt and jacket were pulled up and neatly buttoned.

"Thanks," I said. "What's your name?"

"You can call me A. That guy driving is B. The one next to him never told us his name. A real mysterious type, that one."

"Now, look—"

He gripped my shoulder over the wound and increased the pressure until I groaned.

"Get the idea?" he inquired amiably, and eased the pressure. "You just be a good little birdie and sing only when you're told to."

The car came to a dead stop and from the squeal of tires against a curb I knew it was parked.

"All clear," someone in the front seat said, and I was hustled out of the car and across a pavement into a building. Close behind me, I could hear Leschenhaut cursing under his breath when he stumbled over the doorstep.

There was a flight of stairs to navigate, a few steps across a creaking wooden floor, and then a door slammed shut. When the goggles were removed from my eyes I saw I was in what looked like the dining room of a third-rate *pensione*. A long, narrow room with a few small tables in it and with all its shutters tightly closed. It was lighted by some unshaded bulbs dangling by loose wires from a battered brass chandelier.

Behind a table in the middle of the room sat a man in shirtsleeves examining a folder of papers before him. He was gaunt to the point of fleshlessness, his face skull-like under a bald head, his arms as thin and unmuscular as a woman's. He was smoking a cigarette in a long holder, the holder between thumb and forefinger, Russian style. Still concentrating on his papers, he delicately flicked an ash from the cigarette into a coffee cup on the table. Then, without looking up, he said, "Name?"

I glanced around to see if this was directed at me or Leschenhaut. I found that Leschenhaut and the two men who had ridden in front of the car were no longer in my company. Hawaiian Shirt and I were alone in the room with this inquisitor.

"No name," I said. "I forgot it. I have amnesia," and the heavy hand of my guard clamped down hard on my shoulder again, the pain of it making me buckle a little at the knees.

The gaunt man raised his head now and looked at me with eyes as coldly luminous as a cat's. "Papers?"

I shook my head.

"All right," he said to the guard, "clean him out. Pockets, shoes, everything."

The guard did the job quickly and expertly. My property was laid on the table. A few coins, a handkerchief, a pair of sunglasses, the tightly folded sheets of wrapping paper containing the OEI membership list.

The wrapping papers almost covered the table when they were spread open.

"What's this?" said the inquisitor.

"God damn it, if you tell me who you are—!"

The heavy hand was already on my shoulder again, but its grip slackened when the gaunt man said, "I'll do better than that. I'll tell you who you are, Monsieur Reno Davis. You are an escaped murderer, charged with killing one Louis Metchnikoff alias Louis le Buc. You are an active member of a terrorist organization. On either count—"

"Both counts are false! And while we're wasting time like this, a woman and child are in serious danger. Madame Anne de Villemont and her son. If you let me call the American embassy—"

"Hasn't it dawned on you yet, Monsieur Reno Davis, that you're being held incommunicado?"

"Then you make the call. If Madame de Villemont and the child are there, I'll tell you whatever you want to know. Otherwise, I won't say another word, even if your gorilla here takes me apart piece by piece."

Almost lazily, the gorilla swung the back of his hand against my mouth. I felt the lip split and the taste of blood on it. The gaunt man watched this as indifferently as Georges the chauffeur had watched me being punished for trying to walk out the door of the Château Laennac.

"Not very pleasant being taken apart piece by piece, is it?" he asked gently.

"It's nothing new to me. I used to make my living this way."

"What are the woman and child in danger from?"

"The woman knows too much about the organization. The child knows who Louis le Buc's murderer is. He was in the room when Louis was killed."

The gaunt man opened the folder, riffled through it and drew out a sheet of paper. He skimmed through the paper almost at a glance.

"There were only two people in the room at the time of the murder, you and a Léon Schaefer, now known as Becque. His deposition—"

"He's a member of the organization. His job was to pin the murder on me."

"I don't think so, Monsieur Reno Davis. You see, we know all about Schaefer. He's been investigated very carefully. He was a member of the outlawed OAS and did serve a prison sentence for that. But he was freed under the general amnesty, and his record since then is altogether respectable. Yours, I'm afraid, does not match it."

"If the child is at the embassy, you can speak to him yourself."

"If."

"What do you have to lose by trying it?" I pleaded.

He considered that expressionlessly. Then, with an abrupt gesture, he crushed out his cigarette in the coffee cup and stood up.

"We'll see," he said.

I couldn't gauge how long he was gone from the room. It seemed like hours. It might have been twenty or thirty minutes. While he was gone my guard kept me standing at rigid attention by a casual kick in the ankle whenever I started to shift position.

When the gaunt man re-entered the room my heart sank at the expression on his face. It was all self-satisfaction. The luxurious relish of a cat who has pinned down the canary and is now preparing to devour it.

"Madame de Villemont," I croaked. "The child. They didn't reach the embassy."

"They are at the embassy. I spoke to both of them. They are quite safe now," and when I stood staring at him dumbly, the blood draining out of me with the shock of it, he said sharply to the guard, "Get those cuffs off him and put him into a chair before he passes out on us. And see if you can find something to drink around here. Some cognac."

There was no cognac, but there was wine, and I took down two full glasses of it like water before I could find my voice again.

"This isn't a trick?" I said. "Both of them are all right?"

"Both. But they had a narrow squeak. A man followed them from the Colosseum by car and made an attempt on their lives with a pistol almost at the embassy gates. The police have him now. A Bernard Bourdon. Do you know him?"

"He's one of the organization."

"I thought so. As for the murder of Louis Metchnikoff"—the gaunt man daintily fitted a fresh cigarette into his holder, savoring the moment—"there were not two people in the room during the event as the police believe, but four. Besides you and Schaefer, there was the child himself and a certain gentleman hidden behind the door, gun in hand. Monsieur Charles Leschenhaut, in fact. The boy says it was he who fired that bullet."

"Leschenhaut?"

"Charles Leschenhaut. Someone my service has been trying to pin the goods on for a long time. It seems he's finally made a fatal mistake."

"What service? If you're not the police—"

"So you've guessed that much, have you, Monsieur Davis? But have you ever heard of the S.D.E.C. in France. *Le Service de documentation extérieure et de contre-espionage?*"

"No."

"That's to its credit, I'd say. It is, more or less, a counterpart to your country's CIA. And now that you have heard of it, I'd suggest you forget about it. Let's turn to business instead."

"What business?"

The man laid a pale, skeletal hand on the wrapping papers spread over the table. "This, for one thing. What information does it contain?"

"The organization's membership list. If you use a book called *La Mystère du Tarot* by Sophie de Laennac, I don't think you'll have any trouble decoding it."

His eyes lit up. "In that case, we'll be able to smoke the rats out of the cellar once and for all. I trust we'll get your co-operation in this."

"You will. But right now—"

"Right now, Madame is waiting for you at the embassy, and there will be a doctor on hand to treat your wound without asking troublesome questions. Also some agents of your government and the Italian government who will have questions to ask. One of them has already been picked to act as liaison between us. I'm afraid you and Madame and the child face a difficult time. You'll have to serve as witnesses at Leschenhaut's trial and some others to follow, and that will be a nuisance for all of you until the premises are thoroughly disinfected. Of course, police protection will be provided until then."

"What about Schaefer? He's a dangerous character, and there are some friends of mine he's close to. For their sake—"

"Mademoiselles Eliane Tissou and Véronique Blanchard?"

"You know them?" I said with surprise.

The gaunt man smiled bleakly.

"I know them. They're already under police protection, even if for the wrong reason. It was the killing of Monsieur Adrian Driot-Steiner of the Ministry of Commerce by a speeding car which started the ball rolling. In his files was found an inexplicable requisition to the police for a report on the death of one Sidney Scott. We went to Mademoiselle Blanchard for an explanation of the document, she unwillingly led us to you, and so to the family de Villemont who were already in bad odor from Algeria. Finally, we were led as far as the family Montecastellani here in Rome."

"Was that why your men were trailing me? Because they figured I would lead them to the Montecastellani hideout?"

"Yes. With the kind consent of the Italian police who had to close their eyes to what was going on. And now that I've been so frank, I'd like you to return the favor and explain your involvement with the organization. Everything."

I told him everything. When I was finished he shook his head with a sort of humorous despair. "You mean that concern for the child was the only reason for your taking such an incredibly reckless course?"

"Yes."

"But how could you possibly believe that even a man as ruthless as Leschenhaut—?"

I said, "There was an Algerian—he was the editor of one of those FLN sheets—who lived a few doors away from me on the Faubourg Saint-Denis. I was standing across the street when a car drove by and someone threw a *plastique* at him. It blew his daughter's face off. She was four years old."

The gaunt man sat silent for a while.

"Yes," he said at last, "I see what you mean."

5

I was led out of the room the way I had been led into it, with the opaque goggles over my eyes and a strong hand under my elbow to guide me along my blindly stumbling course to the car.

The car moved off, entered traffic, slowly traveled a bewildering series of twists and turns. It stopped.

"*La correspondance, monsieur.*" The man in the Hawaiian shirt pulled off my goggles, opened the door, and nudged me through it. "Change trains here."

The car sped away as I stood blinking in the glare of sunlight, trying to get my bearings. The sign advertising Stock liqueurs. The Fountain of the Tritone. I was in the Piazza Barberini at the foot of the Via Veneto.

"Glad to meet you, Mr. Davis." A tall, ruddy, crop-haired young man stood before me. There could be no question about it this time. He was as American as Mom's apple pie, as American as a hand-picked agent of the FBI or CIA. "My name's Reardon. Care for a lift to the embassy?"

His car was a black Fiat Millecento, identical to the one Anne and I had been living in the past few days. Evidently, I wasn't alone in my belief that it was the least conspicuous car on the road. As we drew up to the embassy Reardon gestured at the gathering of men on the sidewalk who were carrying large, professional-looking cameras.

"Newspapermen and *paparazzi*," he said. "We had a little excitement here today. Some nut shooting off a gun. Of course," he added, straight-faced, "you don't know a thing about it."

"Not a thing," I assured him.

He led the way, unchallenged, through the busy corridors of the building, a magnificent palazzo with a strong smell of officialdom emanating from it. As I followed him, I wondered with a growing apprehension what the reunion with Anne would be like. She had loved me while we were walking the tightrope together. But emotions were heightened up there, the view of everything around us distorted. How would it be, now that we were safe on the ground?

"That's it," said Reardon, pointing to an open door.

I walked through it and stood there. The room was sunlit and spacious, and at its far end Anne and Paul sat together on a couch talking to some men who all somehow resembled Reardon.

Then I didn't have to wonder any more.

It was Paul who saw me standing there and started eagerly toward me, shouting, "Reno! Reno!"

It was Anne who reached me first.